For The Good Times

David Keenan grew up in Airdrie in the late '70s and early 1980s.
A senior critic for *The Wire*, he is also the author of two previous
books: *England's Hidden Reverse* and *This Is Memorial Device*,
his debut novel, which won the Collyer-Bristow/London Magazine
Prize for Innovative Debut Fiction 2018. It was also a *Daily
Telegraph* and Rough Trade Book of the Year and shortlisted for
the Gordon Burn Prize 2017.

Further praise for *For The Good Times*:

'The blackest of humour, particularly in its exquisite dialogue,
and the constant laughter balances the darkening vision of the
narrator . . . There is a pulsing beat to the prose, accelerating
rhythms built of comic repetition, bawdy vernacular and shocking
collisions . . . A compassionate portrayal of men whose humanity
is deformed by the Troubles.' *FT*

'The driven, furious narrative holds it together, everything
teetering at the edge of comprehension. You can't tear your eyes
away. Which is what it was like. The real thing felt more like *For
The Good Times* than it did like anything else. Under the cosmic
artfulness there is a hardcore authenticity to this telling.'
Irish Times

'Brilliant . . . A white-knuckle tale . . . that is trippy, harrowing
and hilarious.' *Q* magazine

'This fantastic, terrifying novel is phantasmagorical, high-velocity

gothic . . . All the good stuff is there: dark forces, portents, labyrinthine passages, the recurrent idea of the double, inversions of good and evil on an epic scale . . . An unsettling, thrilling read.'
Spectator

'Occult, transformative, difficult, fantastic: Keenan is smashing through so many borders in this novel. It's beyond savage.'
New Statesman

'Keenan writes the violence of the paramilitaries with vividness and immediacy . . . A powerful novel.' *Guardian*

'*For The Good Times* is not simply a fictional account of men in the IRA, or a narrative, but an attempt to capture the sound and fury of the time first hand – a visceral representation that will make readers simultaneously shudder and savour the spark.'
Skinny

'Could well become one of the definitive accounts of the Troubles.'
Literary Review

'Keenan's indelible novel is hilarious, disturbing and surreal – like *The Sopranos* written by Flann O'Brien and edited by Aleister Crowley.' *Mail on Sunday*

'The bad old days of 1970s Belfast are refracted through David Keenan's wild, hallucinatory imagination in *For The Good Times*, a riotous, wise-cracking, gore-spattered account of the Troubles . . . His breakneck storytelling leaves you utterly unsettled.'
The Times

'A nastily funny, ultra-violent account of Belfast . . . Samuel's hyper-adrenalised narrative blends hallucinatory visions, paranoid delirium and graphic descriptions with a Martin

by the same author

England's Hidden Reverse

This Is Memorial Device

For The Good Times

David Keenan

ff

FABER & FABER

First published in 2019
by Faber & Faber Limited
Bloomsbury House
74–77 Great Russell Street
London WC1B 3DA

This paperback edition first published in 2020

Typeset by Faber & Faber Limited
Printed and bound by CPI Group (UK) Ltd, Croydon, CR0 4YY

A CIP record for this book
is available from the British Library

ISBN 978–0–571–34052–1

10 9 8 7 6 5 4 3 2 1

Is there not joy ineffable in this aimless winging? Is there not weariness and impatience for who would attain to some goal? And the swan was ever silent. Ah! but we floated in the infinite Abyss. Joy! Joy! White swan, bear thou ever me up between thy wings!
– The Master Therion, *Liber LXV*

Can the ocean keep from rushing to the shore? It's just impossible.
– Perry Como, 'It's Impossible'

This 'new soul' should have sung, not spoken.
– Friedrich Nietzsche, Introduction to *The Birth of Tragedy*

Contents

Part One: The Swan, In Return

: I'm like an angel, come back into the past, to tell I's Now, that it is here right Now, and that this is Christ Jayzus speaking from the cross, and the screws kept their distance.

He was telling I's about Bobby, who was coming in and out of a coma. Bobby is echoing, He says to I's, by means of time and space; Bobby is lagging.

Christ on a stick – what?!

This is His Father who has forgotten Him, the priest says to I's. His body is here amongst us, lags, he says. His body is here all divided up amongst us. He points to the emaciated boys in the room, to all of the Jayzus to come, and it's like a painting on the wall of a cell in heaven, remembering. And I's are seeing it for themselves.

Ask Him for heaven, one of the lags says to the priest, ask Him how it goes in heaven. *Lags*, Christ Jayzus says to I's, in the voice of a priest in H3, *lags*, He says, *it goes without being*. Then, speaking for Himself now: *I am love in the angles*. This is The Dead Zone: The Place Of Endless Echoes.

Father, He says out loud, *Father*, but it is Himself that is speaking. *Sure is that yourself Father*, He says, and He reaches out as if to touch Himself on the cheek.

And what the priest says is that Jayzus was with The Blanketmen and suffered as they did themselves, which meant that The Blanketmen would likely be in agony till the end of the

3

world. And that a river of gold runs from a garden of Africa name of Belfast called the Free State. And IRA is called after Immortal Revenging Angels. And UDA is called after Under Daemonic Aires. And the earth has only been alive for two thousand year. But there's an eerie atmosphere about the place.

*

And Jayzus Himself, from His place on the cross, which in pity is at the Heart of Time, speaks through the mouth of a priest in H3: *this is an old one, lags*, He says to I's – He calls I's lags, like echoes in time – *so stop me if you think you've heard it before.*

Pat and Mick, He says to I's, this pale Jayzus that we can all see before us and that is lagging like Bobby only on the wall of a chapel in The Maze and not in a pish-stained hospital bed across the way, *it's Pat and Mick and they're away on their holidays*, Jayzus says to I's, and He says it without speaking, without moving His lips or opening His eyes to all of the horror stood before Him, to all of the Jayzus to come, but to hear Him is as plain as the pale light rising beneath His skin, rising up and lightning His skin as if He is give birth to the moon, and His eyebrows raised in a pained expression, rising up at the suffering that His Father brought down on the world (let's face it) so as they look like a child's drawing of a bird and He says to I's, *two old muckers, Pat and Mick, are dandering along the street in America, in eternity, in New York, and they look up toward the sun, the sun is come beaming out of the heavens and they hold their palms up flat to feel the sun on their hands, to feel the sun in the centre of their palms they hold their hands up in salute, and*

4

Mick turns to Pat and he says to him, all in the voice of Christ Jayzus which is the voice of the priest and which is coming from Forever at the Heart of the Cross, *he says to him, sure is that the same sun we have back in the Ardoyne? And Mick says to him, sure Pat I wouldn't know, let's ask someone*, and at this point Jayzus takes one of His pale white hands from the cross and presses it to His face and you can see the wound in the centre of His palm, which is like a beautiful, delicate labia, and He puts it back in place without a word and everyone looks at each other like – what?!

Listen, lags, Jayzus says to I's, *don't give way to wonder, I will pick out your eyes you bastards*, He says to I's, and He goes back to His thing about the two muckers Pat and Mick, and the sun in the sky, and how they're in a new country, in a new life altogether, and they stop the first person they meet, and they ask him if he knows whether that's the same sun they saw in the Ardoyne long ago, the same sun sat up there in the sky throughout the whole fucking shooting match, and now the figure on the cross is lagging in and out of reality, and the first person they meet is speaking in the voice of Christ Jayzus, which is the voice of a priest in the H Block at the beginning of the second hunger strike, in the spring of 1981, and He says to them, *sorry, lads, but I wouldn't know if that's the same sun that you saw in the Ardoyne; I'm a stranger here myself.*

They say that Jayzus's final words were something to do with His Father. But that's the last any of The Boys ever heard from Him.

*

This is the story of Adam's Apple, son, this is how they all became scundered about being naked in front of each other, because up till then life was fucking beezer, my friend, only they couldn't mind anything at all because of that they had no lingo, all except for body lingo, and for making sounds like songs, maybe, like musical sounds, a wee bit, I think, but not actual words, that is until Adam takes a bite of this fucking apple and it meant he could speak the English, just like that, up until then every day had been the same but then Jayzus Himself, or more likely his da (let's face it), let a snake loose in the garden and the snake was the first thing what could talk but it was lonely because nobody else had words that they could use with it, so as the snake tempted Adam to eat this apple, he didn't even know it was an apple till then, he thought everything was a part of himself, he didn't even know how a snake was a snake, so we'll never know how it did it, but basically the snake says to him that the apple was something different from himself and that if he wanted to he could eat it and find out the names of everything, including his wife, who at that point he had no idea was called Eve. After that, he began remembering.

*

Take a look at this photo, would you. Take a look at the state of Tommy. He looks like a fucking negro. The only negro in Belfast. Where the fuck did he get that tan? And those ears. That's me on the left. Silk handkerchief in my top bin. One hand in my slacks. The other arm wrapped around the ladies. I mean would you take a fucking look at that would you. We all thought we were Perry Como. A good dose, a good dose of Como, that's what Tommy says to us, stick that fucking record on and let's get ourselves a good dose because it's Como or nothing, lads, and we'd go to the wooden record booths they had in the shops where you stood in there and you smoked and you ran your hands through your hair and you spat on the floor and when Como came on through a little speaker in the corner it was like a wee fucking time machine that would take you off to some other Ireland or some other Italy, some California or wherever the fuck your man Como was singing from, some other heaven, in other words. And fuck Frank Sinatra. He was a dissolute cunt. But Como never cursed, never smoked nor drank. Plus he was always faithful to his wife.

*

The photo is from Ellen McFadyen's wedding. That's Barney in the middle there, and that's his wife Shona. Poor Shona McFadyen. Died long ago and it was a shame. Died of cancer, and that's Patrick on the far right. Shot through the heart, on his own front lawn, by some bastard, after he was grassed up by his girlfriend if you can fucking believe it. But wait till I tell you. And there's Tommy next to him. Look at him standing there. It's true that we were the handsomest boys in the Ardoyne. All the women loved us, the old dears looked at us like are these guys out the movies or what, the wee kids gazed up at us like that, beaming. It takes me right back there just looking at this fucking thing; happy days.

*

The photo was taken right after the thing in Dundalk. Me and Tommy had gone down there to take care of business, a couple of chatsbys down our trousers, looking like a pair of gangsters. What bollocks we had. That was the surest way to get by the peelers; walk in like you own the place. The peelers treated us like rats, waiting for us to sneak in the back door or shin up a drainpipe, nip down an alley in a black balaclava and a pair of camouflage slacks. Instead we turned up wearing cravats and with gold watches and with Italian handmade suits. That's the reason they used us. We could've sold cheese to the French.

*

We were to do this guy in his house, this dirty lowlife snitch bastard getting plugged in his own home; it had all been arranged. Tommy knew him and he had no reason to suspect that anything was up. We were bringing him a bottle of Bushmills and a trout, this big fuck-off monster trout that Tommy got from a guy up The Shamrock. That's how we did business. Show me the fella that can resist a big fuck-off trout pulled fresh out the river. So as we turn up. Bobby, his name was Bobby, this cunt Bobby. He opens the door and he's pleased to see us. He gets Tommy in a headlock and starts rubbing his hair with his knuckles. His second name was Burns. Bobby Burns. Everybody used to call him Fat Burns. Just for a joke, like. Tommy starts play-fighting him. Cracking all these jokes and he's laughing the whole time, Tommy was really playing with the cunt and laughing, like we were there to shoot him in the head but there was still enough leeway to take the pish.

I watched him mock-wrestling this clown on the sofa. I looked into his eyes and I could tell it was all real. He was *completely there*.

At that moment I idolised him, so I did. He was my hero right then, Tommy was. Then he gets up, cold as you like, and there's a mirror above the couch. The guy's lying there laughing; this cunt's cracking up. I'm unwrapping this huge fucking trout, this fucking dinosaur. I don't know where they found this monster, it was like a fucking Plesiosaurus. And suddenly everything starts moving in slow motion.

I catch Tommy as he's looking at himself in the mirror – just for a split second – a split second that seemed to last forever – and his eyes are smiling, I'll never forget it, Irish eyes just smiling right back at himself; everything they say in the songs is true. And he fixes his hair. He licks his finger and he runs it through his hair and he fixes his parting. All in this film that has slowed to the point where you feel like you could live in it forever. And then he pulls the chatsby out his trousers in one big sweep and he looks down at Bobby and he smiles and he looks back at himself in the mirror and he pulls the trigger and he blows this guy away without even looking at him.

Three shots in the head and the guy's face is a fucking mess. I says to him, ah for fuck sake, Tommy, why didn't you put a fucking cushion over his head or something? But he grabs me in a headlock and starts playing with me the exact same, wrestling me around the room and rubbing my hair, like I was taking things too serious, or what.

We run outside and we're getting into the car. We can see people pulling their curtains over. Everybody knew what was going on, nobody wanted to get involved; good job. But then we see these

9

two unmarked cars at the end of the street. We're in a dead end and these two cars are blocking off the road. It's the fucking peelers, Tommy says to me. To this day I don't know if it was or not but he immediately comes up with this idea, it was insane. Tie me to the roof of the car, he says to me. You have got to be fucking kidding me, I says to him, what in the name of a mad idea is that, I says. Tie me to the fucking roof of the car, he says to me, and I'm not about to argue with him when he's like this. I run inside and I'm looking through all these kitchen cupboards trying to find a piece of rope but I can't find any so as I run out the back and I tear the fucking washing line down and I rush out the front and Tommy's lying on the roof rack of the car with a chatsby in his hand. Tie me down, he says to me. And make it fucking tight.

All the time the cars at the end of the road are just crouching there. There are people in them but they're just crouching there, watching us. The whole place is silent, is eerie. They're waiting for back-up, Tommy says: fucking move it.

I tie him to the roof rack and then he says to me, drive step on the fucking gas: let's go. I head off down the road full tilt toward these cars and I can see the faces inside them, just staring at us in disbelief. They're trying to unlock the doors. Trying to get themselves out in time. And Tommy's just firing away. The windows are popping and people are screaming and we go sailing through and I ram one of the cars out the way and I can hear Tommy shouting up above, I think he's been hit but I keep on driving. We're charging up the main road at this point with this maniac tied to the fucking roof and that's when I realise: he's singing. The fucker is actually singing to himself while tied to the roof of the car. And he's singing Como, *lay your head upon my pillow, hold your warm and tender body close to mine*, all the good stuff. Nobody will ever forget it. Tears were rolling down my face. I'm getting choked up now just thinking about it. He's out to seduce the pants off the world, I says to myself.

Later that night we went up to the Bow Bridge, up at the Whiterock, and sat there underneath it, smoking fags and watching the swallows that had their nests in the girders flying in and out and making that song they have, that summer song, and everybody was coming in and asking if it was true what had happened and Tommy's sitting there like a movie star, not even reacting, just smoking and listening to the birds and the women are crying and all these hard-case IRA men are shaking him by the hand and one kid even got him to sign a plastic bullet. What are you going to write on it? I says to him, and he looks at me and he winks. For the good times, he says, and the pair of us cracked up laughing like the mad Paddy bastards what we were.

*

The next day we're at the wedding in the photo. We're with Patrick and Barney and this cunt McManus, you would not believe this cunt: knob-end. Tommy's got Patricia with him. She wanted to take him to America. She wanted them to have a baby, but first she says that she wanted them to save up enough money so as they could bring her up in New York. They didn't want to bring up weans in Ireland, not with the way things were. Who could fucking blame them. If they had gone back then, Tommy would have been on the silver screen in Hollywood by now, there's no doubt about it.

Patrick was a real snob of a fella. This cunt wouldn't take public transport anywhere even though back in reality he was a promotions man in a fucking supermarket. You know the guy what comes up to you when you come through the door and gets you to take a nip of whiskey and a wee bite of a fruit scone? That's your man Patrick when he wasn't plugging boys for the Ra. But he was a good cunt to know. That was where we got the knock-off booze.

Barney looked like one of them Italian pit bulls, only with a moustache. First thing he says to Patricia is he pulls up his shirt so as it's just his poor suffering chest with the bruises and the purple scars all over it – some of them scars are written on my brain till this day – and he says to her, go ahead and punch me, love. Go ahead and punch me, darling, he says to her. Of course she doesn't want to do it. What breed of woman wants to punch a man in the fucking chest the minute she's met him? But everybody's half-blocked and shouting and Tommy says, fucking bang him one, so as she goes ahead and she swings for him and he just throws his arms wide and he says to her, I didn't feel a fucking thing, he says, and he walks off, like a fucking maniac.

*

None of these boys could read or write; they was all basically illiterate. I was the youngest but at least I had been to school. People like your Tommys, your Barneys, your Pats. All these guys. Their das had them out working since they were seven year old. You should have seen the wedding cards they gave to Ellen and her husband Desi, who was a midget, basically. There were commas after every word, like, this, see, it, would, do, your, fucking, crown, in, or another classic was where they had every word underlined for some unknown reason. Either way, there was barely a word spelt correct between the three of them. It was like they were guessing how the English lingo worked. But it was no problem, because Ellen and Desi could barely read themselves. There was a big banner up in the hall that even spelt their names wrong. Above the door it said Live Musice. Between us we had rewritten the entire fucking world; not bad for a bunch of uneducated Irishmen.

*

Longhairs came late to Belfast. It was 1972 before I ever clapped eyes on a hippy, but there he was right enough, sitting on the ground at a bus stop on the Lisburn Road in the blazing sunshine, with his bare feet and an acoustic guitar round his neck with a piece of string; I could barely believe my lamps.

So as some longhairs turn up at the wedding, some hippy bastards, and they stand out like plums. Tommy starts to making jokes. Look at these fucking women, he says, and he's doing this comedy walk, mincing up and down. I'm sure I recognise one of them but I can't place him. At this point I don't know any of the boys with the long hair. Then this guy who I nearly almost recognise comes over with some of his longhair pals and he walks up to Tommy. Are you Tommy Kentigern? he says to him. Tommy says to him, who wants to know, fucking Bob Marley? and he turns round to us and he's all laughing and winking. The guy is just looking at him. What are you talking about? he says to him. Bob Marley is a Rastafarian. I don't give a fuck what you are, Tommy says to him. Tommy's confused, Pat says, he means Bob Dylan. Don't fucking correct me, Tommy says to Pat, and he turns on him. I mean fucking Bob Marley, he says. What songs does Bob Marley sing? the guy asks him and there was something in the way he says it, something arrogant in his voice, that made me recognise him for who he was. Ah fuck, I says to myself, it's only fucking Mackle McConaughey, this guy's a commandant in the IRA. A killer, a hero, a serious guy. I put my hand on Tommy's shoulder. Tommy, I says to him, take it easy. Take it easy, he says to me, what the fuck is wrong with you? Then he turns back to Mack. Bob Marley sings the song about the wind, he says to him, don't fucking try to cheat me. It's Bob Dylan what sings the song about the fucking wind, Mack says to him, cool as you like. Look, I says to the both of them, who gives a fuck about Bob Marley and Bob Dylan. Excuse me if I'm wrong, I says, but you're Mackle McConaughey, are you not? One of his longhair pals steps up to me. Who the fuck are you? he says. I'm Samuel McMahon, I says to him. Sure, I thought it was yourself, McConaughey says to me. Suddenly he's all friendly, like. How's your ma? he says to me. Ah, she's grand, I says to him.

You're Mackle McConaughey? Tommy says. Now he can't believe his lamps. I'm sorry for calling you Bob Marley, he says. That was unforgivable. Sure, I probably did mean Bob Dylan. Fuck it, Mack says, let's get the green in, and he and his boys head to the bar. I'm starting to breathe again. Tommy gives me a look and under his breath he says to me, is the fucking Ra really coming to this? But we all end up getting half-blocked and at one point Mack actually gets up onstage with the band and sings 'Blowin' in the Wind'.

Now Tommy knew nothing about the rock n roll. None of us did. I mean, we all went to see Bill Haley when he played Belfast. That was just an excuse to rip out the seats. But that night I looked at Mack, who had his arm around Tommy by this point, the pair of them completely blocked and talking into each other's faces, and I thought to myself, the times they are a-fucking changin' alright.

*

Did you ever try the toffee treacle pudding with nothing but cold custard on the top? What?! You've never lived, son. Just a carton of cold custard poured right over the top? The custard has to be cold, otherwise forget it. Some munch.

That's what I miss most in the jail. But there's other things, wee things you get in here that bring back memories, like for instance hot chocolate, you get the hot chocolate in here this weather, and that takes me back to when I was a wee boy in the Ardoyne, that and the carbolic soap, the smell of that carbolic soap takes me right back every time, back to the old house, where we'd all be sleeping in the one bed beneath all these jackets, my da's big coats all spread out on top of us (we never saw a duvet in our lives, are you fucking kidding me) and they all smelt of the carbolic soap, that's what my ma would wash our clothes in, only in the jail they have proper sheets and blankets and stuff like that and they wash them in a washing machine with Persil so as you have to wait till you get into the showers before you can get a good sniff, a good sniff of memory. It's a fucking step up, in some ways.

*

Tommy's da was on death's door for about the space of what seemed like forever. They says that back in the day he had been involved in the Easter Uprising, that he had done time for the cause, but I never knew anybody who could confirm it and besides, what fucking age must the cunt have been? Tommy wore a gold George V sovereign ring on his finger that he said his da had made in the jail but who knows what goes on, they'll tell you anything. When you would go round to Tommy's in Jamaica Street everybody would sit in the kitchen and you would hear his da moaning from behind this curtain they had set up round his bed in the corner. I always thought he just seemed sorry for himself. It was all a big fucking drama. Occasionally this fucking disembodied hand would come out from behind the curtain and grab a cup of fucking tea or a lit fag and then it would go back to moaning to itself. It was fucking disconcerting. You're sitting there trying to eat a biscuit and this guy is wailing like a fucking leper. Everybody would sit and talk to him through this thick fucking curtain. First time I saw it I says to myself, what is this, the fucking *Wizard of Oz*?

At first Tommy's da didn't want us to get involved in the Ra. Get a paper round, he says to us, do something decent with your life. His own da had been involved but then he got hit by a taxi when he was coming home half-blocked and that was the end of that. Tommy's da was just as bad. You should have seen his record. Years later I sent away for it and I get it on a flappy disk out the archive: drunk and disorderly, refusing to do the dishes, no-shows, punch-ups in the canteen. I never knew the Ra used to have canteens, but there you go.

Tommy's ma was alive and well but she was even less of a presence than his disembodied da. A big brooding face with big brooding lamps like big brooding coals plus she was tied to that sink and that stove. I never saw her outside the kitchen except for once at a funeral and once at a hospital visit, but wait till I tell you. I guessed that she must have slept in there beside her man. The toilet was out the back so as there was no need to go ganging up the stair or into the front room. I don't even know if there *was* a front room. And allow me to correct a well-known fallacy: everybody thinks that Catholics, and certainly Republicans, and definitely members of the IRA, hated the Queen, but that could not be further from the truth, my friend. 1977 was the Queen's Silver Jubilee and Tommy's ma was collecting stuff about her. She had a memorial biscuit tin on her shelf and a mug with the Queen's face on it and a badge, as well as a souvenir magazine that she kept in a drawer and that she would pull out when the guests came around. It made no sense to me because Fuck the Queen was my motto. But the mums loved her. My own ma was crazy about her. Even as her friends and neighbours were getting burnt out their homes in her name. The fucking Irish, you want to tell me about it.

Now, so there was a rumour that Tommy's da knew the location of an arms stash in Armagh, and not just any old arms stash, but one that was supposed to have come from Libya or Saudi Arabia –

don't ask me, how would I know – but a big one, by way of some of the big boys, was what they says. Tommy didn't want to bring it up with his da but then Mackle McConaughey leans on him. Don't end up like your da, Mack says to him. Do something with your life, Mack says to him, which is exactly what Tommy's da was saying to us, only the reverse. Personally, I'll take liberating a Libyan arms stash for a bunch of street-fighting nationalists over delivering *The People's Friend* to your agoraphobic ma and I says as much to Tommy but he was touchy about his ma, they all were, so as I dropped it. But he eventually agreed to bring it up, under the stipulation that I did all of the negotiating and that if it was going to bring any heat down on his da then we would make out that the whole story was bollocks and we would say that it was a result of wee dafties talking their gobs off and that there were no arms really, to speak of, and that the whole thing had been nothing but a masquerade.

*

I take a seat in front of this curtain, this black nicotine-stained curtain that smelt of boiled meat and fucking – sadness. Tommy's ma – her name was Josie – gives me a mug of tea with Prince Philip's face on it. Tommy looks over at me. When he was that nervous way of his, he would start with the fiddling with his hair, wrapping it round his finger and pulling it out. He was sensitive about his bald patches but he was his own worst enemy. That's what he's doing right then.

I clear my throat, I'm like that, how are you doing in there, Mr Kentigern? I says to him. It's your man Samuel, I says to him, come to say hello. There's an endless silence, then a coughing fit. Finally he replies to me. How the fuck do you think I'm doing? he says. Aye, it's hard times, I says to him. It's hard times, isn't it, Mr Kentigern? I says. What's so fucking hard about your times? he says to me. We're all struggling, I says to him. We're all part of the struggle. I'm fucking struggling to get out my bed, he says to me. Last I heard you were struggling with some wee bird down The Shamrock.

Tommy's ma looked at me like I was a germ at this point. Aye, there's some cracking wee birds down that Shamrock, I says to him, I'm not about to lie. I see Tommy put his head in his hands. His ma is banging the saucepans this way and that. Don't talk to me about cracking wee birds, his da says to me, and this floating fist comes through the curtain like a ghost in a play.

Has this bastard come to taunt me? he says. Do you think I lie here day in day out because I'm trying to attract the wee birds? he says to me. Then Josie speaks up. He sacrificed his life for the troubles, she says to us. It wasn't all about birds and glory back then. Youse all think youse are a bunch of celebrities this weather. Look, I says, I've not come here to make light of anybody's contribution. Quite the opposite. I've actually come with a commendation. Certain people, let's say, are very aware of the quality of your service and your loyalty and the sacrifices what you have made for the cause (basically I was talking like a prize-winning author). I'm here to say thanks, I says to him, and to ask if there is any way in which we can help extend the great work you did in the past and perhaps, you know, secure your legacy for the future.

I'll cut straight to the point, I says to him. We are speaking here about the arms stash in Armagh. You're the only one that didn't go to jail, I says. And I know you had to deny the existence of any stash. And I also know, by the way, that at that time there were certain factions, shall we say, that were more interested in getting hold of the arms in order to secure their own economic status in certain areas. And kids were getting gunned down. In our own communities. You did the right thing. You took a noble stance. You said in court that the arms did not, in fact, exist. You said it was all bravado and double-dealing. And I know that later everybody gave a statement to the high command that the weapons were actually at the bottom of a river near the border. But I'm asking you. And this is coming direct from the boys up top, boys with no personal agenda or axe to grind, boys what are only interested in guerrilla warfare and in uniting this beautiful country what is where we live. What I'm trying to say, Mr Kentigern, is that you're the one holding the cards. And they're the ones writing the history books.

I sit back and I take a big gulp of tea from out this chipped royal mug. Another long silence, then another coughing fit, and then he replies. Are there going to be any cracking wee birds in it? he says to me, and Tommy's ma cursed him and all of Ireland, and Tommy cracked up laughing, and when I looked into Tommy's eyes, into those laughing Irish eyes, it was like I could see the future, mirrored there, and I says to myself, this is going to be beautiful, so it is.

*

Wait, see if you know this one:

> There's a Irish priest, in a Vauxhall Viva,
> on the other side of the border
> and he's swerving to this way and to that
> across the lanes, so as the garda have got zero choice
> but to pull him over,
> for that.
>
> This is on the road, from Newry to Dundalk,
> I'm sure youse mind the one.
> Have you been drinking, Father? the first garda says,
> and he smells booze on the priest's bad brefff.
> On the passenger seat, he spies a bottle,
> of Blue Nun, emptied, to the last.
>
> Sure, says the priest, but only water has passed these lips.
> Then how is it I can smell wine?
> And the priest looks down, at the empty wine bottle,
>   and he says,
> Christ Jayzus, he's done it again!

*

This is when we get the caravan. This is what they do in Israel, Mack says to me. We're waiting for Tommy at this farmhouse out Newtownabbey way. They have the top brass meetings in the caravans, Mack says to me, and then they scoot the caravans around the place, just so as they can never be found. Tommy says he knew a guy that was getting rid of one, quick style. Top-of-therange one, he says, thirty quid, he says, and he's gone to pick it up with Patricia so as it looked like they were buying it for going away on their holidays but really it was going to be a mobile Ra HQ. Fuck Mossad, Mack says, and he spits in his hands. Anything they can do, we can do better. Mack makes me the offer of a sly bifter. Do you ever urinate on your hands? he says to me. I'm not putting that fag in my mouth if you're pishing on your hands, I says to him. Pish, it's completely sterile, he says to me, and besides, he says, it's not like I don't wash them as well. Don't touch me with your pishy hands, I says to him, and I take a step backward. Gimme your hands, he says, let me see them, and he grabs them and he spreads out my palms, like that. Look at this, he says to me, and he shakes his head. These are the hands of a stillborn baby.

What?!

You want to toughen yourself up, he says to me, and the best way to harden your skin and to firm it up is to urinate on yourself. My da taught me that, he says to me, and he had a pair of hands like cured buffalo hide, he says. We stand there, smoking our pishy fags in silence. Did you ever hear about Barney? I says to him. Fuck is Barney? he says to me. Our pal, Barney Donnen, I says to him. The one what looks like the Italian pit bull? he says to me. Aye, he says, I know the very fella. You know he gets the disabilities on the bru? I says to him. What for? he says to me. I mean, I know he's mental, but still. He told the doctor he was a simpleton, I says to him. Got his wife to go along with it. Went in there and says to him he couldn't even mind his own name and that he thought his house was made of cheese, all this stuff. So as

they send someone out to see if he's really yon disturbed way and
if he qualifies for the bru. Twenty minutes before the fella arrives,
Barney drinks four bottles of water. His wife shows the guy
into the living room and Barney's sitting there on a chair acting
doolally, just completely fucking out of it. The guy from the bru
asks him his first question and Barney just pishes himself right in
front of him. Just sits there in his chair and lets go with this river
of pish running down his legs and pooling round his feet. The guy
can't get out there quick enough. He's on the disabilities for life
after that. Christ Almighty, Mack says, and he shakes his head,
but that is fucking disgusting. It is that, I says to him, but think
of the quality of the skin on those legs. Must be like a fucking
rhino.

*

Just then Tommy and Patricia pull up in this van . . . thing, and
it's painted green and white. He's beeping the horn and waving
to us as they pull in. That's not a caravan, Mack says. That's a
fucking mobile home. Tommy gets out and leaves Patricia in the
passenger seat. What do youse think of the caravan? he says
to us. That's not a fucking caravan, Mack says to him. That's a
mobile home. Don't fucking split hairs with me, Tommy says. I'll
fucking split your lip if you turn up for a meeting with me again
in a green-and-white mobile home, Mack says to him. Do you
want to just write IRA On Tour on the side and be done with it?
Tommy was starting to look a bit sheepish. I almost felt sorry
for him. Give it a good coat of paint, I says to him. A caravan's a
caravan, I says, at least this way we don't need to drag it round
behind a car. Good for quick getaways and that. Exactly, Tommy

says, that's what I'm talking about. I'm out of here, Mack says. I got youse in on good report, he says to us, after your performance in Dundalk. Now don't fuck it up. Get that caravan sorted and make sure youse are in Armagh next week, at the Keady campsite. Youse are going to move on the weapons. And youse better be on top form. Because the sketch is complicated. That's what he says. Then he walks off. Oh, so it's a caravan now, is it? Tommy says. Do you know he pishes on his hands? I says to him. That's as bad as fucking Barney, he says.

*

This is me and Tommy in a caravan park in Armagh, and Barney was there too. The point is to look like tourists, Mack says to us, and in the name of the wee man we gave it our best shot. We sat outside the caravan – radio on, tops off – drinking cans of green that Pat had liberated from Safeways. Up the fucking Rebels, we says, and we gave it plenty. We played card games and we smoked and we listened to the old rock n roll. Dion and Lonnie Donegan and Elvis, that was all fine. But then this song comes on, some fucking harridan woman singing about pishing in a fucking river. It was the time of the punk rockers and Tommy was fucking fuming. I wouldn't sit here and listen to that filth, he says to us, and he gets up and he turns the radio off in a rage. Can you imagine Como singing a song like that? Barney says to us. Never, Tommy says. Wouldn't happen. Como never let a curse word pass his lips, Barney says. He was always a clean liver, he says. Tommy passes me a fag and I just about manage to get it lit in the wind what's coming in from the ocean, must be. Plus he was a good Catholic, Barney says. Barney's sitting on a deckchair in nothing but a pair of blue swimming trunks. I thought he was a Jew? I says to them. Fuck off, Barney says, Como was never a Jew. What about all them Jewish songs he sang? I says to them. That was just him reaching out to the other side, Tommy says. English wasn't even his first language, Barney says. It was Italian. He would only speak the English in the songs. And in the TV shows. Otherwise it was fucking original Italian the whole ways. Nothing was off limits to Como. Even fucking English.

What about birds and booze? I says to him. I thought he drew the line at that? And fucking curse words, Barney says, and he nods his head again, all solemn, like, you forgot those, he says. Fuck Como, I says to them, I've had enough of him already, I says, just for a joke. Hey you, Tommy says to me, fucking cool it. Then he stands up with a fag in his mouth and rubs the suntan lotion into his bare chest. Don't take this too far, he says to me, you're talking to a true believer here. Never forget that. Never underestimate the power of a true believer, he says. Then Barney gets up and starts singing in this mad vibrato style, singing about fucking rain falling, and flowers growing, and prayers being heard, up above, all this stuff. He has his head thrown back and his arms outstretched in those fucking torture trunks of his. Sure, you're murdering that, Tommy says to him, sit the fuck back down. But Barney keeps up with the singing, even as he's backing away from Tommy, who's rounding on him. Tommy was the singer in the group, there was no question. He could have been on the London stage. Tommy takes a run at him. He rugby-tackles Barney and he decks him. They end up wrestling each other on the ground in front of the caravan with everybody watching, the both of them screaming and laughing, but really going at it. Two boys away on their holidays for the first time ever; I mind it like it was only yesterday.

*

Another thing I mind is the sizzlers, these big massive steaks they served still sizzling on a hot plate at the canteen in the caravan park that were the side of a cow, basically, and every day for dinner we had one of these guys each and nothing else until the guy what runs it says to us, don't you guys eat your vegetables, and Tommy says to him, I spent my childhood stealing spuds from the grocer's, he says, from here on out it's steaks and nothing but, big lad.

*

But Mack was right when he said that the sketch was complicated, even if he didn't realise quite how much. Tommy's da, it turned out, had liberated half the stash himself. He had been sitting on it the whole time and over the years he had been digging into it and selling it to local clowns and to gangland headcases and to drug dealers. Anyone, basically, with a couple of quid to run together. As soon as he hears that Mack is asking after it, he comes clean to us, has Tommy's ma leave the room – fuck only knows what she did with herself – and this big pale leprous hand comes floating out from behind this black curtain, this black curtain like hell's gates opening right in front of us, and he makes us shake on it and promise that we would tell nobody while we figure out what the fuck story we're going to come up with for this one. He was Tommy's da, after all. And family is forever.

Luckily, he'd been doing all this through a guy name of Jimmy Smalls, who in turn was passing them on to a guy name of Danny McGonigle, who was the fella doing the actual deal in the first place. So that although the trail was messy, at least Tommy's da wasn't the first point of contact. But still, this left us with several fucking headaches.

Headache number one: it made me look like a plum after my big speech where I laid it on thick about him being a hero of the revolution or whatever the fuck it was what I said.

Second headache: Mack knew exactly what the size of the arms stash was supposed to be. There was going to be questions when half of it turned out to be unaccounted for.

Headache number three: (and this might have been wild speculation on my part but) my big paranoid fear back then was that Mack knew where the stash was the whole time. That he knew what had happened to it and that he was playing every one of us along as part of, I don't know, a loyalty test, or a way of flushing out old corrupt remnants of the IRA, like Tommy's da, or some covert scheme or other.

The point is we were fucked if we did and fucked if we didn't. And did is better than didn't. In my book, anyroads. And this might teach you something about Tommy. He went ahead and he bought that caravan. He got Barney in without telling him the full story. He went through with the whole deal of moving us down to Armagh to this caravan park in the middle of fucking nowhere. All the time knowing full well that the entire set-up was a ruse and that it was his own da's backhanded scheming (let's face it) that we were going to have to go through the masquerade of unravelling.

*

That was a word Tommy taught me. That word called *masquerade*. He was the first person I ever heard use it. He found this mad painting of a fox lying in the woods in a car boot sale. He was convinced it was worth money. He shows it to Barney and Barney says to him, a dead fox, eh? The fox isn't dead, Tommy says to him, what are you talking about? That fox is fucking dead alright, Barney says. It's just sleeping, Tommy says. Tommy's getting all sentimental about this fucking wild fox lying in the fucking woods. It's dead, Barney says to him. It's a dead fucking fox, lying in the woods, dead. It's just sleeping, Tommy says. The fox is just lying there sleeping. And Barney says to him, the fox is fucking dead. Do you think he could have got that close to it if it had only been sleeping? And Tommy says to him, you mugs know nothing about art. And you know nothing about foxes, neither. That fox is just sleeping, he says. That painting is what you call *a masquerade*.

*

Son, did I tell you there was a big picture of your man Mickey Mouse on the side of the caravan? Tommy found it in a skip and fell in love with it. Repainted the van and stuck it on the side. He loved his cartoons on a Saturday morning. This is a piece of art, he says to us, and then he says that he was going to subscribe to the *Reader's Digest* as soon as he has enough money. This is what we should be doing, he says, we should be furthering ourselves. I don't know how he was getting into all this stuff about reading and about art and stuff. For an uneducated Irishman it made no sense.

*

Right, so as there were two plans. The first was Mack's. The arms, according to us, were buried in a field behind a sewage works near the border and so as we could dig them up without arousing suspicion, Mack's idea was that we were to fill the caravan with blocks of peat, which we would then claim we were going around digging up for the fire and the most they would do is chase us off and call us a bunch of halyins. The second was ours and it coincided nicely with Mack's. It was that we would buy all this peat, dig a big fuck-off hole in the ground, dump the arms down into it, fill the hole with peat, dig it all back up again, lay claim to the arms in the name of the Free State, and everybody wins. Only first we had to get the arms off Jimmy Smalls, who in reality had them in a garage in Milford.

*

Jimmy Smalls lived alone with his ma and when we turned up she was making him his crispy pancakes, and sure I love those things, so I do, and she took a few more out the packet and stuck them in the oven, just for us, so as we ate these fucking dynamite wee crispy pancakes and all the while his ma's oblivious, completely clueless, but Jimmy knows something is up. He's chewing all slow like a mad old bull on its last meal and scratching his leg underneath the table and looking up at us with his head down.

Now Jimmy Smalls had a big lump on his coupon. He had been jumped by a gang of Huns when he was coming home from school one day and this egg-shaped lump on his forehead had risen up and had never gone away. Him and his sister Denise were both picked on bad when they was young. Tommy's da says people used to call her Disease Smalls. Ha ha, that was a good one.

So Barney's looking at this fucking lump on Jimmy Smalls's head and glancing over to me and winking and I know he's going to say something. He puts his fork down and he says to Mrs Smalls, sure Mrs Smalls, would you have any vegetables to go with this choice wee crispy pancake?

Ah, son, she says to him, it's only these oven chips, I never knew youse were coming, otherwise I would have got them in special, like. Never mind, Barney says, I'll just help myself to this Brussels sprout on Jimmy's head here. Then he bangs Jimmy in the ribs.

Jimmy's raging. I didn't fucking stick a fucking vegetable up my head, he says, this is a serious fucking injury. All the while he's pointing to this fucking egg thing sticking out his head. You with your fucking baby skin, he says to Barney, you've never seen a day's combat in your fucking life.

Now like I says, your man Barney had anything but baby skin. He looked like he had fallen asleep in the blazing sunshine in a kennel in the Mediterranean. That's how he got his nickname, The Italian Pit Bull. All the time Jimmy's ma is just sitting there smiling, I don't know if she was all there or what. Let me see your hands, Barney says to Jimmy Smalls. Sure, I will not, Jimmy says, and now he's sitting with his hands under the table. Why, because they're all soft from doing your ma's dishes your whole life? Barney says to him. He does his dishes, his ma says. Jimmy's a good boy. Okay, so she's out to lunch. Barney leans over to Jimmy and starts trying to grab at his arm. Jimmy's sitting on his hands now. Let me go, you bastard, he says. I don't need to show you my hands in my ma's own house, he says. There's a tussle. Barney gets up behind him and with his big bear strength he pulls Jimmy's arms up and this thing goes flying out of Jimmy's hand and slides along the floor of the kitchen. It's a tiny little chatsby, a wee fucking snub-nosed handgun. None of us could believe our lamps.

Is this how you fucking welcome us? Tommy says to him, leaping up. With a gun under the fucking table? I came here to save your fucking arse, he says to him. Don't make me fucking bury it. You fucking shady wee bastard, Barney says to him, you're a fucking shady wee cunt, he says. Jimmy's ma gets up. I'll make some teas, she says, you boys make yourself comfortable. The whole thing is fucking weird. Now even I'm starting to see red. We drag Jimmy out to the garage in the back garden and that's when I lose it. Fucking hold him down, I says to Barney and Tommy, fucking hold that wriggling wee bastard still. Then I whip out my dick and I take a pish all over him. You fucking woman, I says to him as I'm pishing on his head, you fucking woman, as he's lying there, crying, like a woman.

That was unnecessary, Barney says to me, you should just have banged him one. I could not believe what I was hearing.

*

It was a messy start, mind. We had to clean him up. I bunged his ma some readies, I don't know why.

You're a wee angel, she says to me, which only made it worse. Then we drive off, in the dark, to this garage Jimmy Smalls had, down a lane behind a petrol station, in the dark, this garage lit up by this broken sign, this broken sign flashing on and off and making this buzzing noise, this buzzing noise that went gar-age gar-age gar-age, in the dark.

*

So there was this one poem Tommy knew off by heart, no one knew how he had learnt it or why. But he must have put the effort in, because he couldn't read it on his own, so as someone must have taught him. When he was nervous he would turn it on and go into it, 'The One Eye of the Little Yellow God', and on the way to the garage in the dark he starts it off, this whole fucking thing about a one-eyed yellow god in the sky, raining down on all the poor bastards below. The one-eyed yellow god was the guy he turned to in a corner. Him and Perry Como, what a team. So Tommy goes on with this poem, and it's a sit-on-your-hoop epic, and Barney's up front with Jimmy Smalls, who stank of my own pish, which was rank, I admit, with Jimmy staring into space like he's already dead. We get to the flashing garage sign, which is buzzing, in the dark, and that's when Jimmy goes and drops the bomb.

I need to get the keys from your man McCaffrey what runs the garage, he says to us, on account of it belonging to the fella. How many people know about this fucking garage? Tommy says to him. Just me and your da and your man McCaffrey, Jimmy says. Does your man McCaffrey know what's hidden in there? Tommy says to him. Sure he knows nothing, Jimmy Smalls says.

Okay, we can't be seen by this ignoramus, Tommy says. I'm going to trust you, Jimmy, to go around there on your own, and to get the keys and come back without a word. You've got two minutes, he says to him, before we blow the place to kingdom come. I looked at Tommy and I could see that he was serious. We get out the caravan and Tommy pulls out a chatsby, puts it up to Jimmy Smalls's head. You were going to shoot me, you wee bastard, he says, and now I'm hotter than I feel inclined to tell. Two minutes, Tommy says to him, then the whole shabazz goes up. I think he meant to say shebang, The Shabazz was an Indian restaurant in Belfast, but I wasn't going to be the one to correct him.

Jimmy disappears around the corner and Barney unbuttons his shirt. I'm sweating like a rapist, he says. It's a clear night and the stars are out. When you get outside Belfast you can really see the stars, I says to them. And what are they saying tonight, Socrates? Tommy says. Something about a one-eyed yellow god, raining down on all of Ireland, I says to him. I didn't catch the rest. Tommy laughed then. Some poem, isn't it? he says. It is, I says to him, the way you tell it.

We stood there and counted to one hundred and twenty under our breath, with the bright stars above us in the sky, until there was no sign of Jimmy coming back, and Tommy says to us, fuck it, and he kicks the lamp post next to him, and the light sputters for a moment, and I look around at Barney and he's standing there, smiling, and I start to laugh myself, I just burst out laughing, it was great right then, that's all I can say, we were going to blow the place sky-high; what a feeling.

*

Okay, so this is a cracker, tell me if you've heard this one before:

> Pat and Mick are in a park off the Falls Road and they
>   find a stash of
> three hand grenades, planked
> beneath a tree.
>
> Pat says, we had better hand these in to the peelers
> but Mick says to him, wait, what if one of them blows
>   up on the way?
>
> Pat says to him, don't worry,
> in that case we'll just lie and tell them
> that we only found two.

*

We go charging round the corner and through the window we can see Jimmy lit up in the night because he's behind the desk

with the cashier and he's on the fucking blower. Barney kicks
the door in and takes a shot at him, hits him in the wrist and
it's like his arm exploded, his hand is blown off and his tendons
dangling down and the phone is still in his hand, hanging there,
and Tommy jumps up and slides over the counter and the cashier
crouches down and starts whimpering and Tommy picks up this
night-duty torch that is lying there on the counter and he starts
beating Jimmy over the head with it, I see his head cave in, I
think he took his lamps out, but Tommy keeps at it, the noise is
disgusting, fucking, stupid, cunt, Tommy's screaming, whapping
him over the head with this fucking thing, we, came, here, to,
help, you, you stupid, fucking, cunt, he's yelling, and now he's
dead, fuck it, Jimmy Smalls is dead.

Tommy to the cashier: who was your man Jimmy Smalls calling?
Quick, he says, and he picks the cashier up by the hair and pushes
him, face down, into the counter. A car pulls into the garage. They
catch light of what's going on and they're out of there in seconds.
I don't know, the guy says, I really don't fucking know. What's he
say on the phone? Tommy says. You were standing next to him
the whole time, what did he say? He said nothing, the cashier says
to Tommy, he said fuck all, he says. He just picked up the phone,
he just dials a number and then he just stands there, listening.
Don't fucking lie to me, Tommy screams at him, but the cashier's
crying, he's sobbing and he's begging for his life. I'm not lying,
he says, Jimmy said fuck all, he says, he didn't speak at all, he
just stood there, listening, in a trance. There's somebody on the
other end of the phone but I couldn't hear them speaking. They
answered but they didn't say anything. And that was when he got
his arse plugged, he says. That was everything what happened,

35

the wee cashier says. That's all I know, he says.

Where are the keys to the garage? Tommy says to him. They're in the till, the guy says, and Tommy gets him to open it for him and he throws them to me. Make sure these keys work and come back and tell me, Tommy says, then he forces the guy back down into the counter and puts a gun to the side of his head. I run out back in a panic.

I can hardly get the key in the lock for jangling but sure enough it works, and I slide the door up, and then I near shite myself. The garage is full of people. Standing there, in silence, staring back at me. It's a fucking set-up. I pull my gun out and I jump back. I take a shot. Bam: nobody makes a sound. I let off a round. Bam bam bam: no cunt's moving.

That's because they're all fucking mannequins. Fuck me but the garage is full of mannequins all pressed up against each other, and here's me having to squeeze through. There's barely any room to get by and their blank eyes are staring, and their cold hands are grabbing, and they smell like they've been imprisoned in here for years.

And I thought about all the mannequins that ever existed, all locked up in garages and in cupboards and with their missing arms and legs, and thrown away, in basements all over Northern Ireland, and I saw myself, right then, floating up, over Armagh, and seeing the rooftops lift off and the walls give way without a sound, trapped faces, looking up, without a word, and me, looking down, just the same.

But I push through to the back and there are boxes stacked to the ceiling and in the boxes there is the stash of your best dreams. Rifles and handguns and fucking anti-tank mines and grenades, you name it. I push my way back through this horrible fucking silent crowd but by this time I am so elated, I'm so high, that I kiss one of the baldy chicks right on the lips. I don't give a fuck.

I run back round to the garage, where Tommy is still holding the guy down by the hair. It's all there, I says to him, let's move it, and Tommy takes a cushion off the chair and puts it over the guy's head and empties three shots into his skull. Then he winks at me.

We cut a path through the cold, staring dummies. Barney's freaked out but Tommy's intrigued. We load the caravan with the weapons and we're out of there in twelve minute flat. I says to Tommy, imagine all the silent fucking dummies, all missing limbs and with their heads all baldy, locked up in fucking empty rooms, right now, just standing there in the dark, saying nothing, just staring into each other . . . Does that not gives you a shiver? Naw, Tommy says to me, and he laughs, that just reminds me of my childhood, he says, and we roar off, triumphant, into the black fucking night of 1970s Northern Ireland, the best decade what ever lived.

*

Tommy had a friend name of Miracle Baby. He said he was a good conversationalist, which was ridiculous, cause of the kid was a retard. Something had happened to him while he was being born, his umbilical got caught round his throat and not enough oxygen went to his brain. He was in the local paper, the headline says Miracle Baby, the name stuck. He would wander round the streets because his own family couldn't give a flying toss and he would talk to people over their hedges and people would feel sorry for him and bung him a few bob or offer him a biscuit. But Tommy actually spent time talking to the lad. I says to him once, excuse me but what the fuck is it that you and this Miracle Baby talk about? He's into every trick, Tommy says, he knows everything what's going on. Tommy actually had him working for him, he had him helping out in his da's garden. I say garden, but really it was a mound of black scorched earth where some eejit had set fire to a car, and about three daffodils. Now Miracle Baby is in there, digging out flower beds and building a very fucking rudimentary rock garden, it has to be said.

You could have fun with him, mind. Sing us a song about the IRA, we says to him, sing us a song about the struggle, and he knew them all. He'd come chiming in, giving it all the history you like, songs about the Bogside and Bloody Sunday. Tommy began teaching him Como. You want to have heard this wee retard murdering 'Tie a Yellow Ribbon'. Just thinking about it makes me nostalgic for the days when you used to have village idiots wandering about the place, what happened to that?

But the point is what happened with Miracle Baby. He became our man. He had access to everybody, inner-circle stuff, and gangsters, and even the British Army. Who else but a fucking retard would go up to armed soldiers in the street and try to engage them in conversation? Everybody knew him and everybody thought he was harmless. The only person what took him serious was Tommy. And he saw how he could use him. Not in a cynical way, because he genuinely liked the wee fella, but the point is this: Tommy was listening when nobody else was.

*

No one saw us leaving the garage with this massive arms stash in the back and a painting of Mickey Mouse on the side of our caravan. I began to think that Mickey was our lucky ghost, that he was making us invisible. We drove back to the caravan park and sweated through a few days, waiting for the law, or the Ra, or who knows, worse, to swoop, but we'd whacked the middleman and we'd severed the connection and the only people that could join the dots between us and the killing now were Jimmy's ma, who was mental, and Tommy's da, who was debatable.

Tommy calls him from a phone box down the road from the campsite. Jimmy Smalls is dead, he says to him. Ah fuck, his da says, and here's me sitting with a bottle of Bushmills for him as well. This is what passed for sympathy with Tommy's da. Still, there was the question of the guy on the phone. Who had Smalls been calling? We sat outside the caravan and debated, debated, debated. What if it's one of they set-ups? Barney says. What if it was Mack that was on the blower? I thought he had a point. But Tommy says it makes no sense. Naw, he says. Jimmy Smalls was selling those arms and had been for ages, selling them to all comers, he says to us, why would he suddenly phone a guy high up in the Ra and blow his own cover? What if it was your man Danny McGonigle? I says to him. After all, it was McGonigle he was selling them on to. Why don't we just fucking kill Danny McGonigle to be on the safe side? Barney says to us. Where'll it end? I says to him. Then who do we kill after we kill him to shut the next one up? Oh, there'll be no next one, Barney says, and all the time he's hoking away at his ear with a cotton bud and this fucking bud would come off and disappear inside his ear and get stuck in there and we'd have to use a fucking hairpin or a bent paperclip to hoke it back out. No cunt likes Danny McGonigle, Barney says to us, no cunt would bat their fucking lamps. In fact they'd be dancing in the streets. Either way, Tommy says to us, for now we go ahead with the masquerade of burying these arms in shite, and of digging them all the way back up again.

*

The arms stash – forgive me, son – the supposed arms stash, was meant to be buried round the back of this sewage works outside of Carnagh. We pull up in the evening, just as the light is settling. We left Barney behind to look after the caravan and so as we could give him a shout once the hole was ready. We couldn't have a Mickey Mouse caravan full of arms parked up at a sewage works in the dark. So me and Tommy borrow a car from an old pal that ran the taxis and fill the boot with turfs of peat. We park the car round the back and leave the boot open so as anybody can see what we were up to. Then we crack out the spades and get stuck in.

We were waist-deep when we struck shite. The stuff was leaking through the ground from the sewage plant, and it was green, green shite, come squelching out. First it's a trickle, then it's a full jet. Ah, we're bollocksed, I says to Tommy. Light some fags, he says to me. This is his solution. Smoke like fucking troopers, he says to me, it's the only way we're going to get through this. So as we clamp a set of fags between our teeth, and we keep to the digging. We're going to end up with fucking trench foot before the night's out, I says to Tommy. Soon we're waist-deep in liquid shite. Right, Tommy says, enough. I climb out and I pull him up after me. This is the perfect cover, he says to me. Who the fuck else would even come here?

We drop the car back at this guy's house, we'll call him Jackie, this boy Jackie, and of course his car is covered in shite. What in the name of all that's holy did you two just do, Jackie says to us, go to a gay disco? He took it well, considering. We called Barney and had him pick us up a few streets away. He didn't take it so well. If youse two get into this fucking caravan with those clothes on we will never get the stench out of this van, he says to us. Take off your clothes, he says, then youse can get in.

Don't fuck with me, Tommy says to him, and he goes to open the door. But Barney peels off and stops further down the street. I mean it, Barney says to us, youse are only getting in if youse take your fucking clothes off first.

Think about it: Barney's proposing that two fucking Irish rebel gangsters strip naked and climb into a Mickey Mouse caravan with a massive illegal arms stash in the back on the fucking main street of a town in bandit country. Fuck this, Tommy says, and he whips his shoes off and he tosses them under a hedge. Shirt, trousers and socks to follow. I do the exact same. Now wipe your hands, Barney says to us, like he's our ma, and we both bend down and wipe our hands in the grass. Curtains are twitching, we're standing there basically bollock naked in the street, but Barney finally lets us in and we go skidding off. We're both sitting in the back in nothing but a pair of Y-fronts, looking at each other, like that. Bring on the gay disco, I says to them. But no cunt's laughing.

That's when it occurs to me. Wait a minute, I says to Tommy, why are we going to all the trouble of digging a hole and burying the arms just to dig them back up again? Tommy looks at me with a vacant expression. He still hasn't clicked. With Jimmy Smalls out the picture, and the guy at the petrol station dead, there's no sinner to say otherwise, I says to him. Why don't we just say that we dug them up and here they are? Do you think anybody's going to go looking for a hole? Tommy looks at me for a minute or so. I'm waiting for the penny to drop, although he might just kill me, there's that too. But then he bursts out laughing. We both do. This is like a bad fucking Irish joke, he says to me, and he shakes his head. Barney shouts back from up the front. If youse want to make it authentic, he says to us, youse could always stick the guns up your arse before you hand them over. That was the punchline, right there.

*

Now, see, I've thought about that word for years, that word called *masquerade*. It comes from the times where the kings and queens of this world would go to their balls in disguise and mix it with the common people with the help of a mask, so as the person you met, you had no idea if they were a pauper, a king or a knave. Everybody, for a single night, could forget their identity. What a relief, I hear you say, but what the fuck does that have to do with a fox asleep, or dead, by a tree?

Okay, so as one day I'm out shopping, in the town, and I pick up this LP, Como, *The Early Years*. And this stuff sounds like Barney has a cotton wool bud stuck in his ear. The quality is murder, but the songs are top-notch. He sings all of the songs on there, 'Girl of My Dreams', 'Faithful Forever', 'Till the End of Time', a whole lifetime of songs. But then there's this other song there too, like a ghost song, come out of the past, and of course you know about ghosts, how they have cold hands, and I feel these cold hands on my head, pulling me awake, holding me under, and this voice comes in, only it's stuck, in the sound, in the clicking and scratching, but then these words, coming out of the background, these words, coming clear as light: *I'll meet you at the masquerade.*

I can feel the cold hands of the ghost, like a snake sliding down and coiling round my wild Irish heart. Ah fuck, I says to myself as Como's voice starts coming to me, and it's like he's trying and he's trying till he's come in, into the room, like a daemon or a spirit, and he's using what he can to come through, and that's when I realise; it's not Como singing anymore, it's Tommy come in, in the voice of Como. *Twelve o'clock is chiming*, he's singing, it's Tommy's come in, and his voice is coming through the air, I see him with his arms outstretched, and I smell him, that manly smell, his precious eyes, brimming over, as he turns and he points to the moon in the night-time sky, and now it is no longer

43

something up above us. *If you unmask your heart,* he sings, *I'll love you, love you. Midnight, shadows fade,* he sings, *no one's left at the masquerade. Everything is through, dear, but my love for you, dear, lives on.* And he holds that one last note forever.

*

But everything goes well. We hand over the arms to Mack, we get our first holiday in a caravan park, plus we're local heroes with The Boys. Tommy's da is off the historical hook, Mack doesn't even ask us about the weapons that were unaccounted for, plus he gives us three massive bags of grass for a present – that's grass as in marijuana – and even I'm starting to think that Tommy was right and that this guy *is* fucking Bob Marley.

None of us has ever done drugs before in our life but now we're sitting there with three fat supermarket bags full of the stuff. It's disgusting, Barney says, it smells like that vomity Italian cheese, he says. It's supposed to be good for listening to the music, Tommy says to us. Come over to mine later, he says, and we can listen to some Como on it and see how he sounds. Como would never approve, Barney says. He doesn't need to know, I says to him.

So as we agree to meet later on at Tommy's and smoke this stuff. I head back home for a bit, I was still living at my ma's by this point but she was away out for the night so as I thinks to myself, I should just smoke myself a wee doobster, just to acclimatise myself to it, like. So I roll myself a wee joint, about two inch long. Mix it with some tobacco. Open the window and take a hit.

Nothing. Nadja. Zip. Then I start to minding stuff. Next thing it's
a flood of stuff. Then it's like too-much-stuff, like a river of stuff,
a river what has burst its banks and what is sweeping everything
up in its wake and plus the waters are filthy in this river what's
coming back to me in a dream. I nip out back to the toilet. We
still had an old freezing outdoor loo in them days. I go out there
and I lock the door and I light the candle and I take a look in the
mirror. Holy fuck. I'm not kidding. There's nothing there. It's like
an ice rink. Frozen. Empty. There's no face, just thick fucking
ice that has frosted over the mirror. I'm stood there staring
into this frozen mirror at my own lack of a face for I don't know
how long. Where's my face. Where's my fucking face, Samuel?
But then these little colours start to form on the mirror, these
spinning little colours coming through the ice. And now I can see
it. It's little girls, starting to appear, little girls come in colour,
dancing and spinning and coming through the ice like in an old
Disney cartoon, in colour. I sit down on the can and I watch them,
beautiful, inside the mirror, is a splash of colour, spinning, and
skating on one leg, the other leg raised into the air behind them,
and some of them are pirouettes, spinning, and there's music,
somewhere far away there is romantic music, and I think to
myself, this is Central Park, I says to myself, it's that ice rink at
Central Park, Samuel, the one from the movies.

> And now it is snowing't
> The soft snowes,
>   falling't,
>   on all the little girls,
>   spinning't this way an
>   that,

I had always dreamt of New York. My ma was in love with America. She had a picture of JFK above the cooker. It's like *Doctor Who*, Samuel, I says to myself. This toilet just went and teleported you to New York, I says. There's one girl in the middle, spinning on the spot. I feel as if I know her. Even though I can't get a good look at her I feel a great connection. Little girl is a whole new possibility, Xamuel, I says to myself. Faceless girl, in a frozen mirror, coming through in colour. And now it's spinning faster and faster. Now the whole place is vibrating. I curl up on the floor and I hold on. I can't move. I'm fixed to the spot. There's nothing I can do. And now it feels like we're flying.

It's a bollocks cold night and there's no heating in the toilet. I'm going to die out here on my own and nobody will know, my ma won't be back to the morning and when she is she'll find my frozen corpse, these are the wild thoughts raging through my mind on this filthy river. But then all of a sudden I get this feeling of calm acceptance. I mean, your ma's toilet is hardly the worst place to die in. I lie there and I think of all the little girls, spinning into colour. And then it's like a minute has passed and I'm back on my feet. I stagger back inside and it's eleven o'clock at night. I was out there lying on the floor completely paralysed for three hour. Where had all the time gone? I missed Tommy and Barney and everything. I was that fucking angry I took all the grass I had and I poured it down the toilet bowl and I flushed it. When Tommy heard what I had done he went furious. He says that when you smoke it time stands still. He says that when you smoke it one Como song could last for eternity.

*

We all got a bit of money out the deal with Mack, a fair bit of money, actually, especially for us, back then, and we kitted ourself out with the tailored suits and the Aquascutum raincoats and the hats. I got a green dog-tooth suit, handmade, that was the envy of the Ardoyne, plus I was the first person in my street ever to have a gold watch. Thank god there's a war on, Tommy says to us.

Barney had this thing for Egypt, don't ask why, there's no point in analysing it. He bought himself a leather folder with pictures of Egypt on the front. I don't even know what the purpose of it was, whether he was planning on walking up and down Jamaica Street with it under his arm or keeping his letters from the bru all neat in it, but when you would go over there he would have it lying out on the table right in front of you, in a house that otherwise had no ornaments whatsoever.

Would you look at the craftsmanship in that, he says to us, look at the Nile picked out there, look at the detail of that, and there's the pyramids, he says, that's the boys right there, sticking up, that's one of the seventeen wonders of the world you're looking at, and that's your man the Giant fucking Sphinx crouched down there by the side. You're a Giant fucking Sphinx, I says to him.

Then he had this cigarette station, I think that's what you called them, carved out of dark wood to look like a mysterious island gone black with the sun. There was a wooden cobra at the front, rising up and getting ready to spit. Then there was a carved elephant's foot you used as an ashtray and another wee elephant that just stood there like it was too young to be there in the first place and an alligator that had its mouth open with little ivory teeth whose back you could use to strike a match on it and this gravestone thing that made no sense where you kept your matches in. If you wanted to smoke at Barney's he would pass you this thing and you would have to go through the whole fucking rigmarole of figuring it out while he's stood there staring at you and explaining about the crocodiles of the Nile and the elephants of Egypt. I don't even fucking know if they had elephants in Egypt, he would have been better off with a pair of camels, I telt him, a pair of dromedaries would have gone a lot better, I says to him, but he didn't want to hear it.

Tommy bought himself another painting. That's where the money is, he says to Barney. This is what you call an investment. Plus it tied in with Tommy's new thing about how as we should be furthering ourselves and always getting better. It was a painting of two fellas, looking away. Two figures in a landscape, setting out on a boat, into the painting, like the horizon was real. Aside from that there was nothing but sea and sky to be seen except for one coloured rock on the bottom right that had what looked like bright seaweed on it. Tommy says he thought it was Chinese. This could be worth serious money, he says, you know what the Chinese are like. You could see what he meant. When you looked at the brushstrokes there was something Chinese about it, which means something light and delicate but deep. Then Tommy says to us: it's allegorical. Where the fuck did he get a word like that? This is allegorical art, he says to us. Barney says to him, aye, well, but there's not much to it, is there? It's not much of a painting at all, he says, if you ask me. You mugs just don't get it, Tommy says to us, and he shakes his head. Then he points to the two figures crossing the sea. Lighting out for another shore, he says to us, and he smiles, like he's explaining something rudimentary to a small child with great difficulty. You mugs just don't have a feel for the arts, he says to us. Mugs like you could never hope to understand, he says. Then he walks out the room, shaking his head at the state of the mugs in this world. It was another insight into Tommy's brain. And it looked like a fucking empty ocean with two Chinese fishermen on it. It's not how I pictured it, I'll be honest with you.

*

Right enough, we start getting jobs, the odd bank heist, the occasional kidnap. We were on our way. We meet Mack at a cafe in town. He orders one of them salads. It was the first time any of us had seen a radish. Barney picks one up to examine it. A wee, perfectly formed one. See if I was a radish, he says to us, I would be this one right here.

I need youse to kidnap somebody for me, Mack says. That got our interest. But it's a woman, he says. Barney puts the radish down. What's she done to anybody? Tommy says. It's not her, Mack says. It's her man. Her man owes us money and the fucker has stopped paying. Did you threaten him with the kidnapping of his wife? I says to him. Of course not, Mack says. This way we've got the element of surprise. What do you want us to do with her? I says to him. Youse just need to hold her hostage, Mack says. I can't have a woman going home with me, I says to them, especially if she's bound and gagged. That got a laugh. We've got a house youse can use, Mack says, but one of youse will have to look after her till her man pays up. And what if he doesn't pay up? Tommy says. I guess we'll just have to sell her off, Mack says, and he shrugs. Everyone's sat there like that: dumbfounded. They're fucking selling women now in the IRA? But then Mack bursts out laughing. You bunch of fucking eejits, he says to us, things aren't that bad. One of youse will just have to marry her, that's all. And keep her imprisoned behind closed doors for the rest of her life. Just like my loving ma and da, Tommy says, and we cracked up laughing all over again.

*

Her name was Kathy M. She worked as a waitress at the Europa Hotel, the most bombed hotel in Europe. She lived on the Springfield Road. Her husband ran some bookshop in town. Every day she walked to the Europa, about a half-hour walk each way. We picked her up in a car on her way home from work and threw her in the back seat. Barney sat on her and Tommy put a pillowcase over her head. I was the driver.

*

> this house they puts us in
> you should have seen this house
> the state of this house
> dirt floors and
> IRA graffiti on the walls
> w/a single burst
> couch on the dirt
> floor

what do you fucking
want,
le Europa? Mack says to us
a fucking carpet would've be nice,
I says to him.

*

At first we tied Kathy to a chair in the middle of the room with
a gag and a pillowcase on her head but whenever we untied
her to let her eat a chinky she just throws the food at us and
kicks at us with her high heels, so as we take the high heels
away from her and try feeding her with a spoon. Then she
just spits it back in our faces. And the lingo that came out her
mouth. Como would've blushed. Let her fucking starve, Tommy
says to us. You're not in a hotel now, love, he says to her. As
soon as we take the gag out she goes ballistic about the IRA.
You're supposed to be fucking looking out for people like me,
you useless bastards, she's screaming, stuff like this. Sure as I
felt bad and all. What's the point in torturing one of your own?
But Tommy says to her, your man borrowed money from The
Boys and he needs to have the gumption to pay it back. The
gumption? I says to myself. What do you think the IRA runs on,
Tommy says to her, buttons? Loaning him money *was* looking
out for him, he says to her, and now he needs to do the right
thing. Is this what it'll be like in a united Ireland, she says
to him, and the tears are streaming down her face. Kidnap,
torture, rape, she's saying, is this what the future adds up to?
Nobody's raping nobody, Tommy says to her. Get me the fuck
out of Ireland, she says to him, get me the fuck out because it's a

madhouse. Every one of youse is the fucking troubles. She kept saying that. Every one of youse is the fucking troubles. I'm going to be your fucking troubles alright, if you don't button your lip, Tommy says to her.

*

Me and Tommy goes to see her husband. It's not a bookshop he owns but a comic shop. We walk in there and there's weans talking at the counter so as we immediately goes to the heads-down style and start with the browsing. And that's when I spot it. Doctor Who's Tardis in the corner of the room. Like a hypnotist snapped his fingers and I'm eating a raw onion, I immediately go into this flashback only it's like I'm back in the outdoors toilet and I'm nailed to the floor while it's taking off into space. I'm holding onto the comic racks to stay on my feet, I'm covered in this cold sweat, I'm seeing this fucking skating rink in the sky, in this fucking frozen mirror, and I put my arms out to my sides and I feel myself taking off, into the air, until I'm on a planet with two moons and the moons have both got a face like Tommy's, hypnotising me, drawing me toward them, and the moons are calling me, Xamuel, Xamuel, Xamuel of Old, they says, and that's when I wake up and I'm lying on the floor of this comic shop and Tommy and the guy what runs it are both looking down at me but I can't tell them apart because *they look the exact same.*

*

Here,
wait a minute,

                hold on a second here,
                see if you know this one:

                how many Irishmen
                does it take
                to change a light bulb?

                two:
                one, to hold the light bulb
                two, to drink till the room spins.

                                  *

Now the whole room was spinning and this guy, who I'm not
kidding looked *exactly like Tommy*, this guy whose wife we have
tied up at a secret location, is holding my head and feeding me
water. Sure, you're alright, he's saying to me, it's just a wee dizzy
spell. You'll be right as rain, he's saying, all of this stuff to raise
the dead. I start to get a bit of sense about me and I can see that
Tommy is agitated. He's looking at this guy and he's freaked out
because the two of them are almost the mirror image of each
other. Tommy starts making excuses. He takes these fits, he
says to his doubled image, I'll just get him back up the road. Do
you want me to shout youse a cab? his double says to him. He's
looking nervously and in amazement at Tommy who is looking
nervously and in amazement at himself. No, you're alright,
Tommy says to this mirrored double, I'll get him home fine on my
own, pal, he says. Sorry about that, pal, I says to this double, I
just took a funny turn, I says. What were you guys after, anyway?
the double says to us. Then he says something weird.

Are you guys from Control? he says to us, and the three of us stop and look at each other for a second, like that. Then: what's Control? Tommy says to him. I thought you might be able to tell me, the double says to him, and then he doesn't say another thing because this big hole opens up in the air between us and we're all looking down into it like, vertigo.

Tommy says to him, we're looking for the Tarzan comics. You got any Tarzan comics? The guy looks relieved or confused or probably both. Sorry, he says to us. I'm sorry about that before, just there, he says. Where? Tommy says. Just then, he says. About what? Tommy says. Earlier, the double says. Tommy says nothing. Okay, the double says. Understood, he says. Then he goes into this whole big fucking spiel. We got this Tarzan comic, we got that Tarzan comic. And here's me thinking there was just one fucking Tarzan comic. Is it in colour? Tommy says to him. Is there one that's in colour? Tommy says to him. A collector, are you? the double says to him. Just starting, Tommy says. Just getting the lay of the land, he says to him, and he presses the back of his hand to his forehead and he opens up his palm, as if he's staring straight into the sun.

The guy looks at him for a second and then he sort of does the same thing, makes the same signal with his hand on his head, only shakily and half-heartedly, so as it was as if maybe he didn't do it as well, like a secret signal that wasn't meant for you and maybe you only imagined it. Then this double, he says to us, *Tarzan, Lord of the Jungle*, that's what youse are looking for, boys, he says, and he pulls out these comics in the plastic bags. John Buscema, he says to us, pointing to the cover, that's your man right there. Who's he? Tommy says to his double. He's the artist, his double says to him. *Silver Surfer*, *The Avengers*, guy's a legend, he says.

I take a look at this one cover myself. I feel like I recognise the artwork and I says to this double, is that your man what did *Doc Savage*? I love *Doc Savage*, I says. Sure, Tommy's double says, your man did the cover of the very first issue of *Doc Savage*. I've got that, I says to Tommy. You ever see his *Savage Sword of Conan* stuff? the double bill says to me and he hands me a bundle of issues. Here, he says to me, free of charge, he says. They'll make you feel better, he says, they always do with me. I don't want to take them. What am I going to do, go back to the house and read them while his wife chokes on a poke of chinky chips? But then he forces them on me. Good to meet a true fan, he says, and then he winks at me, like I'm in the club now too or something.

This is a balls-up, Tommy says when we get outside, a right royal fucking balls-up, and I says to myself, the plot just thickened, Xamuel, as we jumped on the first bus to anywhere, and we looked down at these mad comics in our laps and at each other, for the first time, with suspicion, like who is the true fan here, Xamuel, and what does that mean, or what.

*

That night I go home and I lie in my bed and I read *Savage Sword of Conan* before I fall off to sleep. There's one page in particular, one page what sticks in my mind. Your man Conan is lying on a cushion that's the shape of an exotic seashell, on a luxurious bed, and there's joss sticks burning and it looks like a harem or a whorehouse.

This woman what never opens her eyes, I think she's meant to be a blind, this blind woman, is lying, spread out, on the bed, and she is talking to Conan.

She wears a tiny veil.

At first, she thinks that he is somebody else.

But then she puts her blind eyes up to his face and she says to him: you're not savage enough to be my lover. If thou hadst been Himself, earlier this day, she says to him, He would have torn out yon rival's limbs and fed them to the Aeways Starving't Dawgs. Then she says to him, there's only one thing my lover likes as much as pitiless violence, and she climbs up on top of him and they make savage love.

*

The Old Gods, also known as The First Powers, stand assembled here in conference.

Their true names are subatomic and so unpronounceable by incarnates.

We have given them the name of Father, Grandfather and Son, for they are wedded too.

They are stood in the presence of Fate, who is bound in adamantine chains and imprisoned in the heart of The Singularity.

Fate stands charged with having congress with mortals in the form of a celestial swan.

How can Fate be charged or admonished or in any way chastised when it is his nature – forged, let us not forget, in the turning inside out of our own minds – to shepherd people to their ends? The Father protests.

Is that all we have become? The Son demands. Are we simply shepherds of lambs? Fishers of men? But where is the sport?

It was in sport that I made love to a mortal woman in the guise of a great beast, Fate booms, from his place of imprisonment in the heart of The Dead Zone: The Place Of Endless Echoes.

And now it is too late, The Grandfather says. Divinity has fallen.

As Gods ye have the power to bring time itself to an end, Fate booms, do ye not?

The Old Gods, also known as The First Powers, look solemnly at each other.

What is the name of your son? The Son asks him. What name has she given him? The Calamity? The Troubles? The Fall?

She should have named him Destiny, Fate sighs.

The Father pulls a face.

Instead she has christened him The Anomaly, Fate says.

And what of his powers?

He has become a story. His powers are inexorable.

And where does this story take place?

On the island of Hibernia.

And how long does it last?

Until the end of time.

*Next time: Neutrino, The Anomaly and The X-Ray Kid Enter
The Anti-Matter Universe!*

*

Okay, so it's decided, we're sending Barney to do the dirty, it
has got to be done, whether I'm a true fan or not. I says to him,
see while you're in there, pick me up some more copies of that
Savage Sword of Conan would you? Will I fuck, he says. Do it,
I says to him, it'll be good cover. Besides, I says to him, that's
your excuse to loiter round the shop till the right moment. Plus I
really wanted to get some more issues, is the honest truth. What

the fuck is this thing called, this thing, this *Sexy Sword of Conan* thing, Barney says to me. Fuck sake, don't ask for that, I says to him. It's *Savage Sword of Conan*. Just think about what you're about to do to the boy, I says to him, then it'll all come flooding back.

So as we send Barney packing, but I admit it, I'm nervous. These panic attacks, these flashbacks, they're giving me a weird feeling that I just can't shake, where it's like the past and the future are all mixed up in each other's together. A prophetic feeling, is what you call it. And the guy what looked like Tommy, and what went on between them, but maybe not. All of this has got me on edge, and I'm starting to feel like my head's away with it.

Tommy's gone for the weekend. He's staying in some cottage in Cushendall that some pals of his own. I'm in the dump house with Kathy and the pillowcase is back on her head.

Look, I says to her, I'm taking the gag out if you can be fucking polite for ten fucking minute. I leans in and I take the gag out and she just sits there, in silence. It's a fucking miracle. Are you still alive in there? I says to her. Barely, she says to me, thanks to you. Listen, love, I says to her, I'm the one keeping you alive. I'm the one feeding you every day, I'm the one taking you to the toilet. All of this is above and beyond, far as I'm concerned, I says.

I'm so fucking tired of it, she says to me, I'm so fucking tired of both sides. Her voice is muffled from the white pillowcase that is still on her head. There's a wet patch where her lips have made a circle, so as she looks like a ghost. Youse bang on about civil rights but it's all just a fucking excuse, she says to me, in this voice what's hard to make out and what sounds like an echoes. No one has any rights anymore in Ireland, not unless you can establish them at the end of a gun, she says, in this distant voice. You'll come running just as soon as you get burnt out your house, I says to her. As soon as your husband gets plugged in the back, who you gonna turn to then? The peelers? The fucking Brits?

You're the one most likely to pop my husband in the back, you dirty fucker, she says to me, in this voice like one of them ventriloquists. Why don't you just torch our house while you're at it? she says. I can't believe she called me a dirty fucker. That was below the belt. Still, I keep my cool. Women are different, you have to understand that.

So your man sells children's comics for a living? I says to her. Comics aren't just for children anymore, she says, and her weird quiet voice is really starting to do my crown in, to be honest with you. Fucking superheroes and that? I says to her. Give me a fucking break. Some guy running round in his fucking scants saving people? For the love of Jayzus, what next?

Ireland could do with some fucking superheroes right now, she says to me, and it's barely a whisper now. What, I says to her, Captain Ireland? What would his powers be? Invisibility, she says, at least I think that's what she says, that way he could walk all over this fucking town as he pleased, I think is what she whispered at the end there.

*

Someone spots Barney walking up the Falls Road with a busted head, staggering about all over the shop, it's a taxi driver that we know who works for the Ra and he pulls over and bundles him into the back seat before anyone sees him. He's clearly out of his box. He's taken a right fucking pasting. This fucking man-machine, this fucking man-mountain, was so indestructible that he had walked all the way from the city centre on autopilot, not even knowing where he was, like a crow with a severed claw and with its left eye pecked out.

The driver drops Barney off at his house, his wife Shona is out there in a panic, Shona who was five foot two and made of bullets. They send someone round to the house to get me and I leave Kathy tied and gagged in the living room while I inspect the damage. Barney's got a big dirty gouge out his head. You're going to need stitches in that, I says to him, and then he goes and throws up all over himself, this fucking thick green puke, he's a Tim to his insides, I says to myself, what the fuck is this cunt eating. I tear his dirty shirt off and I ball it up with his stained vest and I run through to the kitchen and launch them out the back window. Thing is, barring his being at death's door, Barney's banned from all the hospitals in Belfast due to his losing the head and causing carnage. I don't want to phone Mack, because then it looks like what the situation is: out of control.

I ask Shona if she's got any Bushmills. Then I ask her for a needle and some thread. She's only got this fucking light-blue wool she uses for the knitting but it'll have to do. I ask her to leave the room. Why, she says to me, what are you going to do to him? What do you think I'm going to do? I scream at her. Take my dick out and dip it in the wound? Get the fuck out of here, I says to her. Okay, Barney son, I says to him, get this down your neck. I pour him a half-pint of Bushmills with two Panadol crushed up in it. I mean, he's incoherent as he is, so it can't do any harm. I tie a small wee knot in the wool and I thread the needle. Then I just pinch the skin around the cut and start sewing. All this fluff is coming off the wool and it's getting into the blood so as it looks like someone has split his head open with a stick of candyfloss. I'm hoping that it doesn't give him some kind of uncommon brain infection. But then it's like that experiment where the guy puts electrodes into your brain and you start to hear things, see things. Barney starts talking like a tape recorder, talking in this fucking disconcerting voice that I have never heard before.

*

Doctor, doctor,
he says.
Who's there? I says
to him.
Is this, what, the butcher shop? he says
and then:
half a pound of kiddlies, please,
he says.
Do you not mean kidneys? I says
to him.
I said kiddlies, diddle I?
he says.

*

I'm cracking up over this. It's like we've tapped into the automatic part of his brain and all it contains are jokes. Irish jokes. My wife's a prostitute, he says to me. I says to him, keep it down Barney, for fuck sake, Shona's just next door. A prostitute, Barney says to me, thank fuck for that, I thought you says she was a Protestant.

Here, I says to him, and I pour him another Bushmills: drink this, it's the law. I finish sewing him up and it doesn't look half bad, apart from it's fuzzy and it looks like he has a weird blue weave in his hair. I put him on the couch and he falls asleep so as I shout Shona through. Some craic, innit? I says to her. But the joke's lost on her. She sees the job I've done on his head and I think she's going to take a fit but instead she just stands there and sighs. He looks like a wee angel, she says to me. It wasn't the first description that came to mind but it's a thumbs-up and I'll take what I can get. I leave Barney to recover, hopefully, who knows, and I head back round to the house. But I can feel that something's wrong. Something in the background there. Prophecy. There's no one's there, I says to myself. She's gone, I says to myself. I'm like a wolf with a dirty rag. I break into a run. I burst through the door and in the living room there's nothing but an empty chair with a pair of stilettos on it. It's like the Invisible Woman hanged herself. Or was raised up, into the air, and disappeared.

*

Of course it was them fucking Conan comics what did it. Of course Barney has gone in there looking like he did and asked if they have any *Sexy Sword of Conan*. Of course the guy says he does, he's got some in the back, and would you give him a minute, would you, and while he's gone Barney locks the door so as it's just the two of them, then he takes out his gun, and he goes into the back room, and by this point the guy is already halfways out the window, this tiny wee window at the top that he can barely fit through, and Barney gets up on the counter and starts pulling him back into the room by the legs, but the guy starts kicking with these boots on, these boots with the steel toecaps, and Barney says he feels it like it's splitting his skull and he falls back off the counter, he falls back out of control, and he fucks his head off the edge of this metal table as he goes. He doesn't remember much of anything else, after that.

But it turns out that not only did he make his way home like a wounded pigeon but that he's somehow had the presence of mind to lock the shop behind him and to take the fucking keys: genius. I says to him, listen Barney, fuck that guy and his foul-mouthed wife. We'll take the shop and its contents and we'll make more money for the Ra than they ever knew they had coming to them. But first we drive round to the house where the guy lived with Kathy and we break in.

There's no one around, of course, they're both hiding out somewhere, obviously, so as we go looting from room to room. A TV, a video recorder – rare as dice in the Ardoyne at the time – plus a bunch of slasher videos; brilliant stuff. I get myself a pair of shoes, a nice pair of tan brogues, the bastard only went and had the same size feet as me. Barney goes through Kathy's panties and takes a couple of pairs from her drawer. You dirty bastard,

I says to him, but he's like that, no, I'm giving them to Shona for an anniversary present. You give your wife dirty knickers for a present? I says to him. Sure, she'll never know, he says. Besides, he says, I'll break them in first myself, if you know what I'm saying. I wish I fucking didn't, I says to him. Besides, I says to him, they'll be a fucking tent on your Shona. Shut it, Barney says. They're elasticated, designed to fit all comers. Then he laughs and he puts a pair of them over his head like a bally. See? he says. You're fucking disgusting, I says to him. Something about it was just really uncouth to me.

When Tommy got back from his holidays, we broke the news. We got our own comic shop, I says to him, all profits straight to the Ra. You wee beauty, he says to us, and he spits on his hands and he rubs them together, like that.

*

It's our grand first day of trading and Barney is only sitting there behind the counter with a fucking bowler hat on. You look like a fucking Orangeman, I says to him, what the fuck. Have you never clocked *The New Avengers* on the telly? he says to me. This is Steed, he says, pointing to the hat on his head. This will appeal to the geeks, he says. They'll lap it right up. Steed is a fucking Orangeman, I says to him. That's fucking heresy, he says to me. Besides, he says, it's this or it's fucking Bagpuss, and he raises his hat to reveal the state of my botched knitting job on his noggin. Either way, I says to him, you look like a villain. A supervillain, he says to me, and he takes his hat off and spins it at me like a Frisbee. Wait a minute, I says to him. Now I know who you remind me of. It's not Steed. It's fucking Oddjob out the James Bond movies. Oddjob's a chinky, Barney says to me, what are you trying to say? And without a word of a lie, Tommy comes in right then and soon as he sees Barney sitting there in that hat, he says to him, alright Oddjob? After that it was all over: Barney was Oddjob, even if in real life he *was* a chinky.

*

It's frightening what fear can do when you think about it. Think about it. We helped ourselves to these people's worldly possessions, we took over their shop, we tied this poor woman up and made her wear a pillowcase for a mask and kept her in a boarded-up house with no floors, just because the Ra says they needed the money and not a sinner raised a finger against us. It was good times, if you were on the right side, or at least one of them. But if you fell through the cracks: forget it.

And not a sinner questioned us about running this comic shop neither. Sometimes weans would come in and ask about where's Davy what runs it but we just says to them he was gone and that's that and they shrugged and bought their comics as usual and left, or even weirder, some of them would catch sight of Tommy and think that he was Davy and some of them even called him Davy, see you later, Davy, they would shout to him as they left. I says to Barney, do you think our Tommy looks like your man Davy? Sure, he looks nothing like him, Barney says to me.

One time the landlord even stuck his head round the door but we just says to him we was under new management and he never called us again because I think he got the message. We spent all day, every day, with our feet up, reading the comics. That's when I got into what they call the underground comics. *Super Furry Freak Brothers, Mr Natural*. Comics aren't for weans anymore, I says to Tommy and Barney. They're still sat there reading Tarzan like a pair of mental defectives. And it was more than comics what we sold. We sold war games. Everything from the Nazis in Europe to the Elves in La-La Land. There was a magazine called *Dragon* where they would talk about rules for defeating dwarves and skills for supernatural sorcerers and with pictures of women with big huge tits in skimpy leather outfits disembowelling priests with double-headed axes. I felt right at home. This is Ireland, I says to myself, everybody's at it, it's just that we're the only ones up front about it. I don't need a map of Middle-earth to find my way into slaughtering a troop of Huns. They called them role-playing games, RPGs for short. These are games where what you do is you pretend to be somebody else. But here's the thing: the point of the game is not to win. The point is to play your part. I mean, you could get points and gain skills and stuff like that, but the real, serious gamers would try to get into the mindset of their characters and make the decisions that they would make, whether it was to their advantage or not. What I'm trying to say is, it was about being true, to a fantasy, for sure, but being true to it all the same.

Now this appealed to me right down to the ground. Think about it. It's not like a game of football where you just try your best. You're given handicaps right from the start. Like, for instance, elves are rubbish at magic. Alright. And then you go along with that. You'll need to figure it out without magic, in that case. Then you have a guy upstair called The Dungeon Master. This is the guy what creates the entire scenario. Only he doesn't get to make the final call. That comes down to the roll of a dice. And not any normal dice, mind. You get four-sided dice and six-sided dice and eight-sided dice and ten-sided dice and twelve-sided dice and twenty-sided dice; all these dice. I thought the roll of a dice was simple. I was kidding myself. The reality is that you roll the dice and you roll the dice again. And you can't lose, really, as long as you play your part. But see as soon as you quit doing that, see as soon as it's all about getting ahead in the game, regardless of what gamers call your characteristics, which is the map of your dungeons, which is the home of your dragons, then the game is up, and it's a bogey.

*

I look up at Tommy and Barney, sitting there, reading the comics. Tommy takes a piece of chewing gum out his mouth, sticks it underneath the desk. He looks up at me and he winks – did you see that, did you see him there? – then he goes back to reading. I hope to fuck we've got a dice that's big enough, is what I says to myself, when I first seen that.

Part Two: The Best Decade What Ever Lived

Once a month me and Pat would go on a night out, just the two of us. It always cost a fortune because Pat would make us get a taxi there and back and we'd go to these expensive bars and then a discotheque afterward. There was this place he liked to go, The Diamond in the city centre. There were some cracking birds in there, to be fair, dancing in the leotards and with the high heels and the leg warmers and the pink lipstick. To this day it's the look that I go for the most, but nobody dresses like that anymore so as all I'm left with is the internet and some fucking unplayable videos from the seventies, so that's me snookered, in real life.

Me and Pat go out for a few beers, meet some of the boys. Pat would fuck anything, no debate, and he's with this chick Arlene, who is as rough as get out, and he's arranged to meet her at The Diamond, so at about eleven o'clock we start making our way over there. I'm dying for a pish so as I nip down this lane and as I'm standing there taking a leak I hear these footsteps, the sound of people fucking charging toward me. Ah fuck, I says to myself, this could be anything. I whip round with my dick still hanging out and there's three guys in black balaclavas headed straight for me. I'm going to get hit, I says to myself. I start panicking; ah fuck, this is it, I says. I can feel my dick crawling back into my scrotum just trying to get away. One of the guys runs right up to me and he says to me: put it away, Sammy, you flasher.

He obviously knows who I am, but the guy's wearing a bally, so as I have no idea who he is, and I don't want to ask. That's the thing about ballys, you forget you're wearing one, and you think that people still recognise you. Anyway, he says to me, how's your ma? Ah, she's grand, I says to him. That's the game, he says. Look, he says to me, we've got to run. Just fucking set a house on fire, so we did. Catch up with you later, right? he says, and then he runs off with these two guys down the lane. I got a fucking fright, I'll tell you that for nothing. And to this day I have no idea who he was. I says to Patrick, did you see those fucking guys in the black balaclavas going past? He saw nothing, would you believe it? I mean he was half-blocked, but still, it only proves that the IRA were like ghosts back then. They could move around Belfast without making a sound. They could float above the pavements and rise up, into the skies, on mass, when they had to. That's how they got away with murder.

*

Patrick's fucking whining, fucking whining about how as Arlene won't fuck him how he likes. She thinks cocks are fucking disgusting, he says to me, in this fucking whining voice. Sounds like a no-use lesbo to me, I says to him. Naw, he says to me, naw, Arlene's not a lesbo. She just thinks it's dirty, is all. It is, I says to him, especially your fucking rancid member. I have two baths a day, Patrick says, my cock's as clean as a whistle, he says, she just doesn't want it in her mouth, regardless. To be honest with you, getting your cock sucked, in Ireland, in the 1970s, was a fucking task. Catholic girls were just not into it back then and a guy eating out a woman? Forget it. Part of the problem, on both sides, was the amount of pubic hair going down back then, but I'm straying from my point, which is to inform you that all this conversation is getting me horny and now I'm popping one.

*

So as we get to The Diamond and they're playing Donna Summers. There are women on roller skates cutting round the dance floor in the fluorescent lights. We get the drinks in and there's Arlene and she's a got a pal with her, whose name I can't even mind now, but she has her hair up in a bun and with the two curls hanging down sexy, like. But she has this voice. This fucking Dublin voice that I just cannot stand. Pat's got Arlene up against a wall and he's whispering in her ear and they're both rubbing up on each other. I can see Arlene's panties through the pattern on her dress. The Rolling Stones comes on. 'Jumpin' Jack Flash'. I take a swatch at Arlene's mouth. You can tell it has never had a cock in it in its life. It's flat and it's tight and it's even got pubic hair on its fucking lip. Her pal is telling me about going to the college, she's a nurse. She's telling me that death is recession-proof, especially in Ireland, she says. What the fuck ever, I'm saying to myself.

Your man Rod Stewart comes on. 'Hot Legs'. Arlene's pal asks me if I want to dance. I don't really want to dance, love, what I want to do is explode all over the front of your dress, darling, but I dance with her anyway. I lift my arm up as she does a pirouette. Her dress spins all around her, like colour into water. We take a seat. She tells me about a car she's saving up for. A Vauxhall Viva. Is that right, love? But I'm elsewhere, darling. I'm looking at all these women on the dance floor, these women dressed so fine. Who are these women? And who are the men they're going home to? I look at Arlene's pal with her own stupid mouth, tight as a mouse's ear. I think of the women in the *Dragon* magazines; in a dungeon beneath Belfast, the prizes. And that's when I see her.

Dancing with another redhead. The two of them in the leotards and the high heels. It's like my dick is going to pop out the centre of my forehead like the Buddha Himself. It's only Kathy M. It's only the fucking girl we kidnapped. And she looks fucking unbelievable. I picture that drawer she had, filled brimming with her panties. I picture Barney rifling through them. I catch the curve of her hips. She has her hair curled round her face like Farrah Fawcett. What's that word for the crease at the top of her thighs. She's laughing and dancing with a friend. What a moment.

I make my excuses and walk round to the other side of the dance floor. I stand there and watch her, in secret. I see her take her handbag and go into the toilet and I don't think twice. I follow her in there. There's no one else inside. She goes to walk into one of the cubicles and I grab her and push her in and lock the door behind us. She's as cool as a kitten.

You look better with your hair long, she says to me. Then she pulls her leggings down and she sits on the toilet and starts to go, right in front of me. I'd never seen a woman take a pish before in real life. Please don't take me away, she says to me, sitting there with this sound, this stream, that is echoing, in the bowl. You ever hear that echoing sound, from a woman? What a sound. And she's all smiling up at me. Playing with me. Don't tie me up, she says to me, along with this sound, that's accompanying her, that's echoing. Don't feed me with a spoon, she says, to this incredible sound.

I want to fuck her so badly.

Did you get my heels? she says to me. I left them for you. Here, she says to me, and she takes out a little mirror from her handbag, have some, she says, and she sprinkles a little magic powder on the mirror. Bam. She leans over and unzips my trousers. She takes my cock in her mouth. She has tight pink lipstick on. I can see it smearing, up and down my shaft, leaving its trail. She hasn't pulled her leggings up. They're down round her ankles, round her heels, spread tight. I put my hands in her hair. This smell comes up, this dark shampoo smell. The music is insides, is banging against, is the walls now. Is Roxy Music. Is 'Love Is the Drug'. I'm going to come, baby, I says, and I pull out and it's like a shotgun going off. I feel like I've damaged myself, like I've used up every orgasm promised me by God Almighty in one fevered religious torrent. There's cum in her hair and on her face. She's laughing, looking up at me. Now it's me that's the prisoner. Now it's me that's being spoon-fed. Now it's me that is set free.

We can keep this between ourselves, she says, can we not? She wipes a little weight of cum from the corner of her mouth. Of course, I says to her. Yes, I says. Yes. Okay, she says. Okay, sweetie. You can ring me. But only at a certain time. We can work this out our way, just the two of us, don't you think? I think we can, I says to her, I really think we can, I says, even though in reality she is talking to a rubbered fucking jellyfish right now. She pulls up her leggings. She wipes her face and her hair with a piece of toilet paper and she says to me, I'll leave you to clean up. She winks at me as she squeezes past, that smell of hers.

When I get out of there she's long gone. Arlene's crap pal has split the scene. Patrick and Arlene are fighting. Fuck this, Patrick says, let's get a fucking taxi called. The entire night is a total fucking write-off, he says. On the way home I'm sitting in the back seat and I pull my cock out and I show Patrick the pink lipstick all over it. He lets out a gasp. The taxi driver clocks it in the mirror. Fuck me, he says, you're an example to us all, my friend. Pat just sat there looking at it with his jaw on the floor like it was an alien come down to earth just to taunt the fucking life out him.

*

Kathy had gone back to her job at the Europa after an extended sick leave where her and her husband Davy had fled their home and moved in with the mother-in-law; she told me this on our first date. Was it a date? She never, explicitly, says that she was doing it to keep the Ra away. And to protect her husband. I never once says that I could. But in the back of my mind, and in her mind too, I believed, there was an element of pay-off, of protection.

But I convinced myself that she was attracted to me. That she saw something in me, something that drew her to me. Something special. We would meet in a room at the Europa; afternoons, early evenings, normally just when her shift was finishing. She had keys to the rooms and she knew what ones were unoccupied, and for how long, and we would make love, and it was the only thing, and it was the first thing, I understood that then. The power of making love to a woman. And sometimes she would change into her outfit for me. A turquoise leotard with white high heels and leggings. At work she smelt of cigar smoke, and of dark liquor, and of black flowers. I would bite her and leave nicks and bruises in her. You did that to me, she would say, and she would point to a little bruise in her night-time thighs, put her tongue between her lips.

I told her we had taken over her man's shop. That he shouldn't go back there. She says that he knew, that one of the weans that came in had told him and he was staying away. This way The Boys get their money back, and no one gets hurt, I says to her. Except for you, she says to me. Except for you, I'll break your heart, she says.

*

I can hear her saying it, here, right now, like she was lying in my arms, next to me, and I could touch her head with the back of my hand that's shaking. Except for I'll break your heart, whispering it in my ear. What a turn. Sometimes she would smuggle food up from the kitchen. Sometimes even a bottle of wine. We'd lie there, on the messed-up sheets, with a tray over our legs, watching TV like a happy couple. We'd watch the news about the troubles and she would say to me, how deep do you go? I'm just a Saturday boy, I says to her, only I says it in the way that somebody who wasn't just a Saturday boy would say it. Do you know about role-playing games? I says to her. Was your husband not into all that? Of course I do, she says. Well, how deep do you go? I says to her. She puts her finger in her hair and she twists a little curl around it and she smiles. I've discovered my own superpower, she says to me. You mind what I said about invisibility? she says. I thought about her high heels, sitting on the chair, when I discovered she was gone. That's my superpower, she says to me. Which means that even when you're not with me, I'm right there beside you. Thing is, it was true.

*

My big sister was killed by Mr Hitler in the Blitz. He's dropped a bomb on our house in Belfast and the family had to sleep out, on a steep hill, in a park, overnight, and she died of exposure. Nobody put her picture on a charity box. No one offered to house them or support them. They slept in a park until our da found them an abandoned house and moved them in. All my cousins moved away, eventually. Looking for work and a place to settle down that wasn't a fucking war zone. They went to Glasgow and Birmingham and Liverpool and London and the Isle of Man. Nobody dignified them by calling them refugees. We were just the dirty Irish, filthy Tims, ignorant Micks, fucking daft Paddies lower down the pecking order than blacks or dogs. And it kept happening, all over again. People were getting burnt out their houses every day of the week. People were getting shot down in the street. People were getting dragged by the hair along the pavement, bloodied and screaming into army vehicles, I saw it myself, locked up for defending your own neighbourhood. I looked at the Union Jack and forgive me, son, but all I saw was a swastika. I looked at the Red Hand of Ulster and to me it was nothing but a blood-soaked *Sieg Heil*.

So as when the IRA moves in and starts protecting us and housing us and taking our plight seriously – they gave my family a house in the Ardoyne – well, I thought to myself, finally, we have an army of our own. I joined up soon as I could. I was gunning for Adolf Hitler and for Brian Faulkner and for Edward Heath and for Harold Wilson and for James Callaghan and for any other bastard what wanted a war, only this time it was our war on our terms and our terms were non-negotiable: a united Ireland, a true Free State, or dead trying.

By the time I was twelve year old I had seen dead bodies. I had seen a soldier shot almost point-blank in the face. I saw bodies at the bottom of lift shafts in the old abandoned buildings up by the Lagan Canal that had been so badly beaten they looked like dead cows. I saw our neighbours crawling on their bleeding hands and knees, the sup-pu-rating legs of poor women, is what my da says, I still mind him saying it, that word, sup-pu-rating, crawling along the streets, beneath mocking British infantrymen with machine guns pointed to their heads. I saw my da and two of his pals whack this guy in the car park of a pub. I watched from the back window of the car as they beat him over the head with snooker cues and one of them snapped.

I thought my da was Jimmy Cagney. What meant that I was Jimmy Cagney's son. What meant that I had to learn to be smart-mouthed, sharp-cut, a cold-hearted killer, a family man, and a swank with the ladies. I'd watch my da and his pals and try to copy their moves. The way they shaved in the mirror. The way they smoked their fags from the very corner of their mouth. The way they greased their side-partings. The way they called the top pocket of their suit the top bin; that was where you kept the fags. The way they smelt of Old Spice; aftershave, you called it, never cologne, not unless you were a fairy. How they fluffed up their silk hankies in their top bin. How to tuck a gun down into the waist of your dress trousers without using a holster. How to always have songs ready, just in case you're asked to sing. How to always have jokes ready, just in case there's a down moment. How to always do the right thing and send a little money back for bullets. How to drive the ladies crazy. How to have class and style. How to wood-panel a kitchen or a bathroom in a single day; that was a key skill. How to foster a network of safe houses, just in case you need to disappear. How to never linger over a drink. How to throw a punch (keep your arm loose till the very last moment). And how to make every day a comeuppance for every single historical slight your family has ever suffered. You call it the IRA, the Provos, Óglaigh na hÉireann. We called it The Boys.

*

Patrick was the first of The Boys I ever knew. He had been involved for a while, but mainly community stuff, as far as I was aware. Area patrols, punishment beatings, shite like that. One time this kid steals a car that belonged to one of The Boys that was high up in command. They tell Patrick to bring him in. I had been angling for a go myself and finally Patrick, who made it seem like you were joining the fucking Mensa, says he would give me a trial run. I mean, the Ra were begging for recruits, but that was your man Pat's style. He had to pretend it was a big deal and of course it was, really. We all looked up to The Boys and we all dreamt of being one ourselves, one day. Look neat, he says to me. Don't go letting the side down. What a joke. You should've seen the state of some of these clowns. But I took it as gospel back then, so as I turn up in a slate-grey suit with cufflinks and with white side-lacing shoes. You've got dandruff on your shoulders, that's all Patrick says to me. Wipe it off, he says. Can't have fucking common car thieves thinking I've got a dry fucking scalp, I says to him, but he just looks at me and at this point he's the boss, so as I shrug and brush my shoulders off. Patrick is wearing an electric-blue suit with snakeskin shoes and a tie with the ace of spades on it. He looks good, I can't lie. He gives me the briefing. Okay, he says, his ma is going to scream and shout, they always do. Ignore her. I'll deal with the parents, he says. You drag the wee bastard outside and we'll kick the shite out him. Sounds like a plan.

We turn up at his door in the evening and his ma answers. We're here to see Roddie, Patrick says. What has he done now? she says. He stole a car and I think he may be using the drugs, Patrick says. He makes up that last bit but it was a piece of genius and I would use it myself for years after, especially when dealing with people's mas. Any suggestion that their kids might be using drugs would be enough to damn them even in their own mothers' eyes. That was traditional Irish Catholics for you.

Drugs, is it, she says, and she goes storming to the bottom of the stair and starts yelling for Roddie. Get your fucking arse down here, she screams. You've brought shame on our house. Me and Pat are just looking at each other. She goes bounding up the stair and we hear a crash and she shouts down to us, he's out the window! He's on the run! We go bollocking round the back and we catch a glimpse of Roddie leaping the fence and heading off down the lane.

Here, Patrick says to me, and he pulls a handgun out the waist of his trousers. He's got a pair of chatsbys down there. I feel it in my hand for the first time. It feels heavy, carrying a gun. Anyone around you could snuff it at any moment. What a feeling.

Let's go, Patrick says. We're gonna scare the living shite out this guy. We leap over the fence and go barrelling after him. I forgot to tell you that Patrick had a moustache. It only added to the appeal.

We're running up all these backstreets and there are always people lurking around the lanes back there in the Ardoyne and they see us with our guns and it's like the sea, parting. People go flying over hedges, launch themselves through doorways, just generally getting the fuck out the way. Provos! Patrick shouts. Provos! Provos! The kid runs into this bin shed up ahead. On the wall, in white paint, it's written: No Trustpassing. There's nowhere left to go. But it's getting dark by this point and we can't really see the wee bastard. Patrick motions to me. He points to a big silver bin. I sneak up and topple it over and it empties all over the ground. Wrong bin, nothing but trash. Then the both of us just start tipping over the bins one after the other till he comes flying out in a flood of rotten vegetables and minking fish bones. He's lying there on the ground and he's whimpering and Patrick is fucking screaming about the state of his shoes. They're fucking ruined, he says to him, thanks to you, you wee thieving bastard. Then he bends down, takes the guy by the ear, and wipes his shoes clean with his hair. What a move.

We drag this kid out into the lane and we hold him up against the wall. The place is silent, is eerie. It's like we sucked all the air out the Ardoyne. There's a time and a place for stealing cars, Patrick says to him, and it's on the Shankill Road and not in our own fucking communities do-you-understand-me.

Do you know whose fucking car that was you stole? Pat says to him. The guy pishes himself right there in front of us, right down the front of his tracksuit trousers. And now he's lying there fucking sobbing.

Look at him there. He's only a wee fucking kid.

You don't want to know whose car you stole, Patrick says to him. Then he toes him in the bollocks. Your poor ma's up to high doh with you, he says. You understand, Patrick says to him, that now we need to make an example of you? Fucking shoot him, Patrick says to me, and he turns his back on the kid and he walks away. I think I see him wink at me but I can't tell. Is this some type of membership test for the IRA? The kid slides down the wall and starts begging for his life. I take him by the hair and I pull his head back. I hold the gun to his throat and I can feel his pulse like a tennis ball. I take two steps backward. The kid covers his eyes and I let a couple of shots off into the air. The kid rocks back like he's been hit but then he realises he's still alive. He starts patting himself all over. Looking for bullet holes. You wee fucking dick, Patrick says to him, if he shot you, you would know all about it. You've got one chance, Patrick says to him. You need to pay back the amount the car cost, with interest, and we'll be up at your ma's door to pick it up in person each week until we feel that you have paid enough. Do you understand me? Roddie nods, but he's still that sobbing way. Come on, Patrick says, and he starts getting all calm and peaceful, like. Let's shake on it, son, he says, and then we can move on. Everybody makes mistakes. Roddie gets up on his feet and offers Patrick his hand. Patrick takes it by the wrist and with his other hand he bends two of Roddie's fingers back and fucking snaps them in two. The sound is atrocious. The kid falls back on the floor and it's like he's running on the spot, his legs kicking up in the air. Always leave them with a memorable injury, Patrick says to me. Rule number one.

Now fuck off, Patrick says to him, and the kid gets up and starts running away as fast as he can, holding his broken fingers and howling at the same time. We turn to walk away and suddenly there's flashlights coming at us down the lane. Somebody shouts something. Ah fuck, it's the Brits. Run like blazes, Patrick says, and we fucking take off down this lane. They must have heard the shots. We get to this high stone wall that leads onto a park. It's our best bet, Patrick says. We can lose ourself on the other side of the park. Quick, he says, I'll give you a footsie up. He lifts me up and I'm straddling the top of the wall and he jumps up toward me. I grab for his hand but I miss him. The fucking soldiers are getting closer. I get him again and I start pulling him up. He's using the wall for support. He's nearly there. And that's when the shots go up.

Sounds like bullets the size of Coke cans. I'm over the other side and Patrick's halfway over, looking down at me. Bam. He takes one in the arse. I see the bullet go flying up into the air. Patrick falls over the wall and onto the grass. They fucking shot me, he's screaming, the fucking bastards shot me in the arse. And then we see this fucking big black plastic bullet come spinning down through the air in slow motion. They shot him in the arse with a plastic bullet. In the Ra these were like good-luck charms, the plastic bullet you were shot with. I see Patrick. He's flat out on the ground in agony but as he spies this plastic bullet he launches himself to the side so as he can catch it. Of course it's really fucking hot cause it has just been fired so as he's lying on his back and juggling this red-hot bullet between his hands. He throws it over to me. Hold this, he says, and he gets to his feet. I can hardly fucking walk, he says, I feel like I just got kicked in the arse by a horse. But we take off, the two of us, staggering into the dark, across this park, and all the time we're juggling this black plastic bullet between us.

We get home, and we're standing there in the driveway of my ma's place, under a street light. Patrick takes the bullet out his pocket and gives it to me. It's for you, he says. They were shooting at the both of us. And besides, he says, I've already got one. And that is the story of how I became one of The Boys.

*

I first met Tommy when he was trying to sell me a set of golf clubs in the street on Christmas Eve. He was selling these golf clubs out the back of a car, in the Ardoyne, in the snow. I says to him, where did you get these clubs from, and he says to me that he shot somebody for them and that he was selling them to pay for his dry-cleaning. Anything else goes back to the Ra for bullets, he says to me.

Of course I never bought one of his golf clubs, but by the end of the day they're all sold and I'm in our local boozer and Tommy's sitting there with this gorgeous bird, holding court and looking exactly the way I wanted to. You get your dry-cleaning paid? I says to him. More than, he says, more than. I picked up this wee number on the side as well, he says, and he nods toward the girl, who was this stunning blonde only with yellow teeth. She slaps him on the arm and she giggles, like that.

Will you take a drink? Tommy says. I order a Bushmills and Coke and we get to talking. Turns out we both know Barney plus Tommy's ma knows my ma. Tommy minds me and he says we were in a fight together once when we went over to kick the shite out the Bone Macks. Oh aye, I says to him, I mind that fight, did somebody not get hit with a spade? That was me, Tommy says, and he's beaming, I just fucked the guy over the head with it, he says.

Now I minded him.

We're sitting there drinking and Tommy whispers something to the blonde and five minute later she comes back with another girl what looks exactly the same, even down to the yellow teeth. They're twins, Tommy winks at me. Two for the price of one, he says.

That's when it finally clicks: it's a pair of whores. I couldn't have told you where you could find a single whore in all of Belfast back then and here's Tommy sitting with two of them what looked the exact same. I thought you were sending all profits back to the Ra for bullets? I says to him. Ah well, maybe you can help me out there, Tommy says to me. I'm looking for a way in myself, he says.

I'm looking to sign up. I've had enough of this shite, he says to me, though looking at him it didn't look like he was putting up with any of it. I'll see what I can do, I says to him, even though I'm only a few month in myself. But I'm telling you, right there I knew it. This guy selling golf clubs from the boot of a car, in the snow, in the Ardoyne, on Christmas Eve, he was fucking born to it.

We drank all evening and afterward, in the snow, round the back of the bar, we fucked these two identical-looking whores standing up against the wall, their tight white dresses pulled up around their waists, as the bells were bringing in Christmas. I was so blocked I missed Christmas Day altogether.

*

The first summer we worked in that comic shop is something like heaven now, in my mind, as I mind it. We were making money, we were looking good in the eyes of the Ra, we were educating ourselves about all sorts of barbarians and planets and elves and superheroes and other ideas about art and life and how things should be lived, plus I was fucking, on a regular basis, unbeknownst to anybody but ourselves, the most beautiful woman in all of Belfast.

If you could travel anywhere in time, Barney says to us one day as we were lounging round the shop, where would you go? I'd stay right where the fuck I am, I says to him. Right here, right now, my friend, I says. But that's no use to him. You can't travel to where you are, he says to me. Well, in that case, how in the fuck do you think I got here? I says to him. I didn't just fucking materialise out of thin air, I says. You're here already, Barney says to me. You don't need the fucking time travel for that. You're in the Tardis, he says to me, and he points to the big police box in the corner that was actually a walk-in cupboard filled with books about science fiction, so where are you going to go?

Where are *you* going to go? I says to him. That's easy, he says. I'm going to Egypt. What the fuck is it with you and Egypt? Tommy says to him. It's where it all began, Barney says.

Where what all began?

This, Barney says, pointing all around himself. Fucking humanity, he says to us. Life. It all began in Egypt? Tommy says to him. That's right, Barney says. We wouldn't be sitting here reading the comics without them. What about The Bible? Tommy says to him. Where did that all happen? That all happened in Egypt, Barney says. That's exactly what I'm talking about. That happened in Jerusalem, Tommy says. And in Bethlehem, he says. That's nowhere near Egypt. Sure it's just across the road, Barney says. Same corner of the world. What about the Garden of Eden? Tommy says to him. Did that take place in Egypt? That was a garden in Africa, Barney says, and he shrugs. Same thing. The fucking Garden of Eden walked out of Africa on two legs, I says to them. I should know, I was balls-deep in it the other night.

That gets a good laugh.

What are these rumours about a blow job we're hearing? Barney says to me. Pat says you had fucking love juice all over your dick.

Fucking poof juice, more like, Tommy says. I met this cracking wee bird at a disco, I says to them. She sucked my cock in the bog. Are you sure it was a bird? Tommy says to me. The only people sucking cock in the toilets of Belfast these days are fucking three-speeds. Oh, it was a bird alright, I says to them. And she was top-notch. What was her name? Tommy says to me. He's got me on the spot. I'm trying to make something up and I'm drawing blanks. Sonja, I says to them finally. Her name was Sonja, I says. Sonja? Tommy says. Bullshit. There's nobody in Belfast goes by the name of Sonja, he says. The fuck is this cunt talking about, Barney says, this fucking *Sexy Sword of Conan* shite is going to his head. He thinks he's fucking Red Sonja. Do you realise that you have to beat her in combat before you can ride her? he says to me. I know, I says to him. I know. Part of the challenge, isn't it? But secretly my head was spinning. It was true. This comic stuff was getting out of control.

*

I told you about Arlene, right, Pat's bird with the mouth that was too tight for a cock? One night I mind her saying to Pat about how when they get married all his Como records were going in the skip. I'm not making this up, dumping fucking Como records in a skip, what a devious bitch.

I mean but Patrick was at fault and all. A tight-mouthed little bitch like that should have been told precisely nadja about what happened with The Boys. But Pat was a fucking show-off and a wise guy and he would probably have been a fucking yuppie if they had got around to inventing that yet.

One night we're at The Shamrock and he's insisting on getting a big fuck-off bottle of champagne for everyone and of course Arlene loves it, of course she does, and she's egging him on the whole way. Go on, she says to him. Sure, you're a high-flyer, so you are. Soon you'll be a commandant.

I picked up on that straight away: oh man. That meant he was telling her things he shouldn't have. Never involve your family, if you can avoid it. It's a sensible rule, son. But more than that, even, do-not-involve-your-new-bird-who-won't-even-give-you-a-fucking-blow-job is rule number one.

As Patrick is walking away – he's got yet another one of his electric-blue suits on, an unforgettable look – I see him mime putting a gun up to his head and pulling the trigger and winking at Arlene, who is all giggles. I couldn't believe my lamps. He thinks he's the fucking executioner now.

I says to Tommy at the time, Arlene knows too much and plus she's a devious, small-mouthed bitch. It's that fucking moustache that gets me, Tommy says.

Okay, so you're probably about to bring up Kathy with me. But that's my point. When me and Kathy met up, it was like we met in another world, a world that just happened to look like a hotel room at the Europa. It might as well have been a spaceship in orbit for all the connection it had to Belfast and the day job and what happened with her and her man. And I made sure to keep it buttoned when it came to anything to do with the Ra. That's where Patrick ballsed up.

Next thing you know, him and Arlene have split up. I meet Pat for a drink and he's clearly agitated. What was I doing with that devious, no-use lesbo? he says to me. It was my fucking cock talking, he says. He laments his own cock talking in a voice that is hard to feel sorry for. Patrick, I says to him, all your cock was doing was fucking complaining, far as I can see.

She went mental when I told her we were finished, he says. She put a shoe right through the kitchen window and then she was standing out on the front step, cursing the day she ever set eyes on me.

She loved you, eh? I says to him. She must've, he says, and he shrugs.

Listen, I says to him, I don't mean to speak out of turn here, but you didn't tell her anything you shouldn't have, you didn't give her any information she could use against you, did you?

Pat takes a blue-and-white polka-dot hanky out his top bin, and wipes his mouth. He leans toward me and with his finger he draws an invisible square on the table. Let me remind you, he says to me, that this is a student–teacher relationship. Don't let the snakeskin shoes fool you, he says to me. Then he gets up and walks out the pub. It was the last time I ever saw him alive. It was a fucking life lesson, that's for sure.

*

Pat was shot in the back while out gardening on what I still mind as being a glorious Saturday afternoon in May, when two gunmen pulled up on a motorcycle in the blazing sunshine and let off five shots, two of which punctured his lungs, one of which got him right through the fucking heart.

I always imagined the bullet flying through the centre of his heart like a rocket, his heart beating in just the right rhythm for impact, closed up tight, like a fist. Another breath in or out, I tell myself, and he might be on a ventilator, but he would still be alive.

His sister Helen heard the shots and found him face down in the pond. I asked Helen for his snakeskin shoes. I want to walk in them, I says to her. I would consider it an honour.

It doesn't take a genius to put two and two together. Tommy rounds up Miracle Baby and we quiz him about what he knew. Who killed Patrick, Miracle Baby? Tommy says to him. We called him Miracle Baby to his face, just like the Buddha. It was the UDA, Miracle Baby says to us. Fucking vile cunts, Tommy says, and he stamped his foot on the floor and fucking crushed the fag he was smoking in his hand. This is fucking war, Tommy says to us, and I don't know if he meant it as in the war had just this minute started because of this affront or whether he was just expressing his angst at the repercussions of this endless fucking battle that had all of us bogged down in it and with eyes in the back of our head in the first place.

Why'd he get shot, Miracle Baby? I says to him. There was a horrible big bogey on Miracle Baby's lip at this point. Encrusted there. Because he shot the guy first, Miracle Baby says to us.

What, Tommy says, who did he shoot? To be truthful, he had probably shot a lot of people but tellingly none of us knew very much about any of them. That's the way it should be. He shot Donny McLaughlin, Miracle Baby says. He shot Donny McLaughlin at the party.

Now, everybody knew about Donny McLaughlin. A notorious UDA hatchet man with a skelly eye. Famously he had been plugged at his own wedding. It was a bold and notorious killing. A sniper had taken him out from a window across the way, just as the confetti went up in the air. The bride's dress was covered in blood. The best man, who the gunman went ahead and maimed just for the sport of it, walked with a limp for the rest of his life.

Tommy and me turned to each other with a look of awe. It was only our own fucking Patrick O'Leary who had killed Donny McLaughlin: legend.

I don't want to ask you anything else, Miracle Baby, Tommy says to him. You know too much. I'm afraid you're going to start telling me my future. Miracle Baby laughed and he clapped his hands.

I can tell that too, if you want me to, he says. The only thing I want you to do for now, Tommy says to the wee guy, is to keep being my secret friend. Can I keep being your gardener too? Miracle Baby says to him. That too, Tommy says, and he gives him a couple quid and Miracle Baby went off to wander the streets without adult supervision as usual.

Fucking Patrick John Michael O'Leary, Tommy says, and he runs his hand through his hair and starts with the whole twirling it round his finger and pulling it out routine. The guy was fucking serious, he says to me. Fucking taking the best man out, I says to him. That was above and beyond. But if *we* didn't even know he did it, Tommy says, then who the fuck did? Arlene, I says to him. Obviously, Tommy says.

I pulled out my gun and I cocked it, just like they do in the movies. She's scrubbed, I says to Tommy. And we'll take her best man with her, just for Pat's sake.

*

When me and my brother were wee my father would take us out the back and we had this big blanket that we would lie down on, me, my brother Peter and my da, and we would lie there, at night, on warm nights in the summer we would lie there and my father would point to the stars in the night sky, every star is a planet just like ours, he says to us, and we would fall asleep, with our heads on his chest, his warm chest, rising and falling, and that smell he had, that manly smell, calm and happy as we drifted off, sure in the knowledge that up above us, and carrying on forever, were planets where fathers and sons lay out in the night on blankets together and pointed to each other, lying there, high, in the night-time sky.

*

So as we round up a meeting with Mackle McConaughey because we want to run it past the top brass. Let us do it, we says to him, let us take revenge. Mack says, naw. It's a pointless civilian killing, he says to us. It does us no good whatsoever, he says. I couldn't believe what I was fucking hearing. Tommy took it better. He was philosophical about it. Fuck it, he says.

I argued the specifics of our case. I says that she gave up being a civilian when she turned into a fucking rat. You've no proof, Mack says. Give me a break, I says to him. Did you know it was Patrick that shot fucking Donny McLaughlin at his wedding? I says to him. If I did I wouldn't be telling you, Mack says to me. Did I tell you Mack had his hair up in a ponytail at this point? Worst look ever. Listen, I says to this ponytailed comedian, none of us even knew. But if anybody did, it was fucking that bitch Arlene. You know what Pat was like, I says to him, he was larger than life. He was a fucking boy. All it would take is some boasting in the bed afterward. We've nothing to go on, Mack says. All this does is open another front that we could do without. Rule number one, he says, no opening of pointless domestic fronts if you can avoid it. I was beginning to wonder just how many fucking rule number ones there were in the IRA.

So there's to be no revenge? I says to Mack. I was disgusted, quite frankly. Revenge comes in time, he says. Till then, hang tight. Then he pats me on the leg like I'm a wee dumb kid and nothing but. You fucking catch that? I says to Tommy afterward. I caught it, he says. I caught it.

Looking back from now I can see the psychology but at the time I was raging. Let it go, Tommy says to me. Miracle Baby might find out about the UDA gunman yet, he says, you never know.

In the meantime, we keep our ears to the ground. Till then, keep punting the fucking comics. I had to laugh, what a mad situation. Tommy put his arm round me and we walked off. But for the life of me I just *could not stop plotting*.

*

I knew Arlene's address, we had picked her up in a taxi a few times on our way to the dancing, and I started going by her house and keeping an eye on her. She still lived with her ma and da at the Glen Road, in a wee house with a brand-new estate car in the driveway. Even that annoyed me. Where did they get the money for a brand-new estate? It wasn't from sucking cock, that's for sure.

I started to get a pretty good idea of her schedule. She worked at a vet's in Ladybrook. She was always taking animals back and forth to the surgery. Maybe she was trying to save them from getting put down, who knows, I couldn't give a shite, because after all, Hitler loved his animals and we all know what he got up to in his spare time.

Most nights I would split from the shop, if I was on the rota, and sit outside her house, sunk down in the front seat of the car, and spy what she was up to. Mostly she stayed in. I saw her da, he was on one of them portable oxygen tanks. Sometimes he would come out onto the step and smoke a fag, standing there double-fisting the oxygen mask and the bifter; fucking chronic.

It was the same warm summer, those beautiful evenings in Belfast where it never goes dark except for the sky goes blue, dark blue, and then purple, and then back to blue again, like it isn't even the sky but the sea up above. One time I watched them having this pathetic barbecue in their front garden, the three of them, the da on the oxygen, the ma in her wheelchair and Arlene sitting there between them, cooking sausages on an old rancid grill. It was probably the fucking dogs from the clinic they were eating. It sticks in my mind, that night. These sad old horrors, slumped in their chairs, in this fucking dump of a garden, not even speaking to each other but eating hot dogs off paper plates and fucking sitting round this white plastic table and fucking . . . staring into themselves in silence, beneath this deep fucking purple sea that was right there up above them. All they needed was a couple of party hats and it would've been a full-blown tragedy. Not that I gave a toss. My intention was that all three of them would be dragging around medical equipment till the end of their days. That is, if they weren't burying Arlene first.

And sometimes I would sit there, outside their house, and watch them before I was due to meet Kathy at the Europa. I was counting my blessings then, the equivalent of staring at a picture of starving Biafrans with flies crawling over their faces and then going to a party in the fucking Hilton. But I kept it up, night after night, and if you were to ask me why, I'd tell you that I did it in order to *keep my hatred sharp*.

*

Paddy from Ireland goes to
the doctor's

complaining of stomach
pains.

Sure, I can't find anything
wrong with you,
the doctor says,
I'm thinking
it must be
the drinking.

Ah, no worries
doctor,
Paddy says to him,
I'll come back again
when yr sober.

*

In the middle of all this we start hearing rumours of a new
bombing campaign. Tommy calls in the one and only Miracle
Baby. Aye aye, he says, it's true. I've heard that, he says. The
plan is to take out multiple targets over the space of a month, all
high-profile tourist attractions. And the Europa is on the list.

A million different scenarios flash through my mind.

Barney's sitting with his feet up on the desk when I walk into
the shop and he's singing 'Happy Days Are Here Again'. I'm
guessing somebody's heard the news? I says to him. We're
upping the game, Barney says. Now's the time, Xamuel

McMahon, he says to me, now is the time to do something great.
Something significant.

By the way, did you hear about our Kathleen's man? he says to
me. No, what happened? I says to him. His brother got lifted by
the UFF, he says. They took him to a fucking romper room. Is he
dead? I says to him. He'd be better off dead, Barney says. They
fractured his skull seven time. The fuck is that even possible? I
says to him. Then they fucking hacked his legs with a machete,
Barney says. Then they fucking left the body in the waste ground
at Sandy Row but everybody was too scared to go and rescue him
in case it was a trap or they got incriminated, so as he was left
to crawl on his hands and knees up till the Donegall Road before
somebody called an ambulance.

These people are fucking animals, I says to Barney. Killing is too
good for them. Maiming, Barney says, maiming and maiming
again, it's the only way. We need to get in on this, I says to
him. I'm about ready to explode, I says. It's time for something
spectacular. It had to be the Europa. And it had to be me.

1977. It was about to be the bloodiest summer of our lives. And I
decided to kick it off in style.

*

Through my own covert operations I had discovered that Arlene
had a new man. And that he was from the other side. Bitch was
in bed with these animals. That's what had cost Patrick his life.
For all I know this was the same guy she had told about the

Donny McLaughlin shooting. I had found my best man.

I saw him come pick her up in a car and drive her to a place off the Crumlin Road, a seedy wee place with a boarded-up window on the top floor, typical UDA rathole. Now it was no longer a civilian killing. Now it was all about eradicating vermin.

I start casing the joint. I would drive by at different times of the day but there was never that much going on. Sometimes boys would come and go but I was confident that he lived there on his own. Plus and now I had a silencer. I lifted it from Tommy's da's legendary gun stash. This was going to be a cakewalk, I says to myself. I start to getting ballsy.

One afternoon I see this cunt leaving the house and locking up, this ugly-looking cunt with the shaved head, disgusting. Once I was sure he wasn't coming back any time soon, I pushed my way through the hedge and I crawled round the back of the house to the garden. Now this neighbourhood was a fucking hotbed of Huns. If anyone had caught me at it, it would've been like Kathleen's man's brother, or whoever the fuck he was, getting carted up the road. There was a window cracked open at the back. I couldn't resist it. I climbed in.

The place is like a morgue in there, or a wax museum, it's so still. I can tell that there's nobody home. There's a little drinks tray on wheels in the living room with a full bottle of Bushmills on it. I go to grab it but then I think to myself, I'll come back later and celebrate with that fucker once I've cut the pair of their throats. There was a pile of video cassettes on the coffee table. *The French*

Connection. Rollerball. I creep out into the hallway and I edge
my way up the stair. I had grown up in a house with the exact
same layout, so as I knew my way about. I checked the bathroom.
Blue with brown carpets. Just like my ma's. Then I spot a loofah
floating in the filled-up bath. The water's still warm. There's still
bubbles on the surface. Ah fuck, I says to myself, somebody's
home after all.

*

I take my gun out and I tiptoe across the hall. I check the two
extra rooms. I'm counting on whoever it is to be in the main
bedroom. Sure enough, both of the other rooms are storage rooms
piled high with boxes. I slip the silencer onto the gun and I edge
the door of the bedroom open. There's somebody in bed, asleep. I
can make out a shape under the covers. I squeeze into the room as
quiet as I can . . .

It's Arlene, in bed. And it throws me for a loop. It's not how I
expected it to be. I can see her breasts, rising and falling, wrapped
in these silk sheets and with nothing underneath. She looks good.
I can see the appeal. The electric blue of the sheets is the same
as Patrick's suits. I'm getting all confused. I should wake her up,
I says to myself, I should tell her why I'm here and why she has
to die. But she might scream, I says to myself, she might cause a
fuss. Before I even know what I'm doing I empty three bullets into
her chest and I hear a sound like air escaping, nothing more to it
than that, and then it's like the room itself is wrapped in cotton
wool.

I did it without a thought, but there was mercy in it, because I had planned to humiliate her, and to beat her senseless, just to make my point, but when it came to it I let her down easy, like the tyre on a bike, and there was little satisfaction to it.

I felt I had to redeem the situation somehow. I sat on the stair and I gazed at the front door. I gave myself up to the lap of the gods. If I'm going to be your executioner, I says to God and Christ Jayzus and all of his fucking angels, lined up, then show me the way. I'm going to sit here, I says to them, till her man comes home. And whichever one of us is meant to go, fucking go ahead and go. You make the call, I says to the angels. I'm abdicating responsibility. That's what I says. Then I lit a fag and I sat there in the gloom. I must have been there two hour at least. Sitting on the stair. Every so often I would hear a sound from the bedroom. Arlene expiring, again, I says to myself. Hopefully she's descending through every level of hell, I think to myself, even though I felt ashamed that I hadn't been able to drag her through every last one of them myself. And then that poem comes into my head, that fucking poem of Tommy's about the one-eyed yellow god, raining down, and I start reciting it under my breath.

A shadow appears in the glass of the front door. I stand up and get ready for the angels. Her man opens the door and walks in with his head down. He walks through to the kitchen without seeing me. I follow quickly behind him. I pick up a bottle of vodka from the drinks trolley and fuck him over the head with it. Then I kneel on his chest and I saw through his windpipe with what's left. He never made a sound. I didn't give him the chance to.

You've never seen so much blood. I went round the room like an artist, smearing bright-red blood all over the walls like your man what does the chaos paintings. Don't ask me why I did that. Then I sat down and cracked open that bottle of Bushmills that had my name on it. The angels had made their call. They were on my side. For now.

*

Next day it was everywhere all over the papers. It gives you a hell of a strange feeling when you're the only witness to something that everybody else is speculating about. You hold in your hands a great secret. You have the privilege of stepping behind the scenes and seeing how history is made. The great bloodied cogs, revealed, in their turning. And plus you get to add your own wee twist, your own gratuitous deformity, which is the closest a man can get to calling himself Christ Jayzus on this earth. Because you're the answer to the question on everybody's lips. Yet you dare not reveal yourself. Because you know you will be crucified for it.

But still there is this secret place in your life that you can revisit, this strange cul de sac, this weird bubble where everything stops dead except for the deed itself, which is forever being replayed, somewhere, offstage, somewhere out of the ordinary, where this one event, repeated, forever, goes on outside of time and space. And whenever you want to, you can re-enter that house, climb in that same window, revisit moments that no one else has the ability to even imagine. Imagine that. You have regrets. Of course you have regrets. But even these are crooked and surprising and not what anybody would expect.

In one way I felt as if it cut me off from Tommy and Barney and from the rest of The Boys. You'll probably say to me that's mad talk, Samuel, sure you were all killers. But each one of us was isolated by it, I says to you, right back. Caught up in our own loops, I says to you. Even as the central loop, the troubles, our troubled Irish history, contained them all.

No one suspected me. Mack joked that I got my wish. That was easy, he says to me. Tommy says that I must have contracted one of them psychic death rays from the comics. In the papers it says that there had been no sign of forced entry. They thought it was an honour killing. Arlene had crossed the lines, they says, and was mixing it up with the other. People get killed for that every day in Belfast. Just like in any other city, in a way.

I told nobody. In my mind it was a promotion. Not in rank, just further into the future. One giant step. I bought every newspaper that I could. I read *every single account*. None of them fit the facts. It was all outlandish speculation. More than that. None of them mentioned her man in terms of the UDA or the UFF. His name was Jimmy Campbell. He was a painter and decorator, was what they said. I began to think that everybody was in on it. That everybody was colluding to keep this cunt's affiliations and identity a secret. I started to think that I had netted myself an even bigger prize than I had thought. I flattered myself, telling myself that the upper echelons had taken a hit. A hit so bad that they had been forced into hushing it up while I disappeared into the night like the Holy fucking Ghost. And I remembered what Kathy had said about invisibility and I realised that Tommy was right, I had caught a superpower, just not the one he thought.

How could he? By this point I had become one of the invisible. But what I didn't realise was that it meant that other people could *see right through you*.

*

It was the first of the summers of blood; you have no idea how many times I had to put up with the one-eyed yellow god what gazes down. It started with the two kids from Athlone, in the heart of the Free State, paid informers, when we dragged their bodies into the middle of the road and called an ambulance that ran over the pair of them as soon as it pulled round the corner. It was an old trick Mack taught us. That's what they do with the junkies in New York, he says to us. How the fuck does he know? Tommy says to me. Maybe he was one of them New York junkies himself, I says to him, I mean, he fucking looked like one.

Then there was the off-duty RUC man from Lisburn who got a kettle of boiling water mixed with six pound of sugar over his head. Then Tommy spots a guy in the street that he says has been harassing Patricia at the dancing. We're on the bus going past and we leap off, bounce his head off a telephone box about ten time without saying a word to the cunt, pop our cuffs, run a comb through our hair, and get back on the bus without missing a beat. Where do you need me to drop you, lads? the driver says to us, without even looking round. A private taxi full of frightened ghosts was the size of our bollocks.

Then we go out on tour. We do a week in Derry, pulling in favours, regulating bootleg booze and fags, kicking the shite out of local dealers and clearing the way for a team of boys from Belfast who the Ra were setting up to make some serious money for the cause. Then we took to using tools. It was the sweetest alibi, a mobile home full of tools and with a painting of your man Mickey Mouse on the side. Who the fuck could object? I broke a guy's jaw with a wrench. Smashed full sets of teeth with a chisel and an iron bar (the sound of bone splintering is like nothing you could ever imagine). Tore a guy's ear off with a hoover. Crippled two blokes with a pair of fire extinguishers. Shot a guy in the leg out the window of a moving car for the wild fuck of it (he had no idea where the bullet even came from). Dropped a guy on his head from the top of a multi-storey car park. That was messy. Buried a guy up to his neck on the beach and took turns toeing his head like a fucking football. That was even messier. Did that thing where you slit the guy's throat with a Stanley and pull his tongue through like a tie, what do you call it, a Glaswegian necktie, but his tongue was too short, and it barely stuck out, and you couldn't see it for the blood and gore anyway (lesson learnt). Forced this car off Etna Drive, stabbed the guy six time in the chest, put him in a bin bag and threw him in the dump. Forced this other car off the Antrim Road, held the guy down, slit his wrists and waited till he bled to death, drove back to his house, kicked the door in and left his body sitting up in a chair next to the fire for his wife to find. Held this guy by the legs off a bridge and made him sing the whole of 'The Boys of the Old Brigade', only he got the words wrong so as we had no option but to drop him. Blew up a row of shops in Strabane. Beat a guy senseless, shaved his head, wrote INFORMER on his forehead and hanged him from a lamp post in front of his house. Cut both a guy's pinkies off, shoved them up his nose and sewed his nostrils shut.

Only joking, we didn't sew them shut. But we would have, if we'd
thought of it.

*

Did you hear about how that war hero Simon Weston
    won the pools?
Only he couldn't claim because he burnt his coupon.
Ha ha.
Fuck him.

*

The whole time me and Tommy are on tour, Barney's looking
after the shop on his lonesome. By this time we had taken to
selling basically anything you could fit on a shelf. There were
dead men's shoes in there – and that is not the name of an
underground comic – old clothes, video cassettes, paintings in
there, cups, jugs, cutlery, plates in there, denim jackets in there,
roller skates in there, radios, TVs, all this stuff that had been
liberated from the dead and the disappeared in there. In fact we
began to get deliveries. The Boys would drop in their pickings,
after skinning it themselves (obviously), but it was all in a good
cause and it made them look like they were giving something
back to the Ra, which they were, of course, only after we had
skinned off yet more of the profits ourselves, because everybody
was on the make, wake up to it, come on. I know there was a war
going on but even the Nazis found time to drink wine, loot gold
and fuck smoking-hot blondes in lingerie.

We watched ourselves on the evening news, the news of the country that we supposedly lived in ourselves, and we saw ourselves portrayed as the worst kind of Fenian bastards. Most people were torn between escaping and standing up to fight. There was no clear outcome, so as people stockpiled. Money, valuables, bolt-holes, provisions. Then you went about your day. With eyes in the back of your fucking head, mind you, still you went about as normal as you could under the circumstances.

But there was always the chance that you could change the game forever. Fight the right fight. Bring down the right target. Hit the right stress points and it was all over. I mean, there had to be an end in sight, right? It was all about the best way to try to bring it down.

I didn't tell them nothing about Kathy when I volunteered us for the Europa job. When Hitler says in the history books that he went about his appointed task with the certainty of a sleepwalker, I understood exactly what he meant. I had privileged access to the Europa. Nobody else knew about it but it was true. I says to Mack, I can do it, I know the Europa well. I told him I had fucked a few whores in there, even though I winced when I says it. I felt for Kathy and I didn't think our relationship was anything like that. Who takes whores to the Europa except for journalists, politicians and fucking Unionist sympathisers? Mack says to me. Exactly, I says to him: meet The Invisible Man.

Everybody loved the Europa. It stood for something in Belfast. For another life. For having enough money to get away or at least only have to come back and visit. Plus and it was called the Europa. It was greater than Great Britain. It was something Ireland could be a part of. But I was as mad as your man Hitler. I'd bring the whole of the Europa down in flames just for the sheer fucking hell of it.

Me and Tommy and Barney get the job. Course we do. But really it was a solo mission. I couldn't let on about the full details of my own involvement and on the other hand here was me having to protect Kathy. I was on nobody's side, really, except for the side of history, which is all you can do, except for the side of the future, which is on its way. But they knew what was coming.

> Come on,
> it was an f-ing game,
> come on

The Boys had hit the Europa within three months of it opening in 1971. And again and again ever since. But nobody had ever levelled it. It was all about coming up with new plans of attack. And here's me eating stolen room service off silver trays, in random rooms, outside the eyes of security, and making love in every one of them; what an opportunity, what a fucking gift.

*

Listen, I'm banging on about the Nazis. I had plenty of time to read about the Nazis later when I was detained at Her Majesty's pleasure, that bitch. I read a ton of books behind bars. Believe me. I read about other wars that took place. Wars in the Middle East and wars in South America and wars in Africa, wars in every language on God's earth. But it was the war with the Nazis that struck me the most and that had the most similarities with our own situation here in Ireland.

Your man Goebbels gives this speech. He was the head of propaganda for the Nazis and he gives this speech at a sport centre in Berlin. All the hard cases are there, all the old fighters. This is in about 1943, I think, when it's becoming clear that Germany is getting shafted on all sides. Goebbels talks about Stalingrad, one of the big crazy Nazi defeats, where they were driven back and massacred, lots of young Nazi soldiers are killed, there's no way to avoid talking about it, so as Goebbels comes up with this thing, it was propaganda but it strikes a chord, he comes up with this thing where he says that all the young men that had died had lived out their mission, he talks about it as if they had solved the riddle of their life much earlier than the survivors, much earlier than the people at the talk in the sport centre. In fact he says that it was actually the people that were left alive who were in limbo because they still had the whole puzzle of their life left to unravel. Think about it. All the young boys that had been killed at Stalingrad had just fulfilled themselves early and even now, even now they were ghosting in the light of eternal blessings, which was not a religious thing, Goebbels was not a religious man, he couldn't give a shite when the churches got bombed, but what he meant is that living out your own life, completely, whatever the story, means to get bathed in this light at the end, the golden light of destiny, this final illuminating moment where all of this stuff makes sense.

I thought about Patrick and all at once I see him in his electric-blue suit, on a cloud, getting his dick sucked by an angel at last, and I thought of how his life had been solved and the story completed whereas mine was still unravelling all over the place. But there was a connecting thread there, something we had in common, something that was running through all our lives and somehow directing them. Our stories were all tied up with each other ever since I whacked his girlfriend and her new man and shacked up with my own in the Europa.

It was like Stalingrad because I was defending several fronts at once, juggling who needed to know what, and what had to be kept secret from who. Goebbels says in that case you fight a Total War, which means that *every single thing* is geared toward the fight. You make it your whole reason for existing, fighting this fucking war. And how do you know when you're winning? Okay, so as this is the best bit.

Goebbels says that you can't judge anything by the mood that you're in when you're in a state of Total War. So he goes ahead and he replaces the word 'mood' with the word 'bearing', as in how you hold yourself. Now, I had to laugh. That was me and Tommy and Barney and your man Pat right there. No matter how heavy anything got, no matter how much blood we had on our hands, no matter how dangerous the situation became, we never once lost our bearing. We carried ourselves like movie stars. We modelled ourselves on Perry Como. Our bearing? You want to know how our bearing was? Our bearing was toward the future. We intended to seduce the fuck out of it.

We're sat around the shop, brainstorming the approach. We still had a trickle of kids coming in to buy the comics and Barney had even made pals with a few of them. There was one kid that did his own comic strip, fantasy stuff like *Savage Sword of Conan* only set in Ancient Ireland (Ur-lan't, the kid named it), that was called *The Fomorians*, who were creatures with superpowers that originally lived in Atlantis after it got sunk but that were tempted into leaving the waters by just how beautiful Ur-lan't was and now they had to defend it against another race of evil superheroes called the Partholons.

This kid that drew the artwork and wrote the adventures himself, he was a wee genius, so he was. Now Barney has taken him under his wing and is buying the original drawings off him. These are going to be worth a fortune one day, Barney says to us as the kid's leaving the store. You're a wee f-ing genius, he shouts after him, this kid with the red hair and a duffel coat, this kid that didn't even look round and that was obviously completely embarrassed. I have only the fuzziest memory of what he looked like. He always had his hood up, as I remember it, and he would leave or look the other way when me and Tommy showed up. This wee kid is as good as your man, Barney says to us.

Who's your man? Tommy says. Your man, Barney says. Your man what did all the paintings. Plenty of guys did the paintings, I says to him. That doesn't fucking narrow it down much. I'm talking about your man Picatsto, Barney says. That kid is as good as your man Picatsto. What the fuck do you know about Picatsto? Tommy says to him. I know plenty, Barney says. Like what? Tommy says. Like, for instance, he painted in the wee squares and triangles. That's what you call cube-ism, Tommy says.

I have no idea where he was getting these terms from.

Exactly, Barney says to him. Cube-ism is drawing in wee fucking squares like in the comic books. That is exactly what the point I'm saying is. That kid is as good as your man Picatsto. Then Barney shows us this picture that he had done, this picture of a guy with the head of a reindeer, it looked like, the head of a reindeer on top of his own head and with a tattooed face, and with a bow and arrow, standing on the top of this mountain, and behind him there are all these ships, like Viking warships, raised up, and floating up, into the air. Fuck me, Tommy says, but that's better than your man Picatsto. Give me a boy with imagination every time, he says, and he shakes his head. Do you think he would draw me?

Fuck that, Barney says. He should draw all three of us. He should put us in an adventure, he says. He should make a comic book out of us. Sure, you couldn't print half of what we get up to, I says to them. Well, we could always make something up, Barney says. A fantasy story. Or we can tell him a story from our past, something that wouldn't get us arrested, and he can write it up and draw us into it.

What are you trying to say? I says to Barney. Have you done something legal in the past? That got a good laugh. Then we get back to the brainstorming.

A bomb in the elevator, Tommy says. Think about it. Going up! A bomb in the water tank, Barney says. Think about it. Flood the fucking place! A bomb in the basement, Tommy says. Think about it. Bring it down around their fucking heads! Bomb Bomb Bomb, I says to them, that's a fucking punk rock song right there. What degree of headcase works in a place like that anyway? Barney says. They must pay you danger money. Wait a minute, he says. Didn't that wee bird we kidnapped work in the Europa?

I can't remember, I says. So she did, Tommy says. It's a fucking shame we let her slip through our fingers, Barney says. She could have been our way in. Don't forget, Oddjob, I says to him, I was busy saving your life. That's how she fucking escaped in the first place. Maybe we should recapture her, Barney says. Save face and get the keys to the fucking kingdom at the same time, know what I'm saying?

She disappeared, mind? I says to him. Half these fucking shelves are filled with her belongings.

She was a good-looking doll, Tommy says. I wouldn't say no to an hour in a spare room at the Europa with her, know what I'm saying? Then he turns round and he looks at me, without saying a word. That's when all the paranoia about transparency really began to kick in.

*

Me: What is a dip-so-maniac?
Tommy: A guy what can't stop swimming in the sea.

114

Me: What does 'A Rolling Stone Gathers No Moss' mean?

Tommy: That if a stone keeps moving, then moss will never be able to grow on it, obviously.

Me: Why do trees lose their leaves in the winter?

Tommy: Because all of the sap has gone back down into the ground so as that the snow won't break the branches by being too heavy for the leaves.

Me: When was the Easter Uprising?

Tommy: 24th to 29th April 1916. Five days what shook the world. Six. Days.

Me: Where do birds hibernate in the winter?

Tommy: Bottom of ponds and rivers.

Me: In that case, how do they breathe?

Tommy: Through their gills.

Me: What is the best movie what was ever made?

Tommy: *Quiet Man*.

Me: What would the story of your life be called if you could write it?

Tommy: *The Twelve Judases*.

Me: ?

Tommy:

Me: What is the terrible date of Bloody Sunday?

Tommy: 30th January 1972.

Me: How many people were killed by the Brits on that terrible date?

Tommy: That date? Thirteen.

Me: What is the best advice anybody ever gave you?

Tommy: Trap it.

Me: Where does honey come from?

Tommy: Bees. Is that a trick question?

Me: What do you call a baby bird?

Tommy: A younker.

Me: Quick, what's that planet up there?

Tommy: Mars. Jupiter.

Me: What is your favourite line from your man Shakespeare?

Tommy: If'n musice be the foode of love, leade on, MacDuff.

Me: When was the Battle of the Boyne?

Tommy: 1st July 1690.

Me: Who was Abraham in The Bible?

Tommy: King of the Murphs.

Me: What is the best musical ever made?

Tommy: *Jolson Story*.

Me: When was the Great Flood of London?

Tommy: 1066.

Me: Name your man, the poet, what led the 1916 rebellion.

Tommy: Your man Big Patty Pearse.

Me: What is the capital of Scotland?

Tommy: Glasgow. Easy.

Me: What is the best way of getting God's attention?

Tommy: Pain.

Me: What is the animal that has the most fun, probably?

Tommy: Dolphins. After that, dogs.

Me: What is the correct term for a man what has no hairs upon his head?

Tommy: Balledosit't.

Me: Name three paintings by your man Picatsto.

Tommy: *Nowhere Known*, *The Face*, and *A Bowl of Plums*.

Me: What was Christ Jayzus's first words after he rose from the dead?

Tommy: You're on a hiding to nothing.

Me: Does the Pope shite in the woods?

Tommy: Is a bear a Catholic?

*

When we were kids my da loved to take me and my brother to the reptile house in the Belfast Zoo at the Cave Hill. I was never a fan of snakes, but I always loved that bit when you walk through the door and you're plunged into darkness and it takes you whole minutes to get your eyes accustomed to the light, that bit when you have your arms out in front of you to steady yourself and all you can see are these aquariums floating in mid-air, all of these colour tellies from hell.

My da always says to us that snakes are the most innocent creatures in the world. Look into their eyes, he says to us, take a good look and be honest with yourself. There's not a bad bone in their bodies, he says. I didn't even know snakes *had* bones in their bodies.

Then, one day, he brings one home, as a present, for my brother. He brings a real-life snake home as a pet and starts feeding it on live hamsters, live hamsters that he's breeding in the garage and that never see the light of day outside of when he marches across the back garden with one of them squirming in his hand on its way to getting eaten whole.

I need to teach you, he says to us, then he would sit us down, in the dark, in Peter's room, in front of this lit-up aquarium, like we were at the movies, and he would educate us. A snake is just doing what it does, he says to us, with no malice whatsoever. It's playing with it, Peter says to him, look, it's taunting it. Snakes don't taunt, my da says, what are you talking about? Then the snake would pounce and its big hinged jaw would go back and it would swallow half the body of the hamster, whose legs would be kicking out behind it as its head disappeared down this great black throat and endless belly that God Himself had created, that's what my da says, God Almighty Himself created snakes, he says to us, and then Saint Patrick kicked them out of Ireland. Beat it, Patrick says to them, go on.

But that was your man Saint Pat's big mistake, my da says. Saint Paddy's original balls-up was booting the snakes out of Ireland in the first place, because that meant there was no one left, no thing left, is what he meant to say, no thing left to get victimised, no thing left to take all of the blame for the suffering of the world, and so the Irish turned on one another. In the absence of snakes they just fucking went at it, but they went at it as innocent as snakes themselves, with that same look in their eyes, that same look that says, what about you?

If snakes could shrug, my da says to us, they'd be at it all day. But you need shoulders for that.

So you see, that's why, in The Bible, there's a snake in the Garden of Eden what takes the rap for everything, my da says to us, and when Peter would say to him, but wait a minute, da, wasn't it Jayzus that was supposed to take on all the sins of the world, wasn't that his job, then my da would look at us both and he would laugh with those eyes of his, eyes like a happy snake that could shrug all it wanted, and he would grab our shoulders and he would kill himself, he'd be cracking up, as if we were the most naive kids in the world, and he loved it, but one day we were going to have to wake up to the reality of Christ Jayzus and snakes and what goes on in Ireland, and in Eden.

My brother came out as a gay when he was eighteen year old. My da threatened to beat it out him. What about snakes, I says to him, what about innocent snakes? We were having this big fight in the living room the night Peter dropped the bomb. Snakes don't turn gay, my da says. You don't know anything, Peter says to him. All snakes do it up the arse. My da knocked him halfways across the living room for that one.

In the end Peter moved to Canada just so as he could get away from the fucking Garden of Eden. But it's true, I found out later, Peter was right, all snakes do it up the arse.

When my da was killed a few year later, Peter didn't even come back for the funeral. No snakes in Ireland, he says when I called him on the phone, remember? The night Peter left my da took the big fucking snake that he had bought for him and forced it down the toilet. I watched him do it, just feeding this massive fucking thing head first into the bog. The thing made a dash for freedom.

Just fucking scooted round the U-bend, never to be seen again. It would rather sleep in a sewage pipe for the rest of its days, I remember thinking, than spend another night in my da's house with an endless supply of live hamsters. That says it all.

Then another snake came along and killed my da. A snake what hit him over the head with a fire extinguisher in a pub, and what snapped his head half off his body. Years earlier, when me and Peter were still living at home, his own da had died and his body had lain upstair at my gran's house in an open coffin. Do you want to see your grandfather? my da says to us, and he has a gleeful look on his face like he is asking us if we wanted to bunk off school and drink a can of cider in a car park. It was another opportunity to teach us, this time about the big one. He took both our hands and led us into this grey room with the last of the light coming through. There was my grandfather, lying there, dead. It's alright, my da says to us, it's okay. Have a good look, he says. Take it all in. You need to learn.

I can't even remember what he looked like. I can't even remember my grandfather's body lying there in his coffin at all. All I can remember, and it's clear as a dream, is me and Peter, standing there, holding hands with my da in this grey room, next to a coffin, and him smiling and saying to us, go on, don't be scared. There's worse things to take to your grave, I'll tell you that.

*

So Tommy goes ahead and subscribes to the *Reader's Digest*, which he can't even fucking read, which tells you all you need to know about Tommy right there. He would sit in the shop with his feet up on the desk, and he would flick through the pages and make an act like he was reading. I mean, what he was taking in, god only knows, but he was taking in something, because he would bring all these strange and alluring facts up to me and Barney and he would use them to lord it over us. We'd be sitting there reading our comics. This is what we should be reading, he says to us, and he comes over and smacks me round the head with a *Digest*. It fucking hurt, they were compact wee bastards. We should be educating ourselves, he says to us. Reading up about the world. They're talking about hypnotism in here, Tommy says to us. The Boys should be making full use of this. They do alreadies, Barney says. What do you think the suits and the gold rings are for? Don't fucking cheek me, Tommy says to him, I'm talking about autosuggestions. Don't you know the *Reader's Digest* is funded by the CIA? I says to him. Even better, he says. We're learning from the pros. Naw, Barney says, all that means is that the fucking FBI or the CIA or whatever this mob is just put the idea of autosuccession into your head. You could see Tommy was thinking about that one.

Then the wee kid shops up, the wee midget Picatsto, and he's drawn a comic strip of us. Did you ever see that cartoon *Beavis & Butt-Head*? That wasn't out at the time but that's the only thing that comes to mind when I try to remember what he looked like, this guy what looked like Beavis from your *Beavis & Butt-Head*. So Beavis goes up to Barney – Barney's his mentor and his main collector at this point – and he hands him the strip. He's drawn the three of us as superheroes and the title of it is *The Forever Family*. That was the name of our superhero group. Alright, so try and guess what our superpowers were. Try and guess.

Naw, no invisibility. That was a pity. That was me and my partner in real life, The Invisible Kathy M.

Check it out: Barney was radioactive, ha ha. He had some traumatic accident where he had got caught in the birth of a star or a planet and he had become like a mini supernova giving off all this radioactive power so as he had to be strapped into like titanium-grade armour to deal with this galactic deformity so as that he looked like a goddamned man-machine because he would literally burn up anybody who had contact with him, which made him like The Thing from *The Fantastic Four*, in a way, like tragic and sad and with no way of getting a girlfriend but with the power to destroy an entire fucking planet. But the thing is, he could be in two places at once, because his particles had deformed and gone subatomic so as he was like a one-man army. The name Beavis gave him? Neutrino.

And Tommy? Tommy was The X-Ray Kid. And get this: he had hypnotic eyes. No bull. He could shoot a beam from his eyes that would reveal anything. That could strip a woman's clothes off to her ankles. That could read thoughts. That could see through walls. That could hypnotise you into believing that every star is a planet just like ours. That would mean that all he needed to do was to stare at a copy of the *Reader's Digest* and he could download everything in there and get special knowledge without even fucking bothering to read it. He had to wear these special visors, mind, otherwise he would be going about turning the whole world upside down with a glance. I says to myself, that's autosuggestion right there, The X-Ray Kid is writing the damn book, that's true superpowers, all this mad stuff is real.

And as for me? I'm not going to tell you my superpower. See if you can't figure it out for yourself. But I'll give you my name: my name was The Anomaly.

*

That's when we realised that Miracle Baby could read the future. That was his superpower. Thing is, if you asked him something that he knew, he would tell you the truth, you would get the full story, no problem. But he was just like a Weegie board, because if you asked him something that he didn't know, then he would just start making it up. But then everything he made up started coming true. Only but it takes us a while to figure it out.

We're sitting in Tommy's back garden and Miracle Baby is working on some rock formation he was making for the equivalent of ten pence an hour. Miracle Baby, Tommy says to him, do you know your man Jinksy O'Connor? Very neat, Miracle Baby says, Jinksy O'Connor is very neat. It was true, Jinksy was a pal of Mack's and even though he was half-blind he dressed well plus he was always polite and decent, except when he was sticking you in the ribs with a sharpened chisel, which was his weapon of choice, that and strangulation with women's nylons, it turns out.

Do you think we can trust him? Tommy says to Miracle Baby. Tommy and Jinksy had been set up with some low-key racket

down one end of the Falls Road and Tommy was convinced that
Jinksy was out collecting on his lonesome. Jinksy O'Connor can't
be trusted with his ma's underwear, Miracle Baby says. What?!
He can't keep his hands out his ma's panties, Miracle Baby says,
which is going to do for him in the end, he says. Then he starts
giggling to himself. Fuck is he talking about? Tommy says.
Fucking wee daftie. Then a week later, and I'm not kidding you,
Jinksy O'Connor is discovered, by his own sister, half-naked and
hanging from the ceiling, with a set of tights round his neck and
wearing a pair of his ma's panties. The stupid cunt only went
and asphyxiated himself to death in one of these accidental sex
murders; what the fuck just happened.

We round up Miracle Baby, pull him into a car as he's walking
down Jamaica Street, his face all snottery and with ice cream
all down his top. Tommy's driving, I'm in the back seat. Miracle
Baby, how the fuck did you know about Jinksy O'Connor?
Tommy says to him. Everybody knows about Jinksy O'Connor,
he says. No fucker knew about Jinksy O'Connor: fact. Miracle
Baby was become prophetic, he was pulling this knowledge
out of the air, which is what it means, prophecy, to get your
information from the future. So as we started asking him all this
other madness.

Will there ever be a united Ireland? Naw, never, he says. That's
fucking mutinous talk right there, Tommy says to him, but guess
what, he's still right. Will I get laid at The Shamrock on Saturday
night? Yes, Tommy, he says, but that didn't take a fucking mind
reader. Wait, I says to him, do you think the Ra are going to hit
Mad Dog McPaik? He's a dead man, Miracle Baby says, and so

he was, a week later. Who killed Arlene McDaid? Tommy says to him, and time stops dead.

I'm looking down at Miracle Baby, who is lying on the back seat with all of this pink ice cream down his jumper, and with snots and saliva on his face, and he's writhing down there, like a terrible grotesque nightmare he's wriggling, and he looks up at me, and he sticks his tongue out and he crosses his eyes, but before he can say anything else I says to him, wait a minute, I says, wait, I've got a better one, let's get fucking serious here for a moment why don't we, is the Europa still standing, I says to him, and he says it right back to me: the Europa is a mighty fortress. What the fuck.

Does anybody die in the Europa? I says to him. Does anybody die when we bring it down around their fucking ears? The Europa is still standing, Miracle Baby says, and it's like his eyes have frosted over, like there's a film over his eyes that has blotted out his pupils and he says to me, no one dies, with his blind eyes he says to us, no one dies. Tommy looks at me in the rear-view mirror. I know what he's thinking. No one dies. The Europa is a mighty fortress. We walk in there with a suitcase full of Semtex and we make our mark without taking a single fucking life. Clean, and easy. We pull over to the side of the Alliance Road, give Miracle Baby twenty pence for more ice cream, and scream off into the future that had been promised us by a retarded baby.

*

1977, son. That's when it all gets fucking serious. Changes at the top, my friend. Martin McGuinness and Gerry Adams are moving up, plus they had guys like Tom Hartley in there, the Falls Road Think Tank they called it, but there had been too much thinking, we all knew it, even for these guys, even though they couldn't stop thinking, and producing books and pamphlets, and taking over local newspapers, even though we all knew that we had been held up, that things were too quiet, that the stand-off would never last, that the Brits would only respond to a massive and concerted show of force.

Everybody gets given these fucking *Green Books*, have you seen these things? They call us in, me and Barney and Tommy, and they attempt to scare the living shite out us. The IRA was the law. They were the true government. They were the voice of the people. So obeying orders to the point of laying down your life was something that was expected of every one of us. I mean, there was talk from some of The Boys about building a Socialist fucking Republic and all of this nonsense, but that meant nothing to me and less than nothing to Tommy and Barney. They couldn't fucking spell socialism and were disinclined to try. We were motivated by more immediate concerns: protection, resentment, ambition, revenge, honour, sex, money, style, class – okay, I'll give you that one – plus a history of violence that ran through our veins and that (let's face it) was one of the only things holding the generations together. So as when they take us in and they hand us these *Green Books* and they says to us that we must be capable of murder, we must be capable of cold-blooded killing, without regrets, we could've laughed in their faces, if we weren't all in on the joke in the first place. Killing without conscience: that's what being one of The Boys was all about. A state of Total War like your man Goebbels: that was the legacy our families had handed down. Total War was our first-born and best-loved. Attrition, *The Green Book* says to us. Bombing, it says. Curbing, it says. Sustaining, it says. Defending & Punishing, it says. It was like a roll-call at school. We knew all these wee bastards. We grew up with them.

*

The first fight I ever saw in real life was when we went on holiday with my ma and da to Dublin. I must have been four or five year old. My ma was washing her hair and my da says to us, let's go down the arcades and get a shot of those penny falls while your ma's getting ready. My da was addicted to the penny falls. We get down there and it's busy as hell, everyone is squeezed in around the machines, it looks like they're going to tip, and my da gives me a handful of pennies. Get in there, he says, and win us a wee fortune. There's an old dear playing right next to us and next to her is stood a shady-looking silhouette, now, in my mind, a featureless ghost, hiding out in my past. The old dear looks like she's going to tip the pennies. And this shade starts pushing into her, starts trying to claim her place. My da steps in. Play the game, he says to this blank silhouette, to this gap in my mind, and he holds onto the machine so that he can't push in any further. But the shade leans in to him, and pushes back, and he accidentally skiffs my da's chin with his hand. My da draws back, takes a hammer from the inside of his coat – it's the first time I realised that my da always carried a weapon – and starts fucking the guy over the head with it. The side of his skull caves in and he falls forward but my da catches him with another blow and sends him flying backward, through the window and out into the street,

127

and now there's blood and glass everywhere. Me and Peter are both crying. My da steps up to the penny falls, calm as you like, drops a penny in, and he's won, with a single penny, the money starts tumbling out, and he turns to the old dear, it's all yours, he says to her, and then he says to us, move it, let's go, and he grabs our hands and we run off and we have to duck into doorways on the way as the peelers go screaming past and after about half an hour we go back to the scene of the crime and we spy on the arcade from across the road and the body is gone but we spot the old dear and she's talking to the peelers. That bitch is going to grass us up, my da says to us. Trust no one, he says, and don't tell your ma, neither.

It wasn't till years later, at my da's funeral, that I telt this story for the first time, and my ma had no idea it had even happened. He was some man, she says to me as we stood at the side of his grave. Wee bastard thought he was Robin Hood. I still think of that ghost every so often, that shade lying in the glass and the blood on the pavement, and I wonder if he's alive or dead. I think dead, probably.

*

Then Bobby Sands goes down for fourteen year. I mean, we didn't really know him. He was up in Rathcoole and we were down in the Ardoyne. But my ma knew his family and he was a good guy by all accounts, a bit of a soft touch when he was a kid, that's what I heard, and of course he looked like a fucking hippy and had no sense of style whatsoever, which meant he was onto plums, in our book anyroads, and even years later when they got that mural of his on the wall of the Sinn Féin, my Aunt Betty goes past and is like that, he was some man, she says, but could he not have combed his hair and got a jumper what fit him?

Bobby gets fourteen year for bombing this carpet factory in Dunmurry, out Lisburn way. He doesn't go down for the bombing, mind, he goes down for possession of a chatsby. He gets lifted by the peelers afters a ten-way firefight where they get their car rammed. He gets sent down to the Crumlin Road Gaol. And what happens is he kicks up a fucking storm.

I heard he was getting taunted. I don't know if it was his hair or what but next thing we hear they've got the poor cunt on boards, what means they took every single item of furniture out his cell and just fucking sat him there. Then they stripped him bollock naked. Then they started starving him. This is the British government what's doing this. That was when a lot of people turned. I mean, it may be hindsight. It may be all that Bobby Sands stands for this weather. But now I mind it as the moment that something snapped. That something was loosed. And besides, in Ireland history isn't written. It's remembered.

*

If there was one thing *The Green Book* hammered into us (The Holy Bible, some of us called it), it was that we were engaged in a glorious struggle, that we were the heroes of the future, that we were fighting for a legitimate cause, and that we weren't just fucking common criminals anymore, which was some laugh, believe me, because a lot of us were just that, or at least had been, until the day they beat us over the head with this fucking *Green Book*. But back then it felt like a calling, like fate or destiny had played their pish-stained hands, and I never forgot what Mack said about thickening your skin and toughening yourself up. Now I understood what he meant. He was telling me in code. He was speaking just like Miracle Baby spoke. The struggle was making us all into oracles. Making superheroes of criminals. Making gods of murderers. Making legends of men. There's a new world coming. What a time to be alive. 1977. God Save the Queen. We mean it, man.

*

I'm in the shop one day on my lonesome. There's a father and son in there reading the comics. The da seems a bit simple. The son is obviously retarded. But they're bonding over the comics. It's a shared interest, isn't it? The da is reading *Daredevil*. The son *Justice League of America*. Da, the son says to him, Da, why do you have to sacrifice yourself for someone else? The da says to him, you give up your life so as someone else can live. Is that like saying sorry? the kid says to him. Is that like saying, I'm sorry? Then the kid starts shouting it, I'm sorry, I'm sorry, I'm sorry! The da puts his arm around him and manoeuvres him out the shop. I'm sorry, his da says to me as he goes. I sat there and thought about it for the longest time.

*

Choppers were all the rage in the Ardoyne in 1977 and everybody wanted one, believe me. Miracle Baby's birthday was coming up and he had asked Tommy to get him one for a present. Tommy knew the rag-and-bone man that would come through the Ardoyne with his horse and cart and he says to him to look out for a Chopper for him and one day he shows up with this three-wheeler, which is what you call a tricycle, and he says to Tommy, here you go, I got you that Chopper you were after. But Tommy says to him, that's not a fucking Chopper, it doesn't even say Chopper on it, plus it's got three fucking wheels. Sure, it's just as fucking good as a Chopper, the bone man says to him. Besides, he says, the wee retard won't even know the difference. Here, give him a balloon as well, the bone man says, and he gives him a white balloon with a black clown's face on it. So as Tommy gives this bike to Miracle Baby and the wee soul's over the moon. Sure, I got you that Chopper you were after, Tommy says to him. Oh my god, the wee guy says, it's a three-wheeled Chopper, oh – my – god. And he's off, speeding along the pavement on this fucking tricycle like he's king of the wheels with this fucking balloon tied to his handlebars.

The next day me and Tommy are sitting drinking cans of green in the garden when we see Miracle Baby getting chased by a bunch of boys on actual real Choppers. They corner him and they cut the string of his balloon and it takes off (a single milk-white teardrop, rising up) and we can hear them taunting him, that's not a fucking Chopper, you mong, they're saying to him, that's not a bike, that's a fucking wheelchair. Me and Tommy go barrelling over and they take off in fright. Wee Miracle Baby is crying. It's not a Chopper, he says to Tommy, you made it up, they don't do three-wheeled Choppers. And Tommy says to him, no, you're wrong, what you've got is a deluxe Chopper, imported from

London. What you've got is the best bike of all. But it doesn't even say Chopper on it, Miracle Baby says to him. That's cause they're fake Choppers, those ones that the bad boys have, Tommy says to him. That's why they had to write Chopper on the side of them, otherwise nobody would believe them. Why would they need to do that if they were real? And somehow Miracle Baby is convinced. Now I feel sorry for them, he says. Don't burst their bubble, Tommy says to him. And don't let on about the three-wheeled Choppers to anyone. Let's keep it to ourselves. And Miracle Baby races off on this top-grade bicycle that was rescued from a midden and that was probably worth about ten pence, if that, even.

*

Then I see Kathy in the street with Davy, the two of them sat on a bench in Bankmore Square, off the Dublin Road, with the leaves falling from the trees, so as it must have been October of '77. She's wearing a short fur coat and she's lying up against him on the bench and she's got her head on his shoulder, maybe she's sleeping. He's reading a newspaper and wearing a pair of dark sunglasses. It's too late for me to turn around. I have to walk past them. I start to whistle to myself. Back then everybody was a whistler. This weather you would probably get lifted for it. But I start to whistle this tune, 'The Old Bog Road'. Davy looks up at me as I pass. I'm standing as close to him as you are to me but it's like I'm not even there. It's like he's looking right through me. He doesn't recognise me at all, just goes back to reading his paper. Kathy shifts on the bench but doesn't open her eyes. Before I know it I'm past them and I'm walking away. And that's when I hear it.

Davy has picked up on the tune I was whistling and he's carrying it on himself. A ghost, I tell myself. I'm a ghost, come in. Then I hear him sing. He even sounds a bit like Tommy. He starts to sing the words to the song.

> Each human heart must bear its grief
> Though bitter be the 'bode
> So God be with you, Ireland,
> And the Old Bog Road

There are all sorts of ways to destroy the heart. When you get older you realise that. When I was young I was scared of nothing. Nothing outside of a knife or a gun or a fucking bomb blast could have put the fear in me, and even then. But as I got older it was the things you couldn't see that began to worry me. Things that can put their hands straight through the flesh of your chest and grab hold of your heart and take it out and beat it to a pulp and put it back there without leaving so much as a scar. Women, chanters, snakes and ghosts. And not necessarily in that order.

*

Finally we get the nod from the top brass and Mack meets us in the Mickey Mouse van, somewhere outside of Belfast. The Europa gig is on and everybody's celebrating. Mack pulls a gold packet of twenty B&H out his top bin and passes them around. What a cigarette. All the top brass smoked B&H. That was their style.

Have youse read that fucking *Green Book* like I told youse? Mack says to us. Fuck me, Tommy says to him, next thing you're going to need a fucking degree to join the Ra. Specialist subject: the murder of dirty Huns, Barney says. That's not university, mate, Mack says to him.

What are you talking about?

That's *Mastermind*, Mack says to him. That's *Mastermind* where you have a specialist subject. In university they call it your major. That's America, I says to him. That's what they call it in America. In the UK it's different. Aye, well, we're not in the UK, Tommy says. Maybe you haven't read the fucking *Green Book*. That reminds me of my favourite joke, Barney says. Paddy from Ireland goes on *Mastermind* . . .

For fuck sake, Mack says to him, cut it out. This is supposed to be a high-level briefing about a devastating attack on the forces of oppression, not the Royal Variety Performance. I'd blow the fucking Royal Variety Performance sky-high, Barney says. Now there's a fucking target. Stop! Mack says. Just fucking stop talking for a minute here, would youse, he says. Do we actually have a plan? I've got a plan, I says to him. I know the Europa like the back of my hand, I says. I don't believe you've ever been in there in your fucking life, Tommy says to me, and he fixes me with a dead-cold stare. Aye, I have, I says to him. The fuck do you know? Listen, I says to Mack. I've been doing a little research, leaning on a few cunts, setting a few cunts up, get the gist of what I'm saying? They're starting to get to know me in there, is what I'm saying. If they knew you, they'd ban you in two seconds, Tommy says, but his eyes have calmed a bit now. Look, I says to Mack. What I'm saying is that I'm happy to do it. I'll need a bomb with a timer on it, mind. Something that I can trigger quick like but that isn't going to go off in my hand. Something sturdy enough to drop down one of the ventilation shafts. They have them on every floor. All you need to do is shoogle the grille off and it'll be like dropping a match into a drum of petrol. Just as long as I've got time to get back out, mind. Before the entire edifice goes ka-boom. Shouldn't be a problem, Mack says to me. You would not believe the boffins we have behind the scenes this weather. They'll be inventing remote-control bombs that you can fly into a ventilation shaft from a mile off before anyone knows it, he says.

And we sat there for a second, marvelling at all the possibilities that the future had in store. One day we'll be redundant, boys, Tommy says to us, and he shrugs. Enjoy it while you can.

*

We'd be making love in the Europa and I says to myself, this can't last forever, Xamuel, her legs wrapped around me and lost in her smells and her tender fingers in my hair are like the words of the song come in, *upon my pillow, hold your warm and tender body close to mine, hear the whisper of the raindrops blowing soft across the window, and make believe you love me one more time*, as I pictured us wrapped around each other, and raised up, as the hotel dissolves all around us and all around us Belfast is in ruins, Belfast lies in ruins beneath us, and the two of us, entwined, stand at the beginning, all true lovers are the first lovers, forever, we tell each other, with our eyes, we see each other, as returned, and then, of course, I start to hear the voices, they would interrupt my reverie, fucking Tommy and Barney are a pair of bastards, standing there in the ruins, shouting up to us, get back down here, you no-user, they'd be shouting, what are you, some fucking woman, they're shouting, get back down here from up in them airs, and we are raised up on secret umbilicals, the two of us, and using my powers, my secret superpowers, I spy us an island off the coast, just beyond the horizon, a secret island where we could be naked together, and where we could live without smoking ruins and twisted metal and upturned cars and soldiers in the streets, an island where we could start the whole game all over again, but even then, even as our bare feet touched down on the grass, this soft grass that has never been trodden, can you imagine such a thing, I knew that beginning all over again meant the same things forever, meeting only to be parted, building to destroy, rising up just to fall back down again. Where are you? Kathy says to me. I'm on a virgin island of Ur-lan't, I says to her, right back at the beginning. Can we live there forever? she says to me and I think of her curled up on a bench with her husband, and I says to her, no, not forever, we can't live there forever, honey, but for a summer, maybe, I think we can manage a summer, a summer before we burn it to the ground.

It's too dangerous to work in the Europa, I says to her. You need to get out. Do you know something I don't? she says to me. I know it's a target, I says to her. Doesn't take any insider knowledge to know that it's a target. I just don't want to see it coming down around your ears, that's all. She rolls onto her back, she's naked except for her black bra and her earrings, the sight of her soft skin, there in the lamplight, her long red hair upon the pillow. She sparks up a B&H. That's a habit I got her into. Does your man not notice you've changed your brand? I says to her. What,

you mean from geeky bookish types to suave gangsters? she says
to me. Anyway, she says to me, the Europa is a mighty fortress,
and she takes a long draw on her cigarette.

I says to her, what, wait a minute, what did you just say? I'm just
saying, she says, that the place is impregnable, Sammy, that I'm
safer here than anywhere. The whole fucking city could go up
at any moment. I could get snatched by the Ra on my way home
from work and imprisoned in a safe house and tortured by a pair
of gangsters. Sure, you were never tortured, I says to her. Now
you're just getting into sexual fantasies. I pounce on her and she
pretends to fight me off before we make love one more time, but all
the while I've got this phrase in my head, the Europa is a mighty
fortress. There it is again. But what is it that's speaking? You need
to go, Kathy says, rushing me out, and I'm still doing up my tie as
I walk along the corridor. I'm high. I'm feeling great. I'm bouncing
along on that soft carpet with the pattern they had. I take the lift
to reception and I'm about to step out when I see Tommy. Fucking
Tommy's standing at the desk, at reception, talking to one of the
girls. He's pointing to something up above him and she's nodding.
He points up, again, toward the ceiling, and the doors of the lift
close and I take it back up and I get out, randomly, on the fifth
floor. And suddenly everything is up in the air.

*

Wait, what about this one, listen to this one, this is a classic:

> Paddy's wife comes home from the doctor's and Paddy says
> to her, did that doctor tell you what was up with you, and his

137

wife says to him, no, the only thing he says was that I had a beautiful pussy, and Paddy says, what the fuck, and he loses it, and he goes battering over to the doctor's and he barges in on him and he starts laying into him, he starts giving him a right pasting, and all the time Paddy's screaming at him, don't dare you comment on my wife's pussy, how fucking dare you, he's saying, and the doctor he says to him, Paddy, you've got it all wrong, all I says to her was that she had acute angina.

*

We're up The Shamrock, it's Saturday night, and Tommy's up onstage giving it plenty. One singer, one song, some cunt shouts. I never knew what the fuck that meant neither. I'm sitting next to Patricia. Look at that wee bastard, I says to her. I think his da was a fucking negro, I says. Where the fuck did he get that tan? Working in the streets, that's where he got it, Patricia says. Working in the streets since he was seven year old and his da made him go out and sell newspapers down the bottom of the Crumlin Road. Let me tell you, darling, I says to her, but there is no sun in Ireland strong enough to inflict that degree of tan. That's fucking genetic, so it is.

That would mean his da wasn't his da, Patricia says. That would mean he was a bastard. He is a wee bastard, I says to her, what did I tell you?

She was a good-looking doll. And smart too. She was in the Mensa. Plus she was obsessed by all the popes. She studied them, read all the books. She knew everything about the popes. Plus she was in love with Tommy. Crazy in love with him. All the ladies were. Women would walk up to him, this is in the street, this is at the fucking train station, and they would ask him if he would like to take them out for a coffee. You ever heard of a woman asking a random guy out at a fucking train station before? In Belfast it was un-fucking-heard-of, believe me. Till Tommy started the trend. Everybody was uptight before that. Till Tommy came along. They talk about the Swinging Sixties and the free love. The era of Tommy was the era of free love in Ireland. When he was born it was the equivalent of the Beatles shopping up in Belfast. Only he had short hair and a handmade suit and a floor-length Crombie and a slouch hat and he would've shot a hippy in the fucking face as soon as look at him. Plus he never touched drugs. Except for marijuana. And LSD, once. But wait till I tell you.

There he is onstage: look at him there in the spotlight. Patricia's mouthing the words along with him and the women are weeping, no word of a lie, the women are wiping their made-up eyes with their beautiful silk handkerchiefs, and it was so sexy, all of the boys from back then, all of the boys have a thing to this day for silk handkerchiefs, ask any of them, it was like lingerie for your face, weeping into your lingerie like it was wet between your legs, and of course we would get them to wank us off with their hankies, these silk hankies, these ladies of Belfast, what a turn-on, and then Tommy starts up again, he opens his arms up and out, just like Como when he's reaching for a crescendo, and he starts to sing.

Don't look so sad, I know it's over
But life goes on and this ol' world will keep on turning

Let's just be glad we had some time to spend together
There's no need to watch the bridges that we're burning

It's the song that came over me in the hotel room with Kathy.
Only Tommy has turned it right back to the beginning. He's
singing how it began, I says to myself, and how it ends.

I felt dizzy, like somebody had shuffled the cards of my life and
everything was in a different order. Then he skipped a verse.
He skipped the verse whose arms I had lain in at the hotel room
(leaving a little gap in the song) (a little gasp) and went on to the
next verse.

I'll get along, you'll find another, and I'll be here if you should find
you ever need me, don't say a word about tomorrow, or forever,
there'll be time enough for sadness when you leave me.

Patricia passed me one of her silk handkerchiefs. It was damp
and I could smell her perfume. I held it over my mouth and my
nose and I closed my eyes as tight as I could.

*

The morning of the big day. We've arranged to meet at the shop,
just like normal. I walk in and Barney is playing this music,
this fucking hippy-music bollocks. What the fuck is this? I shout
through to him. It's *Dark Side of the Moon*, he says. Pink Floyd.
It's a concept LP about life, he says. I'd take life behind bars
before I had to sit through this pish, I says to him.

Barney's in the back room, going through boxes of comics. We're sitting on a fucking goldmine here, he says to me. Look at this stuff. This is all original Gold and Silver Age material. What's the Golden Age, I says to him, what's that mean? Gold is the best, he says, when it was all new. Silver is when they knew a bit more about it. What then? I says to him. Bronze, he says. What's that? I says to him. Average, he says.

What age is Ireland in, do you think? I says to him. Gold, he says without a pause. And how do you figure that out? I says. Because we're making it up as we go along, he says. Because we're right here, at the beginning. These are the golden years, my friend.

We should do one of them conventions, Barney says. Beavis says we'd clean up. Barney, I says to him, I cannot believe you sometimes. We're trying to bring an end to the fucking future and you're making plans to go to some fucking comic geeks' meeting? Have we not got nothing more important to be thinking about, don't you think? Anyways, Barney says to me. There's Tommy.

We can see him through the window, across the road. He's with Mack. Fuck is he doing with Mack? Barney says. No one says he was coming this morning. Tommy and Mack are killing themselves laughing about something or other as they cross the road. When did they get so friendly?

Alright, Oddjob? Mack says. Barney was still wearing that fucking bowler. Excuse me but what in the fuck is this music about? Tommy says to him. It's *Dark Side of the Moon*, Barney says. It's a concept LP about life. Fuck you know about concepts?

Tommy says to him but Mack's big into it. Fucking Floyd, man, sweet, he says. Tommy takes this leather briefcase that he's carrying and slaps it down on the desk. Fuck me, go easy with that, Mack says to him. You're telling him not to bang it off a desk but you're telling me to drop it down four fucking floors to the ground without it going off? I says to him. We open it up, the briefcase. It's like a fucking homemade abortion in there. I thought you said these guys were boffins what could float a nuclear bomb through your granny's letterbox? I says to Mack. Look at the state of this. There's a lump of Semtex with blue packing tape wrapped around it and there's a couple of wires attached to a gold wind-up clock that your old dear might have had on her mantelpiece. This is it? I says to them. I cannot believe my lamps. Does the trick, my friend, Mack says to me. Who put this together? Barney says to him. Jimmy McFlint, Mack says. What?! Barney says. McFlint with the squint? Not bad for an uneducated Irishman. Look, Mack says. This is guerrilla warfare we're engaged in. It's all about improvised explosives. You mean making it up as you go along, I says to him. That's what I says, he says. Naw, you never, I says to him, you says improvised. You're trying to make it sound smart when really you're fucking busking it. Alright, Mack says to me, fucking busking-it explosives, you shower of cocks, does that make you feel more confident? We're running a fucking rebel insurgence here, he says to us. Excuse me if it's just not professional enough for you.

I could have taken Mack right out the game then and there, only the repercussions weren't worth thinking about. Alright, I says to him, alright, I'm just fucking concerned for the fucking reality of this fucking assignment, I says. Look, he says. All you have to do is you set the fucking alarm on this clock, which is easy, like, just turn this knob and it moves the wee hand here, see, then pull this wee knob out and that's it ready to go off. Sure, that sounds just like my average Saturday night, Barney says to him, but by this time Mack is in no mood for jokes. Stop acting like fucking clowns, he says to us. I'm telling you, he says, see if the IRA could dispense with Irishmen altogether, we'd be one fuck of a formidable fighting unit.

*

Saturday afternoon. Kathy doesn't work weekends, so as I know she's safe. We leave Barney in the shop and me and Tommy go about setting up a false trail. We visit Tommy's da and talk to the foul curtain for a bit. Everywhere we go we're cat-rough and deliberately announcing our presence, setting up a sneaky alibi just in case it's needed, drawing attention to ourselves as much as possible.

We dropped into The Tim's Harbour and drank a pint of porter and got into a mock brawl so as the landlord had to separate us and chuck us out. Now we're on Great Victoria Street and there isn't a cloud in the sky. The colours of the trees against it, like blue blood. What a feeling. And now the trees are shaking. There's no breeze but the trees are shaking. I start to getting the shakes myself. The fucking shivers, more like. The shadow of the Europa, running toward us. That's where it will fall, I tell myself. It's all mapped out. It's all written in the stars, Xamuel, down to the silhouette of its dead body lying there on the street. No one dies, I hear Miracle Baby say. The Europa is a mighty fortress. It's the biggest day of my life. One man can make all the difference in the world.

We walk past the entrance. I peel off from Tommy without a word. I turn on my powers of invisibility. I start to whistle to myself. I push open the door and walk through the screening area. Nothing happens. No alarms go off. Nobody even looks at me. I catch a pair of peelers out the corner of my eye, talking to each other, on the other side of the glass. They don't even turn around. I've got the briefcase clasped, tight, beneath my arm. Then I float across reception like the Holy Ghost. This is how the IRA got bombs into buildings. With the blessings of the Holy Ghost Himself.

I see this wee bird on reception, this wee bird that knows me. Now she's looking over at me. I can feel my invisibility fleeing. I can feel it running down and out through the soles of Pat's snakeskin shoes. It's harder to be invisible with women. The Virgin Mary is higher up the pecking order than the Holy Ghost. Fact.

She cries out my name. Xamuel. I can't believe it. Xamuel. We've barely spoken before and here she is, fucking shouting for me across the reception area. Xamuel! People are looking round. Tourists in fur coats and with expensive luggage stood around in groups are looking at me. The pair of peelers manning the door turn to face me and now they're looking at me all shady, like. A valet dragging a pair of cases comes to a dead stop in front of me. There's a split second where I think the game is up.

Sharon. The wee bird's name is Sharon. Somebody left something for you at reception, Sharon says to me. Becoming a regular round here, she says to me, and she winks. The peelers turn away. The tourists start talking again. The room starts moving. Something in me wants to say something to her, tell her to get the fuck out while she can. But it would risk everything. So I says to her, when's your lunch break, love? Another half-hour yet, she says to me. Here, love, I says to her. Here's a couple of quid. Treat yourself to a pizza pie.

I'm breaking every rule in the book. Except one. Except for the most important one. Rule number one of all rule number ones. Walk in like you own the place. Besides, I says to myself, no one dies. Sharon hands me a letter with my name on it. Xamuel, it says, with an X. My name underlined, twice. I take it to the lift. I want to get the fuck out of reception as soon as possible. The door of the lift closes. I'm in there on my own but the mirrors are making me look like I'm surrounded by endless versions of myself myself myself. Which one of youse is going to do it? I says to myselfs and they says it right back to me. Which one of youse is going to do it? they says. Not one of you cunts will take responsibility, I says to them. Fuck youse, I says to them. I'll fucking do it myself. Then we're all in on it. We put the fucking briefcase at our feet. And we all open the letter at the same time. That's when the explosion went off.

*

Neutrino, The X-Ray Kid and The Anomaly enter The Anti-Matter Universe.

Neutrino activates a second self which stays outside as a safety measure in case they need to beat a retreat.

They pass through a fissure and enter a space and time where everything is inverted.

Backward takes you forward, down is up, thought follows actions, the future gives birth to the past.

They are in search of The Singularity, the creation of a mad demiurge that stands at the centre of The Anti-Matter Universe like a mighty fortress.

They enter The Entropic Garden, a place where their actions give birth to terrifying stresses and strains all around them, causing the stars to bleed, the ground to give way.

They do battle with The Equator, who causes their limbs to be swallowed up by the air.

With every move fleshy wormholes open all around them, suppurating sores on the body of reality itself, which becomes an all-devouring mass that swallows and regurgitates at the same time.

Even Neutrino's armoured bodysuit is no match for its appetite.

The X-Ray Kid focuses his eyes and sends a beam of light as far ahead as he possibly can.

But there is nothing beyond, nowhere to escape to.

They have walked into a trap.

It was The Singularity that had come in search of them. Now there is no end to the flesh.

Neutrino's struggles are causing him to be swallowed all the faster.

The X-Ray Kid focuses an intense eye-beam on the ghastly folds that have Neutrino in their grasp but even as it howls in pain – before the beams have even struck it – it seems to grow stronger with the attack, gaining force and fury from what, in The Anti-Matter Universe, is merely the transference of powers.

Then The Anomaly makes his play.

He stops moving. He surrenders.

He gives in to the back and forth, to the trap of the flesh, to the calling of The Singularity.

He refuses to resist.

The flesh around him recoils and extends itself in horrifying reconfigurations.

It opens huge waste pipes around him and exposes the great effluvial channels that run beneath the universe. But The Anomaly refuses to be drawn into wonder.

Even as Neutrino screams and appears to be on the verge of being torn and quartered by the force of their assailant.

Even as The X-Ray Kid appears to turn on The Anomaly himself, his eyes tearing through him in an attempt to rearrange his cells for what he perceives as a moment of mutiny or just a lack of heart for the battle.

As The Anomaly renders himself motionless in the tumult, the tumult itself accelerates, to the point that it starts to feed on itself.

The great Canals of Slurry that run beneath become super-heated and trigger a series of elemental transformations.

The waters start to run clear.

The sound of teeth rending the air.

The sound of the air swallowing itself.

Neutrino drops to the ground with a klang!!! as the endless flesh turns itself inside out in a series of shuddering orgasms.

Don't fight it, The Anomaly commands his brothers.

Neutrino and The X-Ray Kid are stood in wonder.

Is it not beautiful, Neutrino says, as he himself is lifted up by his own power.

He goes to take his helmet off.

*No! commands The Anomaly. Don't go too far! There are
temptations on all sides, he says, even as the great Canals of
Slurry now flow like the rivers through Eden, pure and bright
and slow, even as the flesh gives way to soft grass and lush trees
and the sound of birds appears on the horizon. Even as they walk
forward together and the vegetation parts and a great smoking
tower is revealed to them, a great smoking tower that is in great
pain, even as they realise that truly this is a mercy killing and that
The Singularity tricked them with the notion of a mission, with
the idea of a quest, for good against evil, when really the universe
was upside down and they arrived, truly, as a relief force, as
warrior monks in the charge of the sacred flame, not so that others
could live, but so that they could finally die.*

There is so much longing not to be built.

*They look around at each other and for the first time realise the
gravity of their mission.*

They have been called.

*The X-Ray Kid locks the three of them in a beam from his eyes and
they rise up above The Singularity and gaze down into its blasted
heart.*

*Every breath, the constant circling of blood inside this great black
tower, feels like a pained eternity. Together they let go.*

All of their muscles loosen.

All of their thoughts dissolve.

They enter The Singularity and they raze it to the ground.

Before them stands a new tower.

One that their destruction has wrought.

But this is a tower that rises down, into the earth.

The three heroes look at each other.

Who tricked who?

Next time: Origins Of The Anomaly!

*

A bomb went off on the second floor of the Europa that day, blowing a hole the size of a truck in the side of the building. I was trapped in the lift halfway between floors and had to force the doors and climb up and out. By this point I'm in a panic. Is it a set-up? Did The Boys just try to blow me to kingdom come? Was it something to do with me and Kathy? I make my way down a back stairwell. It's chaos all around me. There are people with head wounds and covered in dust and with blood on their clothes. I can feel the building shaking. I picture this huge mouth, this huge fucking hell mouth opening up beneath our feet and swallowing the building whole. I've still got the briefcase with me with the unexploded bomb. I can't leave it behind. It's got my fingerprints and probably my fucking DNA all over it. Now I'm in fear for my life.

I get down to reception and the peelers are starting to arrive. I put my hand in my pocket and I've still got one of Patricia's silk hankies from the other night in there. I hold it over my face like I'm wounded and I pretend to stagger outside. Somebody goes to put an arm around me but I tell them I'm alright, I'm alright, and all I can smell is Patricia's perfume as I cut over to Brunswick Street, this heavenly woman smell, and now I've got a hard-on. I've just popped one. It's like the whole city just spread its legs in front of me.

*

I'm supposed to meet Tommy back at The Tim's Harbour where we set up the ruckus in the first place. But I've got this fucking bomb in my hands. I head back to my ma's house in Jamaica Street instead. Nobody's in. I run up the stair and I slide the briefcase under my bed. I'm not thinking straight. I turn on the news. Some fucking dissident organisation, some fucking unofficial Republican terror cell has claimed responsibility. The FSV. Okay, what the fuck. How do I play this?

I look out the window and I can see Billy McNab's weans playing in their back garden. The boy has a toy gun and is leading the two girls into a shed at the bottom of the garden with blindfolds on. The whole fucking city is at it, I says to myself. Okay, okay.

I take a packet of twenty B&H from my top bin, crack it. I neck two cans of green, one after the other. I always had a set of cans stashed under my bed in case of emergency even though they would get mouse shite all over them. Probably pished on them too. The mice, I mean. Fuck it. Might make it taste better.

I'm going to tell them it was me. I make the decision. It's a gamble. Mission accomplished, I'll say. The dissidents are a bunch of *fucking lying rats*. I was there. I had a bagful of explosives on me. It was a mad coincidence, I says to myself. We'd both gone to hit it at the same time. Then on the news, they says it. They says it exactly like Miracle Baby says they would says it. No one died. *The Europa is a mighty fortress*. That was it. That's what sealed it for me. This is how it is written. I called Tommy's from a phone box. His ma answered. Have you heard about this thing at the Europa? she says to me. I have that, I says. Brave boys, she says to me. Brave boys. Aye, he was, I says to her. When Tommy gets in, tell him to come and pick me up from my ma's house, I says to her, and I hang up the phone. I try to have a Tom Tit in the outside toilet but for some reason I just cannot go so as I go back up to my room and I sit down on the bed with the unexploded bomb underneath it and I watch Billy McNab's weans, mock-executing each other outside in the garden.

*

You get these turds, these turds off the telly, asking how is it possible, to kill, to maim, and to protect the killers afterward, to treat them as heroes, even, in their own communities. All in this fucking whining fucking voice. I want to say to them, it's fucking elementary, my dear tosspot, have you never heard of loyalty? Have you no concept of friendship? Have you never had a family you would protect with your life? Do you not admire bravery? Have you never felt the calling of your own blood?

Thing is, we all know it. We all understand it just fine. But only when it's our own side we're talking about. Well, I'm from the other side, and I'm here to tell you it's the fucking mirror image of your own. Except braver.

All we had was the fucking *Green Book*s telling us what we did was legitimate. All we had was a bunch of criminal longhairs patting us on the back. You don't go down the fucking Job Centre and they suggest a career in the IRA the way they do with the fucking British Army. They don't erect war memorials or have a fucking national holiday for all the brave boys what died on the other side of the war.

But IRA stands for Irish Republican Army, and don't forget it, because we're the ones what should be wearing medals in public. We used to joke with each other and say that one day, lads, and it won't be long, they'll replace Poppy Day with Shamrock Day, and then we'll remember all the brave boys what died, for a cause, mind you, brave boys what voluntarily laid down their lives, not these fucking clowns fresh from the dole office with a monthly fucking wage and two weeks in Spain, but it wasn't a joke and we weren't really laughing, although that day is somewhere in heaven now (let's face it), when we'll greet the Immortal Revenging Angels, lined up, as far as the eye can see, because

Miracle Baby was right, and there's no united Ireland in sight and no memorial for the fallen in this world, so what about the next.

*

I'm treated like a fucking hero but not for long because they want to get me and Tommy out of the country to somewhere we can lay low for a bit. Don't you worry about those fucking Free State Volunteers, Mack says to me. They're fucking scrubbed, he says, and he swipes his hands together. You two go and enjoy yourself, he says. We'll make sure of who gets the glory. Fucking Free State Volunteers, he says to us. Volunteering is for Unionists and for fucking Ulster-ists, far as I'm concerned, he says. Republicans run armies, not charities. This is an IRA triumph, he says to us. How dare they divide attentions.

In the meantime Barney has agreed to run the shop with the help of Beavis. Beavis & Barney, Beavis & Oddjob, you couldn't fucking make this up, so you couldn't, but Barney's getting seriously into his comics and this fucking wee brainbox Picatsto kid is becoming his mentor and he's taking all this Golden Age stuff home with him. This cunt's going to read us out of house and home if he keeps this up, Tommy says to me.

I phone Kathy and I tell her that I can't go back to our days at the Europa. Are you involved? she says to me. We meet up in a wee cafe in Arthur Street. Of course I'm not involved, I says to her. It was the fucking FSV. You're lying to me, Kathy says to me. Sharon says she saw you that day.

That wee bitch, I'm thinking. Aye, she saw me alright, I says, I nearly got my own head blown off too. Do you think I'd be ducking into the Europa if I knew The Boys were planning to blow it up?

Well, what were you doing there, then? she says to me. I was organising a wee surprise for you, I says to her, a wee secret surprise. Leave your husband, I says to her. I don't know why I says that then, maybe it was the guilt talking. Leave your husband, I says to her, and let's you and me get a wee place together. Have you ever heard of a thing called Stockholm Syndrome? she says to me. One of these European diseases? I says to her. No thank you. You can catch it anywhere, she says to me. It's when you fall in love with your captor, she says. I'm your captor, I says to her. Well, she says, I'm not the style of dizzy bitch that happens to at all. She was pushing all the right buttons, I'll be honest with you. Well, what are you in it for? I says to her. You can walk away tomorrow, I says, if you like. Life goes on, I says. This old world will keep on turning, I says to her. Then she says it.

For the masquerade, she says. That word again. It's out of place. That word is out a place, I says to her. That fucking word. A masquerade is a masked dance, she says to me. Did you leave that note for me in the Europa? I says to her. What note? she says. That note behind the desk. That note that Sharon gave me. Why? What did it say? she says to me. Nothing, I says to her. That's the point. Nothing. It was an envelope with nothing inside it, I says to her. That wasn't me, she says. I would at least have included one of my special wee hankies for you.

I leave her in the cafe and I walk to a pay phone. I give Sharon a bell at the Europa. Are you alright, hen? I says to her. What a terrible business, I says. I was just calling to make sure you were all okay. Sure, we're fine, she says to me. It's awful nice of you to call. How about yourself? she says. Ah, I'm grand, I says to her, a few scratches, nothing to worry yourself about. Then I says to her to order a bouquet of flowers to be delivered to Kathy on her next shift. Don't tell her they're from me, I says to her. Just put: Your Secret Admirer. And I walk away, feeling that I've got everything covered. The next day me and Tommy fly to Glasgow, capital of Scotland, to lay low.

Part Three: Bobby Sands Has Come to Pass

Fucking Glasgow, my friend, it's just like Belfast, the same
rivalries, the same segregated pubs, the same flags, the same
halls, the same murals, the same fucking teams; a friendly city
once you get to know it. Plus you're just as likely to get stabbed
for your colours as you are back home, so as you know where you
stand as soon as you're off the boat. Me and Tommy had never left
Ireland before. To us it was like Babylon.

The first night we're there, wait till you hear this, we go to this
variety club and we're paying in and on the door there's this
guy dressed up as a woman. Okay, a transsexual, it's a fucking
transsexual dressed as a woman, and we've never seen a fucking
transsexual in our puff. I mean, no disrespect to the boy, but all
this is brand new to us, and Tommy's staring at him, of course
he is, of course he's fucking staring at him, I mean, come on. At
her. Alright, okay, whatever. Tommy's staring at her, at him,
the point is he can't help himself. The boy just got off the boat,
for fuck sake. But this transsexual starts getting uppity. What's
your problem? she says to Tommy. Tommy's like that, nothing
darling, calm down, fuck sake, he's a bit freaked out, obviously.
Then this crazy bloke, this crazy bitch, sorry, starts yelling at
him, homophobe, homophobe, pointing at me and Tommy and
yelling, homophobe, that's what she's calling us, homophobe, she's
shouting. Next thing the fucking manager comes over and says
to us that we have to leave, that there's no place for homophobia
in his nightclub. We've not got the homophobia, I feel like saying
to him, we're just a pair of fucking hicks. But there's no point
in arguing. We do what we're told, and we leave, and we stand
outside on the pavement for a bit, awkward, not saying anything.
We were both embarrassed. It was like we had failed our first

assignment in the big city. New skills, Tommy says to me, and I says to him, aye, new skills, Tommy, new skills, I says, that's what it's all about these days. It was the first time I realised just how young we were. Over in Belfast we ran the streets, were up to every trick, but in Glasgow we were absolute beginners. I put my arm around Tommy and we walked to a pub across the road and later that night we kicked the shite out a couple wide boys making Paddy jokes behind our backs and felt that bit better about ourselves.

*

Apart from that, we settled in fast. Every afternoon we would go to the movies to see all the latest shows. Tommy loved his action movies, so he did, *Where Eagles Dare*, *The Dam Busters*, all that style of show. We got to see *The Spy What Loved Me* (we were big Bond men), *Smokey and the Bandit* (some show), *Ten Bare Knuckles* (unrealistic), *Tentacles of the Hairy Beast* (mental), *Cross of Iron Gold* (Nazis, brilliant), *Star Wars* (a classic, in my opinion), *Sinbad in the Eye of the Tiger* (what the fuck was that all about?), plus some cracking scud movies at this seedy wee picture house in Jamaica Street, of all places. Who knew there was a Jamaica Street in Glasgow? It was just like being back in the Ardoyne, only with blow jobs aplenty.

*

I mind when Tommy was in hospital, this is back when we was teenagers, when we had only just met, and he had an irregular heart. We had been out for a bevvy, nothing too heavy, but as

we're leaving this bar he starts acting funny and the sweat
is all running down his forehead and he falls to the floor, like
that. At first everybody thinks he's coming the cunt. Get up,
you chancing wee cunt, Wee Steve-O says to him, but once we
realised it was for real I get him round to my ma's house and I
ring an ambulance. He's lying there on the couch, and I'll never
forget it, he just keeps belching, just belching, again and again,
it was horrifying. But an ambulance comes, and we get him to
the hospital, and he starts to recover. The doctors are all trying
to get to the bottom of it. I visit him in the ward and I says to
him, what did the doctor say was up with you? And he just says
to me, come on, he says, god knows what these doctors think, he
says to me, as if to say why the fuck would anyone even ask this
kind of question. We're in the lap of the gods here, he says to me,
like there was really no way of actually finding out what was
up with you in a hospital. I saw him with the doctors and the
nurses and as soon as they arrived on the ward he would start
cracking jokes or he would take the hand of one of these wee
nurses and start singing to her or he would tell some fucking
made-up story about him growing up in the Ardoyne and I says
to him, fucking speak to these people, I says, find out what's
wrong with you, I says, find out what they're going to do about
it. But it was like if he couldn't seduce everybody, then even his
heart wasn't worth asking after. And he would get angry if you
questioned him about it. What's the diagnosis? I says to him.
Mugs like you just don't understand, he says to me. Mugs like
you just don't get it, he says. Mugs like you, meaning everybody
what was actually normal. He had his ma climbing the walls.
But secretly I think his da was pleased with the performance. I
mean, his da never came to visit him in the hospital but when

I would report back to the curtain you could tell he was lying there thinking, that's my boy. And when he gets out he ends up banging one of the wee nurses. I mean, he might have been carrying a ticking time bomb inside him, you know, but fucking . . . mission accomplished.

My point is, that's what he was like in Glasgow in 1977, I saw him then as he was in his hospital bed, with his heart raging and his dick like a fucking radio transmitter, sending distress calls out to the world at large. Because Glasgow was a challenge to him. New rules. We'd be walking about the streets and seeing things like punk rockers for the first time. Here we were, just getting over hippies, and there would be these guys with the torn clothes and the dyed hair and the safety pins. And some of the birds looked rougher than the men. Total fucking culture shock, my friend. And here's Tommy, like one of them rare fucking birds dancing with the big swollen chests on the telly, the fucking mating ritual of the lesser spotted wee hardman, with his poor fucking heart stretched all till its limits.

*

The place we were staying at was on the hill running up from Charing Cross to the School of Art, this cheap bed-and-breakfast place, no stars, plenty of vacancies, you do the sums. Renfrew Street was what you called it. This young couple runs it, this bird what looks like a worn-out Mary Millington porn star: blue eyeshadow, red lips, blonde hair like she's something out of *Charlie's Angels*, is the look. And her husband has got the porn moustache and the greasy, curly hair. Tommy is all over her like a rash, even though she's rough as a badger. Outside of Patricia his taste in birds was excruciating, I have to reveal.

So as it's the Jubilee. And we're buying all this stuff to take back with us, fucking biscuit tins with the Queen's face on it, fucking shortbread tins with the Queen's face on it, fucking plates with the Queen's face on it. Sure, your ma'll love those, Tommy says to me. We're coming back to the B&B with all this stuff under our arms and the fucking seventies porn star chick, maybe her name was Yvonne, it might have been Yvonne, this bird Yvonne, she says to us, are youse two neighbours?

Now that's a fucking scary word. I feel the hair on the back of my arms rising up, like a cat, just at the thought of it. But Tommy's right in there. Sure, we're neighbours, he says to her. Are the two of youse from Belfast? she says to us. Naw, Tommy says to her. Sure, we're from Birmingham. That was always a good bet: lots of Micks in Birmingham. Do youse get over for the parades? she says to Tommy. Oh aye, he says to her, oh aye. I send them money every year, he says to her.

I cannot fucking believe what I'm hearing. She's looking at Tommy like he's a big shot, like he's a player behind the scenes, only on the other side. She's impressed; she's obviously a Hun. We're having some drinks later, she says to him, having a few people over. You and your friend here are welcome to join us. I'm reduced to the fucking friend already. Sure, Tommy says to her. That would be lovely. Lovely, is it? This guy would do your fucking chump in.

We get up to the room and that's when I fucking lose it. Do you know how dangerous this is? I says to Tommy. You're playing with fire right now, I says to him. You don't know who talks to who. You don't know what connections these people might have. We're over here to lie low, I says to him, not to party like we're fucking Orangemen. But Tommy starts getting that aggressive way of his, and there's no talking to him, his heart is fucking pounding out his chest, and now he's talking to himself, about me, right in front of me, he's shaking his head, these mugs don't understand, he's saying to himself, that fucking line that was more frightening than asking somebody if they was a neighbour. I stepped back. There was nothing anybody could do.

We shop up to this fucking back room, this lounge with a telly in the corner and an old stereo and plastic plants and everybody's smoking and drinking and they all seem half-blocked already. The Mary Millington bird is there and she's wearing a white dress and high heels and she's squatting down on the floor there in front of her man, laughing and rocking back and forth on her white high heels. There are a couple other birds too. Here come the boys, her man says when we walk in, and Tommy's got a bottle of Famous Grouse on him. They ask us what we've been up to and I take a seat next to one of the birds, this dark-haired bird with the buck teeth. Tommy takes a seat on the couch next to this other bird with a hairband on and what looks like Wonder Woman, only as soon as she opens her mouth it's like Wonder Woman has been drinking potcheen on the bru for fifteen year. Tommy's telling her about the film we saw in the afternoon, about this scene where a fighter plane fitted with a bomb is rushing toward this huge fucking tower that they're trying to blow up and destroy and how, in the film, the pilot aims the fighter right at the control room in the heart of the tower and the camera cuts to inside the tower and you can see the fighter tunnelling through the air, and all these people start running in chaos to get away and at the last minute, and this is exactly how Tommy tells it, at the last minute the fucking pilot ejaculates out the cockpit. Everybody cracks up.

Oh my god, Wonder Woman says to him, you mean he ejects out the plane, oh my god, you are unbelievable. Tommy's sitting there, beaming. How the fuck does he do it? Breaking the ice by being a complete fucking eejit. So are youse up for it, boys? Millington's man says to us. He raises a can of Export in a cheers. Aye, we're up for it, Tommy says to him. Sure, we're up for anything, he says. Wonder Woman has her arm around him by this point. I'm looking round at fucking Red Rum to my right here, this fucking mouthful of teeth and breath on her like you would not believe. Let's get a sing-song going, she says. Then Millington's man starts with it. He starts to the singing of it.

Do you want a chicken supper, Bobby Sands?

That's what he sings.
It was the first time I had ever heard it.

Prisoners had started refusing food in the Crumlin jail. But this is before the whole hunger strike kicked off. And they're singing this song.

Do you want a chicken supper, Bobby Sands?
Do you want a chicken supper, Bobby Sands?

> Do you want a chicken supper, you dirty Fenian fucker?
> Do you want a chicken supper, Bobby Sands?

Then fucking Tommy joins in. I'm staring over at him but he won't catch my eye and he's singing it along with the rest of them.

> Do you want a chicken supper, Bobby Sands?

I fucking join in myself. What the fuck else was I going to do? And now we're all singing this song, this song from out the future, which is where I'm talking from now, only this is back then, and Millington's man starts making up new words on the spot, calling him Robert Sands and taking the pish.

> Would you prefer a chicken doner, Robert Sands?
> Or what about a black pudding supper, Robert Sands?
> What about a black pudding supper, you dirty Fenian fucker?
> What about a black pudding supper, Robert Sands?

Singing it in this fake posh English accent. It's fucking horrible. But we're acting like it's the funniest thing in the world. Then Millington's man announces it. Alright, he says, so youse are up for it? We're up for it alright, Tommy says. Up for anything. But then I says to him, up for what exactly? I says. The orgy, he says to me. And Millington comes over and stands right in front of me and without a word she lifts her dress up and she's not wearing any panties and she's shaved her pussy, fuck me but she has only shaved her fucking pussy, I've never seen a fucking shaved pussy in my life, you were lucky to get a fucking clean pussy in Belfast, never mind one with all the hair trimmed, and without a thought

I just fucking unzip my trousers and pull her down on top of me and fucking stick her right there. Lucky for me, because then her man fires into Horse-Breath and I see Tommy and Wonder Woman going at it on the couch.

Now she's on top of me and she's making all these noises, mewing like a cat is unbelievable, and I fucking tear her dress down and she says to bite her tits and I shoot my load in two minute flat, what do you expect from an uneducated Irishman, but then she gets down on her knees and starts blowing me and now I'm ready to go all over again. I'm looking over her shoulder at Tommy. I can see Wonder Woman beneath him. I can see her legs either side of him, he's got his trousers pulled down, I can see his arse pumping away. And Wonder Woman's legs are shaking, her whole body is starting to shake. She pushes her legs out, she's still wearing her heels, and she pushes her legs against the wall to steady herself. Stop it, stop it, you're making me dizzy, she says to him, but Tommy doesn't stop it. Then Horse-Breath turns to me and starts kissing me full-on: disgusting. I push her down and tear open my shirt so she can tongue my nips while I'm fucking Millington from behind. Millington's man goes over to Wonder Woman. He looks at Tommy for a second. She can suck my dick while you fuck her, he says to him. Tommy nods. So as she starts sucking his dick while Tommy's pumping her. Me and Millington are all done by this point, I'm over, just crashed out on the couch, watching them. Tommy's on his back and Wonder Woman gets on top. Millington's man gets up behind her and tries to slip it into her arse at the same time. That's when Tommy loses it.

You fucking touched my dick with your dick, you fucking poof, he says to him. He flips Wonder Woman off him in one movement. You fucking dirty poofter, Tommy says to him, and he's struggling to get his trousers up. Calm down, mate, Millington's man says to him, it was just a fucking accident, I must've brushed your cock by mistake. But it's too late for that now. Tommy has flipped. You're a raging fucking arse bandit, Tommy's screaming at him, and he's rubbing his cock with his hand like he's caught something. Then he half-marches/half-staggers across the room, with his trousers pulled to just above his knees, tears this lamp out its socket with one hand and sets about him. Millington's man falls back onto the couch and Tommy's kneeling over him, smashing him in the fucking head with this fucking heavy marble lamp. At one point I see what looks like a bit of skull go flying up into the air. Leave him, the women are screaming, you'll fucking kill him! I leap to my feet and I pull him off. What the fuck are you doing, you fucking nutcase? But by this point he's like a sleepwalker. You cannot wake this guy from the trance. So as I drag him to the floor and I hold him down but then I start worrying that our fucking dicks are going to accidentally collide or something so as I push him away and I yell to him to get our fucking bags, I'm screaming at him, grab our fucking bags, I says, and I push him out the door. Then I stand there, guarding it, with this fucking broke lamp in my hand. Nobody leaves, I says to them. The guy is lying there in a pool of blood. Oh, my baby, my baby, Millington's saying to him, and she's lifting his head and she's trying to talk to him, he's trying to mouth words back at her, and now he's puking blood all over himself and Wonder Woman and Red Rum are lying there with their make-up smeared and their clothes torn and their panties all twisted on their legs and their nylons. Tommy's at the front door. I hear him tearing the phone out the wall. Let's go, he shouts. I look round at the carnage, at the women whimpering, at the guy whose head is pulped, at the hotel lounge that we've completely destroyed. What we did on our holidays, I says to myself, and by five o'clock the next day we're in London, in a pub in Kentish Town, drinking green with a bad bastard name of The Swan.

*

The Swan takes us back to his, you should have seen the state of this place. Tommy's da called ahead and arranged everything, we were bedding down with two blokes from Liverpool in the back room of this squat in Queen's Crescent, four mattress on the floor and bottles lying everywhere and no shower. You can use the YMCA for that, one of the guys says to us, this obvious homo called Rick. No danger. We spend most of our evenings in a pool hall on the Holmes Road name of Paradise, playing for money. What paradise is this we dreamt ourselves into, I says to Tommy, what kind of garden is this, I says to him that night.

*

Swans mate for life, do you realise that, son? That's how The Swan gets his name. The eyes of a swan are inscrutable, this is what this cunt I'm playing pool with says to me. Inscrutable. Cunt name of Blackie, must have been six foot two. The eyes of a swan, he says to me, are as black as hell's gates. The Swan's partner was killed in action, that's all he says to me, none of the specifics. But he has been faithful ever since, he says.

By this point The Swan is half-blocked and has his arm around Tommy and is singing in his ear. I catch a line of it, an old Irish folk song about a widowed swan looking back across its life and recalling the still, faraway lochs that it had sailed over with its long-lost partner, the great flowing rivers that were a part of them and that had delivered them to the future, the green Irish fields, down there, beneath the two of them.

Are there swans in Belfast? Blackie says to me.
And everything feels like it is in code:
being a swan,
a swan in Belfast.

The Swan is on his feet now. I dreamt I was a swan, he's singing, floating on the tide (his long-ago partner and himself) past long-abandoned mansions (like up on the Malone Road) all overgrown with trees (and misty-wet with rain) and with thick vines hanging down, and there is another sort of bird living in this song, a bird that moves to greet the swans (all in this song where they have been expected for such a long time), and they are led along a path (in the shadow of tall fir trees) and isn't it a pity, isn't it a shame, of course it's tragic, of course it is strange, because we're swans, he sings, to the whole room now, and what do swans need with a mansion, with a house with a butler and a maid, and the swans are led into a library, a library all piled high with books, and the swans look around, and on every shelf they see, there is everything they could have dreamt of reading, stories of all their friends as they were growing up, the memories of their parents, as little birds themselves

– birds themselves, birds themselves, he descended down the scale –

poems by their brothers and sisters (bird poems) (poems by younkers), accounts of the uprising of grandfathers, the rising up of old swans, and the things that happened in the moment of them

– the moment of them, the moment of them, he shakes his head as he declaims –

and the swans, this pair, they turn to each other, these beautiful black-eyed birds, and it's like a joke to them, a terrible sad joke, that they were born swans, and had no way of making sense of any of it. For swans cannot read, I says to my lover, and this is The Swan singing now. And my lover looks back at me, with those eyes of his, those eyes of his, as he sings, and my lover, he asks me, whether one day, when he passes, maybe he could be turned into a book. But I won't be able to read it, my lover, my long-lost, I won't be able to read you, my dear, is how sings, The Swan, in return.

*

Back in the flat in Kentish Town, Tommy's chest rising and falling, and the side of his face, in the light of cigarettes, next to me, on the floor, in the dark, I'm imagining us landing on water, together, and how it is soft between our legs, 1977, and how we sail off, silent, and without a thought.

*

In a cafe in Camden Town, The Swan tells me he how he knew my da. I knew your da, he says to me. Then he just lets it sit there. He looks at me like I'm the one that's supposed to ask him a question. But I don't know what to ask about my da. He was some man, The Swan says to me eventually. Aye, I says to him, he was some man.

I'm for the full English, Tommy says. He's sitting on the other side of the table, next to Blackie, drinking coffee. There are stains on his white shirt; we've been hiding out too long. You realise that The Full English is a euphemism? Blackie says to him. The fuck's a euphonism? Tommy says to him.

Euphonism is Greek for lovely-sounding words, Blackie says to him. Euphemism, on the other hand, is a word for another word. Why use one word for another if you've already got a word for it already? Tommy says to him. Because it's funnier, Blackie says to him, and he looks across the table and he says to us, are you sure this guy is a fucking Irishman? The Full English, Blackie says to him, means taking it up the arse. I'm talking about getting raped, by the screws, in the jail, he says.

They don't do that, do they? I says, and I turns to The Swan. They don't rape prisoners, do they? He looks over at Blackie and then back to me. Over mirrors, The Swan says to us. They rape them over mirrors. Christ on a stick – what?! You've never lived, The Swan says to me, and he winks. You know nothing about pain. Then he says to me, pass me that fucking steak knife there, would you, and he takes this big fucking steak knife and he raises it up in the air and he plunges it straight into his fucking arm.

We're both pushing back from the table. Tommy lets out a shout. What the fuck. But Blackie is just sitting there, looking at The Swan, who has this knife sunk up to the hilt in his forearm, and The Swan isn't even reacting, he's just staring at me and Tommy with a look of sadness and contempt and he says to us, you fucking stupid arseholes, he says, you fucking useless bastards, he says to us, and he shakes his head and he starts laughing, and then Blackie's off, and Blackie's laughing too, and the owner of the cafe comes over and he says to The Swan, what the fuck have I told you about ruining my cutlery, and now the owner's laughing as well, and The Swan takes hold of the knife and draws it, slowly, out of his arm, staring at the two of us the whole time, and he hands the knife back to the owner, it's bent, with the fucking force it is bent that he stuck it into himself, and he holds out his hand to the owner *and it is Christ displaying his wounds which are like beautiful delicate labias* who grabs him by the wrist and pulls his entire fucking arm off. The Swan has a prosthetic limb. The owner holds it up for us to see. It's punctured and cut and discoloured at the end. It's missing a finger. You think you know about pain, The Swan says to us, you think you are capable of suffering, he says, but do you think they make plastic fucking hearts? Fuck this, Tommy says, I'm sticking with a bacon roll.

*

Did you ever hear of lagging? Lagging. It's a musical thing. Rebel Songs, is what The Swan says to us. Tonight, my friends, we're going to get us some right old Rebel Songs, he says, and he tells us about the basement of this pub run by The Boys (God's Boys, he calls them, and he winks at us), where they play this new style of song, this new style of music that came out of The Maze and Her Majesty's pleasure, and that was sung into bowls, into drainpipes and toilets and along echoing corridors, late at night, this music of longing and of sad sufferation, The Swan says to us, this music of fading and of lagging, he says, sure you'll love it, he says to Tommy, did you never hear the Irish psalm-singing, he says to him, but Tommy says that he just cannot imagine singing Como down a toilet bowl.

The pub is on the Prince of Wales Road, it has changed its name, but back then it was called The Butcher's Hook. We head down the stair, into the basement, and the place is filthy and smells of pish. There are thick black curtains hanging down, blocking off certain areas. This is the fucking orgy scene forever, I says to Tommy. Only there are no birds, Tommy says to me. I hadn't noticed that before, but it was all men (it was fucking ominous) and at the end of the room there's a DJ set up, a dark-skinned guy with the dreadlocks name of John The Gun.

Fuck me, Tommy says, it's Bob Dylan. The master of ceremonies, is how The Swan introduced him. Sure, how did you get your name, Tommy says to him, and John The Gun's face is all covered in sweat, and the sweat is glistening on his dark skin, and the bright white of his eyes, and he says to Tommy, my weapon, that's all he says, and Tommy is just stood there, like that, as the music kicks in, and John The Gun starts with these sounds, like the crackle on an old Como record, coming out of the past, he has an old tape recorder that he is playing Rebel Songs on and making them repeat in strange rhythms and next to him there's an old guy in a bunnet playing the accordion and the first man up is an old Irishman with a circular scar around his head, all covered in rashes and wearing an old brown suit, he takes the mic and starts to sing, there are thirty or forty men in the room, all stood right in front of the stage, the Irish diaspora, they call them, boys as down on their luck as any of us, with their battered hats and their stained suits and their echoing, lamenting music, and now he is singing of place names, and it is like seeing Bethlehem written in letters on a road sign in the Holy Land, it is such a strange sensation, Bally-me-na come in, he sings, just like they did in the cells, into the toilet bowls, to tell The Boys where they had come from, to sing where they had been removed from and where they returned to, still, in dreams, there are tears and there are cries and there are soft lamentations, from Inniskeen till Kildare come in, and the places are echoing, forever, till Derry come in, from Eskra till Finglas come in, we dreamt of the places, and sang of their names, in our own time, overlapping with each other, till Galway come in, till Waterford, till Athlone, till Dublin, till Drogheda and Cavan come in, till Enniskillen come in, till Carrickfergus, till Coleraine and Letterkenny come in, is a cloud of voices, and in their lagging is a song, in London, as it was in the H Blocks, as it will be in heaven, on the arrival of The Boys, in the place of names, which is the place of endless echoes, The Calamity is what they call it, not The Troubles, Calamity come down, they says, as John The Gun starts to dance on the spot, clacking his shoes like in a tappety dance and waving his arms up into the air, and the men in the front have their arms round each other and the Irishman with the scar is singing of place names of Ireland and Ireland is in Bible time and the sound it is risen, in all of us, and here comes the sound (fornighsanfornighsanfornighs(openseyes)fornighsanfornighsanforevers)

and I catch a look at Tommy, and he smiles over at me, and I
can see that his eyes are damp, and I slide my arm around his
shoulders, at this sad sound of others, out of time but beautiful
with each other, and now everybody has joined in, a sound like
soft thunder, and the tape is playing the words back as an echoes,
as a lingo that has fallen, as words that have upped and fucking
died, in Bible time, forever, so no need of books, or storyfications,
or words, for that, or for no memories, neither.

*

Behind the black curtains, hanging down, behind the scenes,
the bloodied gears. The Swan leads us to a curtained area and
down into another basement, into a dungeon lit up with flickering
lights, where what appears to be a man – badly beaten and
bleeding from the head – is strapped into a chair.

This is an Ouroboros working, The Swan says to us and he
points to the figure on the chair. But what is the nature of the
work? Tactical magic is the nature of the work. But what is
tactical magic? Tactical magic is what is spelled (o-u-t) by the
Father. The prisoner's eyes are sewn shut, he is deliberately
blinded. This is the UR-A, The Swan says to us, this is the IRA's
Holy Orders.

Stood either side of the prisoner are two men in black balaclavas
with no mouths or eyeholes. Who is he? One of us? But The Swan
says nothing. Blackie approaches the prisoner. He takes his cock

from out his trousers. Now he is beating the prisoner about the face with it. He is slapping him on his cheek with his cock in order to leave a bruise. Now he is holding him by the hair while he ejaculates into the wound. Jayzus but they are humiliating him, Tommy says. A fucking double agent, must be, he says, and he is turned to me all in glee, and in laughter. Blackie comes over and gestures to Tommy and Tommy steps forward, between the men in the masks, and beats the prisoner over the head with his fist (all around the room men have their cocks out and are stroking their cocks in unison as they form a circle about the prisoner) and kicks him hard in the centre of the chest, which makes a sound, this fleshed sound, this body, that is hollow, is a sound, that is doubled, as a word, as Tommy holds the prisoner's head up by the hair, his blind head, hanging sideways, his white skin, like a grub, as he punches him, repeatedly, in the face, is when the prisoner, like a grub eating its way out of the body, innocently breaking the pale skin, is come a word, and he starts to sing, in a voice as distant as conception, *Bobby Sands has come to pass*, he sings, through cracked and bleeding lips, through broken teeth, *Bobby Sands has come to pass* is his blind no-eyes, *to enlighten the world* is a cock-print on his white face, *Bobby Sands has come to pass* is it is Bobby, is it is Sands, it is revealed, whose time, it has come, but to pass.

*

That was hot, Blackie says to Tommy as he's wiping his shoes on the curtain, but Tommy isn't listening and he walks over to The Swan and he says to him, they do make plastic hearts, and I should fucking know, and The Swan puts his arm around Tommy,

and we drink and we sing and we do other things that seemed
impossible only the previous morning.

*

Mick from Ireland plays the pipe,
and what a con-flag-ra-tion
He plays the pipe, to goes to war
against forced immigration
It is his want
to spend his nights in wanton
con-cu-bation,
boys

But come the day
and mark the hour
of Holy Sufferation
He makes his
way
as martyrs do,
bold Fenians, of a nation
That stand as true
as e'er what do
in Holy
Buggeration.

*

Then I minded a story about my father, about how, when we
were kids, he had literally disappeared. My father had been quite

religious when we were growing up. We went to chapel every Sunday. We had a copy of The Bible on the table between our beds at night, just in case youse need it, my da says to me and my brother Peter, which of course put the living fear in us that during the night we were going to be assaulted by daemons or by the kind of crooked thoughts that only The Bible can destroy.

Then he disappeared. And when he came back he was wearing stigmata. That's what he says to us.

He turns up and his face is all cut-up and bruised, so badly bruised that he was scarcely recognisable. Me and my brother were scared as hell, pushing him away. No, don't touch me, we're screaming, Ma, we're saying, he's a monster, and my da, he says to me, I had to go away. I had obligations, he says to me. You had obligations to your family, our ma is screaming at him, you're scaring the fucking life out of them, she's screaming, you've got them all scared like little white rabbits. One day it will be your turn, he says to us, and then he says to us, don't you remember when Jayzus lifted his hand from the cross to show the disciples his wounds?

Look, he says to us, look at my face. It's okay, he says to us. Don't worry. It's alright. But why did they do it to you, Da? Peter says to him. I did it to myself, he says. Why, Da, why? Peter's crying. Have you never heard of the mortification of the flesh? he says to us. Have you never heard of the imitation of Christ? he says to me and my brother, we're both looking up at him in terror, and he takes down his trousers in front of us, he drops his trousers and his underwear is soaked in blood. He's crucified his cock, I says to myself, oh no can you crucify your cock, please no, and my ma, she says to him, you'll traumatise them for life, you've got them all scared like little white mice, she says, and then he pulls his pants down, and it's the first time I ever saw my father's penis, and it's all wrapped in barbed wire, all round his waist, his groin is wrapped tight with barbed wire, biting down into the flesh. You've never lived, he says to us, and he stumbled then and he put his hands out in front of him, and he fell, and he rolled over onto his side and he passed out and me and my brother and my ma were left to drag him to the bathroom and to wash his wounds and to pick all of the barbed wire out his poor, suffering flesh.

*

In bed, on the mattresses, on the floor, this is 1977, and I says to Tommy, Tommy, I think it's a religious thing, I think it's like your opus Dei, I think my da was involved in it too, it's a religious thing to do with suffering and pain, and Tommy says to me, no, you're wrong, it's not a religious thing at all. But they're onto something, he says. There's a way of telling the future through pain, he says to me. That's the secret of the IRA, he says. And all the top brass is in on it. It's suffering that causes the future, he says. Thing is, he says, you can always call its bluff. And then he rolls over and he starts snoring, quietly, like an innocent little baby without a care in the world.

*

Two Irishmen, Tommy and Sammy, go to an art gallery, in that London, for the first time ever.

This is the equivalent of going on the pull in London, Tommy says to Sammy. Well, you better know something about art if you want to pull birds in here, Sammy says to him, because this is not the most popular spot to pick up an uneducated Irishman. Sure, I know all about the art, Tommy says to Sammy, with my eyes, he says, I know all there is to know. Those eyes, okay, Sammy says to him, let's see.

Okay, Sammy says to him, tell us about this painting here (it's a painting with three trees, huddled close together, with a flock of birds in the background and with shadows across the field, in the evening). That was obviously painted during the olden days, Tommy says to Sammy. And how do you make that out? Sammy says to him. Because it's in black and white, it has been painted in black and white, Tommy says. It's not a fucking telly, Sammy says to Tommy, it's not like they invented colour at a certain point. Of course they fucking invented colour, Tommy says to Sammy, don't be a fucking madman, somebody had to dream that up.

This guy, Tommy says, pointing to a painting of a pale suffering Christ illuminated in his agony and with spectators running all the way into the past and the future; this is the guy what dreamt up colour, he says. Colour existed before this clown, Sammy says to him, get real. There's a difference between something existing and something being dreamt up, Tommy says. That's called art, Tommy says to Sammy. Art's called what? Sammy says to Tommy. When Christ shops up, Tommy says to Sammy, he pulls an audience by the art of illuminating Himself.

But in art Christ Jayzus is not the only one that is crucified,
Tommy says. In the background, he says, pointing to the
painting, and fixed to another cross, he says, in the shape of a
coiled number eight, he says, hanging there like it might be dead
already, he says, there's a brightly coloured snake with all of its
bones broken. How do you know its bones are broken? Sammy
says to Tommy. Because, Tommy says, a blind snake with all its
bones broken is the pain at the centre of the world. How did you
get to that? Sammy says to him. *The Green Book*, Tommy says.
I got it from *The Green Book*. Of course it might just be a plastic
snake, Tommy says, and he shrugs. It might not be real, he says.
How come? Sammy says to him. Because in order to vanquish it,
you must make an idol of it, and raise it up, Tommy says. They
probably stuck a plastic snake up there, he says to Sammy, just
for the sake of it. After that the pair of them saw some more art
but none of it was of much interest except for a beezer painting of
Mickey Mouse by your man Lichtenstein.

*

But I came to understand that Tommy was right, in the end, that
at the heart of the struggle, at the centre of The Calamity (which
really is the centre of the world), there is a network of basements
and bunkers, of outhouses and barns and dugouts, of dungeons
and safe houses, of flats and tower blocks and back rooms and
annexes, of working men's clubs and council houses and squats,
of abandoned mansions and boarded-up shops, in Lisburn and
Bangor and Ballymena and Coleraine, in Claudy and Fintona and
Birmingham, and in that London too, and in Belfast and Dublin,
all lit up with strip lights and with halogen lamps and with

dark corridors leading off, and with (secret) trapdoors and with mysterious stairwells, and tunnels running back and snaking off, tunnels that go deep into the earth, back to the beginning of Ireland, which is the beginning of human history, which is bare two thousand year, and which is where secret crowds gather, still, to watch as Christ Jayzus, as the engine of time, shops up (or what looks like Christ Jayzus, all lit up in pain, and in suffering), to watch as what looks like it might, still, be a human being, but which later will be unidentifiable, which later will look more like the carcass of an animal, a poor cow with tattoos and with black hair and with bright-red nipples, is coloured, as a broken snake with bright-red razored nipples, is raised up, and its blind eyes, taped shut, and bound, and beaten with golf clubs, and its nails pulled out, and its teeth smashed in, and broken sticks forced into its earholes, is a painting, and its orifices opened up and invaded, and its face ejaculated on, is art, and its names forgotten, and its faces misremembered, is a dream of colour, bright, and unworded, all in the cause of trying to keep the future alive, like monks praying in caves, or illuminates on top of rocks, in the desert, this terrible need to put suffering on a pedestal, this cult of pain, is Holy.

Part Four: A Word Set Teeth into Silence

By the time we get back to Belfast there's a war on. Not that one, son, another one. An *internal* war, is what you call it. The Boys had taken out two members of the FSV, two brothers, the McNultys, for running their mouths off and for claiming that the Europa hit was their own and for deflecting attention from the IRA, and they had been whacked at their home by two Ra boys, Shorty Temper – he's dead now, legend – and Rab McSpoons. I hear they even brought them a trout.

Thing is, now there was a vendetta on and people were getting popped all over the place. It was Barney that told us about it. He's in the shop with Beavis and this new wee bird when we get back, this new wee bird that he says he met at a comics fair and that looks like the wee bird from *Scooby-Doo* with the glasses. She's sitting behind the desk pricing up the rare comics for him.

How much fucking money did you make at that comics fair? Tommy says to him. We're in the back room and Barney is cooking a steak over a gas burner for his lunch. Look at the size of that fucking sizzler, Tommy says to him. Where's all the money coming from? Don't worry, Barney says to him. You'll get your share. But considering I'm the one doing all the work, as well as bringing in the outside expertise, I feel I'm due for a substantial bonus. Would you take a look at that, Barney says, turning this charred black steak in the pan. Cooked till it's nice and tender, he says. What a moron.

What's the story with the wee bird? Tommy says to him. Just then Beavis walks in. She won first prize in the costume display, Beavis says. I think it was the first time I ever heard him speak.

What the fuck is the costume display? Tommy says to him. It's dressing up as your favourite superhero, Beavis says, and he picks up a bundle of comics and goes back next door. I had to laugh. Don't tell me it was fucking Wonder Woman, I starts to say, but before I can get a jab in Tommy cuts me dead. You're the one that was boasting about getting your cock sucked by Red Sonja and now it's all a fucking joke to you, is it? he says. Obviously he was touchy about Wonder Woman, so as I says nothing. Who was she dressed as? he says to Barney. Tell me she wasn't going as Conan the Barbarian, I says to him.

What about Supergirl? Tommy says. Naw, says Barney. Think again. Spider-Woman? Batgirl? Wait a minute, I says to him, Catwoman? Naw, Barney says. All wrong. Well, tell us then, I says to him, tell us who she was. She was fucking Robin, he says to us, that's who she was, and he pushes past us with this fucking burnt steak to a crisp that he has stuck between a pair of baps.

Who the fuck is Robin? Tommy says to me but then I'm like that, what, wait a minute, Robin is fucking Batman and Robin. Tommy looks at me in amazement. Our jaws are on the floor. That's quite hot, actually, Tommy says. And so it was.

*

Christmas of 1977 we go to see our first punk rock show and it's a *black fucking nightmare*. The Clash are playing the McMordie Hall over at the Queen's University and Mack gets us tickets. Just a thank you, he says to us. A thank you for what? A thank you for failing to blow up the Europa? A thank you for provoking a civil war? I can say that now. But at the time I had to swallow my tongue and says thanks a lot, pal, you're some man, ah that's decent of you, right enough.

This is going to be an initiation, Mack says to us. He's with this other guy, your man Del Brogan, who it turns out is a singer himself, as well as a newly made commandant in the IRA. I had never heard of the cunt before. We meet up at The Tim's Harbour: me, Tommy, Barney, this pair. The pints of green are flowing. Up the Rebels! and we all drink to that. We're half-blocked already. I better not get spat on, Tommy says. This is a fucking good jacket I'm wearing to this dance. These people are animals, that's what I've heard, Barney says. They wear dog leads and get led about on all fours like animals out their own choice. Sure, it's only rock n roll, your man Del Brogan says to us, expand your horizons, man, he says. He's got his dark hair all cropped short in the style and the pale skin and the wee staring eyes that make him look like a mole come up gasping for light. I mean, youse like a bit of rock n roll, do youse not? he says to us. Aye, I like a bit of your man Bill Haley, Barney says. Well, it's like that, your man Del Brogan says, only not boring.

Bill Haley is not fucking boring, my friend, Barney says to him. We ripped the fucking seats out the place the time he played Belfast. Well, you were a fucking punk before your time, then, weren't you? your man Del Brogan says. What you trying to say? Barney says to him. A punk means a fucking poof. No, it doesn't, Tommy says to him. A punk rocker is a different thing entirely. What does it mean, then? Barney says to him. It means somebody what is anti-disestablishment, Tommy says to him.

189

Exactly, your man Del Brogan says. The IRA is the biggest punk group going. Tommy and your man Del Brogan look at each other, and they nod. Then Mack pulls this little container out onto the table. Going to be a good night tonight, lads, he says. I told you this was going to be an initiation. Welcome to the future, my friends, he says to us, and he takes out these wee paper squares like wee postage stamps that have a drawing of a white snake, it looks like, coiling up around this naked woman with the big fucking tits. Fucking hell, Sammy, Barney says to me, that's like something out your man *Conan*. Have youse ever heard of the LSD? Mack says to us. Is this fucking drugs? Tommy says to him. Aye, it's fucking drugs, Mack says to him. Black Mamba. Black Mamba's white, Tommy says to him. That's right, Mack says. That's cause of in the world of LSD, just like in the world of Northern Ireland, everything is inverted. I can see I'm gonna have to teach youse, he says. Have youse never tripped before? he says to us. I smoked that wacky backy, Tommy says to him. Como never sounded better. You think that's good, your man Del Brogan says, try listening to The Clash on LSD. Will it get you wasted? Barney says to him. That's not the point, your man Del Brogan says. This shite wakes you up. Wakes you up to what? Barney says to him. To fucking life, my friend, your man Del Brogan says. Who the fuck wants to wake up to life in Belfast? Barney says to him. Alright, Mack says. I'll be honest with you, it gets you wasted. Good enough for me, Barney says to him. Hand them over. And he grabs a wee stamp off him and just gubs it, washing it down with a gargle of green. Let it dissolve under your tongue, Mack says to him, what are you doing, take it easy. But Barney just sits there. Nothing is fucking happening, he says. I've heard about these drugs, he says. They put fucking cat food

and fucking washing-up liquid in them and all this shite. How the
fuck can they put cat food into a piece of paper? I says to him. You
need to let it get into your bloodstream, Mack says to him, let it
go, then let it flow, into your brain. It'll be a fucking tight squeeze
in there, Tommy says. That's probably why it's not working. You
need to give it time, Mack says, and by the time we gets over
the road to the Clash show we'll be fucking peaking, Fucking
Peaking, FUCKING PEAKING . . . like this:

*

we get to the show and (fucking peaking) the place is surrounded,
the peelers are everywhere, armoured trucks, lined up, outside
the venue, soldiers (peaking) kids with their machine guns and
the kids themselves, starving, and written on, and surrounded,
and boys take off like balloons, what is called pogoing, in the
lingo, a young man is pogoing, on the spot, in the lingo he is
dancing, a bold one is jumping, up, into the air and it's, he has let
go, it's, he hangs there, it's, he's weightless, now, floating there,
looking down at them, and taunting them, boys are, groups of
boys we are, as boys we lift up Belfast, and there is something
to his throat, a connection, as he is floating into the air, is God's
more, boys, God's more, lads, taking off into the air, one after
the other, and the peelers are making a joke of calling them
home but then Fuck Forever, and in motion, but now the soldiers
are rising up and spitting down on the looking up and from the
yelling, it is clear, that God is on our side, yes, even if he is like,
yo-yos, and dragging them down to earth, through room after
room (within a room) (secret room) as everyone is taking their
clotheses off and removed their belts with the studs and piled

high and Barney is taking his belt off at the checkpoint and he
goes to take his trousers down, he thinks we need to undress
and to be naked weapons, out front, and as we go inside we are
taken up, and propelled, on a wave, blind wave is being lifted up
and Rebel Songs, as a sound begins, a Rebel Song is a sound that
comes and that goes, an echoes, is what is lagging, beneath, in
the form of a snake, blind wave is white snake, grub is father as
mother is riven, flowing, with blinding and passing, and queerer
than the singer, a raven steps out of white light, a black raven
at the white rock is a swan in a terror to transform itself, till
a snake, burrowing out, is come in, in its tearing of terrible,
muscle, is what is spitting, is what is spitting is tearing and
force-eating, its way, outside, is life, on life, is its whole body
convulsing, and by force, revealed, as a snake, black snake as a
hood, worn by Miracle, as a word, set teeth, into silence, as my
father, who holds the microphone in his tiny, dead hands, him
what makes the noise, is the shape of a black snake, coming into
ice as horses into war, as legs reaching up, as hands reaching
up in a great wave of reaching up whose name is Set, Baby,
and what is called Egypt, and what is known as the Free State,
and the terrible thought of God, looking back behind where Art
stood, and seeing only his own face and blackness, his hood like
a blind black bally, is to start to sing, as Miracle wears the crown
like a shroud, and the song becomes as all around it, standing,
staring out of the song, like ghosts come back to the place of
their own murder, is the show, called Family, and is containing,
restraining, as Family Is Forever, these words are the song
that is singing (doth we comprehende all speeds, daemon, as we
cannot see a flye as it moves from here to there, are there not
daemons, I name them, that move faster than sight) and behind

it, this tremendous noise, this screaming metal machine music
(I hate the British army and I hate the RUC) until everything
is locked and frozen, into the half-formed arms of a song that
remembers as Family, as the snake is white, riot, as the sea
is Forever, Family, as the scene is dissolved, as the plug-ugly
guitarist returns, as I slide through a gap in the crowd, Is
Forever, as I hit the floor:

*

and I lie there, like a little baby, until the lights come up, and
a pair of friendly punks drag me outside for air, gasping, in my
lungs, for air. The five of us walk home in a daze. An armoured
car follows us part of the way. They're looking for us to start
something. But we're somewhere else entirely. I thought Saint
Patrick kicked all the snakes out of Ireland? Tommy says to me. I
thought he told them to beat it?

*

Me: Is Christ Jayzus a Catholic?

McManus:

Tommy: Course he's a Tim, don't be so fucking stupid.

Me: How do you mean, of course? How is he not a Protestant?

Tommy: If he was a Hun, then we'd know all about it.

Me: How's that?

Tommy: If Jayzus was a Hun, then he'd hate the look of his own
coupon.

McManus:

Me: How do you work that one out?

Tommy: That's what the Protestants want. They want Jayzus out the picture, basically, so why would your man Christ Jayzus go about telling everybody that he was a Protestant? That would be like me going about saying I was a lesbian.

McManus:

Me:

Tommy: Listen, Huns come out of Tims, the way women come out of men.

Me: What? Men come out of women, what are you talking about?

Tommy: The first man does not come out the first woman, that would be impossible, because who infertilised the woman, so as they had to create the first woman using a spare rib from Adam's body, only he didn't know anything about all of this, at this point, to him a rib wasn't even a rib, so as he was oblivious.

Me: You'd think if you were putting together a woman you'd use something a bit more attractive than a fucking spare rib, like a nice fleshy part of your hoop or the blue pupil out one of your lamps or a bit of long dark hair, even. How comes a rib?

McManus:

Tommy: What the fuck is all these questions about? Because that builds a place for the heart, that's what Catholics believe, have you never heard of the heart of immaculate deception?

Me: Conception.

Tommy: Besides, Jayzus is probably a Zoro-as-trian, in reality.

Me: Zorro, what? Zorro-ism?

Tommy: Zoro-as-trian-ism. That is the belief what Jayzus had his own teaching what is not in The Bible.

Me: Where the fuck are you getting all of this dubious shite from?

Tommy: *Reader's Digest.*

McManus:

Me: And what was Jayzus's secret teaching all about?

Tommy: We'll never know for sure, they are lost in caves and in secret temples and in the winds of time, somewhere around the Dead Sea, probably. But we can take a guess.

Me: Like?

Tommy: Like, for instance, he didn't die on the cross, he had a thing for the women, plus he knew everything that was going to happen ahead of the game.

Me: You're trying to tell me that Jayzus knew exactly what was going to happen to him?

Tommy: He knew he'd be born in a manger, he knew he'd be crying a lot, and he knew that he would have twelve pals, and that his job was to get everybody to repent to his da. But he didn't think about it that much, he just got on with being the Son of God.

Me: So it was all down to his fucking da and here's Christ Jayzus, just going through the motions?

Tommy: You end up martyring yourself to your da's ideas, and that's what happened to Jayzus.

Me: This isn't Zoro-ism, though, is it? What is the secret teaching? Also, how comes it has to be a fucking secret all the time?

McManus:

Tommy: I can see I'm going to have to teach you.

Me: Why can't you just tell me the secret teaching? Right now? If you even know it, that is. What's so hard about it?

Tommy: That's the whole point, you can't tell it. You can't think it. You can't speak it. That's why Jayzus had to live it. You can't tell it any other way than by doing it. And if you put a word to it, then that's not it.

McManus:

Tommy: That's what I'm talking about, right there.

McManus:

Tommy: But I'll tell you this.

Me:

McManus:

Tommy:

Me:

McManus:

Jayzus:

Tommy: See?

Me:

McManus:

Jayzus:

Tommy: And that there were two Jayzus, all along.

*

Then they blew up my ma's house with my ma in it and two of Billy McNab's weans got taken to hospital into the bargain. It was the FSV, is what they says. They've upped their game, they says to us. You're a fucking marked man, they says, that's what comes with being a hero for the cause.

They used a word: inter-necine. That was it. It was an internecine feud that had exploded. But I knew fine well what it was that had exploded. I knew it, and it ate me up the same way the mice under my bed must've ate up the detonator on the explosives and blew my ma sky-high by mistake. It ate me up like the punchline of the worst Paddy joke of all time. While they consoled me and told me they would get the human scum what did this to my poor suffering ma. That it was lower than low, for a supposedly Republican group to target their own like that, and that it had come to this, and that this was fucking despicable. That's the word that Tommy used. He was pacing back and forth. It's fucking despicable, he says to me. What was I going to say? That I killed my own ma with a bomb hidden under my bed, a bomb that I never set at the Europa in the first place, a bomb what had already cost the lives of two members of the FSV? The whole thing was spiralling. Snakes are back in Ireland, I says to myself. There's no doubt about it.

Let's get Miracle Baby involved, Tommy says. What the fuck is a Miracle Baby? Mack says to him. I started panicking right then. I don't want no Miracle Baby telling my mind or reading the future or knowing the past at this point. Miracle Baby is the ultimate informer, Tommy says. All the time I'm looking at Tommy as if to say, no, don't do it, Tommy, don't give away our wee secret source, but really I'm trying to kill the idea dead altogether. Miracle Baby is just a wee retard that thinks he knows everybody's business, I says to Mack. Come on, you, Tommy says, don't talk about Miracle Baby like that. This guy is like fucking Delphine's Oracle, he says. The Delphic Oracle, Mack says.

Whatever fucking oracle, Tommy says to him. He knows everything.

Barney and your man Del Brogan go out and grab Miracle Baby off the street and bring him in. So you're this Miracle Baby, Mack says to him. He looks like hell, his underpants are coming up out his jeans, these ghastly stained underpants with the Six Million Dollar Man on them, and his jumper is tucked into his underpants and there is snot across his face and horrible . . . drool. I'm Miracle Baby, he says. Is it true you have knowledge of other worlds? Mack says to him. Word for word. Miracle Baby stands there silently, just blinking, saying nothing. Are you communicating with the other world right now? Mack says to him. Suddenly there's this smell in the room, this atrocious smell. I just went in my pants, Miracle Baby says, and there's fucking uproar. Get him out of here, Mack shouts, what are we doing with this retard in the first place, and Barney fucking kicks him out the door but not before Miracle Baby turns and winks at me and he says, it smells like a fucking hamster's cage in here, and he laughs, and then he's gone, the fucking snake.

*

Origins Of The Anomaly:

Atop a great mountain, somewhere on the north coast of Ireland.

Ériu, the keeper of the river of the stars, weeps at the nativity of her first-born.

There is uproar in the heavens.

The constellations have realigned.

New fates are written in their fires.

Three blazing suns appear to break from the belt of O'Ryan.

Wait! They approach!

These are no suns. These are The Sons Of Men!

The Sons Of Men, three beings of light, arrive to console the grieving mother.

Ériu, they implore her. Do not weep for the way the stars have turned.

All things move toward their end, in which is their returning.

Why him? she demands of them. Why my first son?

The Sons Of Men cannot answer.

We are merely the effluence of stars, they explain to her. In your heart you know this. We can console and project and we can bathe you in our light but we too are sons with destinies all our own.

And what of the star behind the stars? she thunders. What of our heavenly father who made love to me in the form of a swan?

He crossed the great gulfs of space for the joy of union, The Sons Of Men tell her. He crossed the great desert where even our light cannot penetrate.

He came through the fields of anti-matter where reality is made to stand upon its head and where the air itself hungers for flesh.

You have been given an earthly husband. Return to him and speak not of what has been revealed to you amongst the peaks.

But how can I live with such foreknowledge? Ériu demands of The Sons Of Men.

How can I live when I know his destiny is to suffer and to be a scourge and to be shunned by the men of this island?

How can we live as we hang suspended in space and our father turns his gaze upon us and through the eternal vehicle of our bodies, which we term the fire unsound, the lives and loves of our first-borns are written in heavenly fire? they ask as one voice in return.

In the folds of his body every one of us is entwined.

It is as the body of a mother, The Sons Of Men sing together.

It is a body of love, a love that it is not ours to understand.

I will tear the umbilical with my own teeth, Ériu replies. I will gorge myself on the placenta. I will become the air that devours.

The light that does not cast a shadow. And my son will walk in the way of his heavenly father. Free and self-willed. And refute his role in this game of Hibernia.

The Sons Of Men look to each other with empty eyes of silver. Something sparkles on each of their cheeks. They rise as one and as a trio of comets return to their station as the girdle of the warrior, leaving a trail of soft, silent tears across the skies as they go.

Ériu leans into the woven basket where the baby lies sleeping.

They shall call you The Anomaly, she says.

Next time: The Tower That Rises Down!

*

Summer of '78, I remember virtually all of their names, except for some of them, mind, except, for example, for the guy what got his head caved in with a baseball bat, now that was showing off, you had to go out your way to get a baseball bat in Ireland, that's when you think you're in the movies, that's when you're whacking people like a Hollywood gangster.

That was Tommy, of course, who whacked him, who took a baseball bat from under his Crombie and who caved his fucking head in on the spot. Then Tommy clutches his chest and collapses on the ground right on top of him. His heart is playing tricks on him again. This is at the bottom of Royal Avenue, and now there's a pile of bodies at my feet. A wee old woman passing asks me if they're alright. Sure, your man's had a heart attack, I says to her. She spots the blood flowing out from beneath him and she lets out a scream. Tommy's lying on this guy's caved-in head so as you can't see he's had his melt panned but all the blood is starting to flow out onto the pavement and the old dear is standing there, screaming, like that.

Listen, I says to the old dear, I need you to help me out here, love, I need you to run over to that phone box, love, and to phone us an ambulance, would you do that? At this point Tommy wasn't banned from the hospital like the rest of us. Soon as she leaves I pull Tommy's body off this poor bugger with no name and I check to make sure Tommy's still alive. He's breathing, but his heart is all over the shop. Now there are these big industrial bins down the side of this place that sells the pizza pies. I start to drag the man with no name over to them. I'm trying to dump this body, in broad daylight, before the ambulance comes or before somebody sees us. It's seven in the morning, so it's still quiet, because we were trying to catch the unknown soldier on his way to work. I drag this guy with no face and no name over to these bins but I can't lift him up. I rest him against the side of the bin, I've got my arms around him, his poor caved-in head is leaning on my shoulder, I've got my arms up under his oxters, his jumper is all torn and he has a bit of black masking tape wrapped around the bust-up toe of one of his shoes. This guy's had it rough, I says to myself. I couldn't even tell you now why we had to whack him. Not a clue. I don't think he was FSV. Was he a Hun even, who knows? A foot soldier, at best, judging by the nick of him. So as I've got him up over one shoulder but he keeps sliding off and back down onto the ground and I'm cursing him, under my breath, when I hear this voice, coming from the back of the bins. Do you need a light, pal? it says. Do you need a light, my friend? You believe this? There's this fucking tinker, lying in there, behind the bins, on a bit of cardboard, still blocked, and he thinks I need a fucking light, and now he's sprung into life, and he gets up and he comes staggering out with this fucking lighter in his hand, ready to go.

I pull the unknown soldier's torn jumper up round his head so as he can't see his messed-up face. Your man's in some state there, this old ancient tinker with a purple face says to me. Aye, I says to him. I'm fucking thinking on my feet here, so as I says to him, aye, we've been at it all night, I says. This cunt's on his stag do, I says to him. Give us a hand, pal, will you, I says to him, he's getting married in the morning so I'm going to dump him in this fucking bin so as when he wakes up he has no idea what the fuck just happened. Nice one, the wee tinker says to me, ha ha, pal, that's a nice one, he's fucking killing himself like it's the best one ever. Sure, that's some laugh, he says, sure that's the best laugh I've had all week, he says. Give us a hand, I says to him, and the two of us'll fucking launch him right in there. I thought you wanted a light, pal, the wee tinker says to me. Aye, mate, I do, I says to him, we'll get us a bifter in a minute, and between the two of us we hoist the unknown soldier up on our shoulders and we topple him into the bin but it catches on the waist of his trousers and he's left swinging there, with his legs up in the air and his head and shoulders in the bin. But the wee tinker is getting creative. This wee bum is inspired, and he goes and gets a wee box to stand on and he's instructing me by this point, like, sure, your angle is all wrong, or like, shoogle him this way, that's what he says, shoogle

him this way, I've got his fucking shoulders, he says to me, we're a
ball hair off now, he says, one, two, three, heave him up, there we
go. I get down underneath him and I put my shoulders in between
his legs and I can feel that he has pished himself. The unknown
soldier has pished his pants. That's what happens when you snuff
it. It's all in his taped-up shoes, all soaked into his trousers that
are all patched up and worn through, and at first I'm disgusted,
but then I says to myself, poor sod, poor fucking sod with no name,
getting tipped into a bin on Royal Avenue in his best clothes with
the help of a friendly tramp, what a sin.

*

And dominoes is the scene that comes to my mind, it's dominoes,
tumbling, one till the other, as far back as the eye can see, and I
think to myself, what was the first domino, and in that case, how
did it fall, and I imagine this big finger, this big fuck-off finger
coming down and parting the clouds, this deathly hand flicking
the first one, and setting it all off, and then sitting back and
watching the carnage, as one domino tips the other into the other
into the other into a plastic bin up on Royal Avenue and stops
for a laugh and to light a bifter and then goes and drags another
one up the street a bit, away from the bins and the blood on the
pavement, and props it up against a shop window, and waits
for an ambulance to arrive, driven by another pair of dominoes,
and denies all knowledge when they show up, says he has never
seen this guy in his life before and that he collapsed, right there
in front of him, but that he looked in his wallet and saw that his
name was Tommy Kentigern, and they speed off with him in the
ambulance, and barely a week later your man Davy Boyle gets

sliced in a back alley in the Ardoyne as a reprisal, an incident
that saw Frankie Mullen and Mike McMasters strung up and
hanged with their own belts in a house in the Whiterock a few
days later, and that led to the killing of Richie Pollock in a drive-
by in front of his ma and da in a park off Donegall Street, which
is what caused Pete McIver to end up with brain damage after
being assaulted with a dumb-bell in a boxing gym on the Shankill
Road, which is what led to the death of Tony Stuart and Vernon
Forsyth, you must have read about it in the paper, the pair of
them kidnapped and held to ransom in a loft in a safe house,
starved, beaten naked, shot in the head, and dumped on a country
road in South Armagh, that set a trail that led all the way back
to poor fucking Jimmy Papps, who got his genitals removed with
a chisel in the back seat of a car, a car what was then set on fire
and rolled down the hill, into the front garden of his house, in full
view of his wife and kids, with their faces pressed up against the
glass as it exploded right in front of them, killing their da, and
which led to the murder of the two boy soldiers, Roger Sutherland
and Jimmy McDuff, the two boy soldiers on the news, killed
by snipers, McDuff choking on his own blood after being shot
through the lung, and then it's our turn, and we get the call and
we step in on this off-duty peeler, this fucking man-mountain
that rises up in my inner eye, the next domino, teetering, and
that took three of us, going at him full tilt, to get him out the bar
and round the back into the waste ground where we put a plank
with a nail in it through his soft fucking skull and Tommy took
out a sharpened pine stump, who the fuck thinks up a fucking
sharpened pine stump, and fucking impales the guy with it, like
a vampire in a horror movie, and me and Barney and Tommy,
how many unmarked graves did we dig, did the Big Man with the

finger oversee all of that too, did he sit there and watch us, in the fields outside Belfast, in the fields out by the Neagh, up behind Randalstown, in the woods, down by the water, in the dark of the 1970s, at Bellaghy, in this van with Mickey Mouse on the side, scattering bodies across the fields like seeds, bodies I can't even remember now, bodies with no faces and no names, bodies with no limbs at all, sometimes, bodies that nobody will ever find again, bodies with pine trees growing straight from their fucking hearts, I mean sharpened pine stumps, who even makes that up? The fucking Big Man, that's who. Ask me why and I will tell you, dominoes, fucking dominoes: that's why.

*

Right, this is a fucking
belter,
listen to this:
Pat and Mick are walking down the Falls Road, in
Belfast,
when they passes this store, what was selling antiques,
what was displaying knick-knacks
outdoors, on the pavement,
and that style of stuff
and there's a mirror, lying out front,
on the pavement, and Pat's like that,
he picks it up, and he looks into it,
and fuck me, he says,
I know that guy, I knows that guy in the mirror, he says
and Mick's like that, he grabs it off him
and he looks into it

Himself
and he says to Pat, of course you fucking do,
that's me in there,
you eejit,
that's me, you fucking
tit.

*

Turns out your man Del Brogan is some chanter. We're up at The
Shamrock one night and he gets up onstage. Tommy's there with
Patricia. McManus might have been there too but that's irrelevant
to this story. Barney's on his own because he hasn't the bottle
to bring Wee Robin, at least not yet. By this point his poor wife
Shona has been in the hospice for a few month, it was a sin, so
it was. Mack's there with a couple of birds of his own. Your man
Barney comes offstage, he's up there giving it a version of 'The
Way We Were' but he's a fucking chronic warbler, I says to him,
too much yon fucking warbling, son, and your man Del Brogan is
laying into him and all, go easy on the vibrato, he's telling him,
you're giving it too much, he says, and Barney says to him, what
the fuck do you know about how the old tunes should be handled?
You're a fucking punk rocker, what do you know about the
chanting? And your man Del Brogan just says to him: get me to
the stage. Just like that. Get me to the fucking stage, that's all he
says to him, and Barney looks round at me and he winks, let him
go, he says to me, give him enough fucking rope, he says.

Your man Del Brogan walks onstage and whips his yellow tie off,
he's staggering a little, the cunt's half-blocked, obviously, and he

whirls his tie above his head and throws it to a couple of ladies in the front row. Then the music starts up on the karaoke; it's Bruce Springsteen, 'Thunder Road'. And your man Del Brogan is giving it a bit of that. He's got the rasp down. Fair enough, he has got the rasp down. He's strutting his stuff up there. Fuck me, Tommy says, but your man Del Brogan can sing. Patricia's dancing in her seat. The ladies down the front are holding his tie in the air and swatching it from side to side like it's a team scarf. Barney's shaking his head, it's just power pop, he says, what the fuck is he talking about, but people are up on their feet by this point and then he launches into a ballad, your man Del Brogan is playing us at our own game here, straight into a ballad, and by this point his shirt is all unbuttoned and he's standing there and with his eyes closed he's singing our song,

> Lay your head upon my pillow
> Hold your warm and tender body close to mine
> Hear the whisper of the raindrops blowing soft across
>   the window
> And make believe you love me one more time
> For the good times

This is fucking sacred ground he's on here, Barney says. Barney's furious. These punks shouldn't be touching Como, he says. He gets up and he starts shouting at the stage, hands off, you bastard! But everybody's shouting him down. Shut it, Oddjob, stuff like that. Barney sits back down because your man Del Brogan is nailing it. The silk hankies are raining down on the stage. You can smell the little bursts of perfume as they hit the floor. Your man Del Brogan picks one up, a lavender-coloured one, holds it over his mouth and nose, closes his eyes, takes a great big sniff, slides it inside his shirt, and launches straight into the next verse without missing a beat. By this point there isn't a dry seat in the front row. I looked over at Tommy and I could see he was entranced. Right then your man Del Brogan was his hero, so he was.

*

Now wait till I tell you. Next thing you know, Tommy is managing your man Del Brogan. I know. They're making a fucking hit record together, you believe this. But here's the deal: Tommy's funding it but only if your man Del Brogan sings some of the old songs on there. It can't be all this fucking Bruce Springsteen fucking punk rock style, Tommy says to him.

Now your man Del Brogan had a voice like your man Dick Hucknall, your Simple Reds man. The Simply Reds. You know the one, 'Holding Back the Years'? That came out later but that was the style of chanter he was, that was your man Del Brogan's style right there. He could have been as big as your man Dick Hucknall but you should have seen the fucking record they come out with. You can't get it anymore, it's out of print, this weather it's probably a collector's item. They call it *Daddy's Little Girl*. There's a photograph of your man Del Brogan on the cover, with his daughter, she must have been six year old, and he's got his arm round her and it's like a fucking hostage situation. He's sitting there staring into space all profound. His face is beaming like fucking Jayzus Himself on a communion card and there's this wee girl, her name was Eden, Eden Brogan, all done up in what looks like her communion dress, and she's looking to the side, like she's given up on ever escaping the clutches of her psycho father, no joke, it's a pure paedo situation, in other words, but none of them can even see it. What are you talking about? Tommy says to me when I bring it up to him. You're a fucking paedo, he says to me, you've got a sick fucking mind. And the songs, alright, okay, so there's a few Rod Stewart numbers on there, 'Hot Legs', 'Maggie May', but then there's all this other stuff, stuff like 'The Rose of Castlerea', 'The Cliffs of Dooneen', 'Come Back to Erin' and 'My Wild Irish Rose'. Plus he's got this washed-up compere that used to stand in at The Shamrock and run the karaoke, your man Pony McAllister, to write all this pish in the sleeve notes on the back about your man Del Brogan's 'intimate style' and his 'professionalism'.

But then there's this: 'As the record revolves,' Pony writes, 'we are aware of being part of one big family and as he serenades his young daughter Eden, "Daddy's Little Girl", in the character of his voice, in his mellow vocal tones, in the quality of his expression, Del Brogan makes us realise that family is forever.'

*

Mick from Ireland pulls into the Co-op car park, ah bollocks, it's completely full.

He looks up to the skies and he says until our Lord Himself, Christ Jayzus, he says to him, help me out here, will you, my friend?

Christ Jayzus, I says until thee, right the now, he says, in the presence of all what is holy, if you can just see your way to getting me a wee parking space then I promise to come to

church till every Sunday morning is done and dusted and in
its proper place, at the end of days, and without fail, and like a
good Catholic, he says.
Lo and behold, but a parking space opens up, right there in
front of him.
Never mind, Irish Mick says to Christ Jayzus, I found one
already.

*

My father used to take us up the Cave Hill when we were weans.
One time he says to us, get down on your hands and knees, he
says, and get yourself a drink of that water. We're down there,
cupping the water out this river, with our hands, drinking it
and looking up at him, my father, and nodding and saying, it's
beautiful, Da, it's the best water we ever tasted, Da, and he says
to us, you'll never taste more beautiful water than that, boys,
that's the purest water you'll ever taste. Then we climbed further
up and there was a dead dog, lying in the river.

*

There was nothing to put in my ma's coffin but bits of bone, a
framed picture of JFK, a souvenir magazine with the Queen's face
on it, a clump of dark hair and a clasp. Plus there was no upstair
to put the coffin in. I remembered my da telling me it would be
alright. Holding my hand and telling me not to be scared when
my grandfather died. And now here we were.

Me, Tommy, Barney, my Uncle Sam and Terry McGillicuddy

lowered a half-empty coffin into a hole in the ground. We buried her in the rain, as usual, in the mud and the rain, as ever in them days, and this guy is come out of the rain that's coming down in thick sheets, this big lad I've never seen before walks out of it, takes a handful of dirt, and throws it into the grave. Goodbye, Edna, he says.

I goes up to him afterward. We're at the wake and every bastard there is half-blocked and telling jokes. They haven't started with the singing yet. That'll come later. I don't believe we've met, I says to him and I get a good look at his face for the first time. He looks familiar to me, it's odd, like looking into a darkened mirror. I'm Danny McGonigle, he says to me. A friend of your father's. And my mother's, obviously, I says to him. Aye, he says, aye, of your mother's too. It's a sad day, he says. Losing your ma is murder, he says to me, but even the Pope has to die, and he's God's best pal. I don't know if that's any consolation, he says. And that's when it clicks. Danny McGonigle was Jimmy Smalls's pal that was selling the arms for Tommy's da. Sure, were you a friend of Jimmy Smalls? I says to him. He looks a little nervous. Aye, he says. Aye, I knew wee Jimmy. Hold on a second, I says to him. I've got somebody that would like to meet you. He's looking even more nervous at this point. I goes and I grabs Tommy. Fucking Danny McGonigle is here, I says to him. Tommy goes over and puts out his hand. McGonigle, is it? he says. Good to put a face to a name, he says to him. You know, he says, just for future reference. That's all he says. McGonigle immediately starts making his excuses. I'm sorry, lads, he says. Forgive me. Please accept my condolences. But I should really be going. He puts his drink down and he turns on his heels.

That's how you tie up loose ends, Tommy says to me. That's how you leave a clean fucking trail, he says. Then he looks at me funny, just for a second. Don't you think that cunt looked a bit like you? he says. Sure he looked nothing like me, I says to him, and I pick up my drink, and I walk away.

*

Now I hadn't seen Kathy in months. Kathy M. Things had petered out after the attack went down at the Europa. We had nowhere left to go. Besides, I'm banging this wee chick Moira, Moira McCutcheon, from the Falls Road, a wee cracker. But I'm walking into town. I'm going to this market that I goes to, to do my shopping, and I get talking to this taxi driver that I vaguely knew, a guy what does the tours, Pete McComb, tours of the war zone. The Boys are becoming a tourist attraction, McComb says to me, I thought youse were supposed to be bringing the tourist industry to its knees? What can you do, I says to him, we're fucking superstars this weather, is the problem. Talking of superstars, he says to me, I had your Tommy in my taxi the other day. What the fuck is Tommy doing taking a fucking tour of Belfast, I says to him, he fucking invented the place. Aye, McComb says to me, we were even up at the murals at the Shankill, just for a minute, like. He was giving his new bird the full history, a tour of Tommy's greatest hits. His new bird? I says to him. Sure, him and Patricia have been together for years. Is that right? McComb says to me. Maybe it's his bit on the side, he says. Forget I says anything, he says to me. Don't tell Tommy I says a thing, he says. No, but wait a minute, what did she look like, I says to him, this new bird of Tommy's? Ah, I'm murder with people's faces, McComb says, but I heard Tommy calling her Kathy. I didn't get her second name. Remember I says nothing, McComb says to me. I'll deny it if anybody asks. Everybody's entitled to get their hole on the side. Tommy's probably fucking half of Belfast, anyroads.

He walked away and left me standing there with three apples in my hand. Are you gonna pay for them or are you gonna fucking fondle them all day? the stallholder says to me. Your wife will be fondling your balls in a fucking jiffy bag when I post them through your front door, I says to the cheeky cunt.

*

When my brother Peter was just a kid he thought it was the words that gave you an erection and not the thoughts or the touch or the sights or the imagination. One time I climbed up to the loft and I could hear Peter and his friend (through the trapdoor) and they were repeating the words fanny, fanny, fanny, and I heard Peter say, you've got to keep repeating it, or it goes back down again. In other words, it's the speaking of the words that gets you hard. And of course I loved the stories in the scud mags, never mind the pictures, the stories were what it was all about, so as it made sense to me, these sexy words. And you want to have heard Tommy trying to read these porn stories out loud, it was like a witch's tit, all smoking't hot ass't, lickt niiplels, like he was telling you the language of sex that other people outside of Ireland used in the world of free love for everybody, which in our lingo we called The Future:

brush'te agin, agin to'ward
her hot, nekkid sins, frae head's thrill twarts,
ah fuck't it
ah fuck't it, yeah
hole, precious spunk't it,
an's as boner
to splay's, on yer titses

her pussy's w/juice,
o'er her trampling't, arse't,
sex-jolt,
hits my hards
ah, baby's,

in an out ma sticky holes, he says
fuck me,
but who writes this fucking stuff, he says,
it's genius,

your brother was right,
he says
pussy's w/juice and hole precious spunk't
who'd a thunk it?

*

On New Year's Day 1979 Tommy's da died. This is the news.
The funeral was the first time he had been out from behind that
fucking curtain in years. Tommy never cried at the funeral. He
seemed to be taking it well. Fact it turned into a laugh riot when

everybody began telling mad stories about his da back in the day. About his terrible record with the IRA. The guy that played the organ just gives up, turns round in his seat and joins in with the craic. But then Barney told me that Tommy had broken down. Not in front of him, mind, but in front of Wee Robin, Barney's wee bird on the side, when they had been alone in the shop together. She says he was sobbing. That was hard to take.

But now there was this seed planted in my skull. Eating away at me. Tommy and Kathy. Kathy and Tommy. I remembered how I had seen Tommy in the reception of the Europa that time. I thought about the blank note that had been left for me, and I began to wonder, I began to wonder if the note hadn't been some kind of delaying tactic, you know, something to get me to hang around the reception area long enough to get blown up, or long enough to avoid getting blown up.

It was a web of lies we were all caught in. It's the default position of the Irish. If in doubt, lie; if asked, make it up; if questioned, deny it. It had been drilled into us since we were kids, tell them fucking nothing, but it meant that every single relationship in your life was up for questioning. It meant that there were things you wouldn't even tell your own reflection. And that's when the phone calls started.

I had been set up with a new house in the Ardoyne, after my ma died, after I blew our own fucking house sky-high, everybody had gathered round, and everybody had sorted me out, because The Boys were good like that, you could rely on them, but then the phone calls started happening, with no one at the other end, and at strange times of night. I'd pick up the phone and there would be silence or sometimes the sounds of a room, maybe, the sound of movement in a small room, an echoes, sometimes even the sound of breath, but no one would speak. I'd yell at them, what the fucking what is this, you shower of bastards; no change, in the sound, or the breath, or the silence, no change. I'd be sitting on the stair, with a chatsby in my hand, in the pitch dark, looking out through the frosted glass on the front door, into the night, listening to this faraway sound, this floating sound, it seemed to me, on the other end of the line, and I would fall asleep sometimes, on the stair, in the cold, and I would wake up in the morning, with the sun streaming through, and the receiver on my chest, and for a minute I would forget what had happened, or I would be confused, like my dreams were bleeding into the day, and I would recall a talk on the phone that I was having, with my ma, in heaven, and with my da there too, and they were speaking in these calm sounds that weren't really words, but that were more like somebody humming a tune, while you slept, humming 'The Old Bog Road', so as not to wake you, but to take you deeper, and sometimes they would still be there, on the other end of the phone, when I woke up, maybe they had fallen asleep too, and I would think to myself, do I sound like a song? Do I sound like a song on the other end? And I would imagine them lying there, on the stair, with the receiver curled up on their chest, and the sound of my breathing, like the tide coming in, and out, and the tide coming in, and out again, and I says to myself, it's the same person, the tide, on the other side, it's the same person what wrote me the note, it's the same silence what's speaking, and I says to myself, is it Tommy, is it as close as we came to saying what we had to say, to each other, to these silent phone calls, a saying that began in the spring of '79, and that continued for most of the year, and that at first scared the living Jayzus out of me, the living Jayzus, if I'm being honest, scared but then a comfort, a strange, scared comfort is what it was, in the night, on my own, in this empty shell of a house, this empty cell, and I took to thinking, for the first time, maybe, a little, I know it sounds crazy, mugs like you just don't understand, mugs like you will never understand, but I took to thinking for the first time about certain things, analysing what I had been doing, asking myself these serious questions, for the first time ever, and that's dangerous.

Because that was one thing we never did: we never asked ourselves any questions, in fact we lied. We lied to ourselves more than we did to anybody else. You had to. How else do you do this stuff, day in day out? If you had a working brain you would be finished, and then I says to myself, it's me on the other end, hello, is that you, Xamuel, I says to this silence on the end of the line, and I says to it, Xamuel, and it echoes, right back to me, and I lie down, and I listen to it, and I fall asleep, and maybe get connected, to heaven, maybe, where everybody is waiting for us, and where I's didn't need to be I's anymore, in the end, I's no more, and where we could step out of the game, and have a right old fucking laugh about all these I's, in the end.

*

Have you ever heard the story of Pablo's Dog, son? I can see I'm going to have to educate you here. This guy Pablo, this Spanish guy, obviously, he makes this maze into which his dog has to live in, and in order to get his food served every night in his bowl,

Pablo's Dog would have to find his way through this maze built by this Spanish madman and ring a bell with his paw, he would have to ring this bell that was connected to a system of wires and pulleys and electricity and it would drop a lump of dog food into the bowl from a hatch that was hidden in the ceiling, and Pablo's Dog was the first ever smart dog that got taught by a human's invention, because wait till I tell you, every time that dog hears a bell he would start salivating because Pablo had used the bell to program the dog so as that every time he rang it the dog would automatically get hungry.

Now, imagine if Pablo had been an Irishman. Imagine if that had been Paddy's Dog. And they had built a maze. And they were making them hungry. Like in an experiment. Just to see. Fuck me, but it doesn't even bear thinking about, right?

*

The guy what painted all of the famous Sniper At Work signs, you must have heard of this guy, he was a legend. We sparked this scheme to track him down because every time we would drive through South Armagh, Tommy would be pointing the signs out to us and one time we tried to steal one but a farmer saw us climbing up and trying to unscrew it and he came out with a shotgun and let loose at us with it, and Billy McNab, who was there because he needed some extra money, Billy McNab from round the back of me, got shot through his big toe, nightmare, so as we jump into the car and go skidding off but McNab can't get in and the farmer's taking these shots at us and Tommy won't slow down and now we've lost McNab. In the rear-view mirror I

can see him, bouncing along the road, and the farmer coming up
to him, with his shotgun held up to his eyes, and the two of them
disappearing in a cloud of smoke.

Ah fuck, we've got to go back, I says to Tommy, but Tommy's
freaked out, he probably thinks we're British agents, he says,
who else would be mad enough to go taking down Sniper At Work
signs just because they appreciate the artwork. Look, I says to
Tommy, we can go back and explain the situation and just say
that really, it was because we were so in awe of the artistry
of said artist's work, that we just had to have an original for
ourselves. And that we're proud *Green Book*-carrying radical
Fenian bastards to a man. You tell him, Tommy says. I'll stand
well behind you with my shirt as a flag.

So as we drive back and we pull into this empty farmyard. The
wind is blowing through these gasoline tanks that are all rusted
and standing there. Hello, I shout to the winds. Hello, we're the
boys you shot at. We're Provos, I shout out to this empty yard.
We're IRA boys. A voice comes from a broken window, high up.
That's an executionable offence, is what it says.

What, I says, appreciating the artistry of our own side is now
punishable by death, is it?

Can you imagine going into Auschwitz and removing one speck
of dirt? this fucking disembodied voice cries out. Auschwitz is a
memorial to the dead, I says to this voice from out of nowhere.
So is South Armagh, it says to me in return. Look, I says to it, I
just came back to clear up any potential misunderstandings and

to pick up our good friend what fell out of the car in a state of some distress, I says. Your pal lives, the voice says, but on one condition. What? I says to it. What? This isn't a matter of life or death here, is it? We police our own round here, the voice says to us. Tommy's standing behind me with his vest on waving his shirt around, on a stick, in the fog, like we're at the trenches. Look, I says to the voice, we come in peace. Well, you're in the wrong place in that case, the voice says in this mocking tone. Your pal lives, it says again, but on one condition. Okay, I says, what's your condition? That you answer a riddle, it says. I look round at Tommy and he's like that, it's the Giant fucking Sphinx, where's that cunt Barney when you need him? Alright, I says, alright, but are you seriously trying to tell me that my pal dies if I can't work out the answer? That's right, it says. By this point we're that scared we're ready to believe anything. After all, this is South Armagh. Different rules apply. Okay, I says, okay, what's this riddle needing solved? And the voice it says to us, I'd like to hear your views on art. You tell me youse are cultivated Fenians with an eye for the canvas of improvised road signs, it says. What, in your mind, is the purpose of art?

We stand there for a moment, in this silent fog, and ask ourselves some big questions. Like, what the fuck is going on? The purpose of art, in my opinion, I says to the voice eventually, is a process of raising one's self up and improving one's self. You talk like a pansy, the voice says. The purpose of art, I says to the voice (I'm taking another tack here), is to change the world, I says. You're you, the voice says, so who's going to do the changing? Can't we dream of a better world? I says to this mocking voice from out of nowhere. Oh, we can dream alright, the voice says, just don't waste my time making me look at a pretty picture of it. You, in the back there, the voice commands out of nowhere. Tommy's like that, what, me? he says, pointing to himself. You there with the white flag of surrender, the voice says. What's your take on art? I take it you don't get many visitors round here? Tommy says to the voice. It doesn't say anything in return. Voice is embarrassed, I says to Tommy. The purpose of art is to scare the shite out you, Tommy says to it. Ha ha, the voice says, that's a good one, but it doesn't say anything else. Try again, I says to Tommy. In my opinion, art is all about illuminating, Tommy says. Illuminating what? The voice is back. Yourself, Tommy says.

Art is a burning up, the voice says, and I almost felt it sigh as it says it. Look, pal, if that's the answer, can we get our friend back now? I says to it. Are either of the two of youse familiar with the term immolation? the voice says. If you're talking about what they do to them poor young kids in the homes then you can fuck right off and take Billy McNab's life while you're at it, Tommy says to it. Tommy's confused, I says to the voice, I know what you mean, you mean to pass through fire, I says. So as there's nothing left of you but a little mound of ashes, the voice says in return. Then a door opens in front of us and I look to Tommy and he nods and we walk in.

From outside it looked like an abandoned farmhouse. But as we creep through this darkened corridor we come out on a long rectangular room, the walls of which are covered in drawings and sketches, pictures of judges and juries, pictures of weeping witnesses and cold-hearted killers, men with their faces in their

222

hands and women screaming in accusation, men with their hands tied and held by armed guards. I'm in here; I get this terrible feeling that there's a drawing of me here somewhere. We're in here somewhere, I says to Tommy. I've just got that feeling, I says. This is the work of a courtroom artist, I says to him, he might have come across us, or somebody we know, at some point.

At the end of the room there's a shadow behind a table. It doesn't move or signal or otherwise make a sound. We get closer. It's Billy McNab, and he's tied and gagged in a chair. Plus he's bollock naked. Fucking hell, he stripped McNab, Tommy says. McNab's signalling with his eyes, up above, and now there are footsteps, dragging and banging footsteps, going across the floor above us, and approaching the top of the stair. Boom. Schlup. Boom. Schlup. Boom. Schlup. It's like the walking dead. A figure appears on the stair. He's carrying something heavy in his arms. Tommy pulls a chatsby from the band of his trousers. What the fuck is this? he says. Don't be stupid, the voice says. I'm no threat to you. I was just pulling your leg. Who the fuck ransoms hostages with riddles about art?

And then he reveals himself, as a burnt man, with no skin on his face. There is something cradled in his left arm, something moving. In his right hand he holds a crumpled leaf. He holds the leaf out in front of him. Here, he says, I offer you an old wrinkled leaf for a prize, he says. Tommy puts his hand out, I can see he is shaken, but he puts his hand out and the burnt man drops the shaking leaf into his palm. In his left arm the man is holding what appears to be a child in filthy blankets. Balanced on the child's head is an old paper plate to prevent the ashes from the cigarette that is fixed between his lips from falling onto the baby's face and burning it. Who did this to you? Tommy says to him. Art, he says. Art did this to me. I am the one what paints the sniper signs, he says. We've always wanted to meet you, Tommy says.

It's okay, Ron, the burnt man says, and the farmer who we saw earlier and who had shot at us in the road comes out of a back room with his shotgun. Fix our guests some drinks, he says to him, and the farmer nods and goes through to the kitchen and brings back a bottle of Bushmills and some glasses. Sure at first I thought youse were just exceptionally brave members of Special Branch, the burnt man says to us, but then I thought to myself, there is no one that brave in Special Branch. We all had a good laugh about that one. That's why I went ahead and tied up your man, though, the burnt man says. Just in case. You can go ahead and untie him, he says to us. Sure, we'll just leave him like that for a bit, Tommy says, and he sits down next to McNab at the table and cracks open the Bushmills. McNab is signalling with his eyes but Tommy's having none of it. Please yourself, the burnt man says.

How did you get into the painting of the signs, Tommy asks him, and the burnt man takes us back to the year of 1972 and the wake of the Bloody Sunday massacre when a crowd of 20,000 people converged on the British embassy in Merrion Square and burnt the fucking building to the ground. I was an art student, just graduated, this burnt man says to us, and I went along to the demonstration. The occupants of the building were quick to flee and the word went round that we were going to torch the block. I had my paints with me. Me and a girlfriend, we climb over a wall round the back and jimmy a window. We find the stair and make our way up to the top floor, there's an attic level. I'm a war artist, I'm telling myself, I'm Eric Ravilious in a spitfire over Iceland, I says to myself, I'm going to paint the building as it falls, I'm going to capture revolution on the canvas as it happens, I want my canvas to be licked by the flames, I'm enflaming myself with all this talk and I tell my girlfriend, go, lock me in, don't let me chicken out now, and she obeys, we had rehearsed this, we both knew it would be hard, but we had agreed that we would not allow me to back out, we agreed to burn all of our bridges so that we had no choice but to witness history, and to capture it, in its passing, and so she locks me in, she wedges a chair up against the door so as there is no way I can leave and says she'll come and free me at the last minute and she goes back downstairs and joins the mob and all the while she says that she feels like she is in two places at once and the thing is, that is exactly how I felt myself, that I was out there, participating, and yet in here, recording, what a feeling it was, right then, and I heard glass breaking and shouts and the crowd were squeezed all of the way down the street and were moving in one motion, it was all of us, moving as one, only with me looking back at us at the same time, and I started to paint, I started to mix the colours and I started to apply them to the canvas I had brought with me, this recycled canvas, where I had been painting over and over and over again, so that there were all these layers already on it, and I look down at the faces, looking up, I'm looking down at the faces down below, some of whom are singing, some of whom are screaming, some of whom are lighting improvised petrol bombs and hurling them through the windows, it's a carnival of destruction, and the faces are screaming and contorting and that's all I can see, I can't see history anymore, I can't see a myth or a legend, just faces that are screaming, but I've come to paint the scene and how can I, and then I give it two eyes, it just comes to me, I reach out toward the canvas and I give it two eyes, dot, dot, just like that, with two gestures I give the scene a face, I draw a slit of a mouth in a single gesture, a crude triangle for a nose in an unbroken line, waves for hair, basically I have painted this wretched childlike face and now I'm paralysed, I came here to draw history, I came here to paint an epic and all I can come up with is the crude mocking face of a five-year-old, and it was terrifying. I could feel the walls melting, I could feel the floor below giving way, I could hear the cracking of the construction, the crumbling of this edifice. And all that it stood for was this contorted face, looking up, and screaming in anger and frustration. I took my fingers and I edged a tear in the canvas where the mouth was, by this point the smoke was coming in under the door, I tore a hole where the mouth should be and I forced my fingers through the gap, and then I clenched my hand into a fist, and then I buried my arm as far as it would go down the throat of this grotesque, primitive face, and then I felt it, soft in my hand, I felt my fingers touch it, and I went to recoil but no, I pushed myself to embrace it, and I felt the skin give way, and what was inside the skin was soft and bright, and scared, and at that moment I felt myself step out of my skin altogether and leave the old skin behind, there on the floor, which was art, art is the skin you step out of and that you leave behind, I had been purified, in other words, and cured of art, in that moment, and what was soft and bright and scared had been brought to light, and I spent many months in hospital, received skin grafts and specialist care beyond compare, my girlfriend visited me loyally and never once did she look at me in fear, or in sorrow, or in pity. Rather, she looked at me as a hero of our time and I said to myself, is this what it takes, does it take the turning inside out of what is human to be a hero these days, does it take the change into a terror in order to check terror itself, I says to myself, and I became a court reporter, yes, these are my drawings all over the walls, boys, have a good look, you might even find yourselves in there, take it all in, I was the burnt man, sat in the corner of the court, as the Brits condemned wild young boys, boys who would have been artists had they been as uncomfortable in their skins as I was, and here I was again, attending history, only this time I had a new understanding of the face, by which I mean, I understood how faces were worn, or at least, this is what I came to as a court artist, I came to understand that the flesh is a prison and a penance but that there is something, in the face, that is communicating – hear me out – in the folds of the face there is something that wants to break free, but that is fixed there, as a face, which is an alignment of pain, and a direction, as sure as the cross is, my friend, as sure as the cross is, buddy, you better believe it, and in my role of court artist I drew new faces every day, I drew the faces of the condemned, the faces of their distraught loved ones, the faces of victims and the faces of spiteful judges and contemptuous paramilitaries, on all sides, I wanted to understand how to wear your skin, was there a secret to it, could some people wear it better than others, and then I says to myself, what's the rush, there's no shortage of flesh in this world, but there's something there to be learnt, for sure, something about guilt and innocence, and how there is no difference between a guilty and an innocent face, between a face that is true and one that is not, except for one thing, except for one detail, and that I would describe as composure, but then I lost my job, they found

227

out I had lied on my application and that I had been involved in the storming of the British embassy, although really I was a victim of that storming as much as a perpetrator, and they fired me, just as my girlfriend became pregnant, yes, I know what you are thinking, I was still able to have sex even though most of my body recoiled from anything but the softest touch, but sometimes the softest touch is all you need, my friend, and we came back here, to this farmhouse, which was my father's, and his father's before him, and tried to make ends meet, and The Boys came and visited us one day and they says to me, we hear you're an artist, we need artists onside, he says, we need you to redo the road signs of Armagh, we need you to scare the shite out of anyone who shouldn't be down here, if you know what I mean, and I says to them, okay, so why don't we make them run the gauntlet, why don't we paint all of these implied threats and stick them up on road signs at odd spots in order to set the fear of God in them, or the fear of a sniper, at least, and I says to myself, I'm a war artist at last, but still I was haunted by these faces, these faces that would come staring at me in dreams, these composed faces and these screaming, twisted faces that were taunting me and that were caricatures of faces, what was I to do with faces, faces, faces, and that's when I realised, I'm painting memorials, South Armagh is one great big war memorial, and that's when I began incorporating the faces, look, take a look at this, the burnt man says to me, and he hands me a Sniper At Work painting, a red-rimmed triangle with a figure holding a rifle, looking out, and the figure has the face of a child's drawing of a little girl, a crude little girl like a doodle in the margins or the wall of a toilet. The sniper has the face of a little girl, I says to him, I never noticed that before, and he says, she is the daughter of a Republican prisoner,

228

he says to me, and then he shows me some more, I draw a new face every day, he says to me, the drawn faces of snipers are all of children, he says, and he has painted them like strange angels from children's scrapbooks, and now it's clear that they are leaning on clouds, they have rifles along the battlements of the clouds, that the burnt man has painted the snipers of South Armagh as a band of feral children with crude, mocking faces, defending the ramparts of heaven, and I says to him, what happened to your girlfriend, and a little drop of ash falls from his lips and hits the paper plate he has sat on his poor baby's head, and he says to us, my girlfriend is an artist in the women's prison, where she is handcuffed to another woman twenty-three hour a day, it's a durational work, is what the burnt man says, a work that will take many years to complete, he says, and that will remodel her face and her body. An artist, in wartime, is taken prisoner, he says, because an artist, in wartime, is the one that must draw the fire. In order to burn it down? Tommy says to him. Does the artist draw the fire so as he holds it in his hands and he can use it himself? But the burnt man doesn't answer, even as his crooked body takes the form of a question mark in front of us. Illuminating, you called it, he says to Tommy. Lighting up, you says. It is the state of my body, he says to us, and just then McNab has somehow worked the gag out his mouth with his tongue and what the fuck is this, he says, can I just remind you that I am tied up naked right next to you with a burst toe as youse are having this conversation about the meaning of art. Listen to the fucking *Mona Lisa* here, Tommy says, and he points to McNab, that enigmatic smile is well overrated, he says to us. Can we buy a painting off you? Tommy says to the burnt man. I've always wanted to own an original Sniper At Work, he says.

And that is the story of how Tommy came to have an original
Sniper At Work above the mantelpiece in his bedroom with the
face of a screaming Miracle Baby that the burnt man had drawn
specially. But when I went back to the farmhouse with Barney,
a few month later, to introduce him and to get him to do one
with his wee cousin in it, he was gone. The farm was completely
abandoned, and all over the walls there were these gaps, these
stained squares where all of his court drawings had hung.
Whatever happened to that baby, I says to myself, and was it
even a baby at all, and then I looked on the floor and I saw that
there were folds of skin, like he had stepped out of his burnt skin
altogether, and left it behind, and I thought about his face, his
burnt gums all peeled back, his lidless eyes and his missing ears,
and I imagined taking my fingers and working them into his
mouth and down his throat and what I would find there, would it
be soft and light, and could I hold onto it, could I put my fingers
around it and bear its touch? And I thought no, no, I can't bear
it, and I says to Barney, wait for me here, I says, I feel something
like a panic attack coming over me and I run round the back and I
take a leak and I pish all over my hands and I rub them together
and I says, thank fuck for skin, and what we can touch with, and
what we can keep apart with, amen.

*

I take to following Kathy round the streets but at first I never
saw anything out the ordinary. She would get out of work at her
usual time, which was about four or five in the evening, she'd still
be wearing her uniform (the one we used to make love in) and
normally she would head over to the Bankmore Square and she'd

meet her husband Davy there, he'd be sitting on a bench, reading the papers, waiting for her, and they'd kiss, and they'd sit there a while, before heading off, but as the nights started drawing in she was more likely to get a taxi, and there were times when I asked a taxi to follow her, a taxi I could rely on, a boy that I knew, and we traced her back to this house, this new house they had, out Ballygomartin way.

Then there were the nights when she would walk home on her own, seemingly aimlessly, taking different routes every time, and I would follow her, and I'm not kidding you, there were times where she just disappeared into thin air. Like, for instance, I would let her get round a corner, just a little bit ahead of me, but by the time I turned onto the street she would be gone, this long street with no turn-offs and she has just . . . risen up, and floated away. I would search in the doorways and behind the cars and down the lanes but there would be no sign of her, and once, and I swear to Christ this actually happened, I saw her disappear right in front of my eyes.

Walking through the Woodvale Park in the evening and there's plenty of people around. I'm following Kathy from a distance. She's walking in front of me and she's looking round, looking round like she's about to open a secret trapdoor and disappear but she doesn't want anyone to see its location, in back of things, but then that's exactly what she does, she steps through a secret trapdoor, she walks past a tree and then she doesn't come out the other side. At first I think I'm caught, that I've been nabbed, that she's seen me and she's hiding behind the tree to try and surprise me, but I circle round the other side so as that I can get a good look, and there is nobody there. She opened that secret trapdoor in mid-air and she stepped right through it. But here's the weirdest thing. I'm standing there and I can hear footsteps. I can hear the click of heels but there is *nothing making the sound*. I hear the footsteps go right by me, it's her, and she's invisible. And I think back to her escape, when we kidnapped her, how as when I had gone back she was just a pair of heels on a chair, and I says to myself, was she really there, was she there the whole time, is the invisible right in front of us, can't they still be seen, and of course she says that being invisible was the greatest power you could ever have, in Ireland.

I listened as the heels walked off, on their own, right past a group of people, these invisible legs that I had once had wrapped around me go marching past, and nobody paid it any attention whatsoever. And that's when I realised that Belfast is full of ghosts, that Belfast is haunted in the daytime and that nobody pays any attention to any of them, no one bats a fucking eyelid when a disembodied woman goes by them in the park, because it's just another ghost of Belfast. But then I think it's all the superheroes and the comic books we've been reading, it's starting to come off the page. Or maybe it's just that it makes you start noticing things that other people don't, like invisible forces, or maybe it's the invisible forces that start seeking you out, you know, because they see they've got a soft touch here. These guys are primed to believe in me, they're saying to themselves, with these guys I can get away with murder. Daemons. Maybe there are invisible daemons swarming all around us. Think about it. If you were a black daemon, where is the first place you would go? Where would you be most at home? Where would you find the most people willing to do your work? Northern Ireland. Belfast. It makes perfect sense. Fucking invisible daemons. There's a war in Ireland alright. In fact there are thousands of them.

Then one night I see Tommy. I'm following Kathy as usual. We're back in the park where she was took invisible and I catch sight of Tommy up ahead. He's sitting on a bench, reading the *Reader's Digest*, or pretending to. I freeze. I turn away and light a fag. I keep my distance. I look back round and Kathy has gone straight over to him. She leans down, and he kisses her on the lips, and my heart is in my throat and it's choking me half to death. She sits down next to him. How long has this been going on? Since the days of the Europa? Kathy gives Tommy something; it's all wrapped up like a present. He opens it but just stares at it. Whatever it is, he doesn't take it out. Then he leans over to her and they embrace. Is that Kathy crying there? She has her head on his shoulder. I can't make it out. They sit for a few minutes, talking. They kiss on that bench. Kathy puts her hands round his head and looks straight into his eyes. Then she gets up and she walks away. Tommy sits there, watching her go, watching the way her hips move, the way her hair runs down her back, the way she holds her handbag, high, on her shoulder. We're both watching her, only I'm watching Tommy, watching her, and I'm thinking, she was mine, once, but not anymore, and I feel a terrible sense of vertigo, and hopelessness, and I go tumbling into the past, where there is no love anymore, only lovers.

*

I start to obsess, I sit up all night, and I remember, I don't know what to do, crazy me but I start to wondering. I start to wondering, because I didn't say but after that last time, when Tommy collapsed in the street there, he got fitted with an artificial heart, I mean a pacemaker, for his weak heart. They put this thing inside him that shocks his heart every time it's starting to take a funny turn on him, but he didn't like to talk about it, you couldn't bring it up with him, because he wasn't under the control of his own heart, is what I'm sat up all night speculating.

*

Then one night I follow Kathy and she heads off on her old route over to the Bankmore Square. Her man Davy is waiting for her. But it turns into a scene. They start having this argument. Davy gets up and starts pacing up and down in front of her. He's agitated. She has her head in her hands. Then at one point he turns on her. He leaps at her on the bench and he gets her by the throat. Now he's screaming in her face. You fucking stupid bitch, he's saying to her, I can hear him from where I'm standing, you fucking stupid bitch, he's shouting. I starts to run toward them, and it's like I take off.

It's like I take off and I'm speeding, through the air, across the park, I'm flying at incredible speed, people's heads are turning, you've seen this ghost, alright, go shooting cross the park like a dart and take her man Davy straight out the game. I slam into him at speed and the bench goes over and the three of us collapse on top of each other. I pick Davy up by the lapels of his jacket and

I drag him to one side. I push him down into the ground. With my left arm I crush his windpipe and with my right I'm pummelling his face like a fucking piston.

Kathy's behind me, trying to pull me off. Stop it, you're going to fucking kill him, she's shouting. I keep at it. He's unconscious and I'm still pummelling him. His head is fucking sinking into the dirt. I'm burying this cunt alive. I can hear people shouting in the distance. Somebody is calling for the peelers. I get up and I touch Kathy on the shoulder. I did it for you, Kathy, I says to her. He was attacking you, I says to her, he might have killed you. I did it to protect you, darling, I says to her, but she pushes me away. Don't call me darling, you fucking headcase, she says to me. I can see people running toward us. A fucking headcase, that hurt, because I was starting to feel like a fucking headcase. I'd completely fucking blown it, I was seeing ghosts disappearing into thin air, and now I could fly. I did it for us, I says to her, and then I take off, into the air, like a bullet, and I don't look back.

*

We get the word that Barney's wife, Shona, has passed away from the cancer, at the hospice. It's a sin, so it is. I drop into the shop the next day. I'm hoping to speak to Barney on his own. I'm thinking of bringing all of this up with him. Wee Robin is sorting through the comics behind the desk. But Tommy and your man Del Brogan are already there. They're in the back room looking at some painting that your man Del Brogan has recommended Tommy should buy. He's a local artist, I hear your man Del Brogan say from behind the glass.

I'm sorry, Barney, I says to him, and I put my hand on his shoulder. He barely looks up from his comic. She's in a better place, he says to me. Sure, it was a long time coming, he says. That's all he says. Then he goes back to reading his comic. I knock on the door at the back. Is this a private auction or can anybody bid on this pish? I says to them. What do you think of this? Tommy says to me and he holds up this painting of the *Titanic* that your man Del Brogan is acting as the agent for or something.

It's a painting of the ship, out at sea, and with a single passenger on the deck, a passenger that looks more like a pilgrim, more like one of the Founding Fathers of America, than a passenger on the *Titanic*. What the fuck is that on the deck, I says to them, fucking Benjamin Franklin? It's a naive work, Tommy says to me. That's deliberate. Then your man Del Brogan corrects him. It's more of a neo-expressionist work, really, your man Del Brogan says. Aye, Tommy says, squinting at the picture, aye, you're right, actually, he says.

In the painting the *Titanic* is heading directly for this great iceberg that is rising up out of the water, this iceberg that looks like a daemon and that is rising up, white, like the moon, from beneath the waves. I'll take it, Tommy says. I'm a fan of the abject impressionists, he says. Neo-expressionists, your man Del Brogan says to him. That's what I'm saying, Tommy says to him. Sure, it's a shame about Shona, isn't it? I says to them. But the two of them are just sat there, staring at this painting, in silence, and neither of them says a thing.

*

A week later and it's my birthday at The Shamrock. Everybody is there. Tommy has booked your man Del Brogan to sing and he's fucking selling his records from a stall in the lobby for him. Tommy was spending more and more time with your man. We didn't see him as much as we used to. Here's your present, you bellend, he says to me. Pay good heed, he says, and then he hands me this cardboard-tube thing. I've got Moira with me. Barney's there with Wee Robin, he's brought her along, he doesn't sit about, this one, but she's a hit, and she's talking away with all the other women, joking with Moira and Patricia. Robin has got some mouth on her, Moira says to me. She's some laugh, so she is. Sure, Shona hasn't even decomposed yet, I says to her. Away and wheesht, you morbid bastard, she says to me. I see Mack, he's with a bunch of boys I don't recognise. I wave but he just stares right through me. Maybe he couldn't see me. I get a pint of green on the go and I open this present of Tommy's. It's a scroll, what you hang on your wall, and on it there's a poem by your man Mr Kipling called 'If'. Your man Del Brogan is up onstage. He's singing 'It's Impossible'. One of Como's best. Tommy's got him singing Como now. He'd fucking convert anybody. I sit there and I read this fucking poem, this fucking poem about how you have to harden your heart and be a man.

Everybody is communicating in secret. Everybody is speaking in silence. I sit there and I look around me. Barney's stocious. The women are having a right old laugh. Tommy's talking to your man Del Brogan by the side of the stage. Mack's hunkered down with the boys. Everybody's plotting, I says to myself. We're all fly.

We end up leaving early, it all starts getting a little messy, and we get home and Moira is so blocked that she just passes out on the couch. I go up the stair and I lie down on my bed, in my empty room, in my empty house, and I feel like I can hear footsteps . . . coming up the stair, walking around the kitchen, opening the door and sneaking out the back. But when I go downstairs to check, Moira's just lying there, snoring, on the couch, with her clothes on. I stick on the telly, *King Kong*, what a show. The biggest monkey that ever lived has a tiny little woman in his hands and is standing on top of the Empire State Building trying to swat airplanes. He loved that woman, so he did. He was just acting on instinct. Everybody is communicating in secret. Everybody is speaking in silence. I get up and I hang the Mr Kipling poem on the wall above the mantelpiece, then I fall asleep, next to Moira, with the TV on.

*

I need some time away, a chance to relax, I feel like I'm going round the bend. I take a job down South, an easy job. I borrow the van for two week. All I need to do is to bring back a wee arms haul from Galway. See you later. They wave me through the checkpoint on the border. Fuck, okay, that's never happened to me before. The key to being invisible is to stand out so completely that it's like a fucking optical illusion, is what I'm telling myself as I glide across the border in a van with a painted Mickey Mouse on the side. The drive is sweet. The sun is beaming out the heavens. I thank God I'm alive to see a day like today. I drive down through Dundalk and on to Dublin and I'm about to scoot across the M4, just nip across the country, when I change my mind and take a detour.

I mind how we used to go our holidays to Kilkee. We used to stay in the caravan. Summers down there would break your heart. I decide to revisit it, even though this is the autumn, now, that I'm seeing it in.

I pull up at the beach in Kilkee and I walk along the front, smoke a fag perched up on an old stone wall. I'm staring out to sea. I'm watching this young girl changing into a swimming costume beneath a towel on the sand, a pale Irish beauty in the soft light of the South, a little smudge of colour in the distance. There's nobody else around except for a pair of old dears, sitting in their car, drinking their tea. Even the ocean is quiet this afternoon, sneaking up on us with a whisper. I watch as the girl walks out into the water. She doesn't pause for a second. She keeps walking without looking back until the water is up to her armpits.

Then she dives into the waves ( ).
These moving waves (what breaks/like a silent) mirror.
These silent waves (what moves/without making) sound.
Doesn't she feel the cold?

I get back into the van and I drive further down the coast because I'm heading for Loop Head now, in my heart, although I hadn't planned it. But now I want to see the lighthouse there. My father would drive us to the lighthouse when I was a kid. The two of us had a secret cave nearby, where we would build stone monuments in the summertime. On the way down I pull up to a town that's barely a single street in the rain and take a walk around the graveyard. Now it feels cold enough to snow. A young couple are taking photographs of each other beside the stones. Get in the photo, I says to them, and I take a picture of the two of them in the cold rain together. I could've almost swore that it was the same young girl that had disappeared into the sea earlier. But that would be impossible. I make it to Loop Head just as it's starting to get dark. The fog is coming in from the sea as I pull up. There's another car in the car park, some clown is doing the karate moves in the headlights while his girlfriend sits in the car and reads her magazines. I park up on the other side and I sit there and watch him for a bit. He's facing the car, doing all these moves in slow motion, and behind him his shadow is huge on the fog. He gets back in the car and they switch the lights off. I can't see them anymore in the dark. I'm guessing they're planning on staying the night, which is what I'm planning to do myself. I dig the wee black-and-white portable out the cupboard and I make myself a big bap and cheese and crack open a cold green one; the news is on. The lighthouse starts up. The light sweeps through the van as I sit there, in the dark, drinking, and now it's the H Block protests. Wing shifts in the Blanket Blocks, punishment beatings, rectal searches over mirrors, sugar on your porridge if you behaved yourself, prisoners being forced to parade naked, the use of torture as standard procedure; we knew all about that, everybody did. But the woman on the TV says nothing about any of it. Instead she talks about screws being executed when they're off duty, and she compares their killers to animals. It was animalistic, this killing, she says. I killed the TV dead and I walked outside and I stood there, in the dark. The beam of the lighthouse, lighting up the fog in the clouds, is what heaven used to look like in the bibles they would give you back when you were a wee kid. Across the way I can hear the young couple screwing in the back seat of their car. It's heaven for them alright.

And I thought about all The Boys in the H Blocks, sitting there, freezing, in their blankets, getting the shite kicked out them on a regular basis. Boys I grew up with. Boys what were just like me.

For some reason, when you're in Belfast, you don't tend to spend that much time thinking about this stuff. You don't get philosophical about it, for this reason or for that, but mostly because there just isn't time. Because Belfast will get you in its teeth as soon as welcome you. But see as soon as you get some distance from it, that's when it hits you. That it's madness. That it's complete madness. That this is not what God's earth was made for. What was God's earth made for? God's earth was made for pulling up next to the sea, in the dark, and shagging your bird in the back seat of your car. That is what God's earth was made for. And look what we did with it.

*

In the morning the car is gone and I'm on my own. I take a walk along the edge of the cliffs, trying to find where me and my da climbed down to the cave. There's a little path at one point but it wasn't anything like I minded. The way I remembered it was like climbing down this sheer cliff with your fingers and toes, grasping, and with the sea, crashing, miles beneath you, but this was more like a series of steps cut out of the rock, but there was a cave down there, right enough, a cave you had to climb back up and into, a cave with a ledge that stuck out into the sea, and I climbed up and I walked back in there, and in the corner there was a tower of stones, big stones running to small stones, till about half the height of my body. I couldn't say if it was the one that me and my da built so long ago now in the past. I really couldn't say, though probably not. How could something as precarious as that last so long? Even so, I make another tower next to it, about half its size again, and that was me and my da, then, me and my da, standing there, staring out at the Atlantic Ocean together. Who knows, maybe no sinner ever came here. Maybe it was just for us.

*

One night I've got the telly on, in the camper van, in County Clare, in the dark, at the foot of this lighthouse, and it's the usual flagrant pish. The usual wilful misreporting, the usual foul propaganda. A crackdown in the H Block 'caused' by the popping of an off-duty screw in Belfast. It's late. I change the channel. The boxing is on. There are two kids climbing into the ring, two brothers with their arms round each other, a fighter and his trainer. On the back of both their T-shirts it says the word Dad. I close my eyes. I'm starting to drift off. I can feel the beam of the lighthouse passing over my eyelids . . . every few seconds in time . . . and I feel myself . . . going under . . . Then I hear a noise, like a kitten, like a kitten miaowing, and I open up my eyes. I look around but I can't see anything moving. Then I hear it again. It's coming from inside the television. That's when I realise they're showing a whole different programme altogether.

*

Kathy's on the telly, or inside the telly, and she's all tied up in there, bound and with a silk hanky inside her mouth, is a gag,

baby, a baby-blue silk hanky stuffed in her mouth is a gag, her
long red hair run wild, baby her lipstick is smeared, and she is
making the noise of a kitten. And she looks outside the screen,
toward me, and in her eyes it's as clear as any dream, it's a
masquerade, in her eyes, red lady, it is all a charade, and as soon
as it comes to me this music starts up, with this crackling noise,
this music from out of the past, and Como's voice is come in, on
the back of it, or is it Tommy, come in

> lady, dressed in jade,
> hold me tight at the masquerade
> if the music halts here,
> then my heart will waltz here,
> right on

things is a pretend. An awful smile, she smiles, as willing victim.
It's unmistakable, around her soft, wet, blue silk gag. And from
out of the screen a pair of hands can be seen, spread her thighs,
part the lips, of her labia. There's a face buried between her
legs and though her thighs are in the way it is wearing a black
balaclava. Her thighs are tensed up, her legs, tensed up too, her
body, it is rising, in pleasure. And the man in the bally unbuttons
his fly, why, says I, with the bally unbuttons, he's right at the
edge of the screen, and he starts to make love to her, savage love,
forcing himself inside of her, and all the time she's watching me
and she's smiling, even when the face in the bally leans over,
puts its tongue between her lips wet silk, even then she is looking
at me, and she is smiling. As she closes her eyes and bites down
on the silk, her voice is muffled as it echoes in cruelty; stop, you
make me dizzy, she is singing, you make me dizzy, in cruelty, is

her song. And the man gasps, he holds himself inside her, then withdraws. Someone else steps up and puts his cock between her legs. At first I think it's Tommy, it's only fucking Tommy, somewhere in my lonesome mind, screwing her there, but then I think it's Davy, it's Kathy's man Davy, who has been orchestrating the entire thing, and I'm watching her legs, tensed up, he's slapping her tits, her teeth, pressed against her lips, the soft wet silk of her mouth, and her red nails, in his back, as he penetrates her, and black eyes, black eyes as inscrutable as any swan's

> twelve o'clock is chiming
> on the clock up above
> now, if you unmask your heart
> I'll love you,
> love you

the after-image through the noise and the static, before it re-forms: there is a scar between her breasts, a deep scar, between her breasts, as she looks toward me and she opens her mouth

> ba-by,
> she looks to me,
> bites her lips,
> gives her tits up
> to Tommy's dead ringer
>
> and the place in between
> you and I can be seen
> as a prising apart
> with your fingers,

taking hold of the heart,
and grasping it, hard
in your fist,
is the work
of a singer

and its armoured skin,
as it wriggles
within,
baby, feels like the first time,
forever

and something appears in its place, a face that has malformed
as Miracle Baby, talking noise in a lingo that is impossible to
understand, a grotesque face, a howling face, a horror show, but
then I catch a word of it, here and there, and it's the Irish lingo,
Miracle Baby is transmitting in the Irish lingo so as we cannot be
intercepted and no one must know, and though I couldn't speak
the Irish lingo back then, still I catch the names, your man Del
Brogan, Davy, Tommy, and I says to myself, the masquerade is
up, the game is over, it is finished.

*

The Anomaly awakens to the cosmic darkness.

He rushes forward, blind, his arms stretched out in front of him.

He rises off the ground in a straight line.

He plunges forward through the air.

The darkness is limitless and impenetrable.

Wait!

High above him he can make out a single source of light.

Where is he?

He is in the inverted tower.

The Forever Family had entered the negative space of the inverted tower.

The same tower that they had razed and buried.

The Anomaly's memory was shot. What happened after that?

He had a brief vision of The X-Ray Kid turning his gaze on him. Of his bones turning white-hot with pain. Of his insides boiling. Of The X-Ray Kid parting the darkness like flesh and stepping through it. It was a trap!

As he flies toward the light high above him he starts to make out details.

There is something hovering in the pupil of light.

There, suspended in the centre, is Neutrino, crucified, and in great agony.

Hold still, my brother, The Anomaly booms and his words echo across the vast gulf of the inverted tower.

He flies through the cavernous void toward him.

Neutrino's hands and feet disappear into the reflective luminescence that holds him.

Hurry, Neutrino screams, I am impaled by the light.

Who did this, friend? The Anomaly demands of him.

The Sons Of Men, Neutrino says. The Sons Of Men have given up their girdle around the waist of the warrior and have come down to earth. I saw them! Ye Gods, I saw them! They were in conference with The X-Ray Kid. I disturbed them. He has brought the very stars to their knees.

Quick, free me, Neutrino cries.

The Anomaly plunges his hands into the great reflective field that holds Neutrino suspended above the void. It burns his hands like acid.

How? How has he done this? The Anomaly demands. How has he come to have conference with the souls of the stars?

By an act of disobedience so great that the entire universe stands rearranged, Neutrino says.

Thought bubble: truly this was to be my fate, The Anomaly thinks, this is the fate that was predicted for me when I was first given my name.

Neutrino's arm comes free. It burns and pulses as if flitting in and out of reality.

Then the other arm. He slumps forward onto The Anomaly's shoulders.

Hold fast to me, brother, The Anomaly tells him. Then he turns and with Neutrino on his back he rockets into the darkness, tearing Neutrino free from the coruscating field of light with a great cry.

They circle back around and survey the destruction they have wrought.

A tiny fissure hisses and pops with otherworldly radiation.

The X-Ray Kid is not the only one capable of rending the very fabric of reality, The Anomaly announces. As long as I have my name that destiny is still mine.

Then they pass through the tear, like crossing transdimensional razor wire, and begin their pursuit of the one that has betrayed them.

Next time: The Fury Of The Stars!

*

Tommy was shot in the head and killed instantly on his way
to The Shamrock on the 13th October 1979. He was with his
partner, Patricia, who was drenched in his blood and his brains.
It felt like the end of the world.

*

His ma collapsed and ended up in the same ward as Patricia
suffering from the civilian equivalent of shell shock. The Boys
called a meeting and Mack was in tears when he stood in front of
us. Barney's sat there weeping next to me. How could it happen
to Tommy, how could it happen to our golden boy? Your man Del
Brogan was there. I smoked a fag and stared at him and says
nothing and I'll tell you, the cunt seemed uncomfortable. Where
were you when Tommy got hit? I says to him. Don't start, Mack
says to me, don't even fucking start, the last thing we need is for
us to start infighting. This cunt's not even upset, I says to him.
We all express it in our own way, your man Del Brogan says.
Where were you when Tommy got hit? he says to me. You believe
the fucking balls on this cunt? Fuck youse all, I says to them, and
I storms outside.

Barney comes out after me. Come on, Sammy, he says to me. We
need to pull together here, we need to stay cool for Tommy's sake.
We need to make sure his murder doesn't go unavenged. I sat on
the wall outside his house in Jamaica Street and I cried that hard
it felt like I was crying blood.

We received a communication from the FSV: nothing to do with them. In fact they were calling off hostilities. In the wake of Tommy's death everybody was coming together. Fuck me, there'll be peace in Ireland next, I says to Barney. Don't fucking count on it, he says. Turns out that the screw what had been popped, the screw whose death had caused all of the beatings and recriminations in the H Block that I heard about on the telly in Clare, turns out it was Tommy what had taken him out. Best bet then was that it was UDA or UDF or UVF men working in collusion with the Brits that had popped Tommy in return. But how did they know it was him? There had been no witnesses to the shooting. The getaway car had been destroyed. Tommy even wore a bally when he did the deed. Somebody had talked, we had a fucking squealer in the ranks, and I was sure I knew who it was.

That night I go home on my own and I sit on the couch and I look at that Mr Kipling poem Tommy had given me. That poem that he probably couldn't even read himself. Where did he even hear about it? Then I read them lines, them famous lines, and I realise. I realise what he was trying to tell me. Make of your heart a mighty fortress. It was the most beautiful gift anybody ever gave me.

*

Tommy's funeral was a week later and we got to go and see him at the funeral home where he was lying there in a coffin, in a room of his own, with the lid propped up against the wall, just like my old da, and his da before him. Thomas James Kentigern, it says, in gold letters. The kingdom of heaven awaiteth Thomas James Kentigern. I looked down at his face, it was a heartbreaking mess of stuff and I couldn't bring myself to touch it. I tried but I couldn't. I'm so sorry, Tommy. Everything my da taught me was out the window with that handsome face and now it was a jigsaw puzzle. I could see the cellophane wrapped around his arms, sticking out from the sleeves of his suit. This beautiful dog-tooth suit. And everybody had put photos and notes and mementoes into the coffin like it was Como himself that had passed on. I took a silk handkerchief out my top bin and dropped it in. I says to myself, as human beings we've been doing this forever. It's a cycle that's been going on since the first day of God's creation. So how come it doesn't get any easier?

> In the silent Tomb we leave him
> Till the Resurrection Morn
> When his Saviour will Receive him
> And Restore his lovely Form

Thomas James Kentigern was buried with full military honours, with a pair of black gloves and a beret on his coffin and a tricolour flag led by a lone piper. Three masked soldiers let off a volley of automatic weapons over his coffin before disappearing into the Ardoyne.

*

Warm prunes. I have such a strong memory of warm prunes.

*

The next morning I drive round the Ardoyne in the car until I spot Miracle Baby and I bundle him in. Tommy's gone, he says to me. Tommy's gone away. I know, son, I says to him. I know. It's awful hard for all of us. What can you tell me, son? I says to him. Can you help us get the people what took Tommy away from us? Sure, we can just ask Tommy, Miracle Baby says. Son, Tommy's gone, I says to him. We can't talk to Tommy anymore. He's been taken away to heaven. We can talk to him in heaven, Miracle Baby says. Okay, I'm about to boot this wee retard out the car by this point. Maybe it was only Tommy that was able to get the vision out him. Then I says to him, were you sending me transmissions? Miracle Baby just giggles. Were you sending me fucking transmissions while I was down in the County Clare on my holidays? He's sitting there laughing. Sometimes my pictures go out of my head at night, he says to me. Sometimes they float away. Did you catch them? he says to me. Then he bursts out laughing. Did you catch my pictures? he says to me. Do the pictures in my mind make me a bad boy? he says but he's laughing the whole time he's saying it. You're a bad wee bastard, I says to him, if that's what's going on in your mind. By this point we're both laughing. Okay, I says to him, tell me how do we go about reaching Tommy in heaven, because I'm willing to believe anything by this point. Table-rapping, Miracle Baby says. The fuck is table-rapping? Then I realise he's talking about conducting a fucking seance. Table-rapping is what the old witches called it.

You're seriously talking about speaking to the dead, I says to him, and he says to me, I do it all the time, inside my mind. Okay, so okay. How do we do this?

We need a circle, he says, plus we need people. Five is best. Two and two and one. I'm the one, he says. You're the two and two. Who the fuck am I going to ask to do this? I can't ask any of The Boys because they'll think I'm mental. Besides, who knows what Tommy might say? Okay, so Barney I can trust, and what about his wee bird Robin, she's got him burning the joss sticks in the shop this weather, so she's probably into all this shite as well. Then I mind Beavis, our wee fucking comic book genius. That's us, two and two. Of course, I will need to tell them that I will have to fucking execute them with extreme prejudice if they reveal anything about what goes on, but I'm sure they'll understand.

*

What do you call
two Irish three-speeds?
Patrick
Fitz-
gerald, an Gerald
Fitz-
patrick,

ha ha, fucking fruit merchants.

*

A week later we meet up at the shop, after hours, and Wee Robin locks the door and gets one of her joss sticks going and we dim the lights and everybody sits round the table in a circle

Miracle Baby
Me
Barney
Beavis
Wee Robin

if any cunt can jimmy the gates of heaven, it's that wee bastard Tommy, Barney says to us. Shoosh, Wee Robin says to him, we're trying to get the atmosphere going here. We put our hands on the table so as our fingers are touching. Miracle Baby closes his eyes but I keep mine open. I'm watching everything in the room and I'm looking for signs. But nothing happens. You can hear the traffic outside. People coming and going in the street. I look at Miracle Baby and at first I'm like, for fuck sake, no way, he's got the ectoplasm coming out his neb, but then as I realise it's probably just snot, he opens his eyes, and he says to us: he's here. Tommy's here, he says.

Everybody looks around them. Not here, Miracle Baby says: here. And he points to the table in front of us where we've got one of they Weegie boards set up. He's trying to communicate, Miracle Baby says. You can break the circle now, he says. I thought you were never supposed to break the circle but I do as I'm told cause we're in the spirit world here, after all.

Okay, Miracle Baby says, everybody put a finger on the speller. Then let him talk. We put our fingers on this heart-shaped wooden speller. And the blasted thing starts moving. And it's not as if anybody is pushing it. It's more like it's hovering, like it's floating back and forth, across the letters, though unfortunately it's just talking rubbish and nonsense words and making no sense whatsoever. Ah, we're bollocksed, Barney says, this is pathetic, so it is. Wait, Beavis commands him. He's sitting there with his curly hair and his wee round glasses on and he's starting to take charge. You don't understand the spirit world, he says to us. You have no experience of travel in alternate dimensions, he says. Youse need to give it time. The recently deceased are unused to walking in the ways of the spirit. That's what he says to us. Imagine your own first primitive attempts at speech, he says to us. Let the words form, in time.

We settle back down. Everybody is silent. Watching the speller move this way and that. Everybody is silenced. As it stops. And it starts again.

>:- w-h-i-t-a-b-o-o-t-y-e -:<

Barney laughs. That's fucking Tommy alright, he says, and he still can't spell to save his fucking life.

Tell him we're grand, I says. Answer him. Sure, we're grand, Miracle Baby says to him. How are you?

>:- g-r-a-n-t-i-d -:<

He's grand, Barney says. He's saying that he's grand. How can the wee bastard be grand? He's just died. Ask him how it goes

in heaven, Wee Robin says. What's it like in heaven, Tommy?
Miracle Baby asks him.

>:- i-t-g-o-s-w-i-t-h-u-t-b-e-i-n-g -:<

What?!
then

>:- a-m-l-o-v-e-i-n-t-h-e-a-n-g-l-e-s -:<

The angels, he's fucking getting off with the angels, Barney
bursts. This is fucking Tommy for sure.

But that's not what he says, I says to them. He says: I am love in
the angles. He says: in heaven it goes without being. Maybe it's us
that don't understand. Then Beavis asks him a question. Tommy,
he says to him, what is it like to die?

The heart-shaped speller stops moving. It just sits there and
vibrates on the spot. I think to myself, he shouldn't have asked
him that. We're going to lose him. But then he's off. The speller
starts moving in these wee delicate loops, in these wee circles,
spinning from one letter to the next. The room starts to get fuzzy.
Then I hear that fucking music. That crackling hissing music like
it's come in out the past. That music that I heard before. And I
see what he's doing. I'm watching our hands, all moving together,
all coordinated, and it's like a dance. And I see what he's saying.
I watch it come alive in front of us. Then I hear it, and there's no
mistaking

>:- m-a-k-e-l-o-v-e-t-o-l-i-f-e-l-e-t-l-i-f-e-m-a-k-e-l-o-v-e-t-o-y-o-u -:<

He's singing a Como number up in heaven. What a chanter. Then
I think to myself, it's so like our Tommy. Even when he was in
the hospital and you were trying to get a straight answer out
him, even then he'd be trying to seduce you. Now here he was,
in heaven, with all the answers at his fingertips, and it was the
exact same fucking story.

*

I wait for Kathy outside the Europa every night for a week and
then I walk into the reception and ask for her. I don't recognise
any of the security guards but the wee bird Sharon that had
arranged the flowers for me and had given me the blank note
was still on reception. Hello, stranger, she says to me. Is Kathy
around? I says to her. Kathy doesn't work here anymore, she says
to me. Didn't she tell you? We had a wee bit of a falling-out, I says
to her. The end of the affair, she says. She's left a lot of clients
jangling, she says to me. A true heart-stealer, eh?

What do you mean, clients? I says to her. Sure, you don't have to
pretend with me, she says. I knew what was going on. There was
no judgement. I helped her out. We're all adults here, after all.
Naw, I says to her. You don't understand, love. We were having
a love affair, I says to her, there was no money changing hands.
Lucky you, she says to me, and she winks.

What the actual fuck; Kathy was on the game. Who the fuck else
was she sleeping with? Was Tommy paying her? How did he get

involved? And what about all the fucking press and politicians that used the hotel? Was she sleeping with both sides?

I thought about the vision I had in Clare. Kathy gagged, and her man directing. He was pimping her out. But for what? For information, maybe. But who was he working for? I decided to sit down with Barney and tell him everything.

I tell him about sleeping with Kathy at the Europa. About seeing Tommy in there once. About finding out she was a prozzer. Then I tell him that Miracle Baby sent me a message, a vision, to my mind, showing her man Davy, or was it Tommy, and your man Del Brogan, fucking her, I think. Visions, you can't trust fucking visions, that could mean anything, Barney says to me, that could mean that he's just a pervert what gets off on people fucking his wife. Do you know what they call that? Barney says to me. That's what they call a plamf. What are you talking about? I says to him. A plamf is somebody that sniffs dirty knickers, what you're trying to mean is a cuckoo. The fuck's a cuckoo? Barney says. That's nonsense. Naw, I says to him. A cuckoo is what steals eggs from other birds.

That's a fucking magpie, he says to me. Okay, so he's a fucking magpie, I says, so fucking what, the point is that I think it all ties in, I think Tommy's boasting about hitting this fucking screw and she's reported it back to Davy who is a fucking plant and who told his handlers in Special Branch, who then told their people in the UDA or the UVF or the UFF or whatever the fuck ever that Tommy was their man and where to find him. It was a planned execution, we know that. Either that, or your man Del

Brogan told her. Either way, he's a disreputable cunt.

Well, in that case, that leaves us with only one option, Barney says to me. I'm waiting for this masterplan. For this incisive analysis of my theory. Then he says to me, we just need to fucking kill every one of them. Thank fuck there is some cunt you can rely on in amongst all this.

*

We do it ourselves, I says to him. No point involving Mack or the high command. Mack's too in with your man Del Brogan. We start to staking out the house, this new house that I had followed Kathy to, out Ballygomartin way. A few afternoons here and there. The blinds are always down. The only person we ever see coming and going is a wee old woman with a crooked back pulling one of them shopping baskets with the wheels. She must live in complete fucking darkness, Barney says.

That's when I realise we're being watched. Barney, I says to him, see that car parked down the road a bit, can you make it out? Barney looks in the mirror. Aye, I can see it, he says. That car was here the other day when we were here. Two people sitting in the front, just like we are. The fucking peelers, Barney says. Got to be. By the way, I gave your man Davy a doing, I says to him. I forgot to tell you that. I gave him a complete fucking pasting when I saw him beating up Kathy in a park. Quite fucking right, Barney says to me. Cunt had it coming to him. Nice one, Sammy, you wee fucking belter. Aye, but that's not my point, I says to Barney, my point is that maybe they're onto me because of that, I says to him. Maybe they think they've been rumbled. Maybe they think that I've figured out what they're up to. We need to assume that we're being watched, and at all times. What I'm saying is maybe we can't just blaze in and kill them right off. Barney looks visibly disappointed. We peel off as fast as we can and we lose the car that's following us. Then we abandon the stake-out altogether.

*

The only thing I remember about my grandfather, the only time I can see him in my mind's eye, is when me and my ma visited him in the plots to hear that he was dying, on a summer's day. He's getting news from the doctor, my ma says to me (I'm just a wee wean at this point), we'll go and we'll meet him at the plots, she says. I mind walking up there, up this narrow path between the hedges, and the rocks in the ground, and the stones, and I could hear him from far off, from way down the bottom of the hill, coughing his lungs out, this horrible, tearing cough, and he was chopping wood up there, we could hear the axe going down and the cough and the axe going down again. And my ma goes over to him, she goes over there to touch him, but he looks at her in a way that pushes her away, a look that meant that she couldn't come to him, and he just kept at it, the axe coming down, the paralysing cough, the axe coming down again, and my ma says to me, it's a pointless cough, that's the worst of it, and she shakes her head and she looks away but she never cried and I remember thinking, it's chopping wood that's pointless, Ma, it's visiting your da in the plots that's pointless, it's a summer's day in July that has no point at all.

*

Your man Del Brogan is going on tour, Mack says to us, what about that? We're having a lunchtime drink at The Shamrock. Me, Barney, Mack and Fat Tam Fisher aka The Dark Destroller, is what everybody called him, on account of his laid-back ways, and this fella Jimmy The Grunt. All he ever did was fucking grunt. As uncouth as get out. Tommy must be turning in his fucking grave, I says to Mack. What are you talking about? Mack says. Tommy was his manager. Tommy thought he was a real talent. Fucking listen to that record they put out; it's a stone-cold fucking classic. It should have been Tommy that was going on tour, I says to him. Tommy should have been on the London stage, never mind this fucking punk rock comedian with his Rod Stewart disco numbers. Hey, Mack says to me, easy. Your man Del Brogan's brand new. Where did this cunt even come from? I says to him. Your man Del Brogan? Mack says. What's with all the questions? Mack's sitting there with his fucking long hair. He's got a badge on that says Hawkwind. The fuck is Hawkwind? Barney says to him. Hawkwind's a fucking group, you prick, Mack says. A fucking black nightmare, my friend. Sonic attack, he says to him. Barney's staring at him all confused, like. The fuck is a sonic attack? he says to him. It's like a bomb made up of sound, Mack says. That's what you sit at home and listen to? Barney says to him. Aye, Mack says. They're fucking hip. Are they Huns or are they Tims? Barney says to him. What?! The fucking Hawkwinds. Are they Huns or are they Tims? How in the fuck would I know? Mack says. What, Barney says to him, you don't check to see whether they're Huns or Tims before you submit to a sonic attack from them?

Have youse heard that U2? The Dark Destroller says, interrupting the both of them. My boy's into them, they're Tims alright. Was Perry Como a Tim? Mack asks Barney. You can bet your damn fucking life Como was a Tim, Barney says. He was a good Catholic. Never drank nor swore. Plus he was always faithful to his wife. I thought Como was a Jew, Mack says. Don't fucking start this, I says to them. Como was never a fucking Jew, Barney says, he sang all those religious songs. All those religious songs in the fucking Hebrew, you mean, Mack says. He probably did that because that's what they speak in Hollywood, Barney says. Who speaks in Hollywood? Mack says to him. The Jews, Barney says. That's what the Jews speak in Hollywood, so if you want to get right in there, you need to please the right people and press the right buttons. Have you ever seen a Hollywood movie? Mack says to him. Are any of them in fucking Hebrew? I'm talking behind the scenes, Barney says. Don't get fucking smart with me. Besides, he says, Como's Italian. You trying to tell me that's the home of the Jews? The Jews don't have a home, Mack says. That's the whole point of Israel. Exactly, Barney says. The Jews are exactly like the Catholics. So as even if Como *was* a Jew, he was as close to being a Catholic as you can actually be without getting permission from the Pope himself.

Catholics have got their own home country, The Dark Destroller says. It's called the Vatican. The Vatican isn't a country, Barney says. The Vatican *is* its own country, The Dark Destroller says. Its own rules and everything. Me and the missus goes there. You need a passport to get in and out. How many people live in the Vatican? Mack says to him. Couple a thousand, probably, The Dark Destroller says. In that case it's not a country, Mack

says, it's just a state, it's a city state. Same difference, The Dark
Destroller shrugs. The point is, you couldn't fit all the Catholics
in the world into the Vatican, Mack says. Just like you couldn't
fit them all into the Free State. The Free State's bigger than the
Vatican, The Dark Destroller says. Besides, Italy is the home of
the Catholics, we're talking the entire country. The point is that
the Jews and the Catholics have got a fuck of a lot in common,
I says to them. We're both up against it, I says. And that's the
point what Barney's trying to make. Aye, Barney says. That's
right. That's my point exactly. Como understands because he's up
against it both ways. This guy has lived it. So you're admitting
Como's half-Jewish now, are you? Mack says. Jimmy The Grunt
lets out one of his trademark grunts.

Listen, if he's descended from The Bible then he's got a bit of Jew
in him, I'll give you that, Barney says. My point is at least we
fucking know where we stand with Como and your man U2. But
these sonic attacks, my friend. I wouldn't sit through one of them
until I knew, for a fact, that it wasn't the fucking Brits trying to
erase my mind. Hawkwind are totally anti-establishment, Mack
says. Fuck does that even mean? Barney says. Does it mean
they're not into the Queen establishing British rule in Ireland?
Basically, Mack says. Now we're talking, Barney says. But if
they're so fucking anti-disestablishment then why don't we get
them over here and get them doing a fucking sonic attack for us?
Why aren't The Boys looking into these fucking sonic weaponries?

Picture it, The Dark Destroller says. Como shops up in Belfast
and the next thing you know he's doing a sonic attack for The
Boys. 'Magic Moments' reduces history to dust.

Everybody's killing themselves by this point. You should
teach your man Del Brogan to do they sonic attacks, The Dark
Destroller says. Get him into a bit of the Hawkwinds for the tour.
Fucking the Ra's new secret weapon. I wouldn't trust that cunt
with a sonic attack, I says to them. The fuck is your problem?
Mack says. I don't know, I says to them. I just get the feeling that
he's a fucking Hun in disguise. Sure, you can't go around making
wild accusations like that, The Dark Destroller says. That's
dangerous talk. And based on what? Mack says. Did your fucking
Miracle Baby see it in his crystal bollocks? It's just a feeling,
I says to them, it's just a fucking hunch. Somebody is feeding
information to the peelers. That's a fact. And whoever it is is also
responsible for Tommy getting whacked. And when I find out who
it is, I says to them, I'll fucking sonic-attack the shite out them.
Could just as easily be you, Mack says to me. Don't fucking even
go there, I says to him, don't you fucking dare, I don't give a fuck
who you are but if you fucking say that again I'll put my fucking
fist down your throat.

Easy, easy, The Dark Destroller says. Cool it, man. We all need
to calm down. This is what they want. This is how they intend to
divide us. I loved Tommy, I says to them, I fucking loved that guy.
There were no secrets between us. Jimmy The Grunt gives out
a low fucking grunt in response. I stand up and I look round the
table at the lot of them, then I walk out of there without a word.

*

Tinned soup,
that's another one,

there's something so sad about the smell of
tinned soup.

*

Nothing was the same, though. The midnight calls had stopped.
I wasn't going down The Shamrock as much. It was almost like
being in the jail, like a dry run for the future, only more boring.
I would sit there, Moira would be asleep in bed, and I would find
myself sitting on the stair where I used to listen to the echoes on
the other end of the line, sitting there on the stair and watching
the shadows pass by in the street outside and listening, to nothing
anymore, to the sound of my own thoughts, to the dial tone, at the
end of the line.

*

*Neutrino and The Anomaly enter The Dead Zone: The Place Of
Endless Echoes.*

*All around them, stacked in glass coffins as high as the eye can
see, are the bodies of The Vanquished. What is this place?*

This is The Dead Zone: The Place Of Endless Echoes.

Look! Neutrino cries. It's Zorador The Invincible!

*They approach a glass coffin wherein a helmeted bare-chested
warrior stands with a lightning rod at his side.*

So, The Anomaly says. He too is now one with The Vanquished.

This is The Dead Zone: The Place Of Endless Echoes.

Look! Neutrino cries. It's Xerodus!

They approach a glass coffin wherein a man-machine in full body armour stands with a ferocious black beast on the end of a chain.

All around them, stacked in glass coffins as high as the eye can see, are the bodies of The Vanquished. Look! Neutrino cries. Our old foe Metamorph!

Metamorph stands before them, encased in glass, a blaster in each of his eight hands.

So, The Anomaly says. He too is now one with The Vanquished.

I'm sorry, Neutrino says, as they approach a glass coffin wherein a man and woman are fixed holding hands.

It is my mother and father, The Anomaly says.

This is The Dead Zone: The Place Of Endless Echoes.

Is there no end to The Vanquished? Neutrino cries.

At that there is a sound. A slithering sound.

In the distance, at the vanishing point, three stars can be seen.

The stars approach.

Beneath them walks The X-Ray Kid. On his head he wears The Hood of The Snake, what is Miracle.

So, The Anomaly says. He too is now one with The Vanquished.

Behind The X-Ray Kid the body of the snake runs to the vanishing point.

The three stars descend and become as men: The Sons Of Men.

You should not have come here, they warn Neutrino and The Anomaly, in a voice like fire unsound. This is no realm for mortal men.

The X-Ray Kid remains silent. The snake upon his head lets out a hiss.

We followed our brother, who betrayed us, Neutrino says.

That was no betrayal, the stars say, in a voice like cold fire. The X-Ray Kid's quest for The Singularity and his overthrowing of The Tower hastened his arrival in The Dead Zone: The Place Of Endless Echoes. He meant for you to remain on the other side. His mission must be completed alone.

Ye cold stars! Neutrino cries. How can you stand silent sentinel over this abomination? This obscene parade of The Dead?

*This is The Dead Zone they reply, in a voice like silent thunder,
The Place Of Endless Echoes.*

*We have scaled Heaven's Gates to bring our brother back home,
The Anomaly announces. And to free him from the mesmerism of
The Black Serpent!*

*You can no more free him from The Black Serpent and have him
live than you can cut the worm from his beating heart, The Sons
Of Men reply, in a voice like frozen flames.*

*Try and stop me! The Anomaly counters and he draws his flaming
sword.*

*But The X-Ray Kid lets off a blast from his eyes and The Anomaly
and Neutrino are knocked to the ground, their very bones
illuminated by its rays.*

*Neutrino clambers to his feet and attempts to rush The Sons Of
Men but an invisible force field bars his way.*

*You may no more bring The Dead back to life than you may
rewrite your own past, The Sons Of Men cry, in a voice like a far-
off storm.*

*Then damn the stars! The Anomaly bursts as he launches his
flaming sword though the air and watches helplessly as it
rebounds and falls to the ground.*

Just because we are written in the sky, The Sons Of Men sing in unison, does not mean that we too are not written.

These stars speak in riddles! Neutrino says.

The snake is old, The Sons Of Men sing in a voice of uncanny unison. Two thousand year. And his eyes are cold.

The X-Ray Kid steps silently forward and holds his hand up to the invisible force field.

One after the other Neutrino and The Anomaly press their hands to the other side.

Our ancestors spoke of a snake, Neutrino says. And of a Great Return. Tell me, stars, will there be a Return?

The Sons Of Men raise their arms toward the bodies stacked in glass coffins as high as the eye can see. The Sons Of Men raise their arms to the bodies of The Vanquished.

This is The Dead Zone, they say, in a voice like soft wet tears, The Place Of Endless Echoes.

Next time: The Betrayal Of The Gods!

*

I give Patricia a bell and I take her out to dinner. We barely know each other, I says to her, it was all about Tommy, wasn't it? It was all about Tommy, she says. It's not the same without him, she says to me. Aye, Tommy had the gift of the gab, I says to her. It was more than that, she says. Tommy was the love of my life, she says to me.

Did you know he bought a new pair of trousers? she says. Sure, Tommy was always buying the trousers, I says to her, he loved his new trousers, so he did. No, but he went into town that morning, she says to me. He wasn't feeling good and you know all about his heart, his weak heart. Tommy's heart was never weak, I says to her. I don't care if he had a pacemaker. That was a rebel heart he had.

Aye, he was some man, she says to me. But the point is he got up that morning and he says, I'm away into town to get a new pair of decent trousers. That's what he says. I says to him, what for, you've got plenty of trousers in that wardrobe of yours, and he says to me: I wouldn't want to be buried in an old pair of slacks. That's Como talking, I says to her. That's Como right there.

I light a fag for her and I pass it over. We never made it to New York City, she says to me, taking a long draw, we never made it there, in the end, she says. That's where I saw us, she says to me. That's where I always imagined we'd end up. With Tommy on Broadway, she says, and she laughs. Then she brings up *The Quiet Man*. Do you mind *The Quiet Man*? she says to me. Of course I mind it, I says to her, how could I forget it, that was Tommy's favourite movie of all time, along with *Where Eagles Dare*.

I got so sick of seeing *The Quiet Man*, Patricia says. Every time it was on he was dragging me there to see it. Now I'll never be able to watch it again.

Remember, I says to her, remember when Como had his Christmas special and he has John Wayne on there? They were singing the Christmas carols together, Patricia says, and Tommy's stood up in front of the TV, singing along. Mind that? I says to her. The three of them together? That was special, that was, she says. It should've been Tommy, I says to her. I don't even know what I was trying to say, but she understood me anyway. I know, she says to me. It should have been him, not us. We're no match for them, she says. It was a different world. When? I says to her. When was it a different world? Yesterday, she says. Every day till now, she says. When John Wayne was alive, she says. And we both sat there in silence with the traffic going by on Adelaide Street and the windows steamed up. John Wayne's looking for Tommy in heaven as we speak, she says, and once Como gets up there, he's going to find that Tommy has stolen his thunder. We laughed a bit. Patricia cried a little. I didn't have the nerve to tell her that Tommy was already up there, singing. Listen, I says to her. I'll see you right. I'll look after you. I'll make sure nothing happens to you. No, she says, no, I'm alright. I could never have another man after my Tommy. But thanks all the same, she says. I phone her a taxi and I kiss her on the cheek and I get a last smell of that perfume and then I never see her again, except for once, and that wasn't in real life, but wait till I tell you.

*

271

They called it the Daddy's Little Girl Tour and there was another picture of your man Del Brogan on the poster with his mortified daughter in a headlock. Cunt's raking it in, Barney says to me. His shows are selling out. Cunt's big news. He's playing this wee place in Donegal and we decide to go and pay him a visit, though really it was a holiday for me and Barney and we took Moira and Wee Robin with us cause they were best pals by this point but we never told your man Del Brogan we were going, cause we thought we would just shop up, sit there in the front row and scare the living shite out him. He knew I had my suspicions about him and I'd say it to his fucking face, cause I'm not scared.

We drive down there in the van. The Mickey Mouse van. That was hard. Looking at that fucking cartoon mouse on the side was too much like gazing into Tommy's soul. Why did he love that mouse so much? I wanted to take it off. We should get rid of it, I says to Barney, it just brings up Tommy again and again. Over my dead body, Barney says to me. Tommy's memory is in that mouse. That'd be sacrilege. Besides, he says, you were the one what said it kept us invisible.

And it was true. Everywhere we went, the presence of this badly drawn Mickey Mouse immediately discounted us from being any kind of threat whatsoever. After that they never gave us a second look.

*

We stayed in a wee caravan park on the estuary. There was a wee social on site with the live music and the chanting and me

272

and Barney got up and did a few numbers, a few Como numbers. Barney was still doing that warbling, mind you. He murdered 'Tie a Yellow Ribbon' all over again. There's a fancy dress ball on the Saturday night with prizes for the best costumes. We're bollocksed for that, I says to them, if only we knew I'd have fucking rubbed some green dye on myself and ripped my shirt and gone as the Incredible Hulk. I wouldn't mind shagging the Incredible Hulk, Moira says. You think he's got a green cock? Sure, he's green all over, Wee Robin says. You can't have The Hulk with a green body and this fucking pale fleshy cock between his legs. Right enough, Moira says. You can't have The Hulk looking weird. This guy is a fucking green giant that mutates through pure rage, she says. His cock could be any colour. A fucking green giant that mutates through pure rage? Barney says. That's fucking Samuel you're talking about. Pity his cock couldn't mutate as well, though, he says. That's just an angry wee inch, or so I'm told.

The pints of green are flowing. Sammy's got a big cock, Moira says to them. I do, son, actually. That's enough, Barney says, for fuck sake, now I'm sitting here picturing this cunt's big green cock. Listen, Wee Robin says to us. Me and Barney have got a surprise for youse. Ah fuck, I says to myself, he's not gone and married this bitch, has he? But then she says, come back to the van with us for a minute, we've got some presents for youse. We go back to the van and hanging there on the wall are these outfits. We made costumes for youse for the fancy dress, Wee Robin says to us. We made your costume from *The Forever Family*, she says to me. We made you The Anomaly's outfit. And it looks cool as fuck, actually, with the black PVC leggings and a black shield with a black-on-black 'A' on the chest, a helmet with a half-visor and this dark-blue floor-length cloak. I'm supposed to fucking wear this thing? I says to them. But really I couldn't fucking wait. Go on, you daft cunt, Barney says to me, it'll be some laugh, so it will. Besides, Moira says, I'd rather fuck The Anomaly than The Incredible Hulk. Maybe he's got a big black cock. Moira, we made you a superhero too, hen, Wee Robin says to her. You're Alphagirl. She hands Moira this sexy wee number with the black PVC and a boob tube with a Zorro mask. What are you two going as? I says to them. He's Neutrino, obviously, Wee Robin says. I made him the full suit of body armour. But Neutrino doesn't have a partner, she says to me. He's a man alone, trapped inside his body armour and living in a world of pain. Sounds like Barney, I says to her. So I'm just going as Robin, she says. Batman's Robin. Does this mean Robin has joined The Forever Family? Barney says to her. Looks like a whole new line-up, she says, and she winks.

*

We get to the social and it's clear we've got some serious competition; the place is heaving with your top superheroes. It's the most popular masquerade in the country, Wee Robin says. Youse two fucking tricked me, I says to Barney. This is a fucking comics convention you've brought us to.

Barney just shrugs, and he says, it's only a masquerade. That's what he says, it's only a comic book masquerade.

They're queued off the stage and down the side of the room; till Hawkgirl come in, till Superman and The Flash come in, till

Hourman, till The Green Lantern, till Black Terror, till Speedboy and NoMan come in, till Dagar the Invincible, till The Raven!, till The Unknown Soldier and Captain Ireland, till The Sub-Mariner come in, till The Human Torch, till Wonder Woman, till The Thing, till Vampirella and Spitfire come in, and the heroes file onstage, one by one, and they're playing 'We Are the Champions' by Queen (it's a classic, come on, it's a fucking classic) and everybody in the audience is singing along. Superman is bound in fake chains that he snaps in an almighty show of force. Green Lantern zaps a guy dressed in a gorilla costume. Wonder Woman lassoes a chair and drags it across the stage. The Sub-Mariner does a slow-motion walk, like he's walking on the bottom of the sea. The Human Torch has strips of bright-orange paper hanging from him that trail like flames as he runs. Speedboy is a blur as he leaps from the stage and makes a quick circuit of the hall. The Unknown Soldier peels his face off, it's only just a plastic mask and underneath, a dark, black void. And now it's our turn.

Wee Robin picks up the mic and she starts to read. Holy Blank Cartridge, she says. Holy Rats In A Trap! Holy Bowler! Holy Explosion. Holy Escape Hatch! Holy Missing Relatives. Holy Time Bomb.

Holy Waste Of Energy! She's doing Robin from the TV show and everyone is cheering. Holy Nightmare! she says. Holy Shamrocks! Holy Gunpowder! Holy Fireworks! Holy Hallelujah! Holy Holy! Holy Holy! And Barney's up next.

He clanks onstage in the full body armour and makes a signal for the microphone. Then he says to the host, this scrawny wee kid

in specs and a pair of Spider-Man pyjamas, go ahead and punch
me. Swing for me, Barney says to him. Give us your best shot.
Punch me as hard as you like, he says to this goofy little kid. I'm
Neutrino, he says, and I can take a fucking punch. I'm Neutrino,
he says to him, and I'm not fucking scared, and the kid spreads
his legs to steady himself, he holds his hands up in the air like
a champion, and then he swings for him, and drives his fist
straight into Neutrino's body armour, which crumples beneath his
knuckles. There's a moment of silence, with Neutrino standing
there, bent double, and then he turns to the crowd. I didn't feel a
fucking thing, Neutrino says, and the crowd goes fucking wild.

*

The next night we go to see your man Del Brogan sing at a
church hall, in Donegal, and they have a comedian as the
warm-up act, who was quite good, actually, all except for some
stupid joke about dead babies. I take a look around the audience.
Your man Del Brogan is doing well with the middle-aged women,
there's some crackers in here, no debate. We go outside for a
smoke at the intermission and Jimmy The Grunt's out there
selling the merchandise. Fuck me, Barney says, some sales
patter they're gonna get from this cunt. Alright, Jimmy, I says to
him, and he gives me a grunt. How are sales going? I says to him.
He grunts and he nods. Going well, eh? I says. Another grunt;
this guy's fucking chronic. The whole time he's got a cigarette
stuck between his lips and the ash is falling all over the records.
None of Tommy's class whatsoever. He would have sold the lot
by now.

Your man Del Brogan comes onstage, starts off with an Elton John number, 'Someone Saved My Life Tonight'. It's not on the album. Tommy would have advised him against it. Then he's into the Rod Stewart tunes. Barney starts with the booing. Cut it out, Wee Robin says to him, you're ruining it for everybody else. Give us some Como, Barney shouts, and you can see that your man Del Brogan has spotted us in the audience. We've got a few old-timers in here the night, your man Del Brogan says, so as we'll take a trip down memory lane for the pensioners; cheeky bastard. Then he sings 'Make Love to Life', the song that Tommy sang to us from heaven. And now I'm starting to feel a bit funny. Now I'm starting to see the snake.

There's a noise like a slithering noise and a noise like the noise of tearing flesh. I look around myself but nobody else is reacting. There's a movement from the back of the stage. A black shadow, rising up. I'm watching this great fucking snake come in, slithering from behind the stage, and raising itself up. Now the fucking thing is crawling up your man Del Brogan's back and hanging its hooded face down over his head. Barney, I says to him, is it just me, or is your man Del Brogan wearing a giant fucking snake? He's a fucking snake bastard, Barney says. I'll tell you that much.

He wears the snake as miracle.

I need to get some air. Excuse me a minute, I says. I go out through the lobby, and I walk past Jimmy The Grunt who is sitting there at the merchandise table with that fag in his mouth. I make for the men's toilets. I can feel this cold sweat coming over me. My heart is beating out my chest. I stare at myself in the mirror. I'm getting Tommy's heart, I've inherited Tommy's bad heart, in the mirror. And now there's something on the floor. Something is moving toward me across the floor. I can't look round. I'm frozen to the spot. Then I feel its cold touch on my leg. Wrapping itself around my leg and moving up. Its cold muscle. Its coils around my waist and its run up my spine and I get the most feelings, the most feelings, like I could ejaculate and faint at the same time only to come, only to come, right through the middle of my forehead, stroking my spine and making my brain come.

Behind me, mirrored, the head of the snake, puffs, opens its black hood, my brain is going to fucking, spunk, bears fangs in its opened mouth, hoods its tongue, is spit on a mirror, and mirrored is miracle: because I know now why there are no snakes in Ireland. I know now. Saint Patrick told them to beat it because snakes move through time differently from us. Their tails are in the past but their heads are in the future. That's why Saint Patrick told them to beat it. He had to get rid of them. Because if you can read the future then the game is up. And where would Ireland be without the game? But why me? I says to myself. Why has the snake come for me?

And then, the vision, iss, miracled:

*

I'm sitting here, in this lonely prison cell. I'm sitting here in this fucking cage and I'm telling you all about it. I'm remembering something that happened in the future but that is taking place right now as I'm telling you this, in the past. It's like I'm in two places at once and they are both here, right now, in this one place. I walk back through the lobby in this double-minded snake state. I don't know if anybody else can see it. Or the stains on my trousers. I walk past Jimmy The Grunt and he gives me a grunt, grunt.

Your man Del Brogan brings his daughter on. His daughter Eden, in a chair, onstage. This is my heart, he says. Give me a fucking break, Barney says. A little girl can be your heart, for god's sake, I says to him. In this snake glow everything seems perfect. It is here right Now. Your man Del Brogan singing to his daughter is addressing his heart, addressing his fucking heart and no doubt about it, his heart is there in front of him with a white dress on and wearing knee socks just as surely as if somebody had slipped their fingers into the flesh of his chest and torn his heart free of its veins and its arteries and presented it to him, right then and there, his daughter, singing to the audience, is his heart to himself,

> my heart's come back to me
> across the sad and lonesome years
> my heart's come back to me
> darling can you see through the tears
> my heart and I
> returned
> my heart and I

and the audience is beating, audience is pumping blood, this blood that words, inside of us. Can't you feel it rising? Can't you feel it surging and rising and passing through? It's so powerful, this sharing of blood. Aren't you crying?

279

Afterward we go backstage and your man Del Brogan has a gaggle of women around him. Eden is sitting on a stool on her own sucking a lollipop. Fuck me, but that's a bit suggestive, is it not? Barney says to me, and he winks. You've got blow jobs on the brain, I says to him. Everyone in Ireland has blow jobs on the brain, he says. Doesn't Wee Robin suck your cock with her outfit on? I says to him. He shakes his head. She says it's disgusting, he says. Nightmare, I says to him. I bet your man Del Brogan is getting his cock sucked every night of the week, I says. We look over and your man Del Brogan is sitting on the edge of a table talking to this gorgeous blonde number. Speaking of which, Barney says, did you crack one off in the toilet? He points to the stain on my crotch. I had a fucking accident, I says to him, that's all. Do I look weird to you? I says to him. No more than usual, he says. Then your man Del Brogan catches sight of us and waves us over. Fuck me, he says, it's my two favourite stalkers. Are youse looking for autographs, boys?

How's the groupie situation? Barney says to him. Banging, he says. Banging. Better than ever, he says. When Tommy was around I had serious competition. But now I've got the run of the field. I'm getting my cock sucked every night of the week, lads, he says to us. No word of a lie. Fuck me, I says to him, I was just saying that there's a fucking drought on blow jobs in Ireland, always has been. When Saint Patrick ran all the snakes out of Ireland he must have fucking ran all the blow jobs out too, your man Del Brogan says. But they're coming back, he says. Mark my words, they are coming back. For a second I'm caught there, speechless. Can he see me, I'm wondering, the way I saw him? What's coming back, I says to him, the snakes? The fucking blow jobs, you divot, he says to me. The fucking blow jobs are coming back. The fuck you think I'm talking about? Then he winks at me. He fucking knows, I'm telling myself, he fucking knows. The snake means you're marked. The snake means knowledge of the future. But then the blonde comes over and puts her arm around his waist. These are my good friends Barney and Sammy, he says to her. This is Babs. Babs gives us both a really limp handshake and then puts her mouth up to his ear. I hear her whispering to him. When are we getting out of here, Daddy? she says. She's calling him Daddy. Daddy's little girl.

*

Christ Jayzus stands up at the Last Supper and he says to his disciples, before the cock crows, he says, one of you will betray me, he says, and one of you will disown me completely, he says, and one of you will sell me down the river for a piece of gold, he says, and he gives them a commandment, I am commanding you right now, he says, I am telling you to love one another, to love one another like I have loved you, which is like brothers, he says, and to look after one another when I'm gone, because you know I won't be around forever, I'm telling you right now, I'm not long for this world, boys, he says, and then he picks up a piece of bread and he breaks it in two and he says to them, see this bread, he says, this bread is my body, this bread is my broken body after it has been crucified, he says, crucified alongside common thieves, he says, alongside the

281

lowest of the low, he says, and he eats it, he takes a big bite
out this bread, and he pours himself a glass of wine, and
he drinks it down, and he says to them, this is my blood,
he says, this wine is my blood forever, he says, and he says
to them, see every time you eat that bread, he says, you
will be partaking of my body, you'll remember me when
you break that bread, he says, and see every time you
drink that wine, he says, that's my blood you'll be drinking,
he says, and I promise you, he says, I promise you that
whatever one of you believes in me will be granted eternal
life, which is entrance into heaven when you die, where
we'll be united with my da, who is God, the Father of us all,
sitting there, with me on his right-hand side, and where
you will be forgiven for all of the sins you have committed
against me. And Peter gets up, and he says to him, sure,
Jayzus, you're a terrible man when you've got
a drink in you.

*

Your man Del Brogan leaves with this bird on his arm and his
daughter in tow and we're left in the dressing room with his
backing band that consists of a bunch of longhairs dressed up
in charity-shop suits. I never knew hippies played that style of
music, Barney says to one of them, tall guy with the plukes all
over his face. Just doing a favour for the big man, the pluke guy
says, money innit, he says. I thought you guys were all into the
free love and all that? Barney says to him. Where in the fuck you
gonna find free love in Ireland? the longhair-pluke guy says. It's
a good point, I says to him, and I see Wee Robin looking over at

Barney right then. Sure, do youse smoke the grass, the longhair-pluke guy says to us, and Barney's like that, naw, son, we'll just stick to the booze, but of course I can see that he wants to, we both do, but we don't want to do it in front of the birds. How do you know your man Del Brogan? I says to the longhair. Met him years ago, he says. How do you know him? he says to me. Let's just say we're in the same line of business, Barney says to him. In that case, let's just say the same, the longhair says. Alright, we're on the same page now, everybody's talking that wee bit freer. But then the longhair drops the bomb. Sure, I met your man Del Brogan in the jail, the longhair says. We met when we were serving time.

Who knew your man Del Brogan had gone down?

Your man Del Brogan was in the jail? I says to him. Didn't you know? he says to me. Went down for a few year. What for? I says to him. He puts his hand up, makes the shape of a gun, pulls the trigger. And what were you doing in there yourself? I says to him. Same thing, he says.

Okay, so everybody knows that Special Branch recruit their agents in the jail. They enjoy certain benefits, they get out early, they get protected, plus they have the ultimate cover story: they've done time for The Boys.

How did your man Del Brogan get out so early? I says to him. Good behaviour? the longhair says, and he shrugs. This guy with the short hair comes over, it's the drummer. He sniffs the air. Fucking hippies, he says, gimme that. He grabs the joint and

takes a big toke. You look like a punk rocker, pal, Barney says to
him. Fuck's it to you? the wee punk says. I thought punks wanted
to puke and destroy, Barney says, I thought it was all about no
future. There's no future in Ireland, I'll fucking tell youse that
much, the wee punk says, the Pistols got that fucking right, that's
for sure. That's the fucking problem with cunts like you, the
longhair says to him, I mean, if you don't believe in the possibility
of a better future, what exactly are you bringing to the struggle?
An AK-47, the wee punk says, and everybody laughs, except for
the longhair, who is getting more annoyed. You'll change nothing,
the punk says, it doesn't matter. All this fucking nihilism, the
longhair says. It's the fucking disease of the young generation.
But youse were just as bad, he says, and he's nodding to me and
Barney, where the fuck did youse get us? he says to us. Youse
never had a coherent plan in your heads, he says to us. Youse
were political illiterates. Who are you fucking calling il-li-ter-
ates? Barney says to him. Youse never understood that it was
all part of the greater class struggle, the longhair says to us. To
youse it was just a fucking glorified street brawl. I'll fucking take
you in a glorified street brawl, Barney says.

Leave it, Barney, I says to him. Listen, I says to the longhair.
It's the very fucking idea of the future that gets everybody into
trouble, I says to him. It's all this fucking planning, all this
fucking dreaming, all this fucking political shite, all this fucking
tomorrow-will-be-better-than-today bollocks that keeps us all
from living right now. You don't even believe that, the longhair
says. In Ireland there is no now to live in, my friend, he says
to me. There is no fucking present in Ireland. No solid ground.
Our only hope is to literally build the future, so as that when we

get there, we'll have something to fucking stand on. As it is, the ground beneath our feet doesn't even belong to us.

Everybody is stood there, silenced. Then the wee punk, he says to us: youse are all going about it the wrong way. He's walking out the door with his fucking drum kit strapped to his back at this point. And what's your fucking strategy, Mr No Future? Barney says to him. My strategy is fucking infiltration, he says to us. My strategy is the fucking Trojan Horse. And I think of Kathy, and invisibility, and superpowers, and once again, for a moment, before it's pulled from underneath me, I see myself, with certainty, in the future, and I know that when the times comes, I'll be ready.

*

We never made contact with Tommy again and, I mean, I wonder why, because we all says it was amazing, that it was just like Tommy, and it was obviously him. I mean, you can actually talk to people in heaven. You would think we would have made more use of that. But I came to understand something about the dead that is so true, and so simple. You know all that bollocks about the dead living on in our hearts? It's all nonsense, my friend. The dead get further away every minute. Because they have nothing in common with the living anymore. It's the dead that are their people now. I mean, they'll come if you call them. But really, they can't be bothered. Because they have left all worldly concerns behind. That's why even miracles like speaking from beyond the grave have basically zero interest for them; to them it's just a cheap trick.

*

And sometimes I would hear his voice, mostly singing, or I would think of his eyes, when Irish eyes are smiling, or I would picture one of his suits, in my mind, I would see a pair of his shoes, phantom shoes, right there in front of me, I was afflicted by his phantom shoes, and his muscular arms, and his smell, sometimes I would catch a sniff of his smell, Old Spice, from out of the air, and I would feel so sad and lost to despair because I came to realise, son, I came to realise that it was all just echoes, running down. That it was all just after-images, fading.

Being in the jail is much the same thing. Being in the jail is to enter The Dead Zone: The Place Of Endless Echoes. We crossed over as surely as the dead did, and just like them we lost interest in the world on the other side. Visits were denied us anyways, and of course some of The Boys talked about their missus or some wee bird they were banging, but it felt like just talk for show, just talk for show. Because really the jail was the world. And every second was life so intensely. Boys as united in their mission as the dead themselves. And when a prisoner would pass over it was as if we had willed his death through sheer force of solidarity. That we had said to him, die. That he had offered up his body to the miracle of the mass. Even when he had the shite beaten out him, even when he gives himself a heart attack through starvation, even when he was an emaciated skeleton lying in a pool of freezing water; he had gone further, in the name of all of us. I've never known meaning like it, and I don't expect to again, until I take my place in the tombs of heaven, for nobody else to see, but the endless dead.

What's your man Bobby Sands's phone number?

Eight Nothing,
Eight Nothing,
Nothing Two,
Eight.

*

I come in near the end of the first hunger strike. I mind attending
mass in H3 one Sunday morning and seeing men what looked
like they were a hundred year old. Brothers bent double, led in
by their twin, shrouds wrapped tight around the two of them, in
Bible time. Other men touching their pale white skin. Touching
the white skin pulled tight round their faces, and looking in their
dark eyes, and weeping there too. The first hunger strike was
led by a man name of The Dark: Brendan 'The Dark' Hughes. He
was like Tommy. One of these Irish guys what look like fucking
negroes. That's what they called him: Darkie or The Dark.
But everything takes on new meaning in The Place Of Endless
Echoes.

The Boys were being led by The Dark. They were being led by
The Dark across The Dead Zone. And there were communications
between the dead. From the dead that had crossed over into other
regions of The Zone. In December we receive notice that three
women in the Armagh prison had joined us in the hunger strike.
Three women were approaching. Three shades, coming through

from the other side. The priest talked to us about the agonies of Christ Jayzus. How Christ Jayzus will be in agony until the end of the world. But the world had already come to an end. We had left the world behind us. And now there was only a final suffering, a final monumental sacrifice, before we would have no more of this world and every single one of us, echoes, in time. If you could enter the eyes of a dead man, the black, inscrutable eyes of a dead man, at mass, in H3, in the years of the hunger strike, then you would come to know that heaven and hell are just party games played for the benefit of the living.

Part Five: The Ocean and the Shore

The phone rings, in the middle of night. It's Tommy. It's a game of Tommy calling me from the other side, and I sit on the stair, and I pick up the phone, in the dead of this Belfast night, and it's the same silence on the end of the line, the same fucking silence as ever. But now someone is trying to speak. Tommy? Is that yourself, Tommy?

Answer me, Tommy.

Moira's out of bed. Get back to fucking bed and close that fucking door behind you.

Someone's crying. A woman's voice is in tears at the end of the line.

Kathy? I says to it.

Kathy, is that you, honey?

Xamuel, it says.

Xamuel, I'm in trouble.

Xamuel, they are going to kill me.

Xamuel, I'm in trouble deep.

They? Who are they?

The ones what are going to kill me, she says, and the voice, it is Kathy's.

Nobody's going to kill anybody. Not while I'm around.

(muffled noises on the phone)

You need to speak clearly, sweetie.

Will you meet me? she says through the tears.

We can't talk on the phone, she says, will you come to me?

I'll run to you, darling, I says to her, I'll come to you wherever you are, my heart, my sweet heart, I says. Belfast isn't safe, I says to her, so meet me in Carrickfergus, meet me in Carrickfergus by the shore.

Come back across the crackly telephone line, come back to me a song.

In Carrickfergus, my love, I'll meet you in Carrickfergus, I'll meet you in Carrickfergus, by the shore. And what time will we meet?

Tomorrow, at half past three, my love.

I'll meet you in Carrickfergus, by the shore.

*

Next afternoon I'm out there early. Don't dare take the van. Invisibility is wearing off. I eat a fish supper and look out to sea. How come I never visited Carrickfergus before? After all, it's just along the coast. I look out at this sea some more, this sea that has come to me, and that's when I realise. It was waiting for us. It was waiting for us, here, in this moment. I take out my hip flask, and I spot her in the distance, from the swish of her hips, I can make her out, coming back to me, as a gift. Kathy, coming back to me. And what is it they say, about swans, in history, what is it that they rise up, on their wings, somewhere in the world, and they trigger a tsunami?

A tsunami, yes. A tsunami is like a finely calibrated gold watch, which has its time, just as this was the beginning of mine, the time I was to serve, as a prisoner, the time I was to bow down to, the time that is now coming to an end, and that looked so beautiful then, in a dark-blue pencil skirt and high heels. Its long red hair, hanging down. Inscrutable dark eyes, where the future meets the past, like a swan's.

Hiya, Sammy, she says to me, and she sits down next to me and lights a fag. I'm pregnant, Sammy, she says to me, and with her long, red fingernails she pierced the flesh of my chest and grasped me by the heart.

I'm pregnant, Xamuel, she says to me in my arms, on this bench that had been set aside for us by Christ Jayzus and his da at the beginning of time (let's face it), this bench on the shore at Carrickfergus, and I says to myself, let me be the father, please, make it perfect, this moment, but in my heart of hearts, I knew. Even as she caressed it, even as she held it gently in her hands, in this moment, of the two of us, even as I felt it strain against her fingers, I knew who the father was. I tried to make light of it, to turn it into a joke. Don't tell me you're going to give birth to a wee darkie? I says to her. But everything has its season. I held her in my arms then, in the space that was given to us, in the time that was ours, and we wept.

*

The story she told me was this: that she had worked as a whore at the Europa for several year and that it was profitable and safe – at first – and there was a never-ending supply of clients, with members of the press, civil servants, diplomats and international politicians coming and going in those years. There was a circle of girls working there, essentially under the protection of the Brits. Her husband Davy knew nothing about any of this. She says. At first. He had been paying protection money to the IRA in return for being able to trade. His shop was in an area that had fallen under covert IRA control. Kathy mentioned the various diplomats and politicians that she had 'befriended' at the Europa and Davy insisted that she bring it up to them. And so she did.

She mentions it to a few people who shrug and say, it's a problem across the board, there are no-go areas all over Belfast, what do you expect us to do? But she had taken a lover. A man name of Trevor Winter. One of these vague 'protector of the realm' types. And Winter says he'll look into it. That it might be possible to do something, he says. That he would look into what contacts he had on the ground and see whether they couldn't nudge a few of the necessaries. He acted like he was pulling strings. Like the whole thing was a game with just a few people on each side directing the action. He would get drunk with Kathy in a room at the Europa and he would boast about his contacts in the field. The whole game is rigged, he says to her. The whole game is riddled. The whole game is wriggled.

He gets drunk and he goes on about Control. Control says this. Control says that. Control is in control, he says. What is Control? Kathy says. Control, my dear, he says, Control, my darling girl, is whoever defines the term. Are you talking about psychological warfare? she says to him. If you say so, he says, and he winks and he rolls her top up over her small, perfectly formed tits, like little fucking coloured rosebuds, they were. The whole game is riddled, he says. We have introduced contagions. Pathogens of our own making. Psychopathogens, he says. That's another word for a Fenian bastard, he says, and we're flooding the market.

Then, afterward: my husband is being leaned on by the IRA. He has stopped paying their protection money to them out of principle. Principles, Trevor Winter says, and he chokes off a laugh as he lays out a line of coke for each of them in a room with the curtains closed in the spring of 1977. Principles, he says, are the most dangerous contagion of them all.

Give me his details, he says, I'll have some of our men in the field pay him a visit. Perhaps we can sort something out, he says. After all, he says, it's not often that you come across a man with principles in Northern Ireland. It's not often that somebody takes a stand. I do think he should be rewarded, he says, or at least, you know, backed up.

One night Davy comes home and tells Kathy that he was visited at the shop by Special Branch. How do you know it was Special Branch? she says to him. Because that is exactly what they didn't say, he says. They never announced themselves as Special Branch, which is exactly what Special Branch would do, instead they simply says that they had come to see me about *my problem*. That they had heard that I was a man of virtue and of good standing. That that was a rare thing in Belfast, a rare thing in Northern Ireland. Then one of them made a strange remark, her man says to her. He points toward me, he says, and he says to his companion, doesn't he remind you of someone? Yes, his companion says. Yes, I was only just thinking the exact same thing. It's uncanny, he says. It's a million to one, he says. If I wasn't so sure of his whereabouts right now, the first man says, if I wasn't, in fact, so convinced of your integrity, sir, and, well, your honesty, let's just go ahead and say that, he says, if I wasn't so, how do you put it, sold, on your story, my friend, I would be almost convinced that this was some form of elaborate set-up. Some form of psychological double bluff, his colleague says, the conversation snaking back and forth between them. You see, they says that Davy was the spitting image of a sleeping fox. A 'sleeping fox' is a code for a double agent, they says. A sleeping fox that might be willing, they says, to trade places with him.

This could work well for both of us, the second man says. You could take a holiday, as it were, the first man says, while our friend, well, while our friend moves in and, as it were, draws the heat. I thought it was ridiculous, Davy says, a sleeping fox impersonating me, a sleeping fox pretending to be me. I have regulars, Davy says to them. I have close friends that are customers. Sure, he's a cousin, a brother, in that case, the first man says. He's a family member. But the resemblance would be enough to convince anybody that might ask questions. Besides, the second man says, he can look after himself, this sleeping fox, you would have no need to worry about that. He has his own story. We know what we're doing, the first man says. Think about it, he says, as just a subtle sleight of hand.

Counterparts, I says to Kathy. Do you think that everybody has their counterparts out there? Not like their double exactly, but like their opposite number?

That's what Davy says, Kathy says to me. That's what Davy says but only he calls it his alter ego. My fucking alter ego is out there, he says, and then he brings up the story of *Ms Marvel*, which was this comic book that he always went on about. I says to him, what the fuck does your favourite comic book have to do with a sleeping fox? and he says to me, shut up and listen, shut up and wait till I tell you, he says:

*

Carol Danvers is investigating her own alter ego. She is trying to track down Ms Marvel and find out her true identity. But Ms Marvel's true identity, her alter ego, is Carol Danvers. Only she's forgotten or suppressed it somehow. She starts to having these blackouts. There are gaps in her story. Ms Marvel does not know her true identity. Ms Marvel is trapped in a place of no memories. Carol Danvers's shrink puts her under and while she is hypnotised she recalls memories of Ms Marvel and her superpowers. But her shrink dismisses them as ludicrous or as shadow fantasies personified. It's just a complex, he says. Think about it, Davy says.

What if your complexes are not in here but out there?

What if you could come face to face with your own alter ego?

What if your alter ego has forgotten it's your own invention?

I says to him, I'm not indulging any stupid comics-fanboy superhero nonsense, she says. You do not want to get mixed up with these people, I says to him. These people are dangerous, I says to him, but he's obsessing over it. You've been reading these comic books for too long, I says to him. I'm not mental, he says to me, I'm not mad. It's a projection, I says to him. You're projecting onto this fantasy figure, I says to him, but he just laughs at that. Imagine the power of projection, he says to me. That's what you call art.

*

I start to notice changes with Davy and it's like this supposed meeting with Special Branch has inspired him, she says. Can psychological warfare be as subtle as that? Could they have somehow hypnotised him by planting the seed of this idea and then the seed somehow grows under its own power or under the power of Davy's fantasy? Thing is, he stops wearing his sloppy T-shirts and his training shoes and his baggy jeans and he starts

to buying smart shirts and dress shoes. He starts to wearing
a blazer into work and he even starts to wearing the cologne.
Sorry, the aftershave, he starts to wearing the aftershave. I think
to myself, okay, it's good to aspire. It's good to want to better
yourself, if that's all it is, then fine. Then good. He's looking better
than ever, I'll be honest with you. He's making an effort. I'm all
for it. Then you lot go and kidnap me. Then he kicks the shite out
your friend at the comic shop.

*

He didn't kick the shite out him, I says to her, what happened
was he accidentally kicked Barney in the head while he was
flailing about trying to escape. Whatever, Kathy says, what he
told me was that he split that cunt's head wide open. That's
exactly what he says and, I mean, already that wasn't like him.
I split that fucking cunt's head wide open, he says to me. I'm not
going to argue the point, I says to her. It was a lucky kick, but
whatever. So he kicks the shite out your friend, she says, and
then he calls Special Branch and asks for an appointment with
his alter ego. He says that he is ready.

*

The story that he told me was this: how he gets a number and is
told to phone it at a certain time and to use a certain phrase. A
certain phrase that he says he cannot reveal to me under pain of
death.

Don't tell me, I says to him: Flame on!

It's not fucking funny, he says to me, and he fixes me with this stare, this fucking stare where his head doesn't move at all. That's another thing that happened to him when he came back. When he spoke to you he never moved his head. I know that sounds unremarkable but try it yourself. You can move your eyes or whatever but try speaking to someone without ever moving your head. It's fucking disconcerting, I'm telling you. And at first you don't even realise what it is about it until you figure it out. They don't move their heads when they talk to you. You realise that and you get the creeps. That's a Special Branch technique. I'm giving nothing away here but watch out for it. The non-head-moving. Strategic non-head-moving. It's a giveaway. A giveaway that they've had training. So as he calls this number and he utters this phrase. This phrase that he says has the power to unlock the future, is what he utters.

There's no one on the end of the line. When he phoned this number someone picked up the phone without speaking. He's in deep here. He utters the phrase. The person on the other end of the phone doesn't respond. You can hear a transistor radio in the background. It's playing music. What music? I says to Kathy. How do I know what music? she says. What the fuck does it matter what music? It might have been important, I says to her. But carry on.

There's this music playing, this unknown music. And he stays on the phone. Davy stays on the phone and waits for a response but there's none. He listens some more. He listens some more and that's when he says to me that he understood the first lesson. He says that he gets it right there. Listen to yourself, he says. That's the first lesson. The phone call was a feedback loop, he says to me. The phone call was a silent meditation between himself and his alter ego, and he says he felt supercharged. He says he hung up the phone after who knows how long. Long enough to get the message, he says, and he was buzzing. This is dangerous behaviour, I says to him, this is deluded behaviour. But he just looks at me with this fucking stationary-head thing and it's enough to make you jangle.

*

So as he kicks the shite out your friend Barney and he comes round and he rescues me from you lot. He waits until you leave. He was watching the house the whole time. Davy and his alter ego had their eyes on your safe house (I imagine these two fucking motionless heads sitting like Easter Island in the front seat of the car, watching us). He bursts in on me, or it might have been his alter ego, because he's wearing a bally, so who knows. Davy, is that yourself, I says to him. It's me, he says, and it sounds like him, to be sure. I've come to rescue you, he says, and he grabs me, but before he goes he says, wait a minute. Wait a minute here, he says, let's leave them a calling card, and that's when he told me to get my heels and to sit them on the chair. It's like the Invisible Woman hanged herself, he says, and we rush out into the car and we skid off without anybody seeing us.

Was his alter ego in the car? I says to her. Did you get to see him? No, she says, I didn't see anything because he forced me into the boot. Your own husband that came to rescue you forced you into the boot of the car?

He says: get in, bitch. That's what he says to me. Then he picks
me up and he tosses me into the boot and the car screamed off.
We pull up to another house. He gets me out the boot and I'm
kicking and screaming and I'm shouting blue murder. What the
fuck has got into you, I says to him, what in the name of fuck are
you doing? He slaps me hard across the face and he grabs me by
the hair. He drags me across the front grass and into the house
and he throws me on the stair and he tears my tights down and
he rapes me.

I can see us in the mirror, watching myself, getting raped,
watching Davy, raping me. He's tearing my dress in the mirror
and he's holding me down by the hair at the same time. The first
sex we'd had in years and all the time he's calling me a whore,
you're a fucking dirty little whore, you're a slutty little fucking
bitch, so she is.

Then he finishes me off. He finishes me off and he gets up and
he locks the front door and he puts the keys in his pocket. Get
upstair and get yourself fucking cleaned up, he says to me, there's
an outfit for you in the spare room. In the meantime I've got
somebody I need to talk to, he says.

I get up and I'm staggering. I'm covered in bites. He was biting
me the whole time. I go up the stair. I'm in the room above the
living room. I can't hear him talking. I can't hear him moving
around. But after he tells me the story of calling up this silent
contact and uttering this word, I'm sitting, in the room upstairs,
crying, bleeding, sore, and I'm picturing him, down the stair, on
the couch, with the phone up to his ear, sitting there, listening to

his alter ego, listening to the voice of silence. I walk over to the cupboard. There's an outfit hanging up in there. I get dressed and I wait for him in the clothes he has chosen for me, with my eye bruised shut, and with cuts on my thighs. After what feels like an eternity he comes up the stair and he takes me by the hand and he explains what the future has in store for me.

*

Storms toss the kingdom of Hibernia.

The sun and moon rise and fall together.

Neutrino and The Anomaly return to their secret Control Station in the mountain fortress of The Cave Hill.

The future of The Forever Family is in doubt.

Neutrino is alone in the Control Room. He scans absent-mindedly across the surveillance channels. Visions of flood and famine. Whole populations displaced.

He can barely muster a shrug.

In the bowels of the complex The Anomaly paces The Cryogenic Vault.

In his hand he holds a smooth silver cylinder: The Armageddon Artefact.

I was given this by my mother, he says to himself. His voice echoes across The Cryogenic Vault.

I have it within my power, he announces, to bring all this to an end.

To bring all this to an end or once more to join the fray. To battle in good faith, father against son, brother against brother, father against father.

Ah! But have I the heart?

Take heart, a voice says. A voice from out of the air.

Take heart, my son. Take all this with you, all sorrow and foreknowledge of parting, all fate and fortune, and do battle regardless.

For that is what is written. And what is written is The Eternal Warrior.

Is it you? he asks of the air.

No response.

Then: It Is I.

It is I?

No answer.

Outside the elements thunder. Lightning turns the air purple.

The Anomaly steps toward The Crucible. The time has come.

The voice of the silence now speaks. It speaks through The Anomaly in actions.

He takes The Armageddon Artefact and inserts it into The Crucible, which opens like flesh to receive it.

The pod of The Crucible lights up. There is the sound of an amplified heartbeat.

The door slides to one side.

There is nothing there!

Ye Gods, The Anomaly cries. Why have you betrayed me?

Inside the pod: a single coat hanger swings on a rusted metal hook.

Neutrino flicks across the channels. He sees Hibernia from high above. He sees the horizon curving into space. He feels the arc of the planet.

Great plumes of smoke rise up; red smoke and grey smoke and blue fire lick at the clouds. It is the end of days. Hibernia is haemorrhaging into space.

The moon hangs huge on the horizon. The sun boils high in the sky.

Suddenly: a vapour trail rises at an inhuman speed.

Is it a missile? Is it a space capsule?

It tears up into the sky and arcs toward the moon.

Neutrino zooms in.

Ye Gods! The Anomaly, come quick!

The Anomaly thunders into the Control Room. Can it be?

A lone figure tears through the stratosphere.

A lone figure speeds toward the moon.

Sunflower!

Did you activate The Armageddon Artefact? Neutrino asks him.

Yes, he says. But it failed. The Crucible was empty.

But that's not possible, Neutrino cries.

Sunflower is risen! The Anomaly cries. Anything is possible!

The moon itself seems to shudder at Sunflower's approach.

One overthrowing of nature demands another, The Anomaly announces, and he brings his fist down on the control panel.

Then: there is a shadow across the moon.

What sorcery is this?! Neutrino cries.

There is a shadow across the moon.

Sunflower floats high above the dead oceans. Tongues of flame appear like a corona around its edges. Then the moon begins to sink.

It begins to sink toward the horizon.

Sunflower has the moon in her power! Neutrino gasps.

Aye, and she would drown it too! The Anomaly says.

The pair watch, agog, as the moon sinks into the sea.

The moon sinks into the sea with Sunflower at its centre.

The ocean opens to receive them.

The waters rise up and flood the lands before them. The flames are smothered.

The lands are swept clean.

Silence reigns on the face of the earth.

All Hibernia is at peace: drowned and with a silent moon at the centre.

Look! Neutrino says.

Driven deep beneath the waves the moon still shines.

It shines up from beneath the waves and is reflected in the black mirror of the sky.

The Sons Of Men walk the corridors of The Dead Zone: The Place Of Endless Echoes.

They too wear a cloak of silence.

All around them are the glass coffins of the heroes.

The glass coffins all stacked up to heaven.

Each of them now empty.

The covers of their caskets the perfect mirror.

All that sounds is the footsteps of The Sons Of Men.

The footsteps of The Sons Of Men, receding forever.

Next time: Into The Maze!

*

You told me it was me what gave you all those little cuts and
what bruised your thighs, I says to Kathy, you told me it was
me. I didn't want to hurt your feelings, she says to me. By the
shore at Carrickfergus, that's when I says to her. By the shore
at Carrickfergus was where I found out. The news that broke my
heart but made me whole again. How can I explain it? How can I
explain what it did to me?

The tide is coming in and washing all the stones on the beach.
The moon is rising up out of the sea. We're stood at the very edge
of the world, I says to her. No, we're not, she says. Scotland is
just over there. Don't ruin it, I says to her. Don't spoil it for me.
And then I says to her, how did you get pregnant by our Tommy?
She looks at me with a confused expression. What are you talking
about? she says to me. And for a second it's like Christ Jayzus
Himself is holding his breath. For a second it's like maybe I've got
it all wrong. Maybe I am the father. Maybe dreams come true.
Maybe there's a simple way out of this. Maybe we can just walk
away, the two of us. Maybe we're in that song after all, that song
by the shore at Carrickfergus.

And she says to me: who the fuck is Tommy? And I says to her,
Tommy, you know, the one what got you pregnant, my best pal,
Tommy, I saw you both together. You really don't know? she
says to me, and she shakes her head. His name's not Tommy,
she says. His name is fucking Thomas James Kentigern, I says
to her, and it's written in gold letters on his coffin. That's as how
you know him, she says to me. But he was working for the other
side all along, she says. And with a different name.

Wait. I want to tell you the story of my spirit animal, son, which
is a Harry the Hedgehog. It came back to me in a vision of my
father, as to when a time he had found a Harry the Hedgehog
walking in our driveway and he had come running in and with
his eyes all gleaming he says to me, come, quick, it's a Harry the
Hedgehog, and years later, when I had forgotten all about it, my
father, long after he had died, came to me in the spirit world, as
a dream, and he tells me the information that he and my ma had
never really understood each other, and I felt heartbroken and
sad, and I says to my father, my father from beyond the grave,
now, did we truly understand each other, Father? And he says to
me, don't you remember Harry the Hedgehog, and he points up, to
the Milky Way, as a direction.

*

Why did Tommy get whacked? I never asked her his name. His
other name. The name he gave Kathy. The name he was given
by his handlers. His handlers, what a laugh. Who could handle
Tommy? Because the reason that Tommy got whacked, the reason
that I have come to believe why he had to be killed, the reason
that I have convinced myself is true, is that he pushed it too hard.

That would be just like Tommy. He went too far. He embraced
the role a little bit too enthusiastically. The masquerade.
Tommy played the game for all it was worth. No matter whose
side he was on. You would think I might be mad. You would
think I might have felt betrayed by the news that he had been

moonlighting for the other side all along. But really I was in awe of him, all over again. He had every single one of us fooled, and on both sides too. But really he was fooling no one.

What I really believe is that when he was Tommy or when he was this other name that I never asked, this name that his handlers gave him, he was both of them one hundred per cent. And why was he whacked? You're asking me that? Here's what I think. You can't have agent provocateurs – that's the name they use, provisional, provoking agents – out there fucking murdering people left, right and centre. I mean, okay, alright, when we were taking out some of The Boys on our own side then fair play to him, he's just doing a clean-up job and cementing his reputation with the Ra. But then when he takes out that off-duty prison guard from the H Block, I think that's what did it. His cover was too deep for Control. That's the word Kathy used. Control. Tommy was completely out of Control. So as they had no choice but to whack him, is my theory.

I remembered all the jobs we had done together. I remembered that thing in Dundalk. Was the whole thing staged? Himself up on the roof like in a fucking action movie. Me piling through the unmarked cars. Was he working for them back then? Does that mean they were all in on it? Did they set it up like a fucking stunt so as Tommy could go blazing through in all his glory? He loved his action movies, we know that. Did he talk the peelers into letting him set that one up? He thought he was a movie star.

And what about Pat and Arlene? Was it Tommy that had Pat killed or did he know about it? Then I killed Arlene and her man.

And that's when it struck me. It was a fucking duet. Me and Tommy had been duetting together behind the scenes. Think about it: he makes a move, and then I make a move.

For every action there is an equal and opposite reaction. Do you know that one, son? That's Einstein talking. He's talking about dancing. About molecules dancing and about atoms dancing, atoms dancing blind, like me and Tommy, dancing with our ballys on. And I remembered that note. That blank note that had been left for me at the Europa, that note that might have saved my life. And I remembered making love to the same woman, the two of us, in the same hotel, in the same time, and the same place, even though it's all so long ago now. What a feeling.

*

Okay, what about this one:

> Paddy from Ireland goes for a job interview as a blacksmith
>   at a farmyard in County Athlone.
> Have you ever shoed a horse before? the smith says to him.
> Sure, I have not, Paddy says, but I did tell a donkey to fuck
>   off once.

*

The phone rings in the middle of night. This time I know what I have to do. What about you? I says to it, as soon as I pick it up. Then I sit there, and I wait. I sit there and wait for what seems like an eternity. Something is there, in silence, the whole time. I hear the milkboy out doing his rounds. The birds start to sing. And now it is the silence that is speaking, in the voice of my ex-lover.

Tommy turned up to a meeting with Davy that Control had arranged and told him that his wife was a whore. What? Tommy told him that and then he says: we're to put your whore wife to work. Tommy says: we're going to put her to work and that ways we're going to use this bitch for the information.

Davy's come home and he's called me a whore, is what the silence says to me, in the voice of Kathy M. He says that from now on we are going to put it to some fucking use, it says. He says that from now on I would be wearing a device. He calls me a dirty fucking slut, a filthy cunt, a little cocksucking bitch, and he slaps me round the face.

I says to him, you're a stupid fucking prick, it says, in the mocking voice of an ex-lover, don't you know that whores strip off all their clothes? Where am I going to wear a fucking bug?

I'll force that bug up your fucking arse, he says to me, if we get any more of this talk.

I'll be taking it up the arse every night, I says to him, so that isn't going to work.

This silence, turning me on.

You're fucking enjoying this, aren't you, he says to me (in a seductive voice, it says it, without speaking).

My true nature lies revealed, I says to him. My true nature lies in a pool round my ankles. In a cruel voice now. The silence speaks in a cruel voice from now on. And then he takes out his cock, it says, then he takes out his cock and he beats me about the face with it. Then, silence.

The good news is that you were a complete innocent, the silence of my ex-lover says to me. The good news is that if you were to spool back through those recordings made in that hotel room in the Europa, those recordings of all the times we spent there, together, there isn't a single thing to implicate you. You never betrayed anybody. You gave nothing away. In fact your tapes were of no interest whatsoever. No one learnt a damn thing of interest about you in that room.

Now, in a humiliating voice, it says it.

It was Tommy what told me you had a thing for leotards, it says. He told me you had never had a blow job in your life, it says. He says to me, turn up at The Diamond on a certain night wearing a leotard and suck this bastard's cock, or else.

Because he wanted to rule you out, it says. He wanted to make sure you weren't any danger. And you proved yourself not to be a danger, it says. Tommy was a danger. And Davy. Davy became a danger, it says. But you, you were never a danger. You're not savage enough to be my lover, my silent ex-lover says to me, from across the years, now.

I sat there on the stair, with the phone up to my ear, and it was as if I could hear all the way till the end of my life, and what would come after. You're talking to yourself, Xamuel, I says to this silence, give up the ghost. Then: I promise to forget you, darling, it says, in a voice like an absence, I promise to forget you, in a voice like a long-lost love.

*

The last night of the Daddy's Little Girl Tour and your man Del Brogan is headlining at The Shamrock. Look at him, Barney says, drinking before he even gets onstage. Right enough, your man Del Brogan is sat there at a table with a clatter of birds, throwing back the Bushmills and Coke and chasing it with pints of green. Your man Como would never be seen with a drink in his hand, Barney says, never mind chucking it down in full view before the show. We're standing in the lobby with Jimmy The Grunt, looking through the door at the debaucheries. Doesn't he have a fucking dressing room he can go to? Barney says. He's probably skunked out his brain too, he says. There are boys coming over, slapping him on the shoulders and getting their photo taken with him. Who are these cunts? He thinks he's fucking Frank Sinatra, Barney says, and he was one dissolute cunt, as we all know. What the fuck is dissolute? Frank Marby says. Frank Marby was there too. Mad Frank Marby was on loan from Athlone for a job. I think McManus might have been there too: bellend. Dissolute means that you are dissolved in booze, Barney says. Right, Marby says, right. Dissolute cunt, he says. Como never fucking cursed, Mad Frank Marby says, and a drink was never known to pass the cunt's lips. Plus he was always faithful to his wife, Barney says.

Then Jimmy The Grunt pipes up. He's standing there behind the merchandise table and for the first time in living history he doesn't just make this disturbing fucking grunting noise but he actually comes out with a fully formed sentence: youse are talking shite, the lot of youse, he says to us. None of youse have ever seen Como in real life, he says to us. The last time I saw him, he says, he had a fucking glass of whiskey in his hand and he was toasting the crowd, plus and he was half-blocked into the bargain.

Everybody is stunned. Jimmy The Grunt is talking, and he's claiming to have seen Como in real life, with a drink in his hand, and half-blocked. After a couple of confused seconds Barney shouts him down. Bullshite, when the fuck did you see Como? he says to him. At the Kelvin Hall in Glasgow, 1975, on the tenth day of the royal month of April, Jimmy The Grunt says, and on the occasion the crowd rushed the stage, he says to us, and when Como came back on to calm things down he was wearing a tartan bunnet and toasting the crowd with a glass of whiskey and he was very, conspicuously, half-blocked.

We just stood there: vanquished. Fuck me, Mad Frank Marby says, who knew? You should stick to fucking grunting if all you're going to do is go around slandering Como, you carnaptious wee bastard, Barney says to him, and the lot of us walk off in a daze. You fucking think you know someone, Barney says, shaking his head and pulling his lips tight like a maniac.

*

Time for the show, let's go. Moira and Wee Robin have kept us seats down the front. Mad Frank Marby's wife Sheila is there as well. She looks like that serial killer, Rose West, but then he looks like fucking Fred, so as it's a good match. I overhear her talking to Moira and Wee Robin. I didn't get Disney at all when I was a wee girl, she says to them. Disney just went right over my head. What's happening with the shop this weather? I says to Barney. Truth is, I hadn't been in there in months. Nothing much, Barney says, going well. Beavis and Wee Robin run it fine. She's selling all them tarot cards in there, and them Weegie boards, and them joss sticks. Who knew there was such a big market for the future in Belfast? he says. I thought they'd all given up on it long ago. Who would have thought you would turn out to be running a fucking hippy empire? I says to him. Sure, you're like your man Richard Branston. Mind that time we contacted Tommy with the Weegie board? I says to Barney. Fucking classic Tommy, wasn't it? he says to me. You could never get a fucking word of sense out that guy, even when he had shoes, and a body. Never tempted to do it again? I says to him. Never tempted to break out the tarot cards and see what the boy's up to this weather? I don't think he's interested, Barney says, and he shrugs. I don't think he could be fucked at all, he says. The dead don't want a fucking thing to do with the living, that's what I think. All these tarot cards and these fucking Weegie boards are like torture to them. They can't even speak the lingo anymore. To them we might as well be Pakis.

But don't you want to see if he's alright? I says to him. Don't you want to find out what it's like in heaven? They're good questions, Barney says to me, right enough, they're good questions, but that's my point. The dead can't be fucked with all these daft words like heaven and hell. The dead are beyond all of that good-and-evil stuff. That's Neatsy, by the way.

What?

This German bloke, Neatsy, who says that in the future all supermen will be beyond good and evil. In other words they won't give a fuck. Wee Robin is well into him, that's where the character of Superman comes from originally. I might have known he would be a fucking German, I says to him. But at least we know one thing, he says. Even the dead don't lose their taste for Como.

Tommy was like Superman, in a way, don't you think? I says to him. What do you mean? Barney says to me. Beyond good and evil, I says. Aye, well, he is now, Barney says, but the thing about Tommy is, he never had an alter ego. And if you're going to be a superhero you have to have an alter ego because you need to transform yourself into this other thing, this other character completely, this thing what you are actually not. But Tommy was always Tommy; think about it. Tommy was always on. It wasn't as if he had to run into a phone box and change into a different costume. He was always Tommy, no matter what he was up to, Barney says to me, and then he looks me in the eye for a second, just enough to convey . . . something. Does he know?

That's why we'll always admire him, Barney says to me, no matter what. I think about pushing it. I think about asking him if he knows. But then the music starts and your man Del Brogan is onstage and he's got a glass of whiskey in his hand. This cunt thinks he's Como, Barney says. How quickly we forget, I says to myself, as your man Del Brogan launches into 'The Twelfth of Never'. And now he's singing about this love what lasts forever, this love what never dies, and the women are on their feet and they're screaming and it's pandemonium. The curtain comes up and you can see the band behind him with their second-hand suits and their greasy hair and the wee punk rocker on the drums.

Then he's into the usual numbers: 'Maggie May', 'Those Brown Eyes', 'Hot Legs', 'My Wild Irish Rose', 'Come Back to Erin'. But then he starts to changing the lyrics. He starts to changing the lyrics and I'm looking round myself to see if it's just me or if anybody else has noticed, but he's looking right at me, your man Del Brogan is singing right at me, and I hear that fucking noise again, that fucking sound, and the place is darkened, and the band disappeared, and it's your man Del Brogan in the spotlight and this noise, this slithering noise, and he is changing the words of the song, he is changing the words to match the song that we have sung, together

> Come back to the shore at Carrickfergus
> Come back to that fateful Carrick shore
> Come back to the shore at Carrickfergus, ocean
> And greet the girl who couldn't love you more

everyone is singing the words they couldn't possibly know in a voice like distant thunder

> Come back to the shore at Carrickfergus
> And greet the girl who couldn't love you more

it's not Tommy, it's not Tommy, coming back. It's Tommy's daughter. Kathy is pregnant with a little girl. Daddy's little girl, is prophecy, of course, why couldn't I have seen it before? And now the tears are streaming down my face. Then your man Del Brogan does the thing where he sings to his heart and reality is clairvoyant, which means you can *read it like a book.*

*

Your man Del Brogan and his daughter Eden are at the front of the stage. He's serenading her, and calling her his heart. He's down on one knee, as if he's proposing to her. She's sat on a chair in front of him wearing a frilly white dress and with her legs dangling down, her little high-heel shoes, her red hair's on fire and wrapped up in her, and it's like he is asking her for her hand in marriage when how could she ever be true to her father forever, and he falls over, her father, he topples onto his side, her poor da, and he clutches at his chest like his heart has been taken from him, like his daughter has climbed out his chest right there and left him for dead on the floor, like he has given up his heart so as she can live.

Then a hand, a great deathly white hand like a ghost in a play, comes out from behind this great black curtain and drags him back to the other side. The women are on their feet and they're firing the silk hankies onto the stage, silk hankies all misty-wet with women's tears are raining down, and the house is in uproar; cunt gets a standing ovation. It's only later we find out he had died. He had taken himself a heart attack and died there on the spot. What a performance. Nobody will ever forget it.

Part Six: The Hood of The Snake, what is Miracle

I told you Mad Frank Marby was in town, right? Marby's this guy from Athlone with a reputation for pointless torture. I told you he looked like that bad bastard Fred West; big kick-your-cunt-in face. We had never heard of Fred West back then even though he must have been at it at the time, fucking scum, torturing young girls. That would never have happened under the Ra's remit. Things were safer, on the whole. If you stole a car you got kneecapped. Never mind raping some poor young bird and burying her under your patio. But Marby's in town because an informer has been uncovered in the ranks of the FSV and a bunch of the boys had let the top rank of the Ra know. They hadn't blown the whistle yet but they had transferred over to the Ra and had let them know what was going on. It was starting to look like the FSV was a front organisation set up by Special Branch. The whole fucking edifice was riddled with spies and informers. That's the word Mack used when we had a briefing about the situation.

We're at a call house in the Ardoyne, a foul dump of a place. The whole fucking edifice, Mack says, is rotten. The entire fucking structure is riddled, he says. But this presents us with a great opportunity. For information. How do we know it's not a set-up? Big Bik McQuillan says to him. How do we know, if this fucking thing is as riddled as you say, that this isn't some attempt to set us all up? The information is good, Mack says. The information is quality. We have our own sources, he says to us. We have our own confirmed channels. This isn't a one-way fucking street, he says to us.

So what's the game? Mad Frank Marby says. The game is this, Mack says, and he introduces two guys that have come over to the

Ra from the FSV, and one of them is Jimmy McNulty, the brother
of Rab and Joe McNulty, who were taken out by the Ra over false
claims to the Europa bombing. I can see he knows who I am.
That's fucking one of the McNulty boys, Barney whispers to me.

I'm Jimmy McNulty, he says, and this is Pat Allardyce. I'm aware
that there is some bad blood between us and some people in this
room, he says. I lost my two brothers over it but we're all on the
same side. Always were. There was just some dispute over tactics.

Right, and taking the blame for fucking shite you didn't even do,
Barney says to him. Shut your bake, Oddjob, Mack says, don't
start with that bollocks now. But McNulty continues as calm as
you like. That too, he says, that too. Although I'd say we took the
credit more than the blame. Fucking smart cunt, Barney says.
We had our reasons at the time to believe that certain operations
(that's the phrase he used, *certain operations*) had been carried
out by foot soldiers of the FSV when in fact they had been carried
out by the brave boys of the IRA. *Brave boys.* He was pressing all
the right buttons. The *relevant fantasists* have been dealt with,
McNulty says. *Certain operations, brave boys, relevant fantasists*:
that's the story of my life, I'm thinking. Then I says to him: what
about my ma? Are you going to bring my ma back to life? Am I
supposed to work with the cunts what blew up my own ma?

*

Look: it's all out in the open now, now that it's all over, but I'll
tell you this, I never once felt like I was lying. I never once felt
like I was doing anything other than honestly playing the role

that was given to me. I says to myself, what's true? What does that even mean, being true? Could you even fucking handle the truth? Are you really sure that's what you want? Because what if the truth is a stinking pit filled with bodies? What if the truth is the blind pain at the centre of the world? What if the truth is the doubled crucifixion of a snake? Maybe it would be better for us all if we just played the game. I mean, Mad Frank Marby might be a fucking serial killer in private but he knew how to play the game. We all did. I don't know who knew what back in that meeting or who was playing who, but the point was it was all about the playing itself, and we all knew it, was what.

*

Look: see, when you're up onstage and the fucking audience have filed in and you're all given your roles and already the story has gone this way and that, do you just fucking stand up and says, wait a minute, I'm not your man Hamlet anymore? I was never a Pope of Denmark, I can wash the blood out my hands no problem, in fact my name's John the fucking Baptist and I live in Jamaica Street in the Ardoyne? Of course you fucking don't. It's you fucking do-gooders, you fucking investigative journalist types, that are always trying to get to the bottom of things. And the thing is, you have no fucking idea what's down there. Take it from me, son. You might end up disinterring a body. One that you might even recognise. So as when you walk onstage, you're Como, and you live the legend, end of. It's better that way for everybody, believe me.

*

McNulty apologises, he does. This cunt McNulty apologises for
the murdering of my own ma, even though it was me what blew
her up with that fucking bomb under my bed, which is something
I'll take to the grave with me, but okay, at least now we know
where we stand, we're on solid ground at last, although, of course,
we're on no ground at all, we're not on solid fucking ground, not
ever, in Ireland, we're on totally fucking phantom ground because
the very ground beneath our feet does not belong to us, and we're
walking in the air, basically, but there's enough belief there to
support us, can't you feel it, there's a consensus that we can fly, is
there not, son, and so if we can fly, we fly.

*

So what's the game? Mad Frank Marby says it again. We roll up
at The Celt's Head, McNulty says. That's where they all drink
on a Friday night, he says. We roll up there and we cause havoc.
Everybody is looking at each other and beaming. This is what
walking in the air is all about. But there's somebody we need
to take back with us alive, Mack says. He goes by the name of
Danny Whitaker and he's a bad bastard.

*

The week running up to the attack on The Celt's Head was idyllic
in my mind because things were all back to normal and for a
week we were caught up in the old routine. All living together
at the stinky call house. Turning over a shop or robbing a bank
in the morning. In the afternoon maybe we'd do a float, see if we
couldn't take out some soldiers. Plant a bomb somewhere, set a

booby trap. Then in the evening maybe a firefight or two. Happy days.

It was a privilege and a terror to be working with a guy like Mad Frank Marby. He literally did not give a fuck. One night when we were driving back from a fairly successful float – two soldiers shot, one fatally, we later found out – I get to talking to him about your man Del Brogan. Pat Allardyce is with us in the car.

It's a shame about your man Del Brogan, Allardyce says. Fuck your man Del Brogan, Mad Frank Marby says, he was a fucking fruit merchant. I heard he got poisoned, Pat Allardyce says, I heard that somebody spiked his drink, that's what they're saying. Bollocks, I says to the two of them, it was a heart attack. He was hitting it too hard. I heard he was coked out his tits (of course I had heard no such thing but fuck him). It's the fucking Curse of Como, if you ask me, Mad Frank Marby says. What are you talking about? Pat Allardyce says to him. There's a Curse of Como? He fucking took Como's name in vain, Mad Frank Marby says. Isn't that right, Sammy? he says to me and he winks. Right in front of our fucking face he did it too, he says. Disrespectful cunt. That's fucking right, I says to Pat Allardyce, he was trying to maintain that Como took a drink. Bollocks, Pat Allardyce says, that's fucking libellous. Exactly, Mad Frank Marby says, and then the wee cunt walks onstage with a half of whiskey thinking he's doing it just like Como and – bam – God's fucking red right hand comes roaring through the clouds and fuck you; takes him right out the game. Wee shitehawk. God's like that, fucking leaning down through the clouds and letting it be known. One singer, one song, you irreligious cunt.

Did you know Tommy? I says to the both of them. Sure, I knew him, Pat Allardyce says. Frank Marby nods. Sure, I heard he was some chanter, he says. If there was ever another Como, it was him, I says to them. Was he not managing your man Del Brogan for a bit? Pat Allardyce says to me. Sure, he was, for a while, I says to him, up until he died, that is. That's arse-backward, Frank Marby says to me, that's completely fucking back to front. What was Tommy doing behind the scenes with that fucking fruit merchant? Aye, it should have been Tommy, Pat Allardyce says, that wee bastard was like an unknown movie star or something. Your man Del Brogan was more contemporary, I says to them, sure he had all the new songs. Tommy convinced him to do some of the old material but people want to listen to all the disco songs and the stuff that's in the hit parade like Rod Stewart these days. Tommy knew that. He saw the way the future was going. Face it, lads, I says to them, our days are numbered. Men like us are disappearing, fast. We're the old school now. Soon all the hippies and the fucking punk rockers will be taking over.

When you think about what we did for these ungrateful bastards, Mad Frank Marby says, it makes me mad as fuck. It's a different world this weather. The young ones these days have got no respect and all they do is fucking talk and fucking bang on about human rights and all that pish. The leadership is just as bad, if you ask me. I don't know what the fuck is happening to the world sometimes, he says. We've become too fucking soft. I know that much. And I blame the longhairs. When all the longhairs came in and all the punk rockers came in, that's when everybody began mincing around like fucking three-speeds and that's when they began handing these fucking *Green Book*s out about what you can and can't do. I mean, it was clear in the old days that if somebody needed shooting then you just fucking shot them, end of. This new generation has no fucking balls, Mad Frank Marby says, and he shakes his head in disgust and in pity and he spits out the open window into the dark of this warm August night. Just thinking about it makes me so mad I could pish, he says.

That's when I get an idea. It's 3 a.m., we're just down the road from The Shamrock. Hold on, lads, I says to them, let's swing a wee diversion here. We pull up to the front, where there's a memorial to your man Del Brogan. There's a big fuck-off flower arrangement and people have left photos and Celtic scarves and copies of his album and wee handwritten notes to him, as well as hankies, as well as what looks like hundreds of silk hankies. Still mad enough to pish? I says to them, and the three of us whip our dicks out and take a steaming wazz all over the memorial. Feel better now? I says to Mad Frank Marby. Brand new, he says to me.

*

Here, this is the best one yet:

Paddy says to his wife, my arsehole really hurts.
Ring sting, she says.
Paddy says, what the fuck does he know about it?

*

The plan was to hide out round the back of the garages across the road from The Celt's Head and for Shorty McCann to come out the pub and to let us know who was in there and what their positions were and then we get in there ourselves, cause chaos, strike fear into their hearts, break them up for good etc., and get away with Danny Whitaker in a headlock. Then it's down to that bad bastard Mad Frank Marby to taking care of business. How will we know what one is Danny Whitaker? I says to Jimmy McNulty. Sure, he's got the sandy hair like you, and the eyes, he says to me. I'll point him out as soon as we get in there, he says.

Shorty McCann comes swanning across the road. Cunt is obviously half-blocked. You, you wee cunt, Jimmy McNulty says to him, you need to keep the fucking head. Sure, it's not a problem, Shorty McCann says to him, sure this is deep fucking cover for me, he says. Anyroads, Shorty McCann says, they're all in there, lads, and they're all blocked out of their suffering skulls. Where's Whitaker? I says to him. In the snug at the back, in the last booth. He's in there with Benny and that cunt from Meath, your man McPheat. Alright, boys, Pat Allardyce says, and he gives the order to get the ballys on. Then he looks round at me and he winks. For the good times, he says, and I pull a chatsby out of each side of my trousers and all five of us walk calm as you like across the road and through the front door of The Celt's Head. Then all hell breaks loose.

Any concept of a plan is out the window. Mad Frank Marby starts shooting blind, just tearing the place up as soon as we're through the door, shouting and acting ferocious and screaming at everybody. The rule in these cases was always total silence. Do

not speak. Do not give yourself away. I can see by the look in Pat
Allardyce's eyes that he's fucking losing it over Frank Marby but
what can he do, things just escalated. He starts to plugging away
himself.

Two guys sat on stools at the bar hit the floor like skittles. This
big jet of blood is shooting up into the air out of one of their chests
like it's a fucking geyser. Mad Frank Marby steps on it like he's
trying to stem the blood and then shoots the cunt straight in
the face. Everybody's screaming and there's a bottleneck of guys
trying to get into the back room but there's no rear exit, and we
know it, we've got them all fucking trapped in here.

Jimmy McNulty starts wading into this mass of guys jamming up
the doorway and he's pulling people back and cuffing them round
the head with his chatsby. Mad Frank Marby pulls out a fucking
blade the size of his forearm and starts sticking one guy after
the other in this pile-up. There's this fucking smell, this fucking
rancid smell of gutters and of excrement, you would know it if you
smelt it, and everybody is falling to one side and the other and
it's like a passage being cleared, this passage opens up with blood
and guts and torn flesh, and Pat Allardyce looks at me and I just
fucking go for it, I put my head down and I push forward, parting
this mass () of mangled flesh, of bleeding bodies, pushing my way
through this terrible ( ) gap, this gaping human wound ( ), to
get into the back room, to get behind the fucking scenes (   ), I'm
using my arms to squeeze me (   ) through, I'm pulling bodies
to one side of me and the other and then I get my head through
(   ) and then my shoulders ( ) and then bam ( ), I'm in the
back room and it's completely silent in there ().

I can hear the shouts and the screaming from the other room but it's like in a school playground, in a dream, miles away. There are two people stood in front of me. One has a chatsby in his hand, a wee Luger. He lets off a couple of shots and I swear I can see the bullets coming toward me in slow motion -------------------- they're letting off little vapour trails like a jet plane in the sky ---------------- and I start dodging in and out of the bullets as I let off a few shots of my own ------ pop McPheat right between the legs ----------- see his sacs come loose and his bollocks plop onto the floor in front of me. He's trying to hold himself in with his hands. But then as I go to dive to the right a slug gets me in the side of the kneecap.

You ever been shot in the knee, son? Course you fucking haven't, it's fucking no pain like it, it's agony. I go down but I loose another shot and get this other cunt Benny bang in the centre of the chest and he goes over. I lie there on the ground for a second, and I can just see this leg wearing dress trousers and snakeskin shoes. And I can smell him. This smell comes to me. Old Spice. Danny Whitaker is wearing the Old Spice. I pull myself up with the edge of the table and I swing round to get a good look at him. The passage is blocked up with bodies and nobody else has made it through. I turn to take a look and I'm like that: ah fuck.

The guy is the fucking double image of me. More than that: he's me. He's me, sitting there, looking back at me. There's no real expression on his face, he's just looking up at me, there's no fear in him. No fear at all. He's just sitting there, waiting to see what's going to happen next, maybe even with the hint of a smile on his lips. Fuck this, I says to myself, and that's when I do it. Without taking my eyes off him, and with my chatsby still aimed at his head, with my left hand I slide off my balaclava. He sees me, and he lets out a gasp. He starts scrambling to the back of the booth. He's pushing back with his feet and putting his hands up in front of his face. I looks back at I and sees Himself. Mad Frank Marby and Pat Allardyce are pushing their way into the room. They'll be onto us in seconds. I turn back around. And I shoot him, my double, straight through the face.

His face is red and yellow, like the sun. Smoke is pouring from this great round wound where his face should be. Mad Frank Marby and Pat Allardyce come up behind me. What the fuck have you done? Pat Allardyce says to me, and for a second we just stand there, the three of us, with our guns at our sides, while this star man smoulders and spits in front of us, this broiling mess that is like staring into the heart of a star with all the colours of red and orange and yellow, the different degrees of heat, this furnace, and at one point his hands spring up like his body is still going on, his burnt and bloody hands go up, as if to steady himself on the table, and then it's like he's trying to raise himself up, and I see Mad Frank Marby take a step back, Mad Frank Marby flinches then, but one of his arms gives way, and he slumps back into the booth but not before he turns his head around and looks at me with this face like a Cyclops, this face like a blazing sun, and then he falls forward, onto the table, and there's a hiss like water into fire as his head hits the formica and black smoke comes up.

What the fuck just happened? Pat Allardyce says to me. You were supposed to take this cunt alive. I'm sorry, I says to him, I'm sorry. I just fucking lost it there for a minute. He fucking shot me,

I says to them, he fucking shot me in the leg. Let's get the fuck out of here, Pat Allardyce says, and he puts his arm under my shoulder and drags me out, back through this corridor of stinking flesh, out into the street.

You shouldn't have taken off your bally, he says to me. What the fuck were you thinking? The fucking game's up, I says to him. The fucking game is up. I don't even know why I said that then. Just fucking ranting and raving. By this point I was delirious with pain and confusion. What are you talking about? Mad Frank Marby says to me. There's nothing to worry about. Everybody's fucking dead. There's not a sinner left alive to recognise you. But I had been recognised, even though none of us realised it at the time. The dead had recognised one of their own.

*

A gloomy Sunday in December and I had arranged to meet Kathy in Carrickfergus. At the shore in Carrickfergus I sat and I waited and waited. *I waited till dreams like my heart were all broken.* After two hours I give up and I go to leave but before I go I look around and I look at that wee bench one last time, that wee bench that had waited all its life for the two of us, that view that was kept only for us. I go to leave but then I have a mad thought. I've got a chatsby stuck down the band of my trousers and I thought about taking it out and loosing a few bullets into the sea. I thought about shooting the fucking waves dead. I had to laugh. Sure, you're some man, Xamuel, I says to myself, you're some fucking man, right enough. It's not out there, I says to myself, standing there, looking at the wind and the waves, not anymore.

*

See if you like this one:

> Pat says to Mick, here Mick, did you see that Christmas
> is on a Friday this year?
> Ah fuck, Mick says to him, let's just hope it's not the
> fucking thirteenth.

*

Christmas in the Ardoyne and we're all up The Shamrock. The
massacre is all over the papers. IRA Scum Slaughter Their Own.
Republican Feud Culminates In Bloodbath. Behind the scenes,
the bloody gears. But somehow I don't feel like celebrating.

Barney shouts me a pint of green. Fuck's wrong with you, he says
to me, you're a secret hero. But all I do is shrug my shoulders like
a satisfied snake. Who knew Mad Frank Marby was such a top
fucking chanter? Barney says to me, and he nods to the stage.
Mad Frank Marby is up there looking like a rapist singing 'The
Way We Were', with his wife down the front, loving it. Fucking
secret heroes, I says to myself. Listen, Barney, I says to him, I'm
not feeling it, my friend, I think I'm going to head home. You're
losing it, he says to me, and he shakes his head. We're going to
have to put you out to graze, he says. I'll phone you a taxi, he says
to me, and we walk out to the lobby together, me swinging away
on my new crutches.

Jimmy The Grunt's out there. It's the 1st of December 1980. The music is coming through all muffled and Jimmy's selling these Christmas ornaments, these mini Santas, these wee silver angels, and then I spot these decorations, these things on strings that you hang from your tree. Would you take a fucking look at that, Barney, I says to him, it's fucking plastic bullets. It's fucking plastic bullets all painted in the colours of Christmas. Are you selling fucking festive plastic bullets, you daft cunt? Barney says to him and he picks a handful up, but Jimmy just grunts. That's fucking beezer, that is, Barney says, shaking his head. Tommy would have loved that, he says. Then he gives me this big bear hug. God love the Irish, he says to me, and he helps me into my taxi, and I head off, into the night.

*

All the way home I've got one of these feelings, one of these feelings of me and Tommy duetting, behind the scenes, and dancing to this silent music, as I sees myself in that bad bastard Danny Whitaker, and I shoots him in the face, and become like the sun.

*

We're driving through Belfast and it's so – quiet. It's so – peaceful. I pictured everybody lying in their beds as we passed the houses in the dark and the roofs coming off, and the walls giving way, and all the glass coffins, stretching off into forever, in the streets of Belfast, is prisoners in Ireland, is poor suffering souls.

I'll miss the women the most, I says out loud to myself, I don't know why I says that then. The ladies of my life all dancing through my mind, in the late times, is the answer, I think. How, where is it you're off to, Xamuel? the driver he says to me, young boy name of Connell, I knew his family. I wish I had made more room for women in my life, I says to him. That's all I'm saying. This is fucking Belfast, mate, the boy Connell says, there's a fucking drought on women, he says, which is why we're all fighting amongst ourselves. If we could get to the end of all this fighting, he says to me, then all of the women would come back. And what a time that will be. All the women, coming back to Ireland; then you'll see. What, along with all the snakes? I says to him. Aye, that too, he says, that too.

*

The taxi drops me to outside the house. As I hobble to the front door, I drop my keys, and now as I'm trying to bend down to pick them up, there's a voice, calling, from somewhere in the distance: Xamuel, is that Yourself? it says. Aye, it's me, I says to this voice, but I'm struggling with my keys. I'm just struggling, I says. I'm just making sure it's you, says this voice from the air, and it sounds like my old neighbour, Billy McNab. Sure is that yourself, Billy McNab? But there's no answer. Nobody comes to help, so as I'm left to struggle on my own.

*

I get inside, and I shut the door, I'm exhausted, and I leave my crutches in the hall and start to climb the stair, on my hands and knees, dragging my bad leg behind me. There's a banging noise, then another, somewhere out the back. Somebody is knocking pans together, bin lids, running from one house till the next. Something is up, the Brits are on their way. I'm halfway up the stair when the glass of the front door is bathed in light. I'm illuminated and half-blinded. I put my hand up to my forehead to shield my eyes and there's a terrible roaring and a shaking, and the sound of machinery, and the door comes off its hinges and three figures, in masks, come blazing through. I'm dragging myself, backward, up the stair, and the first figure starts to undoing his belt, which is rape, oh Christ Jayzus, he's going to fucking rape me, is my first thought, but then he wraps his leather belt around his fist and starts walking up the stair toward me, real . . . slow . . . like. He's nearly upon me and I can see his eyes, his Irish eyes, are smiling. He takes his belt and he wraps it tight around my throat. Immobilised, paralysed by these laughing Irish eyes and this bright light, I'm taken like a dog by the neck and dragged down the stair, I can't breathe, he's choking me, but I can't speak neither, and I'm grabbing at my throat, when a dark silhouette appears, a shade that raises its leg and brings it down on my splintered kneecap, which is a relief, to enter me, being, enters me, and it is simple, not complex at all, but is light and simple. The belt around my neck seemed to grow, and to extend, till a noodle or a rope is an umbilical, an umbilical running from Adam's Apple, to absorb the light that is all around I's, to take it into our body's mirror, and to speak it.

As they dragged me toward the Land Rover I broke free and I floated up with my arms raised into the air, God's Own Boys are the figures rising up, the umbilical to the throat is our bright

connection, and the vans, and the ambulances, down below, are
humbled, and the military vehicles spread out across Jamaica
Street in the snow, are humbled, and the soldiers, are huddled, in
groups, their guns aimed at the coffins, arrayed all around them,
coffins arrayed, around the ways, and illuminated, by the lights
of ambulances, on this borderline, beneath the frosted roofs of the
old Ardoyne, gathered, as witnesses, in memory, poor bastards,
in memory, now, forever, as I hovered above the rooftops of the
Ardoyne and I cast my light down, on the imprisoned, and as the
three figures moved to open the Land Rover door, I let myself go,
a balloon with the light inside of me is a poor cast for a body, as I
let go of the golden light inside of me, and let it come down

> upon the snowey streets, faye doon,
> > soft raine, ye pome,
> a castes downe aye the pale lighte
> > upon the peoples
> > > aneath me

as it begins to rain, warm golden tears, raining down, on both
sides, as they faced off, as Christmas, of 1980, is long to reign
over us, until there was nothing left inside of me, and I crumpled,
like a balloon, and I floated back to earth where they hid me
in the back of a Land Rover that sped off, in the rain and the
snow, because it was still raining, and it was raining forever,
I told myself, because I knew what I had started would never
stop, because I was aware of being left with one thing, one thing
that was inside me, one thing that they could never wipe out
themselves, one thing that I realised in that moment was my own
to insult and to destroy and to pass through. Then they took me to

The Dead Zone: The Place Of Endless Echoes, which is where
it all began.

*

I come in during the period where the first hunger strike
was coming to an end and the second about to begin, see The
Blanketmen what looked like Jayzus, naked, but for a grey or a
brown blanket, stood there in their own excrement, young men
with the long hair hanging down, brave boys.

I was mirror-searched on my first day, which means being held
spread-eagled over a mirror while thick fingers penetrate your
orifices. They pulled my hair and kicked me around the room
and put their fists in my mouth but when I arrived on my block
a shout went up. New man on the block! And the lags around
me cheered and clapped and they made me feel less afraid. And
I sang what my place was, in Ireland, sang the Ardoyne into the
pipes and down into the toilet bowl, and felt Ireland all around
us, as an echoes, as an echoes, is everything.

In The Maze you must learn to read an echoes. The jangle of keys,
the unlocking of a wing, the approach of a guard, the distant
sound of a beating or the cries of a crucifixion above a mirror, is
as echoes, now, is as lagging ghosts. At mass there were priests
who believed that Christ Jayzus could heal the sick, that we could
cast off our crutches and walk into Jayzus Himself, he tells us,
one Sunday morning, when he announced that Christ Jayzus was
there in The Maze beside us, in the very room where we stood,
that He had come down to greet us, and Christ but He must have

had a strong stomach because nobody was washing, nobody was cutting their hair, and we're all stood there, like all of His sons, come back to Him, all of His Christs, stretching back till forever, which is two thousand year since the beginning of the world, says the voice of Christ Jayzus, as a priest, in H3.

Sure is that yourself, one prisoner asked Him, one young man with his hair down to his shoulders and his face eaten by hunger and with black eyes, is that yourself, he says to a space next to the priest, to an invisible presence, and he reaches out, in silence, to touch Himself on the head. *This is an old one, lags*, Christ Jayzus says to I's, in the voice of a priest in H3, *so stop me if you think you've heard this one before. Two old muckers, Pat and Mick, are on their holidays in New York, in the USA, in heaven's blessed eternity, and Pat says to Mick*, all in the voice of Christ Jayzus who is risen up like the moon on the wall of a chapel in the H Block, *the sun blaring out of the heavens and Pat and Mick hold their hands up to the sun*, as in The Maze we lived in the time of The Bible and were visited by pestilence and plague, by maggots that seemed to crawl out ( ) from through the walls, as if The Maze itself was the rotting, suffering word-made-flesh, *do you think that's the same sun we saw in the Ardoyne, Pat says to Mick, the same sun sat up there in the sky throughout the whole shooting match, and Mick says, sure I've no idea, Pat, let's ask someone*, and the first person they meet is speaking the word that is the redeemer of the blind pain at the centre of the world, *and Mick says to him, excuse me but you wouldn't happen to know whether that sun up there is the same sun we saw in the Ardoyne all those years ago*, which is the voice of Christ Jayzus and he says, *sorry, lags*, as we ran the gamut of the guards on the way back from mass, which was when we took a beating, every Sunday, when even Christ Jayzus Himself was unprepared to follow us out of the chapel and along the endless corridors and into the empty cells where they would hold I's up by the arms and legs and they would kick I's and punch I's and tear at I's bodies, *sorry, lags, but I wouldn't know if that's the same sun you saw in the Ardoyne*, is the voice of Christ Jayzus, *you see*, he says, *I'm a stranger here myself*, and he takes his hand from the cross and he wipes a single tear from his pale white cheek and in his palm there is a hole in his hand, there is a delicate little labia in the hands of the suffering Christ and he says to I's, *listen, lags*, Christ Jayzus says to I's, *don't give way to wonder, I will pick out your eyes you bastards*, in H3, in The Maze, is the sacred heart, closer, brave boys, to the battlefield, and enters History, as a word.

*

The second hunger strike begins in March. I speak to somebody in the cell across from me that had received a comm, a small roll of paper with tiny letters on it that he had secreted inside the eye of his penis and that he had recovered using the graphite shaft of a pencil, saying that Bobby Sands was to lead it and that he fully expected to die. You are talking to a dead man, Sands says, as his fellow prisoners greeted him at mass that Sunday.

We followed the story of the strike with these serial comms, with gossip shouted from cell to cell, with the echoes in the pipes of the place names and the tiny microscopic scripts secreted inside our own bodies. Bobby is coming and going, they says to us, Bobby is leading the lagging.

The no-wash protest comes to an end. The prisoners shaved their heads and their beards. They used soap, carbolic soap that smelt like home but that stung their eyes and matted in their hair.

There were other stories too. The prisoners of The Dead Zone would rewrite books on sheets of toilet paper or adapt books from memory and then read them out the door to the other cells at night. Interminable books, dreadful books filled with terrible words, words like Firepower In Angola and Revolutionary Suicide, so as everything became confused and the comms talked to the books and the books to the toilet paper and the toilet paper to the pipes and the pipes to the songs The Boys would sing, songs by Bobby Sands and Irish folk songs and Victory to the IRA and Victory to the Blanketmen and pop music and punk rock too, until it felt like an echoes of an echoes of an echoes.

That's when I began to learn the lingo that I intend to speak for the rest of my life. The Irish lingo that I have come to associate with the camaraderie of The Maze and with the breaking of the echoes, and the story, best of all, of a hunger striker who had been part of the first protest and who says that he had forgotten what he looked like entirely, that he had literally no memory of his own face until one day as the sun came blaring through the window of his prison cell a warder was sweeping all of the pish that had run out of his cell, all of the pish that had flooded beneath the door and out into the corridor, this warder had swept it back in, and it came in like the tide, washing up around the edge of his mattress, and he has leaned over and caught his own reflection in this glistening wave, lit up by the sun, in these waters of pale gold, and his own face had emerged as that of a stranger's, and he saw

himself, as if for the first time, as if he had woken up and been
given a new identity entirely, that's me, he says to himself, and he
reaches out and he makes his eyes dilate, sets two whirlpools in
his eyes with the tips of his fingers, and says that he felt himself
hypnotised and that he realised that he had come back to himself,
from somewhere that had no name, but that it was there, on the
pish-soaked floor, of this shit-smeared cell, where he had come
face to face with his real self for the first time and it had given
him an inner strength that he never knew before, he had come to
himself and given himself permission to be a hero, the king't ship
of the self, he had said, that's what the comm had read, smuggled
in the eye of a penis, *boys, I, have, been, given't, the, king't, ship,
of, myself*, and wrote like that too, so as that it most resembled
a drunken boat, a royal ship, tossed and raised up over a sea of
pish drops, raining down, this river's made me go where I wanted,
this final crossing, to a dirty mattress, in a shallow pool, from
sea to final sea, is the same place, only Belfast, is the centre of
the world, only Ireland, is a garden, in space, and as they died,
I tracked them, I imagined their real bodies, their final bodies,
these first and last men, spoken, out of Adam's Apple, snaking up,
into the air, and all of the leaving, above The Maze, is a trapdoor,
hidden above these letters, these English letters, written into the
earth, into the page, into the soft, suffering flesh, of this page,
above them, is a gap, and I picture that same, soft, warm rain,
that final torrent of sorrowful drops, raining down, is all that's
left, on Ireland, tears of pity, tears of heartbreak and shame, for
the friends and families, left there, down below, tears of sorrow
for God's Own Boys and their lovers, and a shower of pish for the
rest of the bastards.

But unlike me, the world let them go. Unlike me, their time was at an end, and the umbilical gave way, and they passed over, to a place where they refuse to remember.

*

Tell me if'n youse know this one, sonne't:

> The Dead Zone: The Place Of Endless Echoes is written't
> in lingo, on the face of the
> eartH:_aitch
> is the invisible't letter of the
> English't alpHa-betical
> as Hierophanet sHe is voiceless, as Heth she is:
> bars, fences, divide't aires,
> barbe't wires,
> is a stranger Here, Her-self,
> is closes't to Her, as worde't
> on the battlefiel't,
> brave't boyes.

*

I was visited by Miracle Baby during the final months of the hunger strike. He died, of a brain haemorrhage, in the streets of the Ardoyne, the same week Bobby Sands was elected as the Right Honourable Member of Parliament for Fermanagh and South Tyrone. He came to me that night, in a vision, and he says that he had known, all along, that he had looked into my heart, and read its contents, and that he gave me permission, he reached out and he touched Himself on the head, and he let it be known that it was okay, that I had done what my heart had asked of me, and that now I was moving into a new phase of my life, a new phase that nobody could have predicted but that would require the killing of something inside of me, the erasing of something, deep down, and I knew then, after Miracle Baby had withdrawn his hand from my forehead, his hand from which an extra pinkie grew out of the centre at an angle of ninety degrees (what is love is), that I was capable of my own great sacrifice, though perhaps you will not think so, perhaps you will not think it any sacrifice at all, but from that day forth I can tell you that my relationship changed with the guards and with the speaking of the words, and that I was moved out of my cell and began to enjoy certain benefits, certain indulgences, so that in the wake of the hunger strike and the pointless death of ten young men, ten young men that are now invisible and that achieved nothing but History, I was part of a select group that came to an understanding with the other side and so became aware, for the first time, of the true nature of my powers. I asked you earlier if you could work it out, now can you? Can you guess what my superpower might be?

*

Years later I had access to television, I could watch the news on the TV in my cell, and I told you that I saw Patricia one more time, Tommy's Patricia, I saw her one more time but not in real life and this was when I was watching the news in 1995 and I hear about the murder of a civil rights lawyer name of Patricia Hodges and it meant nothing to me, but with the collusion of the RUC, Loyalist terrorists had placed a bomb under her car,

she had been working for Republican prisoners to ensure that
their trials were fair and she had turned the key in the ignition
of her car and it had set off a bomb that had been hidden in the
undercarriage and she had been blown to smithereens in the
driveway of her home as her husband and her daughter had
waved from the living room window and the news had cut to an
interview with her that had been filmed a few month earlier and
that's when I realised it was Tommy's Patricia, it was Tommy's
Patricia they had killed and that she had found herself a man,
a new man, and that she had dedicated herself to the cause and
that ultimately she had given her life for it and I realised that
Tommy and I, that me and Tommy and Barney and I, would die
for something quite different, that really we were on a different
side altogether, but that there was something quite beautiful
about it all the same, in the disguises we had kept, in the parts
that had been given us, there was something that was justified
and complete and fulfilled, and I thought about Tommy's little girl
and about Kathy and Davy and I wondered if any of them were
still alive and something told me, a voice through the air, that out
there, somewhere, there is a little girl that looks just like him, a
little girl come back, in his name, in secret, a little girl spinning
slowly on an ice rink, in Central Park, her leg raised, her arms
stretched out, a little girl that I will never know and that I knew
I was capable of not knowing, because I knew that I was capable
of not knowing forever, I knew when Miracle Baby visited me
that last time that I was up to it, that when the time came my
powers would not let me down, and now, as I prepare to be done
with this foul language, with these fucking curse words, which is
what I have come to call the English language, this lingo that is
only good for a joke or for a song, I'm telling you all this, how it

all went down, because I never intend to speak it again, because this will be my final telling, because I am to be freed, I am to be freed for good behaviour and according to an agreement, newly made, an agreement bartered, in part, by the dead, I am to be given a new life, gifted with a new identity, and just like the man who saw his own reflection for the first time in the golden waves that flooded his cell, I started when I realised what I had become and what it had all been for. But don't ask me to talk about it any further. These are my last words. Because now I can tell you, if you haven't already guessed, what my true superpower was, my own gift from the gods.

Forgetting.

It is the power of the first and the last man.

But wait till I tell you: